THE GIRLS

The Girls is Montherlant's masterpiece. Seen as the most devastating fictional salvo ever fired in the 'sex war', the book has been the subject of passionate controversy. Simone de Beauvoir even devoted a chapter of *The Second Sex* to denouncing it.

Costals, the narrator, is one of the great fictional creations of our age. He is the cad-seducer, the domineering male, a monster of egotism. The novel describes his relations with four women – Andrée, the bluestocking virgin who writes him a stream of passionately effusive letters; Solange, the ravishing young *bourgeoise* who nearly traps him into matrimony; Thérèse, the crazy peasant religious maniac; and Rhadidja, his teenage Moroccan mistress, an ideal of simple sensuality.

THE GIRLS

A tetralogy of novels in two volumes

=====

1

THE GIRLS
PITY FOR WOMEN

Henry de Montherlant

TRANSLATED FROM THE FRENCH BY
TERENCE KILMARTIN

WITH AN INTRODUCTION BY
PETER QUENNELL

WEIDENFELD & NICOLSON
5 WINSLEY STREET LONDON WI

SBN 297 74727 4

Printed in Great Britain by
Lowe & Brydone (Printers) Ltd., London

CONTENTS

INTRODUCTION

Byron often talked of the letters he received from women. They had begun to arrive in 1812, when he took the London world by storm; and they continued to pursue him during the years of Italian exile until he left Genoa bound for Greece and death. Some were from old acquaintances, like Lady Caroline Lamb, whom he remembered far too clearly; others from admirers he had met once or twice, and was anxious not to meet again; but many of his correspondents were total strangers, and wrote simply because they reverenced his genius and believed that he alone, in an unfriendly world, could give them the appreciation that they felt they needed. Though Byron did not always reply, he seldom threw away their scribblings. He was an inveterate hoarder of every kind of written record; and even the wildest and most ridiculous effusion passed at once into his personal archives.

Those archives can still be examined. Here, among others, are the letters of a mad peeress, an unhappy Swiss governess, an ill-starred actress, a disconsolate housemaid, a famous *demi-mondaine*, and an impressionable day-dreaming girl who addressed Byron as 'My dear Papa'. Some letters are hastily scrawled; some blotted and blistered with tears; some written in a flowing copperplate hand on expensive gilt-edged paper. But all are romantic and enthusiastic; and all do their best to establish an emotional link between the writer and the poet. Every correspondent endeavours to stake out her claim to the great man's sympathy and interest.

Nearly thirty years ago, when I first read through these letters and edited a sheaf for publication*, I was immediately reminded of Henry de Montherlant's sequence, *Les jeunes filles*, *Pitié pour les femmes*, *Le Démon du bien* and *Les Lépreuses*, of which the last volume had recently appeared. Montherlant, too, describes a celebrated writer beset by wild, enthusiastic

---

*To Lord Byron by George Paston & Peter Quennell, Murray, 1939.

7

women, each of whom has managed to convince herself that only she can understand her hero. Costals' correspondents, however, though just as unfortunate, are less numerous and varied than those of Byron, his chief epistolary persecutors being Thérèse Pantevin, a crack-brained country girl who confuses her passion for Costals with her love of God, and Andrée Hacquebaut, a provincial bluestocking, who aspires one day to become his mistress. Both are rebuffed; of many of their letters the recipient notes: '*Cette lettre est restée sans résponse*' Often he does not open the envelope; and, when Andrée eventually visits Paris and makes a forlorn and desperate attempt to force her way into his intimacy, he stages a particularly atrocious scene in which, with another young woman acting as hidden eye-witness, she has her pride demolished and her pretensions humbled. Costals exhibits certain Byronic features; his fund of patience is strictly limited; and, if he is driven too far, his cynical good humour is apt to turn to downright cruelty.

The character of Costals has frequently puzzled critics; and some readers have not unnaturally assumed that it is based upon a self-portrait. This Montherlant has always denied. '*Le caractère de Costals*', he remarks at the head of *Les jeunes filles*, '*est, en partie du moins, un caractère de "libertin" ou de "mauvais sujet" (comme on disait autrefois). Il a donc fallu lui donner des particularités convenables à ce caractère. S'il est sûr que l'auteur a mis de soi dans ce personnage, il reste qu'il y a en celui-ci nombre de traits qui sont du domaine purement objectif. . . .*' The *Avertissement* to *Pitié pour les femmes* includes an equally emphatic declaration: '*L'auteur rappelle ici . . . qu'il a peint en Costals un personnage que, de propos délibéré, il a voulu inquiétant, voire par moments odieux. Et que les propos et les actes de ce personnage ne sauraient être, sans injustice, prêtés à celui qui l'a conçu.*'

Yet Montherlant admits that there is something of himself in Costals; and his reader will observe that many of Costals' opinions on life are also to be found, more or less accurately reproduced, among his published notebook jottings. To judge from his *Carnets*, Montherlant bears as much, and as little, resemblance to Costals as Byron bore to Childe Harold; each fictitious character is a literary *persona*, which incorporates some of the traits of the artist who produced it, but does not pretend to be a full-length likeness. Costals is the moving spirit who controls the story, the exponent of a system of ideas, a voice that denounces and derides, a principle against which the other characters react. Although Montherlant tells us a good deal about his habits, tastes and antecedents, he remains a somewhat enigmatic figure – a personification of the writer's beliefs and prejudices rather than an individual human being.

But then, *Les jeunes filles* has little in common with the average modern novel; for Montherlant rejects the conventions of story-telling that most novelists have inherited from their nineteenth-century predecessors. '*Si ce roman*,' he writes in his second volume, '*sacrifiait aux règles du genre, telles qu'elles sont établies en France, la scène à la cuisine, entre Costals et Solange, y eût été placée à la fin. . . . Mais la vie, qui ne sait pas vivre, prétend sottement se dérober aux convenances du roman français.*' *Les jeunes filles* is not a 'well-constructed' book in the accepted meaning of the phrase, but follows its own rules of construction and possesses its own interior harmony. It includes a mass of exceedingly diverse material – letters, notes, comments, asides, together with long passages of straightforward narrative – and is written, as the story develops, from several different points of view. One is that of the narrator, who sometimes blends into his imaginary novelist; another is the redoubtable Costals speaking in his proper person. Yet the subsidiary characters are also allowed a hearing; and there comes a moment when the ridiculous Madame Dandillot – a commonplace middle-class matron, described as resembling a policeman's horse – suddenly dominates the scene and exhibits all her hidden virtues. Her intrinsic absurdity and vulgarity are redeemed by the unselfish strength of her maternal love; and, as she looks down on her sleeping daughter, she becomes a great and good woman. Although this is an aspect of his prospective mother-in-law that has escaped Costals, and seems to be strangely at odds with the narrator's previous attitude, it inspires him to produce a particularly moving passage on the theme of love and sleep:

9

'*Brusquement elle se tut, comme une petite boîte à musique qui s'enraye.... Elle dit: "Tu dors?" Pas de réponse. Elle alluma. Solange dormait, un peu de salive au coin de la bouche.... Comme la nuit est grande sur le monde, et comme la terre est silencieuse quand on regarde dormir ce qu'on aime! Celui qu'obsède la disparate enclose dans chaque objet, et qui veut y voir une des clefs de la nature, ne méditera-t-il pas sur la tendresse humaine, qui est à la fois le comble de l'inquiétude et le comble du repos?*'

Costals, as it happens, is also a devoted parent; he has an illegitimate son, child of a discarded mistress, for whom he feels a deep, but undemanding, love. Brunet monopolizes his strongest affections; otherwise he distrusts and despises love, more especially romantic love, since he sees it as the arch-foe of his personal integrity and independence; and Costals cherishes the belief that he is, above all else, a free man. '*C'est une de mes grandes forces,*' writes Montherlant in his *Carnets*, '*d'échapper à l'amour en connaissant, mêlées, la sensualité et la tendresse.*' Similarly, Costals has done his best to exclude love – at least, as it is understood by the average woman – both from his life and from his work. '*Je connais bien l'amour;*' he tells Andrée Hacquebaut. '*C'est un sentiment pour lequel je n'ai pas d'estime. D'ailleurs il n'existe pas dans la nature; il est une invention des femmes. . . . Dans chacun des livres que j'ai publiés vous trouverez, sous une forme ou l'autre, cette affirmation: "Ce qui m'importe par-dessus tout, c'est d'aimer". Mais il ne s'agit jamais de l'amour. Il s'agit d'un composé d'affection et de désir, qui n'est pas l'amour.*'

It is the conflict between these two different theories of love that provides the basic drama of *Les jeunes filles*. According to Costals, love, 'the invention of women', is always enervating and demoralizing: moreover, romantic love may lead to marriage; and marriage is the fatal 'hippogriff'; whereas the emotion that blends desire and tenderness suffuses the heart with peace and the mind with energy. In an interview, the author has claimed that *Les jeunes filles* has a definitely 'salubrious' message. Nor will he agree that it constitutes an attack on Woman: '*J'y suis souvent dur pour les femmes.*

Mais, dans toute mon œuvre, ne suis-je pas aussi dur pour les hommes? ... Ce que j'attaque, ce n'est pas la femme, c'est l'idolatrie de la femme, c'est la conception "cour d'amour" de la femme, c'est la situation privilégiée de la femme. Dans Les jeunes filles, *au lieu de cultiver les imperfections de la femme avec une complaisance béate, j'ai voulu la traiter d'égale à égal. ...'*

This, however, though it may be true of Montherlant – his plays present the opposite sex in a much softer and more advantageous light – is not entirely true of Costals, whose attitude towards women is certainly harsh, and who makes very little attempt to treat his female associates upon an equal footing. The personage Montherlant describes is at once a rake and a misogynist; and, as a 'libertin', he belong to the same family as Richardson's Lovelace, Choderlos de Laclos' Valmont or, indeed, as Casanova. Like Costals, Lovelace is a 'marriage-hater'; and he believes that, by conquering Clarissa Harlowe, he is merely reconciling 'herself to herself' and illustrating the 'triumph of nature' over an outworn social code. He, too, is 'noted for his vivacity and courage', and possesses, we are told, 'sound health and ... a soul and body fitted for and pleased with each other.' Though highly educated, he represents natural man as opposed to sentimental, artificial woman.

Valmont, on the other hand, resembles Costals only in his more Machiavellian aspects; but Montherlant's description of how the novelist humiliates Andrée while Solange lurks behind a curtain, and of the meaner details of his treatment of Solange, might well have been imagined by Laclos. As for Casanova, he had more generous feelings than Costals, but often voices much the same opinions. Thus Costals remarks that, if he had a daughter, *'Je la désirerai sûrement un jour'*; and Casanova admits that he could never understand *'comment un père pouvait tendrement aimer sa charmante fille sans avoir du moins un fois couché avec elle.'* But, in Casanova's life, women were the centre of existence; and Costals announces that, *'à la rigueur, je puis répéter à cent ou cent cinquante femmes les mêmes paroles, en étant sincère à chaque coup, parce que la femme reste dans le superficiel de ma vie.'* Casanova was occasionally cruel because he loved too violently and indiscriminately; Costals is cruel because the desire he experiences is apt to conceal a fundamental distaste.

Here he has many distinguished predecessors; a strain of fierce misogyny runs through European thought and writing. Shakespeare himself was not immune from it; and just as Costals is moved to protest against the weakness and untidiness of the flaccid female organism, Berowne in *Love's Labour's Lost* compares it to an ill-functioning piece of household clockwork:

> What I! I love! I sue! I seek a wife!
> A woman that is like a German clock,
> Still a-repairing, ever out of frame,
> And never going aright ...

– an image that Shakespeare apparently derived from a popular sixteenth-century proverb.

Another poetic misogynist was the author of *Les Fleurs du mal*. He, too, attacked *'lidolâtrie de la femme'*, declared that it had always astonished him that women were allowed to enter churches – *'Quelle conversation peuvent-elles avoir avec Dieu?'* – and asserted that in a woman's composition physical and spiritual qualities were inextricably bound up together: *'La femme ne sait pas séparer l'âme du corps. Elle est simpliste comme les animaux.'* In short, Woman was the antithesis of the Dandy; by which Baudelaire, of course, meant not a modern Beau Brummell, but the 'well-born soul', the literary aristocrat, perpetually at war with the world in which he finds himself. To sum up, Woman is essentially a vulgar being; and at this point one recollects Costals' remark on the change that overtakes a woman's personality as soon as she begins to hum: *'Solange fredonna la mélopée des Bateliers.... Costals pensa qu'il y a, en toute femme, une grue prête à ressortir, et qui ressort quand elle chantonne.'*

In *Les jeunes filles* Montherlant expresses his view of the opposite sex more eloquently, forcibly and unreservedly than in any of his earlier or later novels. But it is already obvious in such books as *Le Songe* and *Les Bestaires*, published in 1922 and 1926 respectively. Each introduces a young man who represents the noblest type of human comradeship; and each draws the portrait of a girl who stands for the opposing principle, and who offers, not steady, unselfish affection, but self-centred and self-destructive love. *Gentillesse* – a word difficult to translate – is one of Montherlant's and Costals' favourite virtues; and, among the characters who appear in *Les jeunes filles*, Brunet, Costals' adolescent son, alone exhibits this redeeming quality. Solange puzzles, distracts and annoys; his association with Brunet is refreshingly uncomplicated and straightforward. '*Je n'aime pas*,' reflects Costals, '*ce qui est une occasion de bêtise pour l'homme, et c'est pourquoi je n'aime pas la femme.... Eternelle supériorité des gosses sur les femmes....*' This superiority, moreover, is not only spiritual and emotional; the hero suggests that it is also physical. In Solange's embrace, he notes that her body is strangely scentless, and that even her hair has a weak and faded aroma. '*Pourquoi Costals évoqua-t-il l'odeur si bonne et si vivace des cheveux de son fils? Il ignorait que c'est un règle, que les cheveux des jeunes garçons sentent plus fort et meilleur que ceux des femmes.*' This comparison temporarily deadens his desire; and soon afterwards, for the first time in his relationship with Solange, he feels a humiliating lack of energy.

During the course of an interview on the subject of *Les jeunes filles*, from which I have already quoted, Montherlant admits that he may, now and then, have been inclined to generalize much too widely and too freely – '*j'y dis trop "les femmes" et "les hommes"*'; and that a certain simplification has at times resulted. With this criticism many of his readers will agree. Costals is an extremely dogmatic personage; and, like most dogmatists, he is apt to assume that he has mastered the whole art of living. Besides being entirely self-sufficient, he is, he repeatedly claims, a thoroughly happy and harmonious character; '*la mélancolie est le petit luxe des âmes pauvres*'. Thanks both to his natural lucidity and to his '*discipline d'égoisme*', he can confront the universe without alarm : '*Les gens disent qu'on est malheureux quand on voit trop tout ce qui est. Moi, je vois tout ce qui est, et je suis très heureux.*' The life he leads is 'perfectly intelligent'; he has neither fears nor misgivings.

Such self-sufficiency, a reader may object, is seldom found in real life; but Montherlant the artist keeps a wary eye on

Costals the dogmatic theorist. His hero is slightly incredible only so long as he remains invincible, *'avec sa jeunesse, sa santé, son impudence, son œuvre, son gracieux fils, son collier de maîtresses très jeunes, et tous les avantages de la puissance ...'* But, although Costals never quite vails his sword or drops his intellectual panache, *Les jeunes filles* is still the story of his successive misadventures. He falls into the trap that has been laid by Solange; he becomes engaged; he is nearly overtaken and devoured by the appalling Hippogriff. In the last volume, having temporarily escaped from Solange, he seeks a refuge among the Atlas Mountains, and there suspects that he has contracted leprosy – a symbolic disaster that sends him hurrying back towards a European hospital.

I have suggested elsewhere that Montherlant is a remarkably gifted comic novelist; and the story of Costals' brush with Death, and of his long struggle against that legendary monster, Marriage, is told with wonderfully enlivening humour. Few characters in fiction have been more savagely treated than Andrée Hacquebaut and Solange Dandillot; but Montherlant is far too good an artist to pass a summary verdict on his own creations. The ridiculous bluestocking has a kind of farouche dignity that even Costals cannot quite extinguish; and one reader at least has never lost his regard for the unhappy young girl. Although Solange has a limited, commonplace mind, she is patient, affectionate and good-natured and, despite Costals' ferocious diatribes, by no means altogether stupid.

Style is a quality that seldom ranks very high in the contemporary critic's scale of values; but it would be impossible to discuss Montherlant the novelist without considering his achievement as a modern master of the French language. His prose style is uncommonly rich and various – tart, idiomatic, incisive, when he attacks some typical or controversial issue; measured, euphonious, poetic, when he deals with wider and less transitory themes. He has always loved nature, and shown a deep understanding of the life of plants and animals. What could be more vivid than his description, in *Le Démon du bien*, of the four cats whom Costals meets in an Italian restaurant; or, on another plane, his picture, in *Les Lépreuses*, of the desolate landscape of the High Atlas?

'*Rose rougeâtre de la terre. Blanc de la neige. Bleu des ombres aux flancs des monts. Sur le versant d'en dessous, des oueds avaient oubliés leur mission dans la vie . . . étaient devenus des pistes, encombrées de galets, qu'on ne distinguait plus que par leurs rubans de lauriers-roses; et puis un ruisseau de glace rouge, comme un ruisseau de gelée à la groseille, ou comme une tranchée pleine de sang frais coagulé. Des troupeaux de moutons, qui avaient la couleur même de la sécheresse, passaient au-dessus de leurs têtes, se déplaçaient avec le rhythme des ombres, et le chien croquait la neige durcie. Des bergers momifiés étaient là depuis cinq mille ans. Des sauterelles, figées elles aussi, sur les buissons neigeux, guettées par la fluxion de poitrine. Et de grands faucons blancs qui glissaient et viraient avec des grâces d'almée.*'

Like every genuine style, that of Henry de Montherlant is no mere adventitious decoration, but arises naturally from his subject as he enlarges and develops it. Montherlant's efforts as a controversialist should never blind us to the fact that he is primarily an accomplished artist. *Les jeunes filles* may be read and enjoyed as a deliberately controversial book – an attack on 'the cult of Woman', on the place that Woman has come to occupy in the modern European world; and as such it may have helped to break down many masculine taboos and phobias. But it is also an imaginative work of art, which, having absorbed and digested its subject matter, presents us with something far more valuable and lasting. Circumstances change; social problems vary; one day the unending War of the Sexes may be fought under completely different standards. But, so long as literature continues to play a part in our lives, Montherlant's story of *Les jeunes filles* is a book that will retain its youthful freshness.

PETER QUENNELL

TRANSLATOR'S NOTE

This tetralogy first appeared in France as four separate volumes published by Grasset – *Les jeunes filles* (June 1936), *Pitié pour les femmes* (October 1936), *Le Démon du bien* (June 1937), and *Les Lépreuses* (July 1939). The text I have used is Henry de Montherlant's final version, published in one volume by Gallimard (1959), in the Bibliothèque de la Pléiade.

TERENCE KILMARTIN

FOREWORD

The author would like to point out that in Costals he has deliberately painted a character whom he intended to be disquieting and even, at times, odious; and that this character's words and actions cannot in fairness be attributed to its creator.

The author made the central character of *La Rose de sable*, Lieutenant Auligny, a man endowed with the highest moral qualities: patriotism, charity, a horror of violence, a passion for justice and an acute sensitivity to injustice (to the point of being made ill by it), an almost excessive sensibility and scrupulousness, a sense of human solidarity, an anxiety, amounting to obsession, to put himself out for others and to avoid injuring them, etc.

This character, as central as that of Costals is here, takes up the major part of a work of nearly six hundred pages, and innumerable details lend it that 'autobiographical' aspect which some have claimed to discern in Costals.

One might well wonder whether the critics and the public, on reading *La Rose de sable*, would attribute to the author the same abundance of virtues as they attributed to him of vices after reading *The Girls*.

H.M.

THE GIRLS

Mademoiselle Thérèse Pantevin   to M. Pierre Costals
La Vallée Maurienne   *Avenue Henri-Martin*
near Avranches   *Paris*
(Manche)

    26 September 1926

✝
A.M.D.G.

Thank you, Monsieur and dearly beloved, for never answering my letters. They were unworthy of me. Three letters in three years, and not a single reply! But now the time has come for me to tell you my secret.

Ever since I first came across your books, I have loved you. When I saw your photograph in a newspaper, my passion was aroused. For three months, from November the 11th, 1923, to February the 2nd, 1924, I wrote to you every day. But I did not send the letters, I was too ashamed. I sent only one of them. You did not reply. And yet, as I gazed at your photograph, the look in your eyes, your whole expression, revealed to me my happy fate: you did not love me, no, but you had found a place for me in your thoughts.

With my letter of August the 15th, 1924 – the Feast of the Assumption of the Blessed Virgin – I reminded you of my existence. And a few days later, I caught a certain gleam on your face in that same photograph which told me that my letter had struck home.

On April the 11th last, I wrote to you a third time. But so great was my fear of displeasing you by an excess of boldness that the terms in which I wrote must have left you in doubt as to my feelings. I did not dare tell you of my love, and it was killing me. So then I wrote you a great confession in a six-page letter which I began on the last Saturday of the month of the Rosary and finished on the eve of the Immaculate Conception. But I did not send that either.

I think of you, I suffer, I must tell you all: I love you. I wish you no harm whatsoever.

How I have suffered! When you know me you will understand. I am not a self-sufficient sort of woman. Separated from
you I have been nothing, I could do nothing. I have wept, I
have prayed, I have meditated, but this inner life is all the
life I have had. Why should I take anything out of myself
unless it could be dedicated to the man for whom I was made?
For God created man for His glory, and woman for the glory
of man. Oh! what you could not do for me! Make me live,
my friend, for without you I am incapable of living. All I need
is to be loved, and I feel capable of so much love.

I love you and I know that in telling you so I am fulfilling
God's will. My friend, have you never dreamed of what our
love will be in Eternity?

Soon it will be October ... the last flowers are in the fields.
I could not bear to see them die in vain. I picked them, making
the sign of the Cross as I did so. I put four sprigs of them
from us both on the grave of twin kittens that died two years
ago. I am sending you three sprigs, and am keeping three
more which I shall lay at the foot of my little statue of the
Sacred Heart.

This time I beg you to answer me, so that I may give free
rein to my tender feelings and, if your heart responds to mine,
grow accustomed to my happiness.

My friend, our task is to reconstruct the Kingdom of God.
If you desire this Kingdom, and the kingdom of my heart, give
me a sign.

I kiss your pen, and sign myself

Marie Paradis

for 'Thérèse Pantevin' no longer exists.
(Do not put your name on your envelope.)

This letter remained unanswered.

Mademoiselle Andrée Hacquebaut   to Pierre Costals
Saint-Léonard   *Paris*
(Loiret)

3 October 1926

Dear great Costals,

During the summer I was out of doors nearly all the time,

and the house had ceased to be of any importance to me. With the first cold weather, one fits it out like an ark in which to sail through the deluge of winter, and it is only now, much more than in the spring when my mother died, that I realize what it means to be living in Saint-Léonard (Loiret) with a stupid, deaf old uncle, when one is poor, unmarried, an orphan without brothers or sisters, and pushing thirty.

And yet, this melancholy is as it were swallowed up by the anniversary each October brings. It is now four years to the very day since I first read a book of yours. The power you have over people! Last night I wept – real tears – on re-reading *Fragility*. (Did I tell you I had had an adorable binding made for it in green morocco? The only beautiful thing in the desert of ugliness and mediocrity in which I live. A hundred and fifty francs. Half my month's pocket money....) There are days when I cannot pick up a newspaper without finding your name in it, cannot open my mouth without mentioning you (I pronounce your name more often than a woman pronounces the name of her lover), cannot think without feeling your thoughts intermingled with mine. You are not so much a man as an element in which my life is steeped, as though in air or water. No one else has the 'feel' of you as I have. No, no one, I won't have it! I'm not jealous of the people you love – not even the 'fine ladies' – but of those who love you. Allow me at least the unique position of having loved your work more than anyone. I know it almost by heart, so much so that sentences of yours often spring to my lips or my pen, expressing my thought better than I myself could have done : you speak, and it is myself I hear. This is no doubt the effect of your talent, which conquered me from the very first, but it also has to do with the sort of affinity one notices between oneself and certain persons from whom one might appear to be separated by an abyss. Throughout my life, so joyless and at times so tormented, this mysterious fellow-feeling has uplifted and sustained me. How I have matured through reading you! You have turned over people's souls as one turns over the soil, revealing their own riches to them. For four years, your work has been as it were a mouthpiece for one who has no literary talent, just as your happiness has been

23

a requital for one who is unhappy. Being as eager as you to live life to the full, and yet knowing only self-denial and yearning in this wretched life of mine – wretched and absurdly paradoxical since I have acquired a culture which remains unexploited – fettered as I am by loneliness and lack of money, I had, so to speak, delegated to you all this fervour, all this appetite for life. Far from envying you, as so many others do, I had, if I may say so, something of the feeling of parents whose own lives have been a failure and who live to see their children succeed (so you see you are my son, in spite of your thirty-three years!). Walled in as I was, I was glad that someone should triumph over all obstacles and barriers. That was my recompense. If at any time you had ceased to be yourself, or ceased to be happy, you would have proved yourself unworthy of my trust, you would have betrayed me – me and many others, for I know there were many who felt as I did.

I am proud that you write what you write. I am proud that you live as you live. That a man of your kind should be a success with the public (which is almost unheard of) reconciles me to the world: it means that all is not lost. I could not bear it if you were not loved, and it's now three years since I said to my best friend: 'If you hadn't loved Costals (as a writer), I wouldn't have given much for our friendship.' I am always terrified that you may do something that is not quite 'the thing'. Whenever I read an article of yours in a newspaper I always get the sort of shiver of apprehension my mother apparently used to get when I was a toddler and a neighbour warned her: 'Dédée's playing by the pond.' But what you write is always what I expected, just as, when I met you, you were as I had imagined you. O God, let this miracle never cease! It's a wonderful feeling, you know, to be able to put such trust in a free man.

When I met you! How can I forget your kindness, your straightforwardness, your courtesy! You, the inaccessible Costals! A very big and very famous brother, but a brother all the same. The ideal comrade, with whom one is on an equal footing, provided one holds one's head up a little. I was half afraid you would give me the sort of reception which a writer with your ... all-conquering reputation might give to a young female admirer come to visit him, and anything at all suggestive of physical desire on either side would have humiliated me. Even today I would give you my life, but I cannot imagine myself giving you a kiss. Although religion no longer has any hold over me, something has remained of my very devout and scrupulous childhood (never reading a book on the sly, and never wanting to). Your reserve was an ex-quisite discovery for me : 'reserve' equals 'power', in a man as much as in a woman. And moreover, it proved to me that in your eyes I was not like all the others. Everything you did for me – advising me what to read, finding me that job in Paris, which I lost through my own fault – showed me how kind you were, something one could not have guessed from your books. (Kind when you choose, be it said. There are things about you that upset me a little, as you know. Although of course you have special prerogatives.)

In a month's time, I shall be going to Paris for a few days on business connected with my mother's estate. Tell me you will be there then.

Yours with a solemn hand-clasp,

A.H.

Forgive the length of this letter. I can't help myself. But I promise not to write again for a fortnight.

This letter remained unanswered.

2501 – Girl, 28, blonde, pretty, Catholic, 20,000 frs. savings, would marry gent. in good situation.

2529 – Girl, 25, bronzed, slim, very pretty, good legs, no private means, typist provincial town, would marry gent. with steady job. Seeks above all tenderness.

2530 – Aristocratic lady, 40, only daughter, mildly intellec-tual, living in chateau, 200,000 frs. dowry, would marry dis-tinguished Catholic gent. even without means, pref. nobleman.

2550 – Girl, 21, daughter naval officer, orphan, attractive, light-brown hair, hazel eyes, small, slim, good figure, living Finisterre, no financial prospects.

2554 – Widow, 49, lively, affectionate, sensitive, warm-hearted, rich inner life, distinguished, excellent health, ideal housewife, superior in every way, income 25,000 frs., house-owner, wishes communicate view marriage sincere respectable gentleman similar financial position in order achieve peace and security in mutual trust and affection. Serious. Give exact address.

2563 – Artistic girl, personal qualities, warm-hearted, plucky, independent, living alone, desires marriage nice young man.

2565 – Marchioness, very tall, blue-green eyes, natural blonde hair, good figure, attractive, elegant, distinguished, accustomed fashionable society, good jewellery, would marry good-looking gent. American type.

2574 – Decent, healthy girl, living country with mother, seeks marriage.

2576a – Working girl, brunette, 29, gentle, docile, conscientious, 600 frs. per month, slight curable T.B., would marry gent. under 45 really anxious make her happy. Means unimportant. Would leave provinces.

Extract from *Happy Ever After*,
monthly matrimonial gazette, October 1926.

1899 – Bachelor, thirtyish, fine physique, 5ft 9ins., well educated, every endowment, would marry girl with substantial dowry.

1907 – Clerk, 23, medium height, sportsman, would marry woman who could make him independent.

1910 – Veterinary surgeon, 24, well-to-do, handsome, tall, fine eyes, Ramon Novarro type, seeks, view marriage, sentimental companion with at least 600,000 frs. dowry.

1929 – Widower, 63, elegant, healthy, Belgian, liberal profession, decorated Order of Leopold, private income 4,000 frs., would marry widow or spinster of good physique, fairly stout, loving, not spendthrift, with minimum income 20,000. Has suffered.

1930 – Schoolmaster, Mayenne, 28, due promotion soon, would marry freethinking colleague with substantial means.

1931 – Young man, 5ft 10ins., very smart, very good dancer, fine athlete, wishes meet blonde girl of independent means view marriage. Motor-car trips.

1940 – Gentleman, university graduate, fiftyish, kind, considerate, disinterested, craving tenderness, seeks view marriage young person pref. under 23, genteel, distinguished, well educated, cultured, tender, devoted, character irreproachable, very pretty, good housekeeper, outwardly simple but really seductive, with minimum dowry 500,000 frs. and expectations if poss.

1945 – Colonial warrant officer, clean bill of health, slim, blond, curly hair, aquiline nose, oval face, sensitive, violinist, Tunisian outpost, would marry girl 17-20 with dowry who loves radiant sun, eternal azure of the land of mirages and infinite sands.

1947 – Mechanic, bachelor, 18, seeks view marriage correspondent who could help him set up in business.

1950 – Captain, 33, horseman, promotion imminent, Officer Legion of Honour, fine physique, brown hair, distinguished, elegant, serious, good-humoured despite having suffered, very straightforward, wishes bring happiness to young person even with a child, tall, pleasant, sentimental and ideal, perfectly educated, Catholic, in order build happy durable home based profound affection and high moral qualities. Situation and means immaterial.

1958 – Young man, 21, good-looking, modest means, seeks sister soul with fortune.

1962 – Viscount, only son, 27, certified noble ancestry dating back sixteenth century, no personal fortune at present but substantial expectations, perfect in every way, would marry person with very large fortune, religion and age immaterial, whose parents could provide occupation for son-in-law.

1967 – Road mender, 29, no private means, Paris suburbs, hopes find young woman for marriage.

Happy Ever After, October 1926.

A man reading a page of matrimonial advertisements can give rein, one after another, to several of the different men that are in him: the laughing man, the lusting man, the thinking man; and inside the 'thinking man' there is also a man who weeps.

The laughing man. Ah, yes! he will laugh himself sick. The high opinion most of these poor creatures have of themselves. The importance they attach to blond hair and Catholicism. The regulation height of the gentlemen. The 'expectations' of the young ladies – and what expectations! An inexhaustible mine of absurdity.

On the second page of the journal, 'the editors are at the disposal of their readers to provide them with any help they may need for the success of their plans, and if need be to write direct to subscribers in any terms which may be desired, at a fee of 2fr. 50 per letter.'

On the back page, a box advertising a 'lady detective and her sleuths, shadows, etc. ...' Perfect! One must think of everything when setting up house. (But might not the lady detective be the editor of the journal herself, a Penelope ready to destroy what she has woven?) A good mark, too, for the advertisement for 'quick loans': we all know how expensive women are.

When the laughing man has had a good laugh and a good sneer, etc. ... to the point of thinking, if he is a bit sour: 'Let's have a nice little war to clean up all this riff-raff' (although it's true, adds this deplorable man, that one of the horrors of war, to which attention is never sufficiently drawn, is that women are spared) – when the laughing man has had a good laugh, he turns the switch and the lusting man appears. The man who cannot read 'Girl, 22' without a quiver of excitement.

Behind each of these advertisements a face, a body, an unknown something which, after all, may well be a heart. Behind these printed pages, a hundred and fifty living women, living at this very moment, each of whom wants a man – and why not me? – each of whom, since she is there, is ready for adventure, legal or illegal (the legal being a thousand times worse than the other), each of whom has reached such a pitch of deprivation that she is ready to offer herself to the first comer. The men, for their part, demand 'large fortunes'. We read this, for instance: 'Gentleman wishes meet young pretty woman with large fortune view marriage.' Full stop. You: young, pretty, with large fortune. Me ... well, me, 'a gentleman': aren't you satisfied? Most of the women do at least specify 'gentleman with job' – bed and board. The bed first. And what more natural, what more respect-worthy than this demand? 'You don't feel poverty any more when you're under a blanket', as a Marseilles street-walker once rather splendidly observed. (Sometimes you feel a different sort of poverty. But that's another matter.) The lecherous man, scanning these pages, sees them pulsating as the sea pulsates, swarming as the Roman arena swarmed when the beasts were let loose in it. There are too many of them, and he loses heart – like the art-lover confronted with two thousand pieces in a museum. A herd of women enclosed in the arena. Menacing as the beasts of the arena, and yet, like them, half innocent and defenceless: all victims, even the worst. It is simply a matter of shooting an arrow into the heap. Brutes, cads and perverts, swindlers and blackmailers, all the archers are up there choosing their prey. Every kind of threat against the race of woman. Extremes of candour and baseness, deceptions, disappointments, all the social dramas, even happiness, simmer in the witches' cauldron of a matrimonial gazette. Absurdity and pathos too, as in everything that has to do with life – and this is life itself, a microcosm of life.

As for the thinking man, *he* sees this matrimonial journal, so ridiculous from one point of view, as an extremely valuable piece of social machinery.

The author remembers coming across the alluring phrase *select company* in an advertising brochure for some spa hotel. And one often hears people say to each other: 'You should go to the So-and-So's. You'll make a lot of social connections there.' Whereupon every well-born person draws himself up and recalls the remark of the old aristocratic lady who, on her death-bed, pestered no doubt by tiresome visitors, left her grand-children with this final word of advice: 'Above all, avoid social connections.'

And yet, after this initial reaction, one is struck by all the misfortunes engendered by the lack of connections. It seems a trite thing to say; but in fact it is less widely realized than one might think. One is struck by the vast number of agreeable things people lack simply because they have not known which door to knock at. And it is surely tragic to think of those doors simply waiting to be opened on to gardens of Eden which remained closed because people passed them by.

The people who wait all their lives for the one person who was made for them – *who always exists* – and who die without having met that person: the men who fail to find an outlet for their abilities and waste their lives in inferior jobs: the girls who remain unmarried when they could have made a man happy as well as themselves: the people who sink ever deeper into penury when there are charitable organizations which might have been expressly created for them; and all this because none of them happened to know of this person, that organization, that vacancy – it is a problem that can haunt one.

And it applies to small things as well as big. There is the book which, at a particular moment, might have raised your spirits, but which you did not know about. There is the place that would have made the perfect setting for your love affair, the treatment that would have cured your illness, the scheme that would have enabled you to gain time. They were all there waiting for you, but no one pointed them out to you because you had too few connections. The promised land is all around you, and you do not know it – like a wasp trying to get out of a room, endlessly beating and buzzing against the window-pane although the window is ajar a few inches away. A man is thrown into the water with his wrists tied, and no one has taught him the knack of freeing himself – yet such a knack exists.

This counterpoint of offers and appeals resembles the flight of birds criss-crossing in the vastness of space until at last some of them meet and they fly off two by two. Montaigne tells us that his father would have liked to see in every town 'a certain place appointed, to which those who needed anything could betake themselves. Such a one desires company for a journey to Paris. Another requires a servant of a certain quality. Yet another a master, etc. . . .' And he cites the example of two 'most excellent persons' who died in penury and who would have been succoured if their sad plight had been known. Truly, the man who first thought of using a gazette to help people find what they seek should have a statue erected in his honour. Anything designed to bring people together deserves encouragement, even when they are brought together for sentimental ends, with all the silliness and triviality that implies.

The old lady who enjoined her family with fierce pride, 'Above all, avoid connections', was condemning anyone who took her at her word to all the miseries of non-fulfilment – of soul as well as body – and an agonizing regret for all that could have been theirs for the asking, but which eluded them. Turning in on oneself is bad for all except strong and exceptional natures, and even then only on condition that it is relative and not continuous. Others pay dearly for it. One cannot shut oneself up in one's room with impunity. One cannot live on oneself alone with impunity. One cannot send one's fellow-creatures 'packing' with impunity. And it is right that this should be so, since turning in on oneself – unless it is dictated by high intellectual or spiritual motives – is more often than not the result of idleness, egotism, impotence, in short that 'fear of living' which has not yet been sufficiently recognized as one of the major evils that afflict humanity.

Thérèse Pantevin	to Pierre Costals
La Vallée Maurienne	*Paris*

6 October 1926

†
A.M.D.G.

My Beloved, once again you have failed to answer me! God has not permitted it; blessed be His Holy Name.

Convinced that your silence means that great things are happening – no doubt you are working – I will respect that silence. Yes, until All Saints Day even. On that date I will send you another *De Profundis*.

I kiss your right hand, the one that writes.

Marie Paradis

P.S. Do not put your name on the envelope.

This letter remained unanswered.

Thérèse Pantevin   to Pierre Costals
La Vallée Maurienne   *Paris*

All Saints Day

Quick, let me have something to hold in my hands which
has felt your breath on it! If you only knew the people
around me! If you only knew what a horrible thing it is to
be entirely dependent on a power that does not wish you well.
Only you can save me. Give me life, so that I can be sure of
having it for all eternity.

This is a supreme adjuration. You are the breath of life to
me: do not let me expire.

Marie

I have had my photo taken, and am sending it to you. As
you see, I am young but not pretty. And in fact the photo
flatters me.

(Do not put your name on the envelope.)

Pierre Costals   to Thérèse Pantevin
Paris   *La Vallée Maurienne*

Mademoiselle,

I never for a moment imagined that one day I should find
myself answering one of your extravagant missives. Alas! I
was touched by the most recent ones; the damage is done.
You say that your life is in my hands. We know all about
that. But the possibility that you may really believe it is one
that I must face. Ought I, in that case, to ignore these appeals?

I cannot be so hard-hearted. Let us see what can be done for you.

There is no chance of the feeling you think you have for me ever arousing the slightest echo on my side. Do not persist in it: it would be like beating your head against a wall; you would wear yourself out. And besides, even if you were to reach me, you would get nothing from me, for I have nothing to give to anyone. Let me tell you this once and for all. Do not imagine that I shall ever weaken.

However, if that path is closed to you, it is not the only one. There is obviously a certain force in you, and it would be a pity to waste it on the first oaf you came across, with whom you might become infatuated for want of anyone better. When allowance is made for the element of sentimental gush in your devotion, which comes of your sex and age, what remains is perhaps not wholly bad; though it would be strange if God were to find it acceptable. I do not know exactly what he is, having not an atom of faith. But in him, or in the idea you have of him, you will certainly be better off than in making a 'home'. Homes! Plague centres, every one of them. If there is anything I can do for you, it is to encourage you in this quest, and to follow your progress with sympathy from afar – although, as I say, I believe neither in the divinity of Jesus Christ nor in the divinity of anyone else. But the rarefied heights of non-belief are familiar to me. They will be my prayer for you, if you wish. For it is all the same thing. Luckily.

Do not write me letters eight pages long every three days, as you will no doubt consider yourself entitled to do after this one. I tell you frankly, I shall leave them unread. My interest in you amounts to my being able to read a letter from you about once every three weeks, not every three days. Do not give in to the urge to write to me until you have put up such a fight as will have done you credit. And do not expect me to answer you. I will only answer you if I feel inclined, which is to say that my replies will be few and far between.

Upon which, I remain, Mademoiselle, yours sincerely,

Costals

Pierre Costals   to Mademoiselle Rachel Guigui
Paris   *Carqueiranne (Var)*

6 November 1926

Dear Guiguite,

Could I ask you to post from Carqueiranne (with apologies
for sending it to you in a sealed envelope) this letter addressed
to a young lady in the Loiret who has been wishing me well
(from the Loiret) for the past four years. Since she has literally
nothing else to do but think about me, you can imagine what
a good time she has. Plain, anything but desirable, but intelligent, cultivated, worthy. She is an orphan (her father was a
country solicitor of no standing), she learnt Latin all by herself, etc. . . . in fact altogether most estimable. I have a certain
sympathy for her, being acutely aware of what it must be like
to be a penniless spinster approaching thirty, and of a fairly
superior type, in Saint-Léonard (Loiret) of all places. It's
pathetic to see a woman of this calibre condemned either to
turn into a sour old virgin, or to marry a local shopkeeper,
or to take a lover (which might not be easy, since nature has
not been over-kind to her), and let herself go. I keep up the
illusion of friendship with her, because I know it bolsters her
up. She is coming to Paris in a day or two, and this time I
don't want to see her. A woman who loves you, but whom
you neither love nor desire, is just possible as a correspondent.
But face to face, ouch! I am giving the strictest orders at
home to say I have left for the Midi.

There is another young lady, this time from the Manche,
to whom I've just written after leaving unanswered three or
four letters she has sent me over the past three years. The
other day she sent me her photograph – she's a proper little
peasant, in a black orphan's smock; you couldn't imagine anything more ill-favoured. She's completely mad (in the mystical
mode), and would be nothing without her madness, which is
her only asset. A remark in one of her letters struck a chord
in me, and opened, if not my heart, at least that place deep
inside one where kindness and pity are thought to dwell: 'If
you only knew what a terrible thing it is to be entirely dependent on a power that does not wish you well!' I imagine

she means her family. Since it is not easy, with piety, to distinguish the boundary between madness and sublimity, I have plumped for sublimity and would like her to take advice as to whether she may not be made for the convent: anything would be better than that farmyard with all those cow-hands full of contempt for the little mystic. I'm sure that you, dear Guiguite, who are imbued with the humane spirit of Israel, would have approved of my answering her in the end. I know it was rash of me: good deeds are always rash. But I don't like refusing people the little bit of happiness they ask of you when their paths cross yours.

Nothing in particular to say to you, except to thank you for the pleasure you have given me so faithfully for so many months. Now that you are at Carqueiranne (I hope you had a good journey), you will have seen the fishermen's nets held up on the surface of the water by fragments of cork. My nights with you are like those fragments of cork holding me up on the surface of life. Without those nights, and the nights spent with my other little companions, I believe I would sink like a stone, what with the stupidity of my family, the vileness of my fellow-writers, and the time my friends make me waste.

I hope the latest of your protectors is a fine figure of a man and a nice chap. Come back to me in good form at the end of the month. I don't think I should mind losing you: it would amuse me to have a gap to fill. But on the whole I should be glad if you stayed.

Dear Guiguite, I love the pleasure I have with you, I love the pleasure I give you; in short, you are eighteen and I like you. Good-bye, my dear.

Your devoted servant,

C.

Pierre Costals   to Andrée Hacquebaut
Paris   *Saint-Léonard*

[*Letter dated from Carqueiranne and enclosed with the preceding one.*]

7 November 1926

Dear Mademoiselle,

What a bore! Here I am in this God-forsaken place, where I shall be stuck all the time you are in Paris. If I had been nearer, I would willingly have popped up to Paris to spare you this disappointment. But from here! ...

If you need help of any kind in Paris, a letter of introduction, or anything, let me know at once at Carqueiranne, 'c/o Mlle Rachel Guigui, 14 rue de la Plage.' Mlle Guigui is an elderly Jewess with whom I am lodging for a few days. Incorrigible as I am, I shall no doubt end up by falling into her arms, assuming that one can be inflamed by a person called Guigui, which I find hard to believe.

As I write to you, I can see from my window the irradiations of the zenith multiply themselves in sparkling facets on the shimmering methylene-blue of the sea. Then I think what it must be like to spend eleven months of the year at Saint-Léonard (Loiret).... And the beauty of the sea no longer seems quite so innocent.

Cordially yours,

C.

Well, no! I've just lied to you. I can't see the sea at all at the moment, for the simple reason that I am writing this in a café in Carqueiranne from which it is not visible. Even to tell you this harmless lie would have been painful to me. It is true that, in spite of all appearances to the contrary, it does happen that I do things that are painful to me. Rarely, but sometimes.

Andrée Hacquebaut	to Pierre Costals
Hôtel des Beaux-Arts	*Carqueiranne*
Paris	

11 November 1926

Costals, dear Costals, was your letter from Carqueiranne a disappointment to me? Yes and no. Yes, because to come to Paris and miss you is too idiotic. No, because a little letter like that easily makes up for a few moments of your pre-

sence. Your niceness! Still the same after all these years! So
you would really, if you had not been so far away, have
'popped up' to Paris simply to see me! And your adorable
postscript, the *guilt* I can detect in you for having told me
an insignificant little lie! How could one not love you, in spite
of your moods, your weeks of silence, your harsh words, the
teasing, rather disturbing side of you, the cruel mischievous-
ness, when all this is mitigated and absolved by your truly
divine goodness and delicacy of feeling? I have had nothing
but joy through you.

I am alone in my room in this little hotel. The fire is roar-
ing; down below, Paris stirs and bustles in the rain. Your
letter is on the table in front of me. It will help me to live
through these few days in Paris without you. It will help me,
too, to say to you everything I have to say. For this is a very
solemn letter.

During the summer at Saint-Léonard I find almost acceptable a pattern of life which in winter makes me shudder with
horror. There are, even at Saint-Léonard, nice young men to
go boating or bathing with, to while away the time with, and
they suffice. With the beginning of the cold weather, with
lamps and books, all that comes to an end. The cold makes
me feel the need for the things of the mind. And then I am
drawn to Paris. A few hours in Paris – yesterday Beethoven
at the Salle Gaveau, this morning the Fragonards at the Galerie
Charpentier – and I say to myself: No, it's impossible! I have
no vanity about being what I am, but I must recognize it.
And what I am makes me refuse to marry a nonentity. I have
always had the idea firmly rooted in my mind that a woman's
love cannot be an act of condescension, since in the carnal act
it is she who is the victim.

A provincial girl without means and without connections,
I cannot make a 'good' marriage which would bring me money
and position – for example a marriage in Paris, into a cultivated, well-to-do milieu (to find a cultivated husband I
should have to live in Paris half the year, independently, and
I can't afford that). A 'good' marriage being impossible, I only
want a marriage that will allow me to be overtly in love. If
I were to remain equally lonely and deprived, and in addition

tied for life to a man who bored me but whom nevertheless I
cared for sufficiently not to want to make him feel it, with
all the disadvantages I have now, minus my freedom, plus
innumerable worries, what would be the point? Only a great
love and the knowledge of performing a really fruitful task
would make the sacrifice of my liberty worth while.

There are two or three young men here who would, I
think, willingly marry me. They are not unattractive: young,
pleasant, perfectly decent and well-bred. One of them at least
I could perhaps succeed in loving if I really put my mind to
it. But in what a limited environment – provincial trades-
people – oblivious to poetry, to everything profound or subtle
or disinterested. A married man can perhaps detach himself
from his environment. But a married woman? She cannot cut
herself off either from her husband or from his circle, or even
risk shocking them. Can you imagine how devastating it is
for a woman to be even the slightest bit superior? That is the
crux of my tragedy. The pleasure of disdaining mediocrities
has to be paid for. And liking mediocrities must be paid for
by the mediocrity of the pleasure one gets from them. Ah!
what a wife I would have been for an artist! For to be an
artist's wife one must love the artist even more than the man,
dedicate oneself to making the former great and the latter
happy. And then, how restful to be alone together, to understand each other's unspoken thoughts.

I have a horror of old maids. I pity the unhappily married.
Illicit love revolts me. So? ... And I shall be thirty in April!
Thirty, the crucial age.... My head spins. I'm terrified of
botching everything. Oh Costals, what am I to do with my
life?

One thing alone sustains me: your existence. You alone
give me the poise a woman needs. If I shut my eyes an instant
and tell myself that *you exist*, I feel assuaged. Yes, one must
thank creatures such as you for existing, simply for existing!
Is fire diminished by needing something to kindle it? I love
you like a torch with which I set myself alight. So what has
happened to me is this: you have made every other man
uninteresting to me, for the rest of my life, and every other
future meaningless. I can no longer envisage any normal

happiness – I mean a commonplace marriage – without my whole being revolting against the insipidity of it, because I shall never have the strength to devote my life to a man I scarcely love at all. Imagine a mortal woman who had loved Jupiter, and could not then love any man, though wanting desperately to be able to love one.

How I should have liked to be able to do something for you, for your work! But I can do nothing, nothing! If I could write, I should write articles about you, or a book. I almost wish that you were poor, sickly, unrecognized. I almost wish that you were wandering in search of your life's work, as I am searching for mine. Your weakness would be my strength. But no, you are entirely self-sufficient, you are embedded, as it were, in your solitude, and what makes others hate you – your self-assurance – is for me a matter for regret. There is no hope of my ever being able to feel this bond between us, this unique bond : a conviction on your part that you can put your trust in me absolutely. But tell me, at least, that you will never need such devotion! For if, one day, you did come to need it, how terrible if I could not respond to your appeal because I was bogged down in some dreary task, undertaken out of despair of ever finding anything better to do!

Once, as I was writing to you, this sentence came to the tip of my pen: 'I love you with all my heart.' I did not dare write it, in case you misunderstood. Now that you know me, now that you realize that I am not and never will be 'in love' with you, I can write it with complete confidence, I can write it without the slightest reticence : I love you with all my heart.

You must not answer; you must forget this letter or keep only an impression of tenderness from it, if possible. Above all, you must not make me atone for it by changing your attitude towards me.

A.H.

P.S. I am having a dark-red dress made for the winter, all velvety and light. And I've bought myself a grey coat, very delicate and chic – oh! so chic – which looks as though it might have come from a smart couturier (it is in fact a copy). I shall also buy a tight-fitting grey feather toque, because it

is so kind to the face. .... You see how light-hearted I am in
spite of you.

To be elegant, perhaps even pretty. .... And all for what,
for whom? For the Saint-Léonardins. ....

Goodnight, Monsieur

Pierre Costals   to Andrée Hacquebaut
Paris   *Saint-Léonard*

26 November 1926

Dear Mademoiselle,

I write in answer to your esteemed letter of the 11th inst.
with the regulation fortnight's delay. One week during which
I did not even open your envelope (a little quarantine to which
I submit all letters from women, after which time there is a
chance that they may no longer be contagious). And one week
during which I put off replying to you day after day because
the thought of it bored me. Forgive me, but I find it difficult to
remain completely serious when people tell me they love me.

The fact is that I did not find your letter at all agreeable.
Why leave the nice, friendly plane we were on for the vulgarity and tediousness of 'sentiment'? You have now moved
on to such exalted heights that I doubt whether I shall be able
to follow you. I treated you with complete naturalness, as an
intelligent comrade, if you like. Now I shall have to watch my
step. Now I shall feel I have obligations towards you: an
obligation to show myself worthy of your sublime gift of
yourself, an obligation to treat you with infinite consideration
(of which this letter is already a sample), an obligation to give
you in return something more or less in proportion with what
you have done me the honour of offering me. So many obligations! And obligations, alas, have never been my strong suit.
I'm afraid you have been both clumsy and rash. You should
have kept it all to yourself, so that I could have gone on pretending that I hadn't understood.

To change the subject: you surprised me one day by con-
fessing your ignorance of English literature. I have just inherited the library of an old lady who had, I suppose, a kind

of feeling for me which it should be easy for you to reconstruct by analogy. Would you like me to send you a little
parcel of English literature in translation? I already have the
books in English. And it distresses me to think that a girl like
you might spend her whole life without having been brought
into contact with the genius of England.

Cordially yours, dear Mademoiselle. But keep a tight rein
on yourself, I beg of you.

C.

Andrée Hacquebaut   to Pierre Costals
Saint-Léonard   *Paris*

November 1926

How absurd you are! Imagine thinking that I wanted to lay
hands on you! And immediately you shake with fright, in
your ferocious desire for independence.

What, after all, does it all amount to? As I have told you,
you are like a god to me. And isn't a god more or less a mirror
in which to contemplate oneself and see oneself in a better
light? Does one not create him in one's own image, only
better? That is what you are, my sublimated double, the
strongest, the proudest, the best of me. I have, then, a calm,
cold passion for you. And beside this, my friendship. You are
at once a god and a chum – isn't that delicious?

What obligations does it impose on you? Give me what you
have given me up to now – I ask nothing more. I shall never
weigh more than a feather in your life. How small one would
be prepared to make oneself, in order to remain close to the
man one loves! As long as I can write to you, I shall not be
really unhappy. And what do I care even if you grow tired
of me, since I shall never grow tired of you, and I shall still
have your books? At the worst, even if you no longer gave
me anything more than you give everyone else, it would still
be a noble gift. Hence my attachment to you is calm and
relaxed.

I fancy Mme de Beaumont, who loved Chateaubriand more than Chateaubriand loved her, must have written to him as I am writing to you.

How deep-rooted the idea of mutual obligation is! One tells a person again and again: 'Don't worry. For your sake and for mine, I do not and will not love you. I have a passionate friendship for you, because it gives me pleasure, because I want it, because it makes me happy, because it is gratifying to think about another person, to look after him, to make him happy. I ask nothing of you. You owe me nothing. I love you at my own risk.' And the other person imagines that you love him with an irresistible love and are miserable because it is not requited. Nothing of the kind.

You will not, no, you cannot resent this melancholy half-offering of mine, finer in quality than the offerings of other women. Do not withhold your esteem from me. And write to me sometimes, I beg of you. When you maintain an absolute silence for a long time, I begin to fade away, I lapse into a sort of moral and spiritual lethargy. To understand becomes a matter of indifference to me, if I cannot make you share the fruit of my conquest.

I give you my hand.

A.H.

I accept with gratitude your offer of English books, although I would have preferred not to owe you anything for the moment.

Pierre Costals   to Andrée Hacquebaut
Paris   *Saint-Léonard*

30 November 1926

I recognize, dear Mademoiselle, that loving me is no fun. The moment I realize that someone cares for me, I'm disconcerted and annoyed. My next impulse is to put myself on the defensive. I have had a deep attachment for three or four people in my life, and they were always people I could have

sworn were not even remotely drawn towards me. I think if
they had loved me I should have been inclined to steer clear
of them.

To be loved more than one loves oneself is one of the
crosses of life. Because it obliges one either to feign a recipro-
cal passion which one does not feel, or to cause pain by one's
coldness and the rebuffs one administers. In either case there
is constraint (and a man like me cannot feel constrained without the risk of turning nasty), and in either case pain. As
Bossuet so powerfully put it: 'To love someone too much
is to do him an irreparable wrong.' It's almost what I once
wrote myself: 'To love without being loved is to do more
harm than good.' The consequence is to be found in La
Rochefoucauld: 'We are more prepared to love those who
hate us than those who love us more than we would wish.'
And your humble servant concludes: one should never tell
people one loves them without asking their forgiveness.

Anyone I love takes away part of my freedom, but in that
case it is I who wished it; and there is so much pleasure in
loving that one gladly sacrifices something for its sake. Anyone who loves me takes away all my freedom. Anyone who
admires me (as a writer) threatens to take it away from me.
I even fear those who understand me, which is why I spend
so much time covering my tracks – both in my private life
and in the persona I express through my books. What would
have delighted me, had I loved God, is the thought that God
gives nothing in return.

I am equally afraid, needless to say, of being the object of
a physical desire which I could not reciprocate. I would prefer
to have an utterly passive woman, a block of wood, in my
arms than a woman who got more pleasure from contact with
me than I from contact with her. I can remember some truly
hellish nights. ... There will surely be demonesses in hell who
desire one without one's desiring them. It is inconceivable
that a God who is an expert in torture will not have thought
of that.

I know so well how painful it is to be loved more than one
loves oneself that I have always kept a careful watch on
myself when I felt that I loved more than I was loved. That

has happened to me sometimes, of course, and also to feel that my desire was only tolerated out of complaisance: the person concerned had scruples, or else was frigid. How careful I was then to make my presence felt as little as possible, how gingerly I advanced, how attentively I watched for the first sign of lassitude, in order to go into reverse, to meet less frequently! ... Needless to say I suffered. But I knew that it was vital for my own sake, that I would lose everything if I tried to impose myself, and that anyhow it was I who was in the wrong for loving too much.

I know all about love: it's a feeling I have little respect for. Besides, it doesn't exist in nature; it's an invention of women. If a price were put on my head I should feel safer in the wilds, like a hunted animal, than with a woman who was in love with me. But there is affection. And there is affection mixed with desire, a splendid thing. In *every one* of the books I have published you will find, in one form or another, this affirmation: 'What matters to me above everything is loving.' But it is never a question of 'love'. It is a compound of affection and desire, which is not the same thing. 'A compound of affection and desire – what's that if it isn't love?' Well, no, it isn't love. 'Explain.' ... I don't feel like it. Women do not understand these things.

And finally, I don't like people needing me, intellectually, 'emotionally', or carnally. The inexplicable pleasure which my presence inspires in certain people diminishes them in my eyes. What do I care about having a place in someone else's universe!

I enclose an article I wrote on the subject many years ago. I would write it differently today. It is overstated and lacking in subtlety. But on the basic point I haven't changed.

One word more. You mention Pauline de Beaumont. I suspect Chateaubriand would not have done what he did for her if she hadn't been dying. He knew it was only for a brief moment.

My compliments to you, dear Mademoiselle.

C.

Fragment of an article by Costals

'The ideal in love is to love without being loved in return.'

... For the repugnance which some men feel for being loved, I can see several reasons, contradictory of course, inconsistency being a characteristic of the male.

Pride. – The desire to *keep the initiative*. In the love that others bear us, there is always something which eludes us, which threatens to catch us off guard, perhaps to overwhelm us, which has designs on us, which seeks to control us. Even in love, even when we are two, we do not want to be two, we want to remain alone.

Humility, or, if this seems too strong a word, absence of conceit. – The humility of a clear-sighted man, who does not think himself especially handsome or especially worthy, and finds it somehow *ridiculous* that his slightest gesture, word, silence, etc., can create happiness or misery. What an unfair power he is given! I have no great opinion of a man who is conceited enough to think aloud : 'She loves me', who does not try at least to minimize the thing by saying : 'She's getting worked up about me.' Whereby, no doubt, he belittles the woman, but only because he has first of all belittled himself.

An attitude that I would compare, for instance, to that of a writer who finds it *ridiculous* to have 'disciples', because he knows what his personality is made of, and what his 'message' adds up to. Any man worthy of the name despises the influence he exercises, in whatever direction, and puts up with having to exercise it as the price he must pay for his urge to express himself. *We* do not want to be dependent. How then can we approve of those who would depend on us? It is an exalted view of human nature that makes one refuse to be a leader.

Dignity. – Embarrassment and shame at the *passive* role a man who is loved has to play. For him, the state of being loved is suitable only to women, animals and children. For a man to allow himself to be embraced, caressed, held hands with, looked at with swimming eyes – ugh! (Even the majority of children, however effeminate they may be in France,

45

thoroughly dislike being kissed. They put up with it out of politeness, and because they have to, grown-ups being more muscular than they are. Their impatience with these slobberings is obvious to everyone except the slobberer, who thinks they are delighted by it.)

The desire to *remain free*, to protect oneself. – A man who is loved is a prisoner. No need to dwell on this, since it is well known.

Thérèse Pantevin   to Pierre Costals
La Vallée Maurienne   *Paris*

3 December 1926

†
A.M.D.G.

You have answered me! You have written to me to say that you would be willing to read a letter from me every three weeks! I have read this and kissed these words. Do not let me languish. If you could only see how pale I am! Quick, write some more words for me to kiss.

I crushed your letter against my breast, against my medals, until they hurt me, and the more they hurt the more it did me good. Everything that hurts me does me good. I dream of you coming into my room, but if you really came in I would probably begin to cry.

If I could, I would gladly leave the 'plague centre'. But where could I go? I ought to set out, like Abraham, walking straight ahead without knowing where, in the holy freedom of the children of God. For I dare not go to you. I would not know what to say to you, you would not be able to drag a word out of me ... and yet I await a sign from you, in spite of my terrible fear of disappointing you. But I don't spend all my time in the house; I'm often in the fields. I go to the local town three or four times a year. Last week we went to the fair at N— and I enjoyed myself very much. You see I don't deserve to be a nun, if that is what you meant.

However, do not start thinking I'm a flibbertigibbet. Every day I repose in the Eucharist, as I repose body and soul beside you in the silence of each night, and then everything that exists reposes in me. And I pray for my poor father, who does not believe in God, and who treats me so roughly. Do you know what he said just now at supper? 'It would be better to rear pigs than daughters.' He was looking at me when he said it.

Good-bye, my friend. My heart is heavy with all I have to give you. Love me just one jot as much as I love you, and Eternity will take us to its bosom.

Marie Paradis

Pierre Costals
Paris

to Thérèse Pantevin
La Vallée Maurienne

9 December 1926

Mademoiselle,

If you belong to Jesus Christ, you must not belong to him in a muddled way. Granted that God exists, he has given love to human beings only that they may give it back to him and him alone. Must I remind you of St Augustine's words: 'The soul can only reach God by approaching him without human intervention,' or the mystic (Meister Eckhart) who goes so far as to say: 'Do you know why God is God? It is because he is independent of all creatures.' You dishonour God by mixing him up with me. Such sloppiness is nauseating. When I see Jesus Christ mixed up with the human species (mixed, not juxtaposed, for juxtaposition occurs in all of us), I always think of the Princess Palatine's story of the schoolboy who had pictures of saints painted on his bottom so as not to be whipped.

You tell me you don't 'deserve' to take the veil. Say rather 'I am not destined' or 'I have not been chosen'. That is quite possible. But do not speak of deserving. Just as the love of one person for another has no need to be deserved, so the grace God gives a person to consecrate to him is given to that person in preference to an infinity of deserving persons without his having deserved it. I would even go so far as to say that, if

I were God, what I should like in a person would be my grace, just because it is privilege. This said, you are right not to be too self-satisfied. To be too firmly convinced that God approves of an action is often a clear sign that it is not being done for him and through his spirit, just as it is often a sign that a human action is defective to be too sure that it will be applauded.

Perhaps there are forces within you that could be harnessed to God's purposes. I don't know what you may have to lose by it, but I know it's negligible. It must have been one of the Fathers of the Church who invented the expression: he who loses wins. It pains me to think of you becoming involved in the imbecility of the world. You go to town, you go to the fair, and far from being overwhelmed with disgust by what you see there, you take pleasure in it. If you believe, what are you doing in the world? There is nothing innocent in the world once one believes (to enjoy the taste of a glass of water is to slap Christ's face); nothing that can even be justified. However trifling your activity, it is ridiculous; I should like to see your actions die out one by one, as lights go out at midnight in a town. One of my fellow-writers having spoken of the 'virtue of contempt', an ecclesiastic, writing in some review or other, danced a veritable fandango of scorn and derision: 'The virtue of contempt! A fine sort of Christian!' But the Gospel is full of Christ's contempt for the world; and this very morning I read somewhere: 'What a joy to know how contemptible the world is! How weak one is not to despise it as much as it deserves!' Who wrote that? The 'gentle' Fénelon, the 'swan'. (*Medit. V*) But better still – the last word in fact: the dying Jesus prays for his executioners, and refuses to pray for the world. *Non pro mundo rogo.* 'I pray not for the world.' (*St John* XVII, 9). *There's* a thunderbolt that impresses me more than the one that occurred when he expired. He prays for his executioners, because that is an extravagance worthy of his genius, but he refuses to pray for the corrupt and foolish multitude which he cursed in the Gospel. 'I pray not for the world, but for them which thou hast given me.' Wonderful, shattering words – it does me good to hear them! and now, Mademoiselle, be one of those for whom Jesus does not pray.

The sin against the Holy Ghost touches me deeply. Maybe there is at this moment a religious house waiting for you to bury yourself in body and soul, as I bury myself body and soul in my writings; it awaits you as the earth awaits the morning dew. That you are alive, I can believe. But alive with spiritual life? I have no means of knowing what there is in you; perhaps there is nothing. You have no more pressing objective than to find out what your impulses and inclinations amount to. Only a priest can disentangle them. A good confessor is the foundation of the edifice you must build. Go and see Father M— at the monastery of the — at L—. I know Father M—; he has the distinction of having been the greatest sinner in the world – which means that he will understand your sins the better, knowing what sin is. He will induce in you such a state of humility that the confession of those sins will be as enjoyable to you as the flames were to the martyrs. He will never anticipate the grace within you, supposing it to be there, but will follow it humbly and firmly, after testing it with the greatest care. Although today people no longer enter into religion unthinkingly, as they used to do (and as people continue to enter into matrimony), the Church cannot be too careful in making sure of a vocation. You should not be made a nun by men but by God.

You pray for your father? You would do better to pray for yourself. Have you forgotten how insistent the Gospel is on that point? And you would do better to read the Gospel, and understand it, than to go so often to Mass, to Communion, etc. Abuses are often more dangerous than errors, because one is less on one's guard against them. Piety should be devoid of gestures, like sorrow, and, I might almost venture to say, as silent. How eloquent the silence of Moses before God!

Do not cease to remind yourself, whatever I may write to you, that I am not a Christian believer. Faith is darkness – the expression falls frequently from religious pens; and I am all crude brightness. Do not cease to bear in mind that I have no faith, that I do not miss it, that I do not ever expect to have it, that I do not ever wish to have it. 'There is a road which, though it may sometimes appear the right one, leads to hell.' Perhaps I am that road. In imagination and in hope I have damned myself a hundred thousand times. In action – in the total and absolute fulfilment of my desires – I have damned myself another hundred thousand times. And in memories and regrets I have damned myself another hundred thousand times. And that is part of my glory. And I have helped enough women to damnation to help one in the opposite direction. For I am a spirit of grace, and spirits of grace radiate like grace itself, which assumes every form. And I am – essentially – *he-who-assumes-every-form*.

I have written to you in a language that must be partly incomprehensible to you. You may forage what you can from it.

Forgive me, Mademoiselle, for my presumption.

Costals

Andrée Hacquebaut   to Pierre Costals
Saint-Léonard   *Paris*

24 December 1926

You do not write to me for more than three weeks. Then at last a slender post-card with no more than a dozen words on it brings me your greetings and asks for my news. My news? I cannot go on telling you *ad infinitum* that I'm unhappy. I must, however, find some way out of this state of crisis which is killing me. The day when it is proved to me beyond a shadow of doubt that every outlet is closed to me as far as love is concerned – and that day cannot be far off – I shall persist no longer. It would be horrible to cling on. The only alternative is voluntary renunciation, a pure and dignified life. I belong to the sacrificial generation, the girls whose chances of love were decimated by the war with its toll of young men: we too are widows. As for man-hunting, for adventure, I am not yet ripe for that.

It seems to me that such a renunciation would open up fresh fields for me. 'I'm beaten, it's all over and done with. Therefore, everything that happens to me from now on will be a bonus. Since I no longer seek, it may be that I've already found.' I have often noticed in myself a sudden reversal of this kind when I reach the climax of some experience I've been going through : a burst of furious pride, a sort of emotional desiccation and detachment, a sudden asperity towards fate : 'After all, come what may, I still have myself.'

I still have you, too, of course. In my confusion and despair I have a kind of peace : 'He cannot, he will not be my happiness. But he is my truth. He does not want me to love him – I would fail to please him and would destroy myself. Nevertheless, it fills me with a great peace, in spite of my life's failure, when so many women will never find the man who would make their hearts throb, or will love heaven knows whom out of the need to love, it fills me with a great peace to have discovered at least this certainty : that there exists a man who is everything to me, whom I could have loved with my whole being. I no longer need to search or to wait – the exhausting fate of lonely women.' Yes, telling myself this appeases me. The impression of having *achieved*, of having *had*, of escaping at last from that vague and indefinable torment, from the inordinate appetite for love – the renouncing of a precise treasure, and not innumerable and unknown possible treasures – why, in comparison it's almost tantamount to possessing.

Christmas ! An abyss of boredom and mediocrity with the people among whom I have to spend it. A day of rain and nostalgia and misery. Why are there days when all those hostile things which at other times lie dormant and innocuous rise up and assail one all at once ? It's agonizing to have to undergo this onslaught. And I think of the Christmases of those who love one another, of the adorable Christmas in *Werther*. What a pity I can no longer put my shoes in the fireplace ! I would have put two pairs, because there are four things I long for madly : a husband (with love), a gramophone, a book about Cosima Wagner, and a hat decorated with an aigrette, a hat I won't describe to you, because you would make fun of me.

A Happy New Year ! I'm very fond of you, you know, Costals. And if happiness could be given like a diamond, it would long ago have passed from my hand into yours. Once more I offer you my undying devotion. But when, oh when will you ever make use of it?

A.H.

This letter remained unanswered.

Saint-Léonard. January. Seven degrees of frost. At night, in spite of the stove, the water freezes in the Hacquebaut house.

What is most immediately striking about Andrée's room is that everything in it, furniture, hangings, objects, is at least twenty years old and looks it: for twenty years nothing has been bought, or next to nothing. The only things of any beauty are some reproductions of famous pictures, chosen with taste, and a very unfeminine taste (a taste in which there is a feeling for grandeur).

The sound of a hooter outside. How often this hooter has made her heart miss a beat! In spite of the cold, she opens the window. The postman's big bicycle-lamp lights up the door of the neighbouring house. Then it moves, comes nearer. As the lamp passes Andrée flings out a wish to it as though it were a shooting star: 'O God, make it stop!' But the lamp moves away into the distance. Out there, too, is the man she calls to, who also goes by without stopping.

Already fairly isolated from humanity, she is isolated even more by the cold. The snow-bound atmosphere muffles sounds. Everything lives in slow motion, everything shrivels up. Express trains no longer run. The mail arrives a day late. But what does it matter, after all? Never a letter from Costals. Luckily she knows that in February she will be going to Paris for a month.

She had always suffered from the feeling of having nobody at the other end of the line, from not knowing what person, what cause to dedicate herself to. As a child she already showed symptoms of the disease that Costals, in a neologism worthy of a medical student, called Andrée's 'letteritis'. In those days she used to write letters to herself, rather like the English poet in the last war, who at each port of call on the way to the Dardanelles, hired an urchin to wave a handkerchief when the steamer sailed (Costals professed to find such a trait utterly *repulsive:* he could not possibly have shaken hands with a man with that sort of sensibility). Later on, she had contributed for some time to the correspondence columns of the women's papers, which are the young girl's substitute for men, as lap-dogs are the grown woman's substitute for babies. This correspondence had ceased when she began writing to Costals.

She scribbled page after page to him, for hours on end, stopping only because of cramp in her hand. As with most women, what she wrote in the form of letters was in fact her diary – huge pages without margins, unnumbered, with words scratched out or written over, and lines added in every direction and even across other lines. Whenever Costals received one of these letters, he would weigh it in his hand with a sigh, assessing the number of pages it must contain : for a man who, like most men, could not read long letters, it was an affliction every time. It was unusual for the envelope not to be held together with bits of stamp paper lest it should burst under the weight. Inside, Costals would often find a photograph of Andrée which he would tear up in a rage and throw into the waste paper basket without even glancing at it. Ah! if she had seen him then it would have been like a dagger in her heart. But also, in an instant, she would have seen the light at last. Unless, incurably, she were to think : 'Only love could account for such a fit of rage. What has he got against me today?' Sometimes she would perfume her letters with such a pungent scent that he was obliged to hang them out on clothes pegs for the night; but even this was not enough, and the drawer of his desk would reek for days on end. If he complained to her, she would complain back : how could friendship be affected by such trifles? She was incapable of realizing (1) that there was no friendship, and (2) if there had been, yes, it would have been affected, because in anything to do with the quality of personal relations, there are no trifles. It was the same with her writing-paper, which was of an 'impossible' format. As Costals kept her letters, he had pointed out to her how awkward they were for his files, overlapping them and destroying their neatness. It was a waste of breath – so much so that he was occasionally provoked into throwing some of her letters away out of sheer exasperation at seeing their edges frayed like lace in his files.

From time to time, Costals would send a reply to these letters – illegible little notes, scribbled as fast as he could manage, in which he put down whatever came into his head – literally anything – and in which he always teased her a little, because it was in his nature to tease. *She* believed that one only teases people one loves. In her more lucid moments, she found these notes touching in their goodwill, which indeed they were.

At the beginning, she had also sent him little presents – baskets of flowers or fruit. At first he had been weak or lazy or charitable enough to accept them: 'She would be very hurt if I refused them.' When she sent him a rather elegant cigarette-holder, he sent it back with a friendly letter. For a year she stopped sending presents, then began again – eau de Cologne, sachets of lavender. He wrote to her: 'Dear Mademoiselle, I shall not return your little presents any more. I shall give them automatically to my mistresses' (which was what he had done). That did it. There were no more little presents.

Andrée's other cure for boredom was reading. Books borrowed, books ordered from a lending library, books even bought (mad extravagance – books costing thirty francs!): she read until her eyes ached. Almost always worth-while books. And almost always something interesting in the reflections she scribbled in the margins.

Letter-writing, reading, what else? She ordered prospectuses from travel agencies, catalogues of rare books, manuscripts, records, catalogues from big stores, and thumbed through them interminably, marking what she would have liked to have, almost without bitterness. She did not resent the fact that millions of fools, thanks to their ill-gotten fortunes, could enjoy the art, the luxury, the things of the mind, which were denied to her. She had tried to 'write', but soon realized that she had no literary talent. Sometimes, at the end of her tether, she would go out and walk aimlessly in the countryside, although she had no feeling for nature, at least the nature round Saint-Léonard. She would only have liked it as a background for living people.

There were times when this life was bearable, when, if she did not feel happy, she was not exactly unhappy. Reading a good book, she would say to herself: 'To think that there are women who work seven hours a day in an office!' At other times she was bored to distraction – so much time on her hands that she did not know what to do with – but nonetheless she resisted manual work, from an acute sense of the value of time. While her mother was alive she had never wanted to help her with the housework, to darn, or sew her dresses. 'Imagine making jam when I could spend the time improving my mind, discovering a great writer I haven't read, learning something, no matter what, if only from reading Larousse!' Only an acute attack of misery would drive her to take up a manual chore. Thus, whenever she felt particularly distressed, she took to darning her stockings. It had become a formula: great unhappiness = darning of stockings – so much so that the crimson 'egg' she used for this purpose gave her a twinge when she came across it in her more serene moments. Since her mother's death, she had had to get down to minor household chores – but never without a feeling of vehement impatience. It was something she simply could not accept.

One day Costals had said to her: 'If I had had the misfortune to have a daughter, I should have been stiff with anxiety until she was married off, all the more so if she had no money. Parents are terribly proud of themselves when they produce a brat, and go round trumpeting it to the world, but when it comes to bringing it up with a little intelligence, nothing doing. Of course I realize how awful it must be for decent people to do what has to be done to get a daughter settled – intrigue, entertain, etc. – because everything connected with marriage is unquestionably the greatest nonsense that can happen in the life of a human being. But they shouldn't have got themselves into the mess in the first place! It's always the same – producing children, and then not knowing what to do with them. So much care and attention and conscientiousness about birth, and so much frivolity, blindness and stupidity about education. And then we come to the parents who haven't enough money to get their daughters married off, and go on waiting, waiting for God knows what, waiting until she becomes crabbed and can't afford to be so choosy. I know some really criminal parents, whose daughter was made for marriage, but who condemned her to celibacy in order to keep her with them. All this is simply to explain to you that there is only one thing for you to do – to take a job in Paris that is not too exacting and that provides you with your bread and butter, and to concentrate, to the exclusion of everything else, on *meeting people*, in other words looking for a husband. Your sole aim, for the time being, should be to make social contacts.'

Mademoiselle had taken offence at these words. She was like those bogus artists who rail against the bourgeoisie but who are more bourgeois than anyone. 'Make social contacts' – so that was the advice he gave to a superior girl like her!

'You who despise society, you who wallow in solitude, you tell me that!'

'I live in solitude because I've won and paid for the right to live in solitude. When I was twenty-five *I* "met people" too. It's because I did things that bored me then that I can now do what I like. It's not a question of whether "meeting people" is fun. It's a question of whether you want to remain a penniless spinster in Saint-Léonard (Loiret). If not, you must make a suitable marriage, and you will only make a suitable marriage if you have an inexhaustible supply of suitable gentlemen parading in front of you, like stallions parading round a paddock. Which you can only do in Paris. Find a job there. If you like, I can help you to find one.'

'I'll be saddled with her the whole time,' Costals had thought to himself. In spite of which, in this unfortunate fit of altruism he not only told her, 'I'll help you to find a job', but went further: 'I'll introduce you to people.' She agreed.

If she had not been in love with him, he might perhaps have taken her on as his secretary, his own having just left him. But imagine taking on as secretary a woman who is in love with you! ... Costals had a friend called M. Armand Pailhès, an excellent man, a splendid paterfamilias, who was secretary-general of a big firm of robbers (a company formed for the reconstruction of the war-devastated North). He offered a job as a typist, and so Andrée landed in Paris.

But when it came to doing a job that encroached on her inner life, Andrée bridled – she could not help it. She could not work for half an hour without heaving sighs which infuriated her boss. She would spend twenty minutes at a time in the lavatory reading Nietzsche. She arrived late and left early. After three or four days, with a volume of Valéry lying in her half-open drawer, she would bury herself in 'pure poetry' as soon as her boss's back was turned. Her habit of suddenly closing the drawer if he looked round gave her away. Apart from this, although she considered that her tact was nothing less than heroic, her notes to Costals, at the rate of one every three days ('Won't you come to the concert of Spanish music on Sunday? . . .' 'I'm going to the exhibition of prints at the Bibliothèque Nationale on Saturday. If by any chance you were free. . . .') exasperated him. He excused himself two or three times, did not reply to the next few letters, and finished by tearing them up without opening them. And it must be admitted that he did nothing about 'introducing her to people'. He too considered himself heroic, for having got her settled in Paris, and his heroism was strictly limited. Take Andrée to parties! He would rather die. In short, both regarded themselves as heroic, which is always a bad sign. When, at the end of the month, enlightened about the girl's behaviour, M. Pailhès found a pretext to give her back her cherished freedom, everyone was happy, Andrée included. To live in Paris but to be imprisoned in that stupid office, to have everything she loved within arm's reach but to be unable to enjoy it, was worse than the provinces, where at least, if she suffered, she suffered without irritation. It was almost with a sigh of relief that she took the train back to Saint-Léonard.

In the waiting-room of the War Pensioners' Review Board, awaiting examination, two hundred average Frenchmen, ex-service men, neither bourgeois nor plebeian, but of that intermediate class which is the backbone of France, with their characteristic French tendency to be buttoned up to the eyebrows, and their pallid and, my God, so unprepossessing Parisian faces.

A restless crowd, with men coming and going, edging in and out, like bulls in a herd when they sense a man approaching; the one-legged men in particular stubbornly refuse to sit down. One man jumps at every name that is called; another asks the way to the lavatory : the thought that his request for a renewal of his pension will be refused has upset his inside. But there are also some quiet little men, old lags, reading their newspapers. How wonderfully brave of that one over there to open the *Action Française* in the middle of the crowd! (If they don't reduce *his* disablement scale, there's no government left.) And the doleful faces of the seriously wounded, escorted by their 'good ladies'. And the bourgeois with the red ribbon of the Legion of Honour, sitting not with the common herd but a little apart, on the only chair in the room, in order to make it clear that his respectability has remained intact throughout this grim ordeal. (Costals, on entering, had put his gloves in his pocket so as not to be the only person there wearing them.)

Costals imagined all these men in uniform, and then he loved them, whereas in their civilian clothes he had a tendency, typically ruling class, to regard them as malingerers. 'That fat one, for instance. . . . Is it possible,' our professional psychologist asks himself, 'to be ill and fat at the same time? And this one here with his shifty look, there's obviously nothing wrong with him, absolutely nothing.' Whereupon the man with the shifty look turns round and shows the professional psychologist an empty coat-sleeve.

A wave of respect, hope, fear, a sudden sharpening of attention, as a doctor passes through. Some of them salute him, to remind him who they are, although he has never seen them in his life. He passes by with his cigarette in the air – not that he is a smoker (he is nothing of the sort), but because smoking being forbidden here, it is a sign of his power. To two or three poor devils who are particularly keen saluters he offers, or rather *tenders* his hand, without stopping or turning his head. As he goes through, the man of power moves the men aside by taking them by the arm with an air of affable superiority, as one touches the backs of sheep when one is trying to make one's way through a flock. At first, when they do not know who is taking their arm from behind, they start indignantly; but as soon as they see who it is, their faces light up: the man of power has *touched* them, unworthy as they are! Ah yes, they are in good hands!

If the doctor stops to speak to one of them, he is suddenly surrounded by three or four, then six, then ten, who crowd around him shamelessly and listen, hoping to pick up a hint which will help them to obtain something, or simply hasten their turn. They are suddenly so humble, so insanely, incorrigibly respectful towards people in authority, so ready to accept anything, that it is painful to see.

A placard warns: 'Doctors are strictly forbidden to accept fees on the premises of the Review Board.' Why, O Administration, do you have to put the idea into our heads that there may be something shady about such fees? We know perfectly well that everything to do with pensions is as pure as the driven snow.

What a superb play of expressions on the face of one of the men when a doctor leaves the room by the outer door! He struggles against his natural shyness, finally overcomes it, and quickly makes for the exit behind the doctor, whom he will buttonhole outside; and he lowers his eyes, feigning indifference, so that the others will not spot his game and follow him in order to accost the doctor at the same time.

Some men leave, but more come in – so much so that (utterly convinced as one is that one will be the last to go in) one tells oneself that there will never be an end to it. Which is indeed a very 'wartime' sentiment.

From time to time an assistant appears at the door of one of the consulting rooms and calls out the names of the men whose turn it is. Those whose civilian lives are on a par with their military ones for wretchedness, the eternal second-raters, answer 'Present!' like keen young recruits. When one of the assistants shouts the names in a stentorian voice, some of the men laugh, and the others, realizing that it was funny, laugh too. A great wave of laughter. They are suddenly right back at the Front.

Some of the men hunch their backs on the way into the

consulting-room to make themselves look iller. Others preen themselves and look ingratiating, thinking that this will make the best impression. The room concerned with the 'respiratory and circulatory systems' is much the most popular, because malingering is easiest there. Through the open door, the surgery appears bathed in a limpid, greenish glow, like an aquarium or an oriental night. One can catch a glimpse of what is happening in the consulting-room. One man tries to read what the doctor is writing about him, and goes on talking, lying into the void, while the doctor stands there casually turning his back on him. Another breathes heavily, oppressively. Another comes out pulling up his trousers, and the price-tag is still to be seen on his underpants, bought only yesterday because he was ashamed of his old ones. His furtive look betrays the fact that he has hoodwinked the doctor, or thinks he has hood-winked him, and he walks with his eyes lowered, like a man going to the Communion rail, to hide the gleam of triumph in his eyes which might give him away. Others come out with collars and ties undone, which accentuates the guard-room aspect of the place (on his way here Costals had made the taxi-driver hurry, thinking that if he were five minutes late he would be court-martialled). Some of the men argue the toss as they come out, with their rapacious, tubercular Parisian faces. But they are peaceable rebels, very French. A swig of white wine and it will all be over – or another doctor has only to cross the room for that awful gleam of humility to appear in their eyes again. They hope to get something out of him, so they cease to be rebels. One only rebels when one has nothing to lose by it.

As the hours go by, exhaustion begins to set in. Even the cripples have given up standing. The herd has become stupefied. When one sees how they have acquiesced, how one has acquiesced oneself, in waiting from half-past eight until ten minutes to twelve, one understands how *it* lasted four and a half years. . . .

A blind man came out of one of the rooms, led by a girl – and for Costals the war atmosphere collapsed there and then like a burst balloon. She had slender, slanting eyes – bluish below her black hair, as in Andalusia, and as disturbing as dark eyes in a real blonde; a tiny forehead (ah, nice and stupid!); curls down her neck – and although he had always proclaimed that he only liked clean-shaven necks, the pleasure of contradicting himself (his privilege, like God's) now made him adore these curls. Her skin was stretched so tight that it might have been marble, and it was matt, though her nose shone a little, as marble statues are polished in places where they have been kissed a great deal. She held her head a little to one side, as though to indicate the point on her neck where she should be kissed. He loved the way she patted and re-arranged her hair: the gesture of the midinette. He liked this community of gestures among women. Her body was well-rounded and yet slender: what is known as *morbidezza*, is it not?

As she passed by, Costals sniffed the odour she left in her wake, his nose quivering like a dog's. The couple went out. Without a moment's hesitation, Costals followed them. He would concoct a pretty lie for the head of the Review Board.

He was about to offer to find them a taxi. But they were hardly in the street before an empty taxi drew up. They hailed it, and it was the distinguished novelist who was left standing on the pavement.

He was delighted. 'Now I shall be able to work in peace,' he said to himself.

On the very day she arrived in Paris Andrée went to a concert. In the past these hours of music had meant so much to her in her loveless life. They were a substitute for all the other ecstasies. It was as though thousands of lovers clasped her in their arms. What a let-down it was, afterwards, from this seventh heaven to the Parisian street! At such moments she felt strongly that she could never marry an ordinary person. This time she was bored at the concert – a mixture of dejection and indifference. This music, which she had once loved so desperately, for want of anything else to love, now seemed to her so insipid by comparison with the proximity of Costals.

Costals spoiled her taste for everything else, demolished everything around her, everything she relied on, created a vacuum
as though he wanted her to love nothing but himself. It was
no longer Beethoven, it was he, his 'music of perdition'. Listening to the Pastoral Symphony, with its imitations of bird calls,
she found it puerile. The sounds reached her across a layer of
distraction and boredom. Actually, she was not listening, she
could not listen. The most trashy music would have accompanied her daydreams quite as well.

Costals had invited her to dinner the following night. The
restaurant was a little twenty-franc bistro. They talked of
nothing but literature. Flanked on either side by other diners
a few feet away, she did not dare speak to what lay nearest
her heart. But in fact she scarcely felt the need to. She was in
Paris for a month : there was no hurry. And moreover, now
that she was with him she felt a profound sense of unison, as
though they were brother and sister. (She kept coming back
to the phrase 'brother and sister' – although now she was
thinking 'Byron and Augusta', which was to give it an extra
twist.) Such peace, such well-being, such security, such abandon! An impression of the futility of words, and a feeling
of being marvellously alone, almost more alone than when she
was by herself. . .

She was astonished to find herself unperturbed. It must, she
thought, be due to their profound intellectual understanding,
stronger than love and superior to it. And also because, ever
since Costals' harsh letter, she was trying hard to keep to the
plane of virile friendship on which he wanted her to remain,
and to hold romance at bay. She had no desire, even, when she
was with him, to indulge in those chaste caresses which girls
love, except for an occasional longing to kiss his hand. And
even this did not seem to her to be an amorous gesture, but
rather an overflowing of gratitude, as though she could not
find words to express her feelings, or dared not, or could not
say them.

As for him, at the other side of the table, his eyes never
rested on her, but looked over her head; but she did not
notice it. Besides, he never looked at anyone he did not desire;
always beyond them.

At one point, however, his eyes fell on the girl's bare fore-arms – and he could not take them away. Her arms were dirty. He tried in vain to persuade himself that their greyish tinge was the natural colour of the skin : the illusion was impossible. For a long while he kept his eyes glued to her arms, unable to utter another word. Perhaps, if he had desired her at all, he might have found her even more desirable (a big 'if'). Since he did not desire her, the sight froze him.

The atmosphere of cheerful banter created by Costals (and quickly recaptured) became even more animated towards the end of the meal. Andrée thought it must be the effect of the wine, or even of her presence. In fact this gaiety had sprung up suddenly in Costals the moment he had decided he was going to cut the evening short and pretend he had to get away early : it was the gaiety of the horse that sniffs the stable.

She accepted her dismissal with good grace, and went home on foot. This calm and serenity sustained her at each of their meetings. After the agonies induced by Costals' long silences, during which she longed for something shattering to happen to cure her of her love – silences which might have driven her to all kinds of folly – when she saw him again everything became simple and peaceful, everything happened in the same natural, easy rhythm – so much so that she found herself being almost cold with him.

On leaving her, Costals had said : 'I'll get in touch with you in two or three days.' A week having elapsed, she wrote to him. Costals groaned, but decided that it would be cruel to go on depriving her of another meeting during this paltry month in Paris by which she had set so much store. He had two appointments in the same district, the avenue Marceau, two days later, one at four o'clock, the other at eight. Between them he would be free. He arranged to meet her at half past five in the rue Quentin-Bauchart, on the pavement in front of number 5. He would be leaving this house at that time, after visiting some friends.

On the pavement in the rue Quentin-Bauchart at twenty-five past five, Andrée was already accusing Costals of being late. Obviously he had forgotten their appointment; he had come out early and gone away. She was a little surprised at this rendezvous in the street after dark, on a bitterly cold day in early February. 'Would he make such a rendezvous with a woman he really loved, or who meant anything at all to him?' But he emerged, her heart leapt, and off they went side by side down the dark street with its red and white lights.

'I'm not in very good form,' Costals said straight off. 'The other day I saw in a shop a piece of jade which I coveted. A thousand francs. I decided to go back to the shop that evening and buy it. And then I ran into an old lady who used to keep a flower stall where I bought violets for my girl-friends a few years ago. She's a widow; she told me her two children were both ill, her brother treated her badly, and she was destitute. Crash! There I was utterly disarmed. I was ashamed to buy my piece of jade, and pressed the thousand-franc note into her hand. I haven't got over it yet.'

'What do you mean?'

'I haven't yet got over the irritation I felt at giving her the thousand francs instead of buying the piece of jade.'

'What was to stop you buying the jade as well?'

'Oh! I bought it all right, but it wasn't the same thing. What annoys me is to have given away a thousand francs out of pure charity. It's ruined my week.'

'Nonsense, the satisfaction of ... no, I won't say "of duty done" – that would be too pompous. But after all, don't you feel a certain satisfaction at having given pleasure to an old woman you were sorry for?'

'No. I feel. . . .'

'Go on, say it: you feel regret.'

'Yes, regret. I'm ashamed. And at the same time there's something else that worries me. I feel that a thousand francs. . . . What's a thousand francs? I'm tormented by the desire to give her more.'

'How complicated you are!'

'But you don't know what pity is. It's a feeling that can ruin your life. Luckily I know how to protect myself. I have a

64

very strict egotist's discipline. If I hadn't I wouldn't have written my books. I had to choose. You'll be able to test this egotism one day, God willing. . . .'

'Did he do what he has done for me out of pity?' she wondered. She believed that he was fond of her, but could not make out in what way. Perhaps he would have been just as kind, just as devoted, to a male friend. Yet there were times when she thought to herself that one isn't as helpful and sensitive as that simply out of kindness. Had she not been afraid of annoying him, she would have asked him whether he treated her as he did out of pure comradeship – an exquisite sense of comradeship – or whether there was an element of love in it. In other words – how could she put it? – whether he was attracted to her.

But Costals, having caught sight of a notice-board advertising a flat to let, glanced up at the building and said :

'I've been haunted by the idea of moving ever since I can remember. Would you mind coming with me while I have a look at this place? I've rather fallen for the house.'

A few minutes later the concierge was showing them round the flat. What a strange sensation for Andrée! Almost as though they were a young married couple, or engaged. It made her feel dizzy . . . and it was even more extraordinary when the concierge said to her :

'Everything works very well. Perhaps Madame would care to see . . . the hot water. . . .'

'Madame'. . . . And in the bathroom! Was it really possible that Costals did not realize how provocative it was for a girl – and a girl of whose love for him he was well aware – to be shown round a flat which he thought of making his home? Was it possible that he had no ulterior motive? And she was not too badly dressed to be taken for his wife! Meanwhile he was asking her advice : should that window be walled up, this wall knocked through? She answered mechanically, like a good housewife, but her soul was elsewhere, borne away as though on a gust of wind to a realm so unexpected and improbable that it frightened her.

'Six rooms . . .' she said for the sake of saying something. 'Isn't it rather on the large side?'

T – T.G. – C

'Not at all. Drawing-room, dining-room, my study, my bed-room, a junk-room, and then the other bedroom, the "tomb of the unknown woman"....'

'Tomb? Are you a Bluebeard?'

'No, "tomb" in another sense – a double sense.* The room in which women fall. And the room in which their illusions tumble down.'

Was it really possible that he could be so lacking in tact if.... She felt as though in a dream, in an abyss. On the way downstairs, she was afraid she might lose her balance.

Outside, the cold gripped her. She shivered. Now he was walking beside her, and his long overcoat, tight at the waist, flapped against his legs like a skirt (like a German officer's great-coat, she thought) to the rhythm of his footsteps which rang out with a power and majesty which startled her. His gloved hands were clasped together over his stomach in an attitude which he maintained almost throughout their entire meeting – an attitude Andrée found somehow hieratic. It seemed to her that she was walking beside a Homeric hero.

'What torture all these domestic problems are,' he was say-ing. 'My family are always on at me: "You must get married, you need a woman to look after you." That's a moral way of looking at marriage, don't you think? Marry for social or family reasons, or to make a girl happy – not at all. It's simply a question of having someone there to see that you're not swindled when you buy the upholstery. Fancy getting married on those terms! One might just as well engage a housekeeper, who one can always get rid of if she won't do. Whereas a wife....'

Costals was obsessed with the idea of the wrongness of marriage for a writer – a real writer, who takes his art seriously. He was inexhaustible on the subject. For five minutes, without drawing breath, he railed against marriage, extrava-gantly and, it must be said, tastelessly. Truths, half-truths and sophistries welled from his lips, accompanied by bitter jibes. A great burst of eloquence. He was like a cup full to the brim

---

*Untranslatable pun on the words *tomber*, to fall, and *tombeau*, tomb (*Translator's note*).

and continually overflowing, like the basins of Moroccan fountains.

'You see how I trust you,' he said at the end. 'I talk to you as I would to a man.' Regardless of the fact that almost everything he had said had wounded the woman who walked at his side, numb with cold, hurrying to keep up with him along the dark avenues. Had he not raised her to the seventh heaven, only to plunge her back into the abyss? At first she had ventured a few remarks in favour of writers marrying. She was sure these remarks were sound, but she felt so self-conscious that now she did not know what to say, the words refused to 'come out'; she was like a schoolboy being tortured by a sadistic examiner, knowing the answers perfectly well but standing there like an idiot, overcome with nerves, his mind a blank. Nevertheless, incapable of rejecting the idea that the visit to the flat was not unintentional, she began to think that he was only saying all this to provoke her into taking the opposite view, and to hear it from her lips. She allowed herself to indulge in this fantasy, this madness, this senseless daydream.... Then she thought it would be cunning to switch from wives to children.

'Yes, but what about children! How can a man like you, Costals, who are a sort of fertility god, have no children? I must confess that it's always surprised me. Your personality is incomplete without them. Even if only from the point of view of your work, think what riches you're depriving yourself of!'

To every word she had said before, the fertility god had been ready with a lightning retort: a vicious thrust of the foil, and each time a hit. Now, for the first time, he did not answer. She thought she had found his Achilles heel. She turned towards him, saw his upturned face and his limpid eyes, in which she seemed to see an expression of sadness, intensely moving in a man as overconfident as he. Ah! how she adored him when she saw him weakened!

'Your son, Costals! His little arms around your neck.... Think how he would need you.... All the messages you send out into the void, for a crowd of indifferent people, concentrated on a person who was flesh of your flesh, a person you loved.... No, you're not a complete man if you haven't experienced that. But I can tell that you regret it. No, don't deny it! You can't hide it from me any more. Women have these intuitions, you know. . . .'

He was like a punch-drunk boxer, who can no longer defend himself, his eyes staring into space, those eyes in which Andrée seemed to read a message of defeat. Sensing her opportunity, she brought the conversation round from children to herself. The darkness gave her courage, and the fact of not looking at him. She looked only at their two shadows, side by side, which loomed up, turned, vanished, reappeared, according to the play of the street lamps. And she thrilled at the thought of all the passers-by who knew nothing about them, suspected nothing. For she still imagined that there was something to 'know'.

'Sometimes I think that, whatever you may say, you need to be loved, you don't dislike being loved, in spite of all your blasphemies against love. But something tells me that you may perhaps relent a little. You gave yourself away, Costals, unwittingly: I saw your look of sadness and longing when I spoke to you about that non-existent son and about the element of sterility in your love life. Something tells me that you hanker after another form of tenderness. I can understand how one might feel ill at ease if one were loved the wrong way. But I, for instance, do I love you the wrong way? Isn't my affection for you a source of sweetness and not an infliction? Don't you understand that it's the most ardent and passionate love that is most capable of renunciation and self-sacrifice? Let me love you, so that I can stop having to hold back for fear of displeasing you, saying "affection" when I mean "love". What do I want? More warmth, more life, more activity. Oh, to be able to do things for you – anything! Not to have to go away again in three weeks' time with so cruelly little to treasure. . . . Because what suffices me here, once I'm far away. . . . I should like, for instance – how shall I put it – should like you to call me by my Christian name, or even "my dear". It's been "dear Mademoiselle" for four years! You might be talking to your piano teacher. I should like you to write to me more often – a few lines every fortnight (it isn't much to ask). I should like you to treat me as a little girl, if only a stupid and sulky little girl. I should like to see you in places that are more appropriate, more suited to you – gardens, the country, art galleries. ... I don't know what I want exactly. ... But I don't want things as they were, as they are, as you've wished them to be. I don't demand that it should last for ever, only that I should enjoy you more, be closer to you, as long as it does last. And I should still like an answer to the question : has my affection given you some happiness? Have I the right to think that I'm to some extent necessary to you? Have you felt less alone for the assurance I've brought you of being passionately understood and loved, loved in everything that makes you what you are, in the quintessence of your being as in your smallest idiosyncrasies, your irony, your fooling, your unkindnesses even, God forgive me? If you don't give me the terrible answer Satan gave to Eloa, it will be happiness enough for me.'

'What a fantasy world she lives in!' thought Costals. 'Andrée Hacquebaut's affection giving me happiness! She has a mania for denying the obvious, and another typically feminine mania – wanting me to be unhappy so as to be able to console me. The idea of her consoling me for my alleged unhappiness, when it's she and her kind, meaning all those women who give you a love you haven't asked for, who are responsible for spoiling my happiness! No, the whole thing is too farcical. And yet at the same time one can respect and pity it. How can I get out of it without hurting her?' The thought of the harm he could do her by simply telling her, in one short sentence, *how things stood*, paralysed him – like a man playing at boxing with a child and hardly daring to move for fear of hurting it. 'God, how maddening the girl is! What a mess I've got myself into!'

He was still dragging her along with his long strides. In the past twenty minutes they had passed through one gloomy and almost deserted street after another (rue Christophe Colomb, rue Georges-Bizet, rue Magellan, etc.). These streets, with their blocks of expensive flats and private houses, and very few shops, were almost entirely plunged in darkness. The rare passers-by were hunched up against the cold. Cars were parked along the edge of the pavement. Andrée wondered why Costals did not take her into a tea-shop or a café, as any other man would have done. But no – walk! walk! (Costals had in fact thought of going into a café, but in the restaurant the other day Andrée had got stuck in the revolving doors so that she could neither get in nor out, and the waiters had laughed. And she was so dowdy and frumpish – let's face it, he was a little ashamed of her. So he preferred to let her catch pneumonia rather than suffer an affront to his vanity on her account.) Each new street they took seemed to Andrée even darker than the one before, and, although at first she braced herself against this glimpse of sky amidst her inner clouds, she ended up by thinking that the object of this Wandering Jew act of Costals' was simply to find a suitable place to kiss her; and if the expedition was becoming rather prolonged, it was because he could not make up his mind – a proof that he really loved her. As they turned into the rue Keppler, a particularly dark and deserted street, she was certain that it was there that her destiny would be fulfilled. Never would she forget those details: the terrier seated beside a chauffeur in a parked limousine, staring at her with an almost human intensity; the lantern on a heap of paving-stones, as moving as a sanctuary lamp. But they came out of that insidious street without anything having happened. Then Costals said:

'I've listened to you with great interest, and I'm extremely touched by what you say. But I've already given you my answer. Our friendship was a very excellent thing. But the heart infects everything. On the plane of friendship, or on the plane of sensuality, things are healthy, and wounds, if they develop, are clean-cut. When the heart intervenes, the wound spreads, everything goes wrong. I've seen it happen so often.'

'What you say is absurd. The heart infects nothing; on the contrary, it purifies everything. It's really too idiotic! So it's "the plane of sensuality" that is pure? If I had a great physical passion for you, you'd forgive me for it. If I were provocative, if I gave you to understand that it was only pleasure I was after, you might despise me perhaps, but you'd accept it. But when I offer you love, how embarrassing, how boring! If only people would leave one in peace with their love! When

I offer you my love as the very basis of my life, the life of a
girl still intact and (though I say it who shouldn't) fairly
superior, how dull and ridiculous! You don't care for my
love. You don't want *everything* from me, you only want a
little. And I can't give you only a little. You have treated me
as a sister. You have given me a privileged position at your
side, as a sultan chooses his favourite concubine or his vizier
from the crowd, and now you want me to stay there like a
good girl without raising my voice, and content myself with
what you give me – with delightful generosity, true, but that
isn't enough for me any more. Imagine having the right to
nothing more than friendship! Friendships can be beautiful,
marvellous even – like yours – sweet, consoling, touching,
fraternal, but they are inadequate nonetheless, terribly inadequate. I cannot survive with you through friendship alone, nor
indeed will I. There is something buoyant in me that transcends all that – transcends it utterly. So much inner strength
that remains untapped. . . . I'm brimming over with the desire
to give. I demand everything, and by "everything" I don't
mean necessarily that you should abandon the disinterestedness you exploit so cleverly. . . .' ('Ah!' he thought to himself, 'a touch of asperity! Here's a little mouse who's asking to
be eaten up. That, too, might have been expected.') 'No. I'm
quite sincere when I tell you, as I've told you many times,
that you have never penetrated to the source of my inmost
feelings, or you've touched it only fleetingly, when you were
feeling particularly kind and sweet. What I ask is the right to
love you, to cherish you with all my strength and all my
heart. Your coldness has always restrained me. I cannot love
you if you do not want me to.'

'How can I be so frivolous as to allow you to give me a
love I can't respond to? You see, I've used up all my feelings.
I gave everything in a first love affair, at sixteen. From seventeen onwards I would have answered you as I do today:
"Friendship, yes. Love, ecstasy, the whole shooting match:
too late".'

'Too late! Always the same devastating words: too late!
Ah! well, my life is finished.'

He felt sorry for her. 'When I was seventeen,' he said

gravely, 'and was beginning to move in society, I immediately began flirting a great deal, and I remember my mother saying to me then: "You mustn't excite young girls when your intentions aren't serious. It isn't fair." I'm beginning to wonder whether I haven't behaved badly towards you.'

'Good heavens, you haven't behaved badly towards me at all, not voluntarily. You're the most upright of men. . . .'

'Me, upright! I lie the whole time.'

He blinked his eyelids. Why had this cry escaped his lips? He felt a violent flush rise to his cheeks, and bowed his head.

'Of course you sometimes lie, like everyone else. All the same you're the most upright, the most noble of men.'

'Nobility again! You're going to make me take a violent dislike to myself one of these days with all this talk of nobility, and it would be a bore for me to dislike myself. I shall have to say to you what I said to an Italian servant who had worked for some prince or other and who, when he came to work for me, used to call me "Your Honour" at every turn. "If Your Honour would care. . . ." "I think Your Honour had better. . . ." Finally I got so irritated that I said to him: "Don't keep talking about my honour. You'll end up by making it real".'

'How impossible you are! Always joking at the most solemn moments. . . . Anyway, whether you like it or not, I repeat: you're an absolutely upright man. But you've been guilty of a certain rashness as far as I'm concerned. You shouldn't have let me get to this point.'

It was on the tip of his tongue to answer: 'Haven't I given you enough proofs of my indifference?' but he could not bring himself to do so. What he said was:

'So friendship isn't possible between a young man and a young woman?'

'Oh yes, the sort of impotence such a friendship represents must be possible in certain cases. With a very young girl for instance. When I was eighteen, I should have asked for nothing better than what I have now: a masculine friendship, especially with you, would have been everything I desired. But being the woman I am, a woman of whose age, loneliness, anguish, desperation and need for love you are not unaware, how could I help falling in love with such a magnificent friend as you? I offered you my love; you rejected it. But when I told you I was coming to Paris, far from making it clear to me that you did not want to see me again, as you ought to have done . . .' ('There's my reward!' thought Costals), 'you invited me to dinner. You encouraged me to think about you, you showed me that I wasn't unattractive to you. . . .' ('That's a good one!') 'You've done everything you possibly could to make me lose my heart to you. Because in refusing yourself, dear sir, you offer yourself. And that is what you will not see. To allow oneself to be loved is tantamount to loving. You are wrong in thinking that one can only offer oneself by promises or caresses. You have offered yourself without either promises or caresses, but just as surely, in your good-natured frivolity. . . . Do you know what your trouble is, Costals? Not being able to be nasty to me.'

'Well, well, how profound we are! So that's it, I'm "too nice"?'

'Yes, you are "too nice". In future, Costals, in your relations with women, don't be "too nice". Out of pity for them. And then you should drum this axiom into your head: "No friendships with unmarried girls." Because each one of them will believe you like her best. And because, unconsciously, you will give each of them the impression that you like her best. Even when you aren't trying to seduce, you behave like a seducer – and then you're genuinely astonished and furious afterwards, when the harm is done. You're so extraordinarily lacking in conceit! Perhaps that's what causes the trouble.'

'But after all, I can't pretend there aren't thousands of men as intelligent as I am, and much better looking. Just look around, and you will surely find one who will give you back as much as you give and more.'

'How exasperating you are! I'd like to give you a good shaking. I'm sick and tired of telling you that a woman only loves once, and that for me you are that once, you are irreplaceable as far as I'm concerned. You refuse to face the reality, which is that my true life is my love for you.'

'I don't know which of the two of us won't face up to reality,' he said gently.

'And besides, what a charming answer: "Why don't you look elsewhere?" to a woman who tells you: "I love you more than my life. Or rather, quite simply, you *are* my life".'

'How lucky you are to find that simple. As far as I'm concerned we're in a stew, a real sentimental stew.'

'You talk about love like a schoolboy. You ought to be ashamed of your childishness about such a subject.'

'A man without childishness is a monster.'

'*You're* a monster because you're too childish.'

Her voice was full of tears. Costals went on in a more affable tone:

'You're the one who's absurd, my poor girl, for giving me the power to make you unhappy. Do you know how I'd like you to be? I'd like to be able to say the most cruel and wounding things to you without your minding in the least.'

Her only reply was a shrug of the shoulders. Then she added:

'"My poor girl." Careful, don't start being "too nice" again.'

'Well, I must say you really are maddening! If I'm brusque with you it won't do. If I'm nice to you it won't do. I'm getting fed up with all this slop. After all, what am I doing here?'

Costals had never taken much part in the emotional brawling which women try to impose on any man who comes near them, not even with the ones he liked. And to have to indulge in it with a woman he was indifferent to....

But it was too much for Andrée. The tears gushed from her eyes.

'There, there, my dear girl! Stop crying. If women only knew how much they lose by their whimperings. A man has to be a saint, when he sees they're hurt, not to want to hurt them more. But I am such a saint. Although ... women have to be continually enlightened (I mean one always has to be explaining to them), enlightened, pampered, consoled, petted, appeased. I must admit I've no vocation for wet-nursing or for handling cases of porcelain. I like the things of the heart to be treated fairly briskly, without too much fuss, without going on about it as if there weren't other things in life. I

74

believe that the more one really loves, the less one talks about
it. . . . You silly girl, do you want to kill yourself!' (He had
grasped her by the arm. She was so distraught that in crossing
the street she had allowed a car to brush past her in a quite
terrifying way.) 'Well, you're lucky I didn't push you under
it! It's a sort of reflex I have with women when a car goes by.
Especially with those I like best. However, up to now I've
always resisted the impulse. And in your case, as you see, I
had the reflex to protect you. And yet you complain!'

'No, Costals, I don't complain. I know you're fond of me.
There are moments when I think of you as a kindly father
figure, and of how nice it would have been to be created,
re-created by you from scratch. Have I reproached you? If
so, forget it. I can't imagine what nonsense I must have
talked. . . . I'm not myself today. . . . I don't want you to feel
under any obligation towards me. Even if, one day, by some
miracle of fate, I were to acquire a privileged position with
you, I wouldn't wish for any other bond between us but your
tenderness, never your pity or your charity, as with the
flower-seller . . .'

'What she doesn't want is the one thing I can give her,'
Costals thought to himself. 'And what's this "miracle of fate"
that might give her a privileged position with me? What new
chimera is she riding off on now?'

It was perhaps the third or fourth time they had walked
round the square des Etats-Unis, marked by the dainty feet of
countesses and dotted with statues of Liberators and Bene-
factors and Enthusiasts. The leaves of the spindle-trees glowed
in the nocturnal gloom, as though each manservant daily
polished the foliage opposite the house of his noble master.
The windows with their closed shutters called to mind a row
of strong-boxes in the vaults of a bank. There were a few
humble people about who, in this opulent setting, looked like
prisoners-of-war working for the enemy: black-faced coal-men,
paid to be disfigured; a little butcher's boy bringing the
countesses' meat, slipping down through a tiny tradesmen's
entrance, like a cat through a hole in a door. It was Costals
who noticed these things, because his mind was free. Andrée
noticed nothing. Novelists have always gone into elaborate

detail about the settings in which their lovers meet; but only the novelists notice these details; the lovers see nothing, immersed as they are in their slop.

As they circled the square des Etats-Unis, Andrée noticed only the darkness of its green arbours, its lonely paths, and that almost suspect nook with its benches (just behind the statue of the Enthusiast), and her crazy hopes revived: here she was among these groves at night with this man, and – whether he kissed her or not – he could not have brought her there by chance. And he had called her 'my dear'. Would a man say 'my dear' to a woman he was indifferent to, to a woman with whom he did not feel to some extent intimate? Perhaps he would, after all (when one lives at Saint-Léonard one ends up by not knowing what's done and what isn't). And he had taken her by the arm and said 'Silly girl!' For the first time, he had *touched* her. (At that moment she had raised her eyes to see if she could read the plaque bearing the name of the street, so that for the rest of her life this memory should be linked to a precise spot.) She began to believe that he had held her arm for a long time, squeezing it in a meaningful way, and that a man did not say 'Silly girl!' unless he felt a certain tenderness. All her earlier clear-sightedness – 'You give each one the impression that you like her best' – had dimmed, like a sky clouding over. Passionately she wished that he would take her arm, or that she could dare to take his. But they left the square with its dark thickets, and her hopes subsided. Where was he leading her now? Were they going to resume their fearful chase through those streets in which there was nothing but chemists and flower-shops?* Once, indeed, she had complained of the cold, but he had replied with a winning air: 'A nice dry cold.... Very healthy!'

'Anyhow,' he said, 'we must clear up this question of friendship between men and women.'

'No, no, let's forget it, there's no point....'

'Well then, here we have an intelligent, shrewd (when she chooses to be), cultivated, self-made girl, a girl who knows my work better than I do myself, and knows it intelligently – in

---

*A symbol, perhaps, of the ruling class (*Author's note*).

short, a girl worthy of the highest praise. She vegetates in
Saint-Léonard (Loiret), that is to say in an indescribable back-
water. . . . '

'I beg your pardon,' she said with a smile, 'Saint-Léonard
(Loiret) has three thousand one hundred and eighty inhabitants.
Important textile mills. Birthplace of the great agronomist
Leveilley. . . . '

Now she was trying to adopt his tone. She felt rather
ridiculous being a woman, and thought he was quite right to
be a healthy, cheerful overgrown schoolboy made for bachelor
friendships and easy-going love affairs, whose only fault was
to be too down-to-earth and not to take himself seriously
enough.

'I offer this interesting young woman the sympathy which
is her due. She seems very pleased. For years she goes on telling me in a thousand different ways that I have saved her,
that I "have given her nothing but joy". . . . You see, I know
your letters by heart too,' he interjected, succumbing once
more to his natural imprudence. . . . 'One fine day, I realize
she's going to fall in love with me, and that I shall be unable
to respond adequately to her love, because I'm not a man of
love but a man of pleasure. (Yes, there it is, I like pleasure.
And pleasure likes me too.) So I take up my finest pen and I
write to her and say: "Dear Mademoiselle, I have regretfully
perceived that you were about to fall in love with me. Don't
deny it: I saw it with my lynx-like eye (am I, or am I not,
our 'eminent psychologist'?) And so, from today onwards,
nothing doing. I shall write to you no more. I shall return
your letters unopened. When you come to Paris, 'Monsieur is
away'. I opened the door of enlightenment to you; now I am
closing it again. I dragged you away from the birthplace of the
great agronomist Leveilley; now I am sending you back there.
Good-bye, dear Mademoiselle. The best of luck to you." I ask
you to consider a moment, quite calmly, what you would
have thought of such a letter. You don't answer? Well, you
would have thought this: "He's a swine. What a fine friendship he must have had for me, when it can be destroyed at
one blow! And what conceit! He thinks every woman wants
to fling herself at him. Just like men. You talk to them of

friendship: they assume you mean sex. Afterwards they accuse you of thinking of nothing else." You would have suffered then what you are suffering now, and with good reason. Why didn't I write you that letter? Because I didn't want to lose your friendship, because I knew that my friendship was a help to you, and because I should have loathed myself for plunging a dagger into your heart.... Well, then, did I behave badly in not breaking with you?'

'Of course not, I know very well how kind you are.'

'You'll have to pay a forfeit every time you mention my kindness.'

'Oh, you're really too mischievous,' she said, half laughing.

It was true, she no longer knew whether he was kind or cruel. Now she was rather inclined to think that it was she who was in the wrong. But she no longer really knew; everything was getting mixed up in her mind. What she would have liked would have been to be back at her hotel, alone with herself, decanting all the happiness and all the pain he had poured into her, to see which, the happiness or the pain, would float above the other. What she would have liked most of all was not to feel cold any more. But at the hotel she would still be cold. She repeated to herself a saying of Costals': 'Cold is a disease of the planet', and more especially a remark of St Thérèse of Lisieux, a remark so ordinary on the surface, but in reality most moving: 'You don't know what it's like to have been cold for seven years.' She was worn out (they had been walking for two hours) and her fatigue was befuddling her brain; her eyelids were aching, and she could feel a headache coming on. She said to herself: 'What a night it's going to be!' But having invoked his presence month after month at Saint-Léonard, she could never be the first to put an end to it. She would collapse, exhausted, on to the pavement rather than give the signal for his 'Good-bye, dear Mademoiselle. I'll get in touch with you one of these days.'

In the avenue Marceau the north wind swept out from each side-street with a bombastic flourish. From the top of the avenue Pierre-Ier the Champs-Elysées could be seen below, a valley of light. She longed for him to decide to go down there. She would be warmed by those lights, those human beings, the noise, the movement, the luxury. They would go into a café and listen to some music : she would show him a shop where there were 'ensembles' for 390 francs – incredible, they might have come from one of the big fashion houses ... but no, that would be impossible, it might look like cadging.... Suddenly, for the first time, it struck her that he had not thought of buying her a few francs' worth of flowers at any of the florists they had passed, even though they had stopped in front of one of them. No, not even one of those bunches of violets which, he had so tactfully informed her, he used to buy 'for his girl-friends'. In fact he had never given her anything at all except books – oh yes, he was generous enough with books ('You see, I'm an intellectual girl ... so naturally! ... '). She fought against the unexpected bitterness it caused her, considering it naïve and vulgar. But Costals turned his back on the Champs-Elysées, the Promised Land, and plunged once more down one of the drearier streets, as though he took pleasure in pacing up and down like a caged beast, as though he enjoyed this spasmodic, nightmarish flight, like some legendary descent into hell. Almost fainting, her thighs aching with fatigue, dabbing at a drip on the end of her nose ('I'm sure my nose is red'), biting her lips from which she thought the cold and the pain must have drained all colour, and, with all this, a pressing need to obey a little call of nature, she heard him hold forth ('hold forth' was the word that came to her mind, she was so weary of him) :

'According to your theory, then, the magnificent realm of friendship between man and woman would become forbidden territory. Women would be penned in the "heart and senses" domain, incapable of being raised to a nobler, more rarefied world. And, for fear of disappointing them, a man would have to avoid social contact with any young women not destined for his bed, licit or illicit – in other words, when all is said and done, the vast majority of women. He would have to rush past them with lowered eyes like a seminarist : "*Noli me tangere*, ladies! Because you might think I was in love with you, which I'm very far from being – no offence meant." Or like the young Kabyles. A Kabyle once told me that, in his village, boys who had reached the age of fifteen and were not yet married were packed off by their parents to Algiers, so as not to be an object of temptation to the girls of the village. And whenever they returned to the village for a few days (on the occasion of a funeral, a wedding, or for the feast of A'id) they had to give warning of their comings and goings by shouting "trec, trec, trec", so that the girls could go and hide, such a temptation were boys to them. In future I too shall say "trec, trec, trec", so that the girls can take cover. Or rather I shall have a rattle, like a leper. . . . '

He went on to say something rather cruel : 'Girls are like those stray dogs you can't throw a friendly glance at without their assuming that you're calling them and will welcome them with open arms, and without their wagging their tails and scrabbling at your trouser-legs.'

He embroidered on this. As always when he was talking or writing to someone he was indifferent to, he said more or less anything that came into his head (Andrée had never been aware of this in their relations with each other). Just as matadors regard anything that happens to them in bull-rings outside Spain, successes as well as failures, as non-existent, so Costals, a born writer, really only took trouble with one of his modes of expression – books. Conversation and correspondence belonged to the sphere of relaxation and spare time; in those spheres he did not mind what he said; it did not count.

Suddenly he stopped dead.

'Do you understand what I'm saying?'

'Of course.'

'Well, I don't. For some time now it's ceased to have any meaning – pure word-spinning. If you can't see that, what's the use of talking to you? In short,' he concluded, 'since, according to you, it was my duty to break with you, and I've delayed all too long, it's quite simple. . . . I cannot give you what you want from me. Let us, therefore, cease to know one another.'

'No! No!' cried Andrée, springing up from the depths of her torpor, 'you have no right to desert me now. But you're not serious, are you?'

' "Have no right",' Costals thought. 'Ah, well, as I've always said, the trouble with charity is that you have to go on with it.'

As though she had read his thoughts, she went on:

'Loving commits one, doing good commits one. One hasn't the right to love people in the same way as one dispenses charity, anonymously, without entering their lives. . . . '

'Let's stay as we are, then. Only, from now on, don't complain of the situation. You're the one who wants it.'

'I shall never complain of anything again, I give you my solemn word. There's only one thing I want: not to lose you. . . . You know what the key to it all is,' she said point-blank. 'The fact that you're a man who has always jilted and never been jilted. One can sense it.'

'It's not true. I've been jilted twice, and in the most cruel way.'

'And . . . you were hurt?'

'No, I found it quite natural. What could be more legitimate than to have had enough of someone? I've felt it too often myself not to understand it in others. When I see a woman with whom I've had months of intimacy drop me from her life overnight, no longer want to have anything to do with me, I recognize myself.'

She was silent, as though stunned. But then he said:

'Goodness! I must leave you. I'm dining with some people at eight, and it's now ten to.'

'Shall we see each other again?' she asked, feeling at the end of her tether, incapable of further speech, of uttering anything more than a few banal remarks.

'Of course. I'll get in touch with you.'

'Don't leave it too long. . . . If I write to you, you probably won't answer. To think that you've never given me your telephone number!'

'I thought you were supposed not to complain any more.'

'Sorry.'

'Even if I did give you my telephone number it wouldn't make any difference, because it's permanently switched off: "the silence of those infinite spaces" reassures me. And do you know who drove me to take this step, which is irritating for friends or business people who want to talk to me, and inconvenient for me since I'm liable to miss things that might be important? Women, and women only. Women in general, with their daily or twice-daily calls, each one lasting a quarter of an hour, and always about nothing. And a particular category of women, who are the most dangerous of all: the women who love me and whom I do not love. Result: I get three express letters from women per day, always about nothing, of course. And there's nothing more exasperating than to be pestered with letters from people one doesn't love when one expects every post to bring a letter from somebody one does. Well, good-bye, dear Mademoiselle, and don't catch cold.'

He had spoken to her in a tone that froze her to such an extent that she wondered whether she might not faint. She gave him her hand mechanically. She had no feeling left.

She walked away. He called after her: 'Hey!'

She stopped. He came up to her. Alternating waves of sincerity and trickery, of gravity and mockery, flashed across his features. And it was true that he felt more lively and restless than she, like a mischievous dog jumping round a sheep and having the greatest fun teasing it.

'Am I a swine?'

'I don't know. Leave me alone. . . . Leave me alone. . . .'

'Good-bye.'

He went off, and after a few steps lit a cigarette. He felt ten years younger now that she was no longer there. A woman going away and leaving him alone meant ten years' reprieve if he did not love her. One or two years if he did.

Andrée did not sleep a wink. Lying in bed, she turned over on her right side, and her anguish fell to the right, then on her left side, and her anguish fell to the left, like a lump inside her body. She kept wanting to change the position of her legs, which were still aching after the evening's frantic trek. The too-narrow sheet added to her misery: she kept finding herself uncovered, and felt (or believed) she was catching cold. In the morning, she cried from seven o'clock until twenty-five past. How cruel he had been, and at the same time how gentle! At all costs she must know 'where she stood' with him. She sent him an express letter, telling him she had cried from six to eight, and 'beseeching' him to telephone her at noon at the hotel. Having paid for the letter with a two-franc piece, she left the change to the post office clerk, who muttered a few sardonic words about forsaken women.

Costals did not telephone. The express letter had made him furious. The mere sight of Andrée's handwriting exasperated him. 'She means nothing to me. I owe her nothing. I've put myself out for her dozens of times. I take her out to dinner and then on top of that I give up two and a half hours of my life to her – yes, two and a half hours! I rack my brains trying to find a way out of the ridiculous position she has put me in without hurting her feelings. And now she comes back at me with express letters, tearful letters. So I'm expected to see her three hours running every other day! Well, this time, no.' At noon, he sent her a telegram saying he had to leave for Besançon to see a sick uncle, and would write to her on his return.

Andrée sat and waited in her room on the sixth floor of her squalid hotel (she had asked the prices of six hotels before deciding on this one), with its draughty windows, its stinking bedside table, the drawer in which she had found some old bits of soiled cotton-wool. Sitting on the only chair beside a meagre wood fire, her overcoat round her shoulders, she thought she could never have experienced such an agony of distress. Oh, God! if only she knew what was in his mind! She guessed that she must have irritated him by writing, but it would have been impossible for her not to write. Her mind swung back and forth like a pair of maladjusted scales. One moment she thought of them walking, walking like lost souls along those lugubrious avenues in the frightful cold, and his every word seemed like a knife twisted in a wound. The next moment she was at the other extreme, exaggerating and in-venting as she went along: 'Those minutes will have been the only happy minutes of my life. Even when he teased me, he was so kind, so tender and serious, perhaps unwittingly. He was unhappy about not having any children, he wanted to confide in me, seemed to be looking for sympathy. How touching he was when he talked about his mother! Has he ever spoken to another woman about his mother?' Just as she imagined that Costals had been confiding in her, when he had merely been thinking aloud, no more and no less than when he prostituted himself to fifty thousand readers, in the same way she genuinely believed that, because she had held his hand for rather a long time when they shook hands on meeting, it was he who had held hers. She could still hear the clatter of 'his German officer's footsteps' on the asphalt; she could still see him listening to her with 'the imperceptible smile of the gods' on his lips. The idea that he had contemplated marrying her – even in a moment of aberration – seemed to her less probable than the day before, and yet: 'I know I'm unworthy of such luck; I realize all that divides us, if only from the social point of view; I'm neither crazy nor romantic. So there must have been something for this eventuality, which I had never, never dreamed of, to have suddenly seemed plausible.' She even reached the point of wanting passionately to walk with him again one evening through those gloomy avenues, to walk and walk until she had to beg for mercy; and what had seemed to her 'frightful' and 'lugubrious' a moment before was what she now pinned all her hopes on.

At half past eleven she went down to the reception to wait for the telephone call, her eyes glued to her wrist-watch. Nothing happened. At one o'clock she returned to her room, incapable of lunching, and went on waiting. She was in Paris for only a month, and yet she was waiting for the time to go by! At two o'clock she received Costals' message, and sensed that he was lying. She went round to the avenue Henri-Martin, and inquired of the concierge:

'Is M. Costals in Paris?'

'Yes, Mademoiselle.'

But upstairs the servant told her:

'M. Costals is in Besançon.'

Next morning she went back to the avenue Henri-Martin. She had no doubt that he was there, but could not bear not to know. She needed a verdict one way or the other, however unpleasant, to rest upon a certainty, or die upon it.

'Is M. Costals back?'

'No, Mademoiselle. We don't know when he'll be back.'

She went away and wandered around, unable to bring her-self to leave the neighbourhood, looking everywhere for Costals, wallowing in the bitter thought that he and she were both in Paris and the days were flowing by in an emptiness no different from Saint-Léonard. And soon she would have to return to Saint-Léonard, return without a ray of hope to a hell of loneliness and despair. Her peregrinations (no question about it, she was born to tramp the streets!) were aimed not so much at meeting Costals as at providing her with a sort of opiate: sitting idly in her hotel room she might have had a fit of hysterics. She went into a church, the name of which she did not know, and spent an hour there, half frozen, repeating to herself: 'Oh, no, God cannot make one suffer more than a man can.' She wrote this sentence on a piece of paper she found in her bag, bought a cheap envelope, slipped it inside it and took it round to Costals' concierge.

She paced up and down outside the house for an hour, just as, when she happened to be in Paris and Costals was away, she used to pass underneath his windows nearly every night to see if they were lit up. She went pale when she saw a man whom she took for him. She caught sight of herself in a shop window, and was horrified by her ugliness: 'My God, what have you done to me? Who is this stranger?' (she had not thought of God when she was in the church). She met a woman selling violets and bought a bunch – 'I shall be more generous than he' – and going back to Costals' house, laid them on the floor of the landing against the door of his flat. Out in the street again she realized, too late, that her gesture would only do her harm, that the servant would find the flowers and make fun of her. She thought of going up to take them back, but it would be the fifth time the concierge had seen her in two days. . . . She dared not.

At nightfall, frozen stiff, she made her way to the under-ground. But oh! the temptation to take a taxi. She would have done so for a short trip. But her hotel was so far that it would cost her at least twelve francs. It was typical of her, this habit of stopping short amid the storms of her emotional life to tot up money. In the underground, people stared at her: people wear their sadness as they do a garment. She felt full of compassion, all kindness, weakness and abandon; she offered her seat (an unconscious reflex action, for she could see nothing) to an old man who was standing. She changed trains in a state of utter bewilderment, horrified by the labyrinthine passages, the rush for the automatic gates which shut in your face, those automatic gates that corral people like animals, as though they were a herd of pigs being sorted out by machines in an American factory. And she thought she was going to faint when she finally got off, what with her utter exhaustion, the nervous tension, her sleepless night, and no lunch. It seemed to her that only the strength of her heartbeats sustained her. Her eyelids were aching. All her anguish and distress seemed to be concentrated in this pain in her eyeballs. She went into a bar and ordered a coffee, despite her fear of being taken for a whore. There was a crowd of workmen at the counter. She had to stand behind them, stretching her arm between two men to reach her glass. But she felt that, without the coffee, she could not have stood up a moment longer. Suddenly one of the workmen smiled at her, and his smile eased her pain. But it only lasted a moment; outside, the pain welled up again.

Back at the hotel, she noticed that a forty-franc bottle of scent had been stolen from her room. During the last few days this scent had been her only consolation: she had sniffed it when she was feeling particularly tormented. She also learned from the waiter that she was being charged three francs a day more for her room than other guests had to pay for it (because of her smart appearance, of course!). She attracted blow after blow, like a wounded hen being pecked by the whole poultry-yard.

She would cheerfully have spent hundreds of francs in a single day if she had been happy. When she was unhappy, the thought of money spent – or wasted – gnawed at her, and there were moments when she told herself that she must leave Paris simply in order to stop the leakage.

She wept.... Tears of uncertainty – it was too stupid. After all, it would be time enough to shed them when it all came to an end. She began to think that he was putting her to the test, teasing her rather cruelly, in order to dazzle her the more with joy for all the suffering he had inflicted on her. She applied to him the remark made about M. de Chavigny in Musset's *Un Caprice:* 'He is mischievous, but he is not bad.' In the end she drew some consolation from her suffering, telling herself that it was a decisive test, that she now knew better than ever how much she loved this man, and what the quality of her love was, since she could put up with his behaviour in this way. For all her horrible doubts about him, she had never felt a moment's anger or resentment. She loved him just as much, but simply did not understand. She also told herself : 'Anything that happens to me now will be paradise after all this.' In spite of the grinding neuralgia which had not left her for two days and upon which all the pills in the world had failed to make an impression, she settled down to write him a long letter, scribbling, scribbling away across the calm paper. But the ceiling light was too high and too dim, and she had to give up.

Next morning, at a quarter to eight, Costals heard a ring at the door of his flat. His servant did not come down until eight o'clock, and anyhow had a key. Costals went from the bathroom into the hall with the lather still on his cheeks.

'What is it?' he asked through the door.

'It's me.'

'Who's "me"?'

'Andrée.'

'Andrée? Andrée who?'

He knew only too well. But he wanted to punish her. Ringing at his door at a quarter to eight! And that note : 'God cannot make one suffer more than a man can'! And those flowers on his doorstep, as though it were a tombstone! Enough to cover him with ridicule in the eyes of all the tenants! He had thrown them in the dustbin at once, after crushing them in his rage.

'Andrée Hacquebaut.'

'I can't let you in. I got back last night. But I haven't shaved.'

'What difference does that make? Let me in, please.'

'You must say "for the love of God".'

'For the love of God!'

'I'd be delighted to let you in. Only I'm stark naked.'

'You refuse to see me?'

'At this moment, yes.'

'Is that your last word?'

'Please don't insist.'

'All right. I shall take the eight fifty-six train to Saint-Léonard. You'll have nothing more to fear from me.'

'No, no. I'll telephone you at noon.'

'Yes, just like the other day! Good-bye!'

He heard her footsteps receding. After a while he half-opened the door. He wondered whether he might not find her still there, crouching on the stairs. There was no one. But in front of the door were the fresh imprints of her wet shoes, going in every direction, as though a hunted beast had trampled there.

At eleven o'clock he heaved a sigh and telephoned the hotel. He was told that she had paid her bill and left.

At first he was profoundly relieved. Then he felt remorse. She was to have spent a month in Paris, and it was going to be such a treat for her! As a novelist he was too accustomed to putting himself in other people's skins not to realize how much she must have suffered, and he was moved by it. He wrote to her:

Dear Mademoiselle,

Your sudden departure has left me puzzled. I cannot for a moment believe that it was due to my not receiving you at half past seven in the morning. Once, my mother refused to let me into her room. Being a sensitive child, I was upset and wondered in what way I could have incurred her displeasure. When she came home that evening, she called me in, kissed me, treated me exactly as usual, but refused to explain why her door had been closed to me that morning. Years later she confessed to me: she had run out of face-powder, and did not want me to see her without any powder on. And I was fourteen! When she was about to die, she gave orders that I was not to be allowed into her room after she was dead until they had bandaged her chin.... Well, I'm her son. You accuse me of not being vain enough : and yet, in certain respects, I'm terribly punctilious. This morning, for example, even if you had been in flames on the landing as a result of some heater exploding or God knows what, I probably wouldn't have gone to your help because I hadn't shaved. The fact that I was naked had nothing to do with it, mind you. No doubt you know how men are made : you must have seen statues. And besides, I was dressed.

Your absurd departure has deprived me of the pleasure of taking you to the Monet exhibition, as I had planned. I was so looking forward to it.

Cordially yours.

How very like him Andrée found this letter! Kindliness, jokes, and even a touch of impropriety, which she smiled at without being disturbed by it. And again the allusions to his mother, which she found so moving . . . But she did not regret having returned to Saint-Léonard. She had a feeling that, had she stayed in Paris, he would have continued to make her suffer. Whereas this friendly letter mysteriously – yes, really unaccountably – dissolved her pain. Full, as always, of Costals' books, she remembered a saying in one of them : 'Absence brings people closer.' Why did he understand everything so well in his books and pretend not to understand in life?

One morning, some days after this scene, Costals was in Cannes. The sea could be seen from the villa, still grey after the riotous winter storms. The novelist was reading Malebranche – *La Recherche de la Vérité*.

From the next room came the sound of a clear young voice singing to itself. Costals raised his head. When he heard his son singing in the house, he felt as though the house were flying through the air. Sometimes both father and son would sing, each on a different floor. He listened for a while, then could not resist any longer and made his way to the child's room.

As soon as he opened the door the voice stopped. The boy pretended to be asleep. Costals was familiar with this trick. As with all boys of his age (he would be fourteen in three months' time), Philippe's jokes and gags, though they did not last long, and were buried forever from one day to the next, were persistent while they did last. Even if he had not heard him singing, Costals would have known that his son was not asleep: his face was dry, and he always perspired in his sleep.

'Open your eyes, donkey, or I'll drop my cigarette ash on your face.'

Costals sat down on the bed . . . and jumped up again. He turned back the sheet and found a foil. Philippe had discovered fencing a fortnight before and, still in the first flush of this discovery, took his foil to bed with him – as Cardinal de Maillé, newly promoted to the Sacred College, slept with his red hat, according to Saint-Simon.

Sitting down again, Costals took his son's hands, never quite clean, with their long, delicate fingers (*Les jeunes garçons aux mains larges et limpides*, he had written one day when he had a penchant for alexandrines), and kissed them. The boy had a tanned face and straight black hair. On the front of his pyjamas the stains of breakfast chocolate were proudly displayed. He was still pretending to be asleep. One could see at once that if he had no wings it was because he had wished it so (but what about the cloven hoof?). Scattered on the floor around the bed, like gobs of spittle around an Arab, was a large quantity of small change (Philippe insisted on having his pocket money in this form so that he could jingle it in his pocket – 'But why?' – 'To show off, of course!'), a comb (broken), a mirror (broken), a fountain-pen (broken), a wallet, an empty scent bottle – all the things which boys' pockets are eternally stuffed with, and which slip out whenever they lie down. There was also a padlock, for Philippe did not want his rabbits to be killed, and every time the cook brought their food, Master Philippe had to be fetched to open and shut the hutch himself.

Suddenly Philippe seized his father's head, pulled it down, and kissed it. Then he squeezed it violently between his arms, no longer the caressing child but a child who fancies himself as a wrestling champion. There followed a great deal of horse-play, which he liked best of all, being very sensitive to touch. Whenever Costals warned him that he was going to break something, or that he was ruining the pillow, he replied: 'That's a detail' – it was the catch-phrase of the moment. Finally Philippe pinned down his father's shoulders with his knees (the sheet, by this time, was all over the place), and in that position bent forward and nibbled his nose.

'You've hurt me, you idiot!'

'Cry-baby! Sissy, sissy!' (and he made faces at him).

Eventually the excitement died down. Philippe got back under the sheet and buried himself in *Cri-Cri*.* Costals, stretched out on top of the bed, returned to his Malebranche.

Costals had had this bastard son at the age of twenty-one. The chosen intermediary was a woman who in law was an adulteress so that there could be no question of her having any rights whatever over the child. At the age of six Philippe had been entrusted to the care of an old friend of Costals, Mlle du Peyron de Larchant, a spinster of about fifty, who had all the advantages of maternal love for the brat without any of its grave drawbacks. Although she also loved Costals like a son, she had never been in love with him, and this guaranteed the stability and probity of her affection. Costals had arranged things in this way because it seemed to him disgraceful that anyone but he should have any rights over his son. He was, moreover, convinced of the pernicious influence mothers generally have on children, a view shared by a large number of educationists and moralists, who dare not admit it openly for fear of offending time-honoured conventions, which are always exquisitely chivalrous.

Philippe lived partly in Marseilles, partly in Cannes. Costals spent ten days or so with him every month, being convinced from experience that a highly-strung man cannot love a person with whom he cohabits, or even merely sees every day. The arrangement had worked extremely satisfactorily for fourteen years. Which proves nothing.

Philippe, who was known as Brunet because of his brown

*A boys' magazine of the 1920's (*Translator's note*).

skin (he called his father 'La Dine', a nickname for which no explanation, sensible or otherwise, was forthcoming), was still, at the age of nearly fourteen, physically very much a child: undeveloped, and his voice still unbroken. In character also he was very much a child, but at the same time terribly quick-witted and alert: a little backward physically, very advanced mentally. He was not an adolescent, he was a precocious child: not at all the same thing. One day in Paris at the age of ten, finding himself without enough money to go home by underground, he had gone and sung in people's courtyards until he had made enough for his fare. When he was eleven, Costals, who himself had not been born innocent (innocents do not notice such things), had discovered a hole made by Philippe in the door of Mlle du Peyron's bathroom.

He was not a rebellious or ill-natured or even wearisome child – wearisome as children are in their high spirits. Not one of those children whose mien one studies anxiously when they wake up in the morning to see if they are in a good or a bad mood and whether the day will be possible or unbearable. He was a little highly-seasoned, but he was straight. He was not pure, but he was healthy. He zigzagged violently, but without ever leaving the road. Disinterested; warm-hearted; intelligent, in a down-to-earth way (all Costals' efforts to inject him with a more high-flown conception of the universe – a philosophy of the universe – had failed); and with the restfulness one finds in boys who are not interested in sport. Although at first sight he appeared to be a typical French boy of 1927 – in other words a horrible little guttersnipe – he was not a guttersnipe, for he was never mean or nasty: he never did anything despicable.

The surest way of winning the confidence and friendship of a young boy is not to be his father. Brunet, however, confided in his father far more than most boys. He also lied to him less than is usual. Costals did not always understand his son, and he was sometimes annoyed by this, or rather irritated with himself on account of it. Whereas with women he could tell almost without fail what was going to be produced out of the hat, what was going to be their reaction in any given circumstance, with Philippe he was not so sure. Perhaps it was because women's reactions have something mass-produced, or – shall we say? – traditional* about them. Perhaps it was simply because what happened inside their heads did not seem worth bothering about. He considered them far less mysterious than men, especially in childhood. There is no comparison, from this point of view, between boys and girls. Who was it (Vauvenargues or Chamfort?) who said, cruelly, that one must choose between loving women and understanding them? Costals loved them, and had never tried to understand them, had never even wondered whether there was anything in them to understand.

'La Dine!'

'Shut up! Let me read Malebranche.'

'You make me sick with your branch! I say, I had a lovely dream last night.'

'What did you dream?'

'I dreamt I was eating noodles with tomato sauce.'

'Is that what you interrupted me for? What a pain in the neck the child is!'

There was more horse-play. Suddenly, at the height of the struggle, Brunet, with his face a few inches away from his father's, stopped and studied it attentively.

'I'm looking at you. I'd forgotten your face. Yesterday at the station I wondered if I'd recognize you when you got off the puff-puff. Luckily I remembered your overcoat. It's a pretty awful one! A fifteen-hundred-franc overcoat! Really, you have no taste. I shall have to come with you when you buy your togs.'

'He too forgets faces....' Costals mused. He himself was liable to forget the faces of his mistresses, his best friends, to forget everything, in fact. When one of his own traits came back at him like this from his son, he felt a bit uneasy. 'Nonsense! he's a good kid, and I love him – so we should get by all right.' (Which was anticipating a bit.)

Meanwhile Brunet was still staring at his father. 'I'm fond of

---

*'In France, women are too much alike. They have the same way of being pretty, of entering a room, of writing, of loving, of quarrelling. No matter how often you change from one to another, it always seems to be the same one.' – Prince de Ligne

you, you know. You're a good sort,' he said at last, and kissed him. Costals kissed him back, on his eyelids, rather from a sort of sense of the proprieties, of the necessary reciprocities, than from any keen impulse.

'Is that the way you kiss women?' the boy asked. 'Go on, show me how you do it.'

'Shh.... Now, now.'

'Had you ever kissed a woman by the time you were fourteen?'

'Of course.'

'I kissed Francine Finoune. She said to me: "Give me a kiss and I'll take you to the cinema." So I kissed her.'

'Where?'

'There.' (He pointed to a spot on his cheek.)

'And did you like it?'

Philippe eyed his father as though, by the mere suggestion that this kiss might have given pleasure, he had insulted him.

'Oh, come off it.'

'The day you find you like kissing Francine Finoune, you must let me know, because I shall have one or two things to tell you.'

'Catch me telling you that! Anyway, we've quarrelled. She asked me for ten francs. So I gave her a clout.'

'She takes you to the cinema, and yet you refuse her ten francs. Is that fair?'

'Oh, that's a detail.'

Costals searched his pocket for a cigarette ... and found a roll of peppermints. Hardly a week ever passed without Brunet giving his father some such 'surprise', a little present slipped into his pocket – sweets, a packet of cigarettes, or some such thing. Costals gave the child a light. This was the signal for another standing joke – Brunet blowing, rapidly one after the other, several puffs of smoke into Costals' hair. The latter then had to don his son's beret as quickly as possible. When he took it off, his head would be smoking. Vast amusement, each time as fresh as ever. The smouldering skull of the genius!

'Poor La Dine, I'm wasting your time.'

'It's never a waste of time being with you.'

Costals had stretched himself out on the bed again; having

abandoned *La Recherche de la Vérité*, he was reading *Cri-Cri*
over his son's shoulder. Philippe burst out laughing every other
minute. He seemed to be not quite himself unless he had a
pretext for laughing, and everything was a pretext. He would
throw his head right back, and in the middle of his brown
face, at the summit of his whole being, his dazzling white
teeth, small and regular as the incisors of a cat, shone like
snow on a mountain top. Scarcely for a moment, during the
hour they had been together, had he ceased to laugh –
radiating sweetness and good humour. One could see at once
that he was a child who was rid of his parents. All this was
well attuned to Costals' own constant good humour – the
natural condition of a man of sense.

A wire-haired fox terrier appeared in the doorway, gave a
muffled 'woof' of approval, and disappeared after this benison.
The terrier, who answered to the name Hairynose, was the
only person in the house who maintained a high moral tone.
He often watched with a look of severity as Costals and his
son played the fool; it was obvious that he was judging them.
The examination would end with a deep sigh. Then this
paragon would put his nose to his behind and go back to sleep.

Several times Costals tried to get up, but Brunet held out his
arms towards him, stretching them as a cat stretches out its
fore-paws, and Costals, who knew this gesture well and found
it touching, gave in.

After a time, Brunet crumpled up his *Cri-Cri* and threw it
aside violently, as though suddenly horrified at having enjoyed
it; then he bent down and laid his head on his father's chest.
With him there was always, beneath the playfulness, a desire
for physical contact; he was always finding reasons for rubbing against his father, either in their rough-and-tumbles, or by
suddenly clasping him in his arms and trying to make him
dance the fox-trot, or jumping on his back, or taking his arm
in the street. (And then there was his girlish way of giving a
start and turning away his head whenever anything painful
or cruel was mentioned, such as an operation, or even a
thermometer.) Costals, finding himself close to him like this,
and touched by his need for affection, felt that the least he
could do was to kiss him again. He thought to himself: 'He's

charming, he's cuddly, he smells good, the softness of his skin is not of this world. And yet I haven't the same sort of tenderness for him that I have for a woman. Why? It's strange.' The fact was that Costals was capable of feeling strong tenderness only for people he desired. He thought the bridge of Philippe's nose, just below the eyes, was too wide (like a lion cub, perhaps), and this single small feature that he did not like prevented him from responding with complete spontaneity to his son's caresses. And he watched himself, afraid of appearing cold – for he was very fond of his son – and making sure that, in the matter of caresses, he would always have something to spare. He also wondered, as he wondered about women: 'Why does he enjoy embracing me?' And he could not understand.

At this point Old Mother Hubbard (their nickname for the old lady) poked her head round the half-open door like a little tousled field mouse and beamed at the charming spectacle they presented.

Andrée Hacquebaut   to Pierre Costals
Saint-Léonard   *Paris*

15 March 1927

Not a day has passed since my return without the tears springing to my eyes under the impact of a painful memory. But it only lasts a few seconds. The rest of the time I live, I laugh, I talk, I write. Apparently unscathed. What brings my wound home to *me* is the fact that I can no longer sing. Before, I used to sing all the time, even in my worst moments. Now it not only won't 'come' to me, but if I make an effort it won't 'come out'. Oh Costals, what makes men suffer? There is only one suffering: loneliness of heart. I have made a list of my blessings: freedom, health, leisure, my daily bread (dry bread, but still), comparative youth, and so on. And yet, telling myself that other human beings might passionately envy all this does not make me any happier. Even if the list could be extended *ad infinitum*, I would only have to put down the absence of love on the debit side for the whole of the credit column to be reduced to zero. The truth is that I no longer enjoy **any**thing. Only on Saturday did I find a little peace, when I went to Confession in order not to break completely with the practice of religion. With God and yourself together forbidding me to love you, I ought to be convinced!

I had a dream the other night. Its origin is easy to guess. We were walking through Paris in the rain. And I kept forgetting things – once it was a fur – and I would climb back up interminable staircases while you waited for me below at the corner of the street. I would rejoin you, we would set off again, once again I would find I had forgotten something, I would go back, climb the stairs again, search again.... And, as usual in dreams, the search involved unbelievable trouble, I had to rummage through a mass of things, there was no end to it, and I was obsessed all the time with the fear that you would have got tired of waiting. But I always found you on the pavement waiting for me, your face contorted with impatience, like an angry little cat. This dream consoled me a little, as a sign that you were not lost to me.

And yet, if I were to judge by your silence....

Oh, no reproach intended, no sulking (I know what sulking costs me). I cannot conceive of there ever being the slightest shadow of reproach between us. Whatever you do, whatever happens, *nothing* will ever weaken my admiration for you, my devotion and gratitude. But my affection is beginning to succumb, from anæmia, because it feels wasted. It cannot go on living off itself for ever. That would be a superhuman task, like having to go on filling the Danaids' bottomless barrel, until one collapses. It might be possible for a girl of twenty. At thirty (minus thirty-nine days!) one no longer has the energy. I can sense that you are deeply involved elsewhere. All my enthusiasm is dead. Permanently wrapped up in you as I am, how could I possibly endure without torment those long deserts in our friendship?

What have I had from you? Such meagre oases! Not an hour of intimacy. Two years ago, you had me to your house several times. Since then, always outside – at concerts, in restaurants, in the street. It's as though you were afraid of something. There remained your letters, rare as they were.

(I would have far preferred you to do nothing for me in the practical sphere but to write to me more often. My correspondence with you is an eternal monologue.) But if even the letters disappear! Remove both physical presence *and* letters from a friendship, and what remains? I know there are men who go for weeks, even months, without seeing or writing to one another, and yet remain firm and devoted friends. But I am not a man. Each empty post leaves me crushed for a whole hour, and upsets my entire day. A word from you, on the other hand, is like a drop of oil on a fire : it kindles a passionate fervour in me. . . .

If I am to keep a small corner in your heart, I must first of all write you shorter letters, mustn't I?

> Your
> Andrée.

I have decided to laugh as little as possible from now on, because of my wrinkles.

This letter remained unanswered.

Andrée Hacquebaut   to Pierre Costals
Saint-Léonard   *Paris*

31 March 1927

What does this silence mean – this barrier of silence that I have to break through to reach you? I love you as one loves a child who has a heart disease and is doomed to die at twenty. I know I shall lose what little I have of you, that is to say the right to correspond with you, etc. – your presence in my life, the slight interest you have in me. I also know that I shall make no attempt to cling on to you. All I ask is not to be stabbed in the back : it's the only expression I can think of to describe these appalling betrayals through silence, which leave me floundering in ignorance and incomprehension, groping in the void like a blind man with his stick, or a mystic seeking God in the darkness of spiritual desolation. Even the mystics have need of the sacraments, which are a substitute for the real presence. I love everything about you: even your raillery and your harshness give me happiness, and anyway they fortify me against you; whereas your silence paralyses and destroys me. You can deal me blow after blow and I shall be able to withstand them. But do not take a cowardly advantage of the weapons of silence and absence.

If you only knew what it is not to have any contact with you – either in person or through letters – that is not broken up by these weeks of total separation! The lack of *continuity* between us! All these things that come to nothing, that absence makes abortive, when it was essential to strike while the iron was hot. Everything evaporates through absence, like the heat of a room through an open door. How do you expect anything to develop, or even survive, between us in such a disjointed situation? No sooner have I left you than I find the words I ought to have said to you (such a stream of things I ought to tell you to explain this or that, to rectify the idea you have of me ...), but I cannot say them because we see each other so rarely. So I am reduced to my letters, which irritate you and which have no effect on you, and it is only in my room, alone, that I speak out to you and convince you.

It is not your behaviour I'm complaining of, you understand. It isn't even your indifference to my distress. It isn't *you* at all, it's the uncertainty – that abyss of absolute uncertainty within whose depths anything can lie hidden without one's knowing: accident, illness, changes of heart, ill-founded grievances, misunderstandings. . . .

Write to me anything you like, but write to me. Be it only an empty envelope – like those the Maréchal de Luxembourg asked Rousseau to send him – so that I know you are still alive.

I believe in you in spite of everything, as one must, our preacher used to say, believe in God in spite of everything.

Andrée.

This letter remained unanswered.

Andrée Hacquebaut
Saint-Léonard

to Pierre Costals
Paris

23 April 1927
9 p.m.

I am thirty years old today, Costals.

It is Sunday. Sunday, a bad day for me even at the best of times. The weather has been divine, too divine. Alas, I'm beginning to know them, these desolate springtimes, these summers that go by one after the other like empty baskets: not one of them, not one, has fulfilled its promise. How terrible it is, this sensation of sterility in a season when everything aspires towards renewal. Must one always see these intoxicating things through a horrible veil of deprivation? What is the point of being pretty? (For how much longer?)

This afternoon there was the usual hubbub of the *boule*-players. Seven times, from my room, I heard the hotel gramophone play the famous tune from *Louise: Depuis le jour où je me suis donnée* ... From time to time there were cheers and rounds of applause, for there was some kind of reunion party going on. Before dinner there was a thunderstorm. Now everything at the hotel is lit up *al giorno*, the tables on the terrace glistening, rain-soaked. The soft air brings me the sound of dance music, and the sweet orange smell from a languishing acacia branch. I can see two young men in dinner jackets coming out of the hotel, their shirt-fronts shining, too, and their patent leather shoes in the mud. Their carefree happiness pains me.

I am thirty. That's that. The age of waiting is over, the age of realization has begun : I have reached the turning-point. What I need now is a past rather than a future, memories rather than hopes. This is the age at which film stars in America commit suicide, because they have nothing more to expect from life. I still have *everything*.

In my mind's eye I see myself at the bedside of a dead child or a dead husband. Of course it must be terrible to have had and then to have no longer; but not to have had at all is worse. If only I were younger, or older! Younger, I wouldn't yet have had enough of this purely cerebral life and this purely platonic, intellectual, cold friendship: when I first met you, I didn't care about love, I didn't need it, I was sufficient unto myself, my body didn't interest me. Older, I should no longer be in a position to 'make a life' for myself, I should no longer have anything to lose by resigning myself to friendship pure and simple, I could even be quite happy with it. Thirty, for me, is either too early or too late.

Costals, I tell you quite simply and sadly: I am not trying to cling on to you. I have always known that, whatever I did, I would not attract you for ever. I have lived, I am still living, in the constant expectation of your growing weary of me, forgetting me, and the silence in which you have immured yourself during the past two months confirms my fears. Perhaps this is a psychological error: you have stuck so faithfully to your 'good works' on my behalf for four years! But I don't want to rely on the past as a gauge for the future. And besides, I don't even know if it was a question of 'good works' on your part or a genuine inclination. You have never cared to enlighten me on that point.

This being so, why should I go on being discreet and circumspect with you? Why should I go on being adroit? I'm inclined to think I've been only too discreet, and I know very well that no sort of finesse means anything to you. You get tired of things for no reason, simply because they have 'gone on long enough', because they have 'served their purpose', because 'one must have a change'. There's no point in trying to *deserve well* of you; it's simply a matter of trying to make the best of the short period during which one has a place in your life and if possible turn it into something more solid, beautiful, and happy.

Never, never, never will you be able to accuse me of being the female enemy. Never, no matter what you do, will you see me turn against you, or reproach you. I am your *friend*. But I cannot go on being nothing but a friend. I am like a soul in Purgatory, a woman of thirty, highly-strung, unhappy, with none of the outlets men have: brief affairs, travel, work, vanity, ambition. For twenty years I've walked in a straight line between two high banks. So you must be a little indulgent when you hear what I have to say to you.

What I have to say to you is this. Your friendship can do nothing more for my happiness. It is like a pearl found in the desert by a Bedouin dying of thirst. I am no longer at an age when half-measures and half-attachments can suffice; I must have total happiness or total despair. I am hungry for plenitude, and it is a passionate plenitude that I need. I am no longer interested in all those spiritual values which I prized so highly when I was younger; I am no longer interested in you in that sense; I have had enough of being loved fastidiously. This pure friendship is a beautiful thing, but it isn't a tangible thing of which I can be sure as I am sure of what I eat or what I drink; it's a fleshless thing, arid, stifling, intermittent, spasmodic, and in any case flagging, exhausting itself in the long run – all absence, waiting, emptiness – in which I have all the self-denials of love without any of its benefits. A sterile, spent thing, unless it can be infused with new sap. To be loved is to be at once desired, cossetted, possessed and cherished. All the rest is moonshine.

I should like to have my share of you, to take my fill of you, to be able to live on my repletion. Here, then, is what I propose. I do so calmly and coolly : I've thought a great deal about what I am going to write to you. I propose that we exchange this moribund friendship for two months during which you would give yourself to me passionately, during which I would be entirely yours. I am ready to give you my solemn word that once this time had elapsed you would never hear from me again if that was your wish.

These brief weeks of desperate plenitude (desperate for me) might perhaps give you some pleasure. For me they would be everything – everything, that is to say *something*, in this life of mine in which there is *nothing*, something for me to hold on to, the memory of which would remain with me, inviolate, which nothing and nobody could take away from me, a satisfaction of a different kind from the psychological satisfaction you have, it's true, given me up to now. With such a memory, I could snap my fingers at the banal happiness of married women. Having possessed you once, my life will not have been wasted. What dazzling peace for the rest of my days!

You must not think that, even at thirty, I have an inordinate

need of physical love. A cerebral need, rather. It is really my
conscience that tells me I ought to experience it. To get it
over with. To be inoculated. Appeased. Mentally appeased, I
mean. Like settling down in a train one was afraid of missing.
As far as the senses are concerned, I am still a very little girl.
Everything I have to offer you is fresh and new as at the
break of day, completely worthy, in its simplicity, of your
greatness. I would never forgive you if you forced me to offer
it without love.

And please do not bring up that word 'affair' which you
sometimes use so crudely. For me, everything that comes
within your aura loses its ordinary meaning. Lover, mistress,
liaison, affair – these words no longer mean anything : there is
simply love. And, within the context of love, every liberty,
every audacity, all consumed by its radiance.

Yes, it is I who have written this letter! Only two years
ago, I should have died rather than contemplate the step which
I am taking towards you. But what do I care about the world's
opinion, when I know that what I would give you is radiantly
pure and perhaps sublime?

Andrée

This letter remained unanswered.

The most striking thing about man's – the male's – conception
of happiness is that no such conception exists. There is a book
of Alain's entitled : *Propos sur le bonheur*. But nowhere in this
book is there any mention of happiness. This is highly
significant. Most men have no conception of happiness.

Saint-Preux, in *La Nouvelle Héloïse*, cries out : 'O God, my
soul was made for suffering : give me one that is made for
happiness!' Well, God did not hear his prayer : the soul of the
male is not made for happiness. In his eyes, happiness is a
negative state – insipid in the literal sense of the word – which
one only becomes aware of as a result of a glaring *un*-
happiness; happiness is obtainable only by not thinking about
it. One day you take a look at yourself and realize that you
are not too badly off : so you tell yourself you are happy. And

you take as your guiding principle the famous platitude that happiness comes only to those who do not seek it. To look for happiness, to speak of it as of something concrete, is regarded as unmanly. It was a man, Goethe, who spoke of 'the duty of happiness'. And it was also a man, Stendhal, who made that magnificent remark, so far-reaching it embodies a whole philosophy and a whole ethic: 'There is nothing in the world I respect as much as happiness.' But these were superior men, and it is precisely because they transcend the ordinary human categories that they think like this. To the average man, any-one who admits to a respect for happiness is suspect. As for 'the duty of happiness', in spite of Goethe it has always received, together with the notion of 'live and let live', the worst possible press. You may say to a man, even a young man: 'One empty hour, one wasted hour – think of the remorse, as death draws near, for not having devoted it to the pursuit of happiness!' and he will be taken aback. 'Whose happiness do you mean?' he will ask. 'Other people's? The country's?' And if you answer fiercely: 'No! MINE!' he will be shocked. He cannot understand how you can think of your own happiness; he has never thought of his. The male is always telling himself, quite cheerfully: 'Tomorrow you'll start living.' And if he knows what he means by 'living' it is already quite an achievement. Another young man, almost a youth, with everything in his favour, having heard someone use the word 'living', in the sense of making the most of life, asks him: 'But what do you mean by "living"?' For him, to live means to work, to scratch a living. If he were asked what happiness was, he would no doubt reply: 'Doing one's duty, finding a task to fulfil, a discipline, etc.' In other words, what he means by happiness is the method he has chosen, or, more probably, has had imposed on him, of killing time. And even this is not enough; when men kill time in too easy and pleasant a way they grow sick of it. One has often heard of the sort of malaise that comes over a man when he reaches a standstill, a state of quiescent equilibrium in which he no longer feels any desires: it is similar to the sort of malaise one feels in a motor-boat on a dead calm sea when the engine fails. Whence the fact that the consciousness of happiness gives such a powerful sensation of loneliness. This is often misunderstood.

However, it does sometimes happen that a man has a positive conception of happiness. In this case happiness lies in the satisfaction of vanity (with all kinds of individual variations, of course, since each man's idea of his own happiness is absolutely incomprehensible to everyone else). Vanity is man's predominant passion. It is not true that one can make a man do absolutely anything for money. But one can make most men do anything one wants by appealing to their vanity. Most men would go without food and drink for a whole day if by doing so they were to obtain a sop to their vanity at the end of it. A man without vanity is a bit of a freak : he casts a chill, and is given a wide berth. Thus for men it is not so much a question of *being* happy as of making people believe they are. A young doctor in the North African desert, recently married, once remarked ingenuously, without realizing how splendid his remark was : 'I'm extremely happy. But if only I could tell someone about it.' Most men would be only too delighted with the happiness of the sage. Fundamentally, that is what they like : how they all yearn to go into retreat! But people would not believe they were happy, people would think they had given up, or were incompetent, so off they go on the other tack, giving themselves airs, plunging into the shameful and ridiculous bustle we normally find them in, making lots of telephone calls, and soon a day of happiness for them is a day on which they have made plenty of telephone calls, in other words a day on which they have been very important. And in this way happiness-as-the-satisfaction-of-vanity merges with the happiness-which-comes-without-thinking-about-it which we mentioned earlier.

Women, on the other hand, have a positive idea of happiness. For, if man is more restless, woman is more alive. No woman would ask, like the afore-mentioned young man : 'What do you mean by "living"?' She has no need of explanations. To live, for her, is to feel. All women prefer to burn themselves out rather than be extinguished; all women prefer to be devoured rather than ignored. And in their 'feeling', what mobility, what profuseness of reaction! When one sees how a woman, if the

man she loves seems to love her less – even a little less –
suffers as much as if he no longer loved her at all; when one
sees how, later, if she realizes that he still loves her as much
as ever, not only does she feel wonderfully happy, but her joy
is redoubled by the joy of being forgiven· for having suspected
him – when one sees this and compares it with the sluggish-
ness of men, one grasps the meaning of the word 'alive'.

In fact, the succession of minor pleasures which, according
to men, is what ultimately constitutes happiness, as a mass of
little stars makes up the Milky Way, seems no more capable
of doing so in women's eyes than, for Christians, a thousand
venial sins are capable of making up one mortal sin. For
women, happiness is a clearly defined state, endowed with its
own individual personality, a tangible reality that is extremely
alive, powerful and sensitive. A woman will tell you she is
happy as she will tell you she is hot or cold. 'What are you
thinking?' – 'That I'm happy.' 'Why do you want to do this
or that?' – 'In order to be happy!' (this in such a vehement
tone, with an 'of course' implied). 'I'm afraid of your doing
this or that.' – 'Do you think I want to ruin my happiness?'
She will give you a description of her happiness, telling you,
for example: 'When I'm happy, I don't talk', or 'When I'm
happy I always feel well.' She will know precisely when it
begins and when it ends. There is a book in the Bibliothèque
Rose entitled *A Fortnight of Happiness*. It is a book by a
woman, and this is obvious from the title alone: no man
would ever have had the notion that happiness can be cut
into slices like a cake. And a woman will enjoy this 'fortnight
of happiness' – meaning any limited period of happiness, any
obviously ephemeral happiness – much more than a man
would. For a woman any happiness, however short-lived, is
better than nothing. If you tell a girl you would love to marry
her but for one reason or another it is inevitable that she will
begin to be unhappy within a year, she is sure to reply: 'Well
then, I shall have had a year of happiness.' A man in her
place would think of the threat to his future, and would weigh
up the risks. The idea of happiness is so strong in women that
they can see nothing else; all risks are blotted out.

The only acceptable future for a woman is a happy

marriage. Thus she is dependent on men, and knows it from an early age. However true it is that male adolescents suffer from their impotence, as boys they live in the present, as young men they think of the future as a substance they will fashion by themselves. Girls, on the other hand, are afraid of the future. A boy knows that his future will be what he wants it to be; a girl knows that her future will be what a man wants it to be. Her dreams of happiness during this period of uncertainty will be all the more ardent if this happiness is threatened in advance.

Similarly, women attach far more importance than men to the conditions of happiness. It was a woman who once wrote that, as room thermometers indicate the correct temperature for *orange-trees*, *silk-worms*, etc., the word *happiness* ought to be opposite the 25 degrees centigrade line. When one returns from long stays in North Africa, Spain or Italy to the leprous Parisian winter, ten degrees below, to the darkness, the dirt, the ugliness, the inconveniences, the nastiness, the strained unhealthy life, what astonishes one is not so much this accumulation of horrors as the fact that most men put up with it: thanks to them, life goes on. But women, in the midst of this hell on earth, daydream of other things, pine away for other things, and sometimes fall into despair. There was once a novel for girls entitled *L'Age où l'on croit aux îles*. Women are always at the age when one believes in islands, in other words the age when one believes in happiness.

This positive idea of happiness that women have, and the demands they make on it, no doubt arise from the state of unsatisfaction which is their lot. Not that all women are martyrs by any means! Nevertheless, when one thinks of the condition of the sexes in society, the word that springs to mind for women is *unhappiness*, and for men *worries*. There is a striking custom in the Moslem marriage ceremony as celebrated in Algiers. A woman advances towards the young couple and pours jasmine water into the cupped hands of the bride. The groom bends down and drinks it. The woman proceeds to do the same with the bridegroom; but just as the bride is about to drink from his hands, he opens them and lets the water escape. What an appalling custom – laying it

down as a principle that man should be happy and woman
not. There is something about the picture of the little girl
bending down to drink the water and being refused it that
makes one shudder. True, that is the Moslem world; in Europe
the unhappiness of woman is not laid down as a sacred principle in advance. But even in Europe, whereas the happiness
of women is dependent on that of men, men are not much
concerned about making women happy. It is rare to find a
public man risking his career, an industrialist endangering his
business, a writer sacrificing his work, to make a woman
happy (by marrying her, for instance). In fact, quite apart from
any question of sacrifice, one never sees a man marrying a
woman who wants to marry him more than he wants to marry
her, simply in order to make her happy. Whereas there are
millions of women who dream of marriage simply in order to
discharge an overflow of loving devotion on a husband and
children.

Dreams are born of dissatisfaction: no satisfied person
dreams (or, if he is an artist, he dreams only in a calculated
way.) Where do people (even men) dream of happiness? In
slums, in hospitals, in prisons. Women dream of happiness
and think about it, because they have not got it. If a man
suffers through a woman, he has everything else to console
himself with. But what has she got? A woman can never
realize herself completely: she is too dependent on men. She
therefore dreams continually of the unattainable. A poetess
once wrote a book under the title *Waiting* – a title as feminine
as our *Fortnight of Happiness*. Women are always waiting,
hopefully up to a certain age, hopelessly thereafter. This dreaming of happiness, so peculiar to women, is incomprehensible to
men. They call it naïvety, emotionalism, romanticism,
Bovaryism – always with a suggestion of superiority and dis-
dain. There is an even more contemptuous word: soulfulness.
If a woman admits to being happy, a man will tell her it's
exhibitionism. If she sings all day Jong, a man will say she is
a bit simple-minded – for him, she could not possibly be happy
unless she was simple. If a poet writes that he would rather
not go to the Italian lakes at all than go there without his
beloved, there will always be a critic ready to say: 'Shop-girl's

talk.' (If it is 'shop-girl's talk' for a woman to say: 'It would be absolute torture for me to see, for example, a Titian I like when I'm in the company of someone I dislike', so much the better for shop-girls.) The girl who waits for a husband a little too long, and vainly decorates the unknown beloved's altar in her heart, would simply appear comic to that same beloved: he thinks, or pretends to think, that it is simply a drama of the flesh, when in fact it is the soul consumed with the desire to give itself. (Whether this unhappiness is greater than that of many married women is another question.) A young woman who dreams of a happiness she does not possess interests him only to the extent that he can hope to benefit from it: he has no more respect for her longing because of this. As for the old maid and all her regrets, for them he has only jeers, not to say insults: the attitude of men towards spinsters, in France at least, is a disgrace.

The feminine conception of happiness suffers the fate of all feminine conceptions: it does not interest men. Men are not interested in women when their senses are satisfied, and the day she realizes this for the first time is one of the tragedies in a woman's life. Galatea flees into the willows, hoping to be caught; a moment later the man runs from the willows, but this time it's for good – he does not want to be caught. Men are bored or irritated by women as soon as they have ceased to enjoy them, just as the smoke from a cigarette inhaled with pleasure a few moments ago is bothersome when it rises from the cigarette after one has put it down three-quarters finished with no intention of taking it up again. It is because they have nothing to say to each other that couples quarrel; it is a way of passing the time. A man has to make an effort, out of politeness, or good nature, or a sense of duty, to devote some of his time to the woman who has satisfied his desires; when he does so, he always has the feeling that he is doing her a favour. Only rakes are permanently interested in women, because with them curiosity – the soul of desire – is permanently alive: hence the indulgent attitude of women towards them, even the most serious women. 'The happiness of women,' a character in a novel has perceptively remarked, 'the happiness of women comes from men, but the happiness of men comes from themselves. The only thing a woman can do for a man is avoid disturbing his happiness.' The terrible thing is that women – powerless and naïve – long to do for men what men do for them. A woman who is happy and loved (and who loves) asks for nothing more. A man who loves and is loved needs something else as well. Leaving aside the question of money, a man always makes a present to a woman by marrying her, because marriage is a vital necessity for her but not for him. Women marry because marriage is for them the only key to happiness, whereas men marry because Tom, Dick and Harry do; they marry out of habitude, if not hebetude. Naturally they do not admit this, because they are unaware of it. Thoughtlessness makes men marry, just as thoughtlessness makes them go to war. One shudders at the thought of what would become of society if men began to be governed by reason; it would perish, as we see peoples perish before our very eyes because they are too intelligent.

Man and woman confront each other, and society says to them: 'You know nothing about him? You know nothing about her? Well, have a try. Go ahead and make the best of it.' Indeed, were it not for the mating urge, each sex would stay where it was. Not out of shyness, as in Vigny's poem, but simply like two species impervious to each other and with nothing to say to each other. Nature has made them antithetical, incapable of agreeing, or capable of agreeing only on the ruin of something, and we watch this strange spectacle of beings who are driven towards each other although they seem not to be made for each other.

Woman is made for one man; man is made for life, and incidentally for all women. Woman is made to arrive and stay put; man is made to act and move on: she begins loving when he has finished; people talk of women 'teasing' when they ought to talk of men. Man takes and throws away again; woman gives herself, and what has once been given cannot be taken back, or only with difficulty. Woman thinks love can do everything – not only *her* love, but the love man bears her, which she always exaggerates. She will eloquently maintain that love has no limits; man sees the limits not only of woman's love but of his own, whose poverty he is only too well aware of. Not only are they out of step, but supply and demand are badly synchronized between them. Men seldom feel anything for women except desire, which women find tiresome; women seldom feel anything for men except tenderness, which men find tiresome. Women offer more tenderness than men can stand; fortunately there are children to absorb the surplus, as long as they need it. Women say: 'Ah, how foolish men are to sacrifice, for the sake of ideas, or glory, or money, time that should be devoted to love, to true love! It teaches one so many things! Think how many men fail to attain to the highest spheres (intellectual, social, religious, etc.) because they have not allowed love to live and grow in them!' And men reply: 'How can love live and grow in me? It can only die there. These embers cannot be fanned into flame: artifice is worse than useless. Why ask me to be other than what nature made me? Nature made me a man – that is, a member of a loveless species.'

Such is this hybrid couple from whom spring most of the ills of mankind without either of them being to blame, but only nature, which brought them together without matching them, throwing in the best and the worst as in all her other works, wherein nothing is not muddled, confused, impure, two-sided, *pace* the ignorant and the sage, who never see more than one side.

'What!' you will say, ' "the source of most of the ills of mankind" – what an exaggeration!' But just open your newspaper. Dramas of jealousy, dramas of adultery, dramas of divorce, dramas of abortion, crimes of passion. And all those family dramas which would not exist without an initial couple. And all the things one never hears about. It is not the free union that seems to be cursed, it is the couple, whatever form it takes, and perhaps more especially in marriage. At the basis of it a monstrous gamble: the man being forced to take a partner for life when there is no good reason why it should be this one rather than the next, since millions of others are equally worthy of his love. The man driven by nature to repeat the same words of love to a dozen women including the one who is destined for him – false if he hides the truth from her, cruel if he admits it. The man driven by nature to deceive his wife, with all the lies and baseness this entails – culpable if he yields to nature's commands, unhappy if he resists them. The girl who grows to womanhood in the midst of tears, and to motherhood in the midst of sighs. The child, a natural occurrence that makes woman ugly and deformed. The act which is supposed to be supremely natural, but which can only be performed at certain periods, in certain conditions, with certain precautions. The terror of pregnancy, or the terror of disease, hovering like a spectre above every love-bed. The so-called supremely natural act surrounded by a whole pharmacopoeia which sullies it and poisons it and makes it ridiculous. What man, indeed, if he only stops to think for a moment, will not admit to himself, when he approaches a woman, that he is entangling himself in a mesh of misfortunes, or at any rate risks, and that he is tempting Providence? And yet he wants it, women want it, society wants it, and nature, if she were capable of wanting anything, would want it too. For that is what love is – the thread of fire which binds the living to the earth and justifies the Creation. You will ask me, dear reader, what I am driving at. The answer is that I am simply registering my astonishment at the fact that an impulse so basic as that of one sex towards the other should be forced by its very nature to cause so many ills. It seems to me that what nature should condemn is what is done against her, not what she prescribes. But no, she reserves all her severity for those who follow her and without whom she would not exist. Unless everything is nature's, and we are mistaken in seeing her in one place rather than another.

Pierre Costals   to M. Armand Pailhès
Paris   *Toulouse*

27 April 1927

My dear Pailhès,

A letter from poor Andrée H. She offers herself to me in the most formal terms. If she persists, I shall of course be obliged to refuse her, in no less formal terms.

In so far as I understand the French attitude in these matters, I should guess that her reaction will be as follows: 'A real man does not behave in such a way. Either he's a cad, or he's impotent. It is disgraceful to insult a woman in such a way.'

What do you think? But first of all, here is my defence.

Totally lacking in worldly wisdom, Andrée is incapable of distinguishing the element of civility pure and simple, of complaisance, of good-nature if you like, in my attitude towards her. Where I am concerned, she takes politeness for keen interest, benevolence for predilection, pity for friendship. God forgive me, I suspect that at times she thinks I'm in love with her. If I send a book to a colleague with whom I am on perfectly amicable terms, with the dedication 'affectionate regards', it does not enter his head for a moment that I really have any affection for him. A similar dedication would make Andrée swoon with joy: 'He has declared his love!'

The truth is that I regard her with sympathy, respect, and a certain admiration. That is all, and it's a great deal.

All? No, understanding too. I know that people find Andrée antipathetic. They complain that she thinks herself superior — but supposing she is, in some respects? That she is 'literary' — but in fact, although she is stuffed with reading, she is still perfectly natural, completely devoid of affectation, unlike so many of these female bookworms who adopt, more or less unconsciously, opinions and attitudes which they think will impress. Andrée's writing is also revealing: simplicity itself, flowing like water from a spring. The fact is that, unlike all those others, she has a simple, powerful temperament, she's a *Natur* (and you know that to call anyone *eine Natur* was for Goethe the highest praise). And I even forgive her, up to a point, her lack of dignity. For after all, the girl loves, and love and dignity make bad bed-fellows. She wants to be happy: what could be more natural? I too, when I want to be happy, go at it as hard as I can. In short, she irritates me but I understand her, and defend her when she is attacked, for I could not swear that in her position I wouldn't be irritating too — more discreetly than she, of course, or at least so I hope.

When all this is said, the fact remains that she is ugly, graceless, badly dressed, and utterly unfeminine. As you yourself said to me: 'She looks like a housemaid.' The human face is a curious invention: it must be very nice, or else!

And then, even if she were not obviously unprepossessing, she doesn't attract me, and that in itself is enough to justify my attitude. There are women who have nothing to recommend them, but this nothing arouses my desire. Andrée's nothing gets me down. Drain that cup to the dregs* – no, never!

I am capable of making the gesture of taking this woman. To succeed in something one despises is a noble and difficult thing – because one must conquer oneself as well as others – but it has always been within my power. To succeed in something that disgusts me is something I am also capable of. I should escape with nothing worse than that deadly depression one experiences after having consummated the carnal act with somebody who doesn't appeal to one. But what I cannot do is feign love. In being possessed by me, she would feel my disgust, and it would stab her to the heart. I should have undergone this harrowing ordeal, and to what end? To make her suffer!

Even supposing she doesn't suffer, should one take a woman out of pity? It's 'a good talking point', as my fellow-writers say. Of course it can happen that one takes a woman because one is sorry for her, just as it can happen that one takes a woman because she has made one angry. But there must be a basis of desire, which there is not, and never will be, between me and Andrée. One of my friends, who is very unhappily married, said to me one day à propos of his wife: 'I go on with her out of pity. She's young. She needs it.' I've never forgotten that remark, which seemed to me to be appalling. But you can satisfy a woman out of pity, even though she makes you unhappy, if she is your wife, if she is part of your life, someone you see continually. You cannot satisfy, out of pity alone, a stranger who repels you physically and for whom you feel no affection.

Furthermore, whatever anyone may say, it really is something to make a woman of a well-brought-up young lady, even one of thirty. It creates a bond, involves risks, perhaps responsibilities, perhaps long-term consequences: nothing can

---

*An untranslatable pun here: *Boire cette coupe jusqu'au lit* (bed) instead of *lie* (dregs) (*Translator's note*).

alter the fact that the thing has happened. And so, I consider it the purest folly to incur all this for the sake of somebody to whom I am indifferent. Colette's mother used to say
to her: 'Don't do anything foolish unless it's really going to
give you pleasure.' And I don't want to feel under any obligations to her.

One final reason, a shabby one if you like, but after all I'm
not a saint. By disposition and on principle I have, since
adolescence, kept all my love affairs secret, even the most
flattering ones. By disposition, being naturally secretive (which
goes hand in hand with false confidences). On principle,
because a young woman will yield to me all the more easily
if she knows that nothing will leak out, and because my reputation as a libertine, since no names can be attached to it,
remains on the whole vague enough not to interfere with my
enterprises. And inevitably Andrée, who is as incontinent in
speech as on paper, would go round advertising the fact that
she was my mistress. I have always prided myself on the fact
that, with a few rare exceptions, nobody has been able to
name my women-friends. And the whole of Paris, faced with
an ugly duckling like Andrée, would exclaim: 'Now we know
what excites him', and from this one sample imagine the rest!

And lastly, even without all that, there is something else
which in itself would be enough to restrain me from becoming
her lover: something about the shape of her face and her forehead reminds me of my great-uncle Costals de Pradels, and you
will appreciate that I don't want the family mixed up in
all this ... Who would have believed it? I too have my
scruples. . . .*

Costals

Andrée Hacquebaut   to Pierre Costals
Saint-Léonard   *Paris*
                                              30 April 1927

You have left unanswered the most solemn letter a proud

---

*The rest of this letter has no bearing on our subject (*Author's
note*).

and pure young woman could write to a man. My other letters did not necessarily call for replies; this one demanded one. If you do not answer the letter I am writing to you now, I shall consider that, for the first time, you have *behaved badly* towards me. It will be the first *real* crack in my esteem for you.

I am thirty; I have no experience of love, and unless you change your attitude, I never shall. Because you have occupied too great a place in my heart. Who else could love you as I do? No one – it wouldn't be possible. Not one of your mistresses loves you as I do. (Indeed, this is one reason why you prefer them to me.) You are the being one meets once in a lifetime, the decisive, the definitive being who leaves his mark for ever, without whom a woman's life is bound to be abortive, truncated, without flower or fruit. You are my master. God knows I haven't the soul of a slave, and yet I submit to you without the slightest effort or the slightest humility, remaining nevertheless on the same plane as you, at once your subject and your equal. I do not believe there could possibly be a more delicious sensation than that, for a woman like me, if you were my master in the full sense of the word. Which is to explain that I could not, even if I wanted to, offer to another man a sort of residuum of myself, when all that is best in me belongs to you : in my view, it would be a defilement. And besides, I am now incapable of taking an interest in another man. Men who are not you bore me. They do not dominate me. It is I who would dominate them. And I cannot belong to a man who does not dominate me in everything; it would be impossible, everything inside me rebels against it. My destiny as a woman is to love in submission and respect; I must feel myself transcended. You see, even if I were offered the most tempting marriages, now.... Like women who have a religious vocation, I've weighed it all up. On one side of the scale, all the material goods of this world, and on the other my vocation, which is to love you. And my vocation wins hands down.

You are both too much and too little in my life. Too much for me to be able to love anyone else. Too little for me to be fulfilled and satisfied. You give me too much for me to be able to break off relations with you without a terrible wrench. You give me too little for it not to be as painfully inadequate as nothing at all. Your friendship is a torture to me, and the rupture of that friendship would be torture too. You are like a knife in my heart. To leave it there is painful; but to pull it out would be to drain my life away. I am torn between my friendship for you, my spiritual need of you, my need to be loved spiritually by you – and my desire for love, my desire to *live*, if only for a few months: my flesh, too, has a legitimate need to be loved. If I do not want to lose you, I must sacrifice my flesh. I must die a virgin, or forget your very name. I must forgo marriage, sexual pleasure, motherhood, a healthy, normal life, and exhaust myself in a hopeless passion for someone who is fond of me, no doubt, but who has no need of me, either as a person to give to or as a person to take from. For you do not want even my self-sacrifice. You want nothing of me.

You once told me that women who looked at you with melting eyes 'sent you up the wall'. Have you ever seen me look at you like that? Do I ever foist myself on you or cling to you? If that were the case, I would understand your resistance: one owes nothing to people who bore one. But it is not the case, and I would take good care that it wasn't: a man's boredom is far too humiliating for a woman. My love is a loving comradeship. I do not desire you, but you are the only man whose desires I could accept without revulsion. I repeat, I can only love someone who is superior to me. I would rather be tortured by self-denial than give myself beneath me. I would prefer marriage, even a mediocre marriage, to a mediocre love affair. What then? Marriage, and your friendship on the side? First of all, no husband would tolerate such a friendship. And then, the mere thought of a man touching me sends me back to you, and I imagine all the heart-rending regrets for what might have been.

I have wanted, and I still want, with all my strength, your well-being and mine. Is it possible that it has all been to no purpose? Hurt me, if honesty demands it of you, but do not let me down. Let us assume that in these two months of intimacy there would be no pleasure for you who are surfeited elsewhere; they might at least be a psychological experiment from which your books could reap some benefit. I should be your guinea-pig, a guinea-pig of a particularly rare and precious species: a thinking guinea-pig, a guinea-pig which could if necessary take notes on what it felt and pass them on to you. In default of pleasure, you would be furthering your work, and as for me, if I knew that I was contributing towards it in however small a way, my happiness would be redoubled. And then, who knows, pleasure may come: your catalogue of women perhaps does not include a thirty-year-old provincial girl, as cultivated in mind as she is intact in body (and much prettier in body than in face). You have so often written that a man's only motive in love is curiosity, how could you not feel curiosity for that sort of object? And after all, me or another....

One of two things. Either you have a genuine affection for me, in which case no harm would be done, for you would know you were making me happy, and your affection would be gratified; and perhaps our relationship, begun in friendship, would end in friendship; love would have been deliciously enclosed between two layers of friendship, like a jewel between two layers of tissue paper. If not, if you are indifferent to me, then what have you to fear? It would cause you no regret to see this experiment detach you completely from me.

I have the impression of beating against a wall. The wall hasn't given yet, but by dint of perseverance.... You have no idea what a woman's will-power can be.

Andrée

Pierre Costals   to Andrée Hacquebaut
Paris   *Saint-Léonard*

2 May 1927

Dear Mademoiselle,

This is to acknowledge your two March letters in which you complain of my silence, and your two April letters in which you offer yourself to me. So you see that I've read you.

You are obsessed with the idea of happiness. So am I. You have no idea how keenly I feel the tragedy of a situation in which neither body nor soul obtains what it desires. I could write page after page on the subject, even more forcefully than you. If in this matter we are in complete sympathy – *sumpathein*: to suffer with, to suffer from the same suffering as – it is because, from this point of view, *I have been you.* Not only during adolescence, bound hand and foot as I was by my shyness and my ignorance of the world, but even later, when I was already a man, during certain desolate periods of my life. True, they did not last long. Today I have everything I like, and I like everything I have.

And so, I repeat, your suffering is not of the kind I need to imagine in order to be able to sympathize with. I know what it's like; it's intolerable, and your situation is intolerable. You are really very unlucky.

That said, if I understand your last two letters aright, you wish to give yourself to me. Allow me to say, dear Mademoiselle, that this idea does not seem to me a happy one.

1. Physiologically I am somewhat peculiar. I only desire: (a) girls of under twenty-two years of age; (b) passive, bovine girls; (c) long, thin girls with raven hair. So you see that you do not at all fulfil the required conditions, which are an absolute *sine qua non*. Whatever your attractions, upon which I will not expatiate – you know them only too well – I do not feel capable of responding to the desire which you do me the honour of conceiving for me. Nature (the wretch!) would remain deaf to my appeals. And, as they say, you can take a horse to water but you cannot make it drink.

2. (Just for the record.) The act which you have in mind would be an immense disappointment to you, especially after the way you have worked yourself up to it. You have no idea what these apish antics are like. A love-scene overheard through a partition sounds like a session at the dentist's. I don't know whether you have ever heard the things a woman murmurs when she gives herself. No? Well, it's a pity, because you would have become a Carmelite there and then. (But let's be fair; I ought to add '. . . and what a man says when he's trying to pick up a woman?' Surely not, because you would have shot yourself long since.)

I must also put you on your guard against your belief in the efficacy of desire and will-power. You know my views on the ineptitude of women. One example of this seems to me to be their faith in the power of persistence. No doubt there are men with whom it works. But I belong to the opposite species. And I tell you: no, never!

Come now, be brave! Please believe that I am whole-heartedly with you in your affliction. But anyway, why be so set on me when the world is full of gentlemen with multifarious assets whom you could make supremely happy? You beat against me like a bird against the window of a lighthouse. You will not break this window. You will break yourself against it, and you will fall to the ground. Good-bye, dear Mademoiselle. I hope I can still count on your friendship, with no ill-feelings. You know I am determined to be forgiven everything.

Sincerely yours,

C.

P.S. – You did not put enough stamps on your last letter. It is the fourth time at least that this has happened, and it's inevitable with the packed envelopes you send me. So I have to pay exorbitant surcharges. You should buy yourself some scales.

Pierre Costals
Paris

to Armand Pailhès
Toulouse

2 May 1927

... Another letter from poor Andrée, offering herself right, left and centre. She loves me so much I'm amazed she hasn't yet murdered me. But let her try! She'll get a hot reception. I'm not so easy to get rid of. And I would leap at the opportunity getting rid of *her*. I don't blame her. I understand her and pity her. She once wrote to me: 'To understand is to love. If I understand you so well, it's because I love you.' Well, I understand her and I don't love her. I'm profoundly indifferent to her; even the thought of making her suffer gives me no pleasure. Which is why I will not give her her two months of love. Or a week of love ('charity week'). Or a night of love. Not even 'an hour with'.*

I wish you had read the letter I wrote her! Not wishing to give the poor girl my reasons, which could all be summed up as follows: 'I will not love you and I will not take you, because I do not love you and I do not want you', I racked my brains to find a way of refusing her without being too wounding.

This is not the first time I've been in such a jam. As a young man I had to get a doctor friend of mine to tell an over-enthusiastic American lady that the Venus of the streets had not left me unscathed – which was pure invention. Three years ago I was pestered by the Baroness Fléchier, a woman of fifty years and more. One evening, around midnight, at the end of a tête-à-tête which until then, by sheer strength of will, I had managed to maintain on an exalted level, she put her scrawny old arms under my nose and said: 'You're the first man I've entertained at such an hour who hasn't kissed my arms.' In this predicament, I naturally had to concoct some excuse. I was ashamed of the one I had used against the lady from Alabama, so I told her that unfortunately I was not attracted by women. Since I keep my love affairs a dead secret, I thought this might get by. She believed me, or at any rate pretended to, and I, in a fit of good humour at the thought of my let-off, went and overdid it by swearing to her that never in my life had I held a woman in my arms! On this basis we remained good friends.

I was loth to give either of these excuses to a 'young' girl, and I wrote to Andrée the most unbelievable nonsense. I told her I only liked tall, thin, twenty-year-olds with raven hair, and that they must also be totally inert. And I told her the act of love was apish. Which it is. But it's also something else.

And to think that it's all so simple! A single spark of desire, and the thing would have happened four years ago. You know my cosmogony? 'In the beginning was Desire.' Yes, and if

---

*The reference is to a well-known book entitled *Une heure avec* ... published in the 1920's – a collection of interviews with famous people (*Translator's note*).

there's no desire, there's no beginning.... Incidentally, I saw a stunning girl at the Doignys' last night. Such a ravishing little creature! I had noticed her and followed her for a moment last February at the Review Board, where she was escorting a blind man (an orphaned cousin, she will tell me). While everyone else was jabbering away and paralysing me with compliments, she said nothing. To say nothing to me is, as you know, the surest way of 'saying' a lot to me. Simplicity always scores a point with me – especially after 'remarkable' persons of the Andrée type. I guessed from the very first that this child was not very intelligent, because she's too pretty. (You know I've never – never – found the two things together in a woman: intelligence and beauty.) Eventually she addressed a few words to me – banality itself, of the choicest kind. Naturally I couldn't help teasing her.

'You say you've read me. What have you read of mine, Mademoiselle?'

She thought....

'Let me see.... Ah, yes. *Rien que la terre.*'

'Sorry. That's by Morand.'

She was quite unruffled:

'I know I've read something of yours. I can't remember either the title or the subject, but I remember liking it.'

Bravo! But her ordeal was not yet over. I threw her a sombre look:

'And ... and ... have you any reservations about my art, Mademoiselle?'

She opened her eyes wide. 'No, you haven't any reservations, have you?' I repeated in an impassioned voice. She shook her head. So all was well.

And how ravishing she is! A little round head, like a bird's, and perfectly made hands, literally translucent at the fingertips, like onyx. The beauty of these extremities, and of her nails, would suggest that she was of noble blood, which unfortunately she isn't.

I contrived to leave with her, and we found ourselves in the avenue de Wagram. Her conversation was as flat as the pavement, and her acidulous voice made a bad impression on me. But I was touched by her little mule's steps as she walked along beside me – I walking like a mountain, and she like a shrub (there's a good pair of similes for you). All the women stared at her – without warmth – and men turned round. And as for me, there was that prompt familiarity which showed that she attracted me. And the old, vulgar vanity of walking beside a pretty girl knowing that one is taken for her lover. 'Yes, but they must realize from the sound of her voice that she's still a virgin.' And that was a bit of a dampener.

I felt slightly awkward not knowing her name. When you desire a woman whose name you don't know, learning her name is a kind of preliminary sketch for the act of possessing her. The name is already a soul. She is called Solange Dandillot. *Sol*: ground, and *ange*: angel – the two extremes, and I'm equally at home with both!

And she's the granddaughter of a public prosecutor! That alone would have been enough to make me want her.

She told me a little about her life, with a characteristically French directness, very refreshing after the eternal self-romanticizing of German virgins. I escorted her home to the avenue de Villiers. Good address; that helped to make me love her. (Oh! . . .) She tells me she has no girl-friends. And there's nothing better for a girl than to have no girl-friends – except to have no parents. I offered to take her to the Piérards' next week, and she accepted. I wrote at once to the Piérards, simply for the pleasure of writing her name.

Why am I telling you all this? Because here is an angel who will not get away from me. Her wings are weighted with lead; all one has to do is to leave her to tire herself out. And this is the answer to the divagations of poor Andrée, who spends her time seeking God knows what God knows where. The Andrée story can be summed up in a single phrase, which would make a good title for a light comedy: *If only she had been pretty*.

(I put 'angel' in the feminine. And indeed, since angels are pure spirits, I don't see why they are invariably represented in male form, unless it is to satisfy the unacknowledged homosexuality of the human species.)

Andrée Hacquebaut   to Pierre Costals
Saint-Léonard   *Paris*

Friday, 4 May

I once showed a letter of yours to one of my friends who is a graphologist, without telling her who the writer was. 'Beware of this man', she told me. 'He is of the race of serpents.' And it's quite true: you are the masculine serpent in all its hideousness. Another of my friends once swallowed a snake's egg while drinking from a well. The egg hatched in her digestive system, and it was not till long afterwards, when she was X-rayed, that they found she had a snake inside her body. In the same way, I let you into my heart some time ago in all innocence. And now I see the reptile there.

Treacherous and hard-hearted killer! Oh, no complaints, it's a nice clean job. No blood, nothing compromising. And a wonderful alibi: 'What, me! After all I've done for her! I who even now am "in complete sympathy" with her, I who understand her suffering so well, I who have lavished encouragement and condolence and consolation on her!' Your condolences make me want to slap your face – your charitable advice, your insulting detachment, your disinterestedness, which is nothing more than impotence or sadism. 'Never!' you say. And why? Because I'm thirty years old, because I'm not 'passive', etc., etc. The most squalid street-girl has enjoyed your caresses as she might enjoy those of any other man, whereas a woman for whom you are everything, a woman for whom those caresses would have been the summit of human happiness, not for what she would have received from you (you're not God's gift to women), but for what she would have given you.... The woman of the gutter or the brothel, whom you despise, gets that from you, whilst I, whom you love with your heart, with your kindness.... Your kindness! What does it amount to? The kindness of a man who watches his friend drown without lifting a finger! But it isn't even a question of kindness, but of fairness. Fairness means responding to the love that is offered to you with an equal love.

'I can only love girls of under twenty-two.' Rubbish! In *Fragility*, Maurice says to Christine: 'You no longer have the

124

eyes of a girl, but those of a woman. Now there's something
behind them' (p. 211). That is not the sort of thing one tosses
off idly. One must have felt it. You can only love 'passive,
bovine' women? Do you want them made of wood, or stone,
or iron, or reinforced concrete? But anyhow you're lying. Remember what you wrote about the Polish girl: 'I love the
(physical) pleasure I give her. Even if that were all, it would
be enough' (*Purple*, p. 162). You can only love 'long, thin' persons? That's a good one! Must I remind you of the description of Hélène in *Fragility* or Lydia in *Purple*?* And my 'persistence'? Me, persist! Me, want to intrude on your life, when
I spend my own trying to extricate myself from you and you
from me; when I have reached the point of longing for you to
offend me even more deeply than you have already, so that
my wounded pride may assuage the pain of losing you, when,
in exchange for something durable, our friendship, I offer you
the means of getting rid of me for ever! 'The act which you
have in mind would be an immense disappointment to you.'
Why? That's a typically masculine idea. Woman excels in en-
larging, ennobling everything with her imagination and heart,
while man belittles everything with his carping spirit, not to
say his natural pettiness. A woman loves more than ever after
being physically possessed, especially by the man who initiated
her. The opposite is unheard of, if my friends are to be
believed. And even if it did turn out to be a disappointment,
wouldn't this be infinitely preferable to the slow poison of
unfulfilment, which makes it impossible to free yourself from
the other person? And even if it did turn out to be distasteful,
what a relief to have got it out of one's system at last! No
more Costals! Disappointment, I welcome you! Disgust, I
welcome you! But of course such a solution would offend
your pride. You do not want me, since you cheerfully allow
me to disappear from your life, but you want to lose me with
all the honours of war. No woman must be allowed to see you
as other than a hero. You're afraid of being deglamorized,

---

*A number of quotations from Costals' work, all with the same
object of proving his inconsistency, have been omitted here. They
occupy two whole pages, back and front, of Andrée's letter
(*Author's note*).

poor angel. Well, I can tell you that the true hero is the man who dispenses happiness. And if I were to be disgusted by anything, it would not be 'the act of love' with you, it would be your cowardice in avoiding it. My admiration for you has been shaken, for the first time, by your pathetic excuses. Yes indeed, I have nothing but pity and contempt for your miserable affection, which is too lukewarm to assimilate the flesh, for fear of having to cope with its ferments. There's my fertility God! People envy you, and yet your life is mean and shabby – yes, do you realize that? Oh, all those 'superior' men! Impotent parasites! It would serve them right if the common people, the horny-handed sons of toil, cut off their heads – and other parts as well, since they don't know how to use them to give happiness to those who need happiness more than life itself. Ah! why did you not take me if only to humiliate me? You could cure me of a love that is killing me, and you won't! So one must suffer 'nobly', eh? One must be sublime. Monsieur is very strong on sacrifice – the sacrifice of others, of course. 'In any case we'll remain friends, won't we?' In other words: 'It would be the simplest thing in the world for me to give you the happiness you desire. But I do not wish to. Nevertheless I want you to remain in my life, just enough to gratify me without inconveniencing me or complicating my existence. I don't like your face or your body or your appearance; you can give that vulgar part of yourself to whomsover you like. But please, dear Mademoiselle, keep the more ethereal parts exclusively for me. Not to mention (*for the record*) the right to make you suffer.' Well, I've had enough of heroism. You've cured me of heroism. For life.

I used to have dreams of a man dominating me, sweeping me off my feet. I chose a conquistador, a solitary prince, a man ten times more masculine, more intelligent, more self-sufficient, more wonderful than anyone else, the man who said in reply to the Catholic interviewer who reproached him with having abused the gift of pleasure: 'Well, what of it! I've rejoiced in God's creation.' To him I would have given my mind, my youth, my virgin body, my lips which have never once been kissed. Him I should have been only too happy to obey. For him I was ready to sacrifice everything, my life, even my honour. I offer him all this, and he will have none of it! I foresaw everything, accepted everything: *during*, the loss of my peace of mind; *afterwards*, the wrenching apart, his infidelity, his neglect, my despair, my lost reputation. I foresaw it all, except that my offering might be rejected. I foresaw everything that would happen *afterwards*: what I did not foresee was that there would be no *afterwards*. I wanted your embrace, and all I got was your 'kindness' and your pity: either a patronizing and paternal old man, or a capricious, teasing boy. My psychology was that of simple, humble people, who believe that desire is inevitable between a man and a woman who are young and normal and fond of each other. I hadn't thought of the affectations of the upper classes and the 'intellectual élite.' There, you make me talk like a Communist.

Saturday

'Never!' Your 'never!' You know, even if you knocked that 'never' into my head like a nail, I should still rebound under the hammer. For if I really believed in that 'never', there would be nothing for it but to lie down and die: there are things one could die of, literally, without much effort; one has only to let oneself go. But I don't believe in it, I can't believe in it. One day you'll suffer, you'll pay the penalty for never in your life having forgone a single desire, not even a passing whim, and for having forced a creature who adores you to forgo a desire that for her was unique, irreplaceable, vital. And when that day comes, Costals, there will be no more 'nevers'. No, I cannot believe that if, one day, I were reduced to crawling at your feet and begging you to give me, not two months, but a single week of illusory happiness, you would refuse me. It's not that in itself it means so very much to me. But to know that it will happen some time, some day. All I ask of you is one week, and then it will be finished for ever, if you so wish. During that week I should be capable of burning up my whole life and dying, like Lucifer, in the flames. No, no, no, I cannot believe you will go on refusing me forever. Even if you took me without either love or desire, like a woman you picked up in the street....

Sunday

It's First Communion Day. Bright sunshine. A dazzling May morning ... I wept as I listened to those little girls' voices. A few years more, and, like me. ... I flung myself on to my knees beside my bed, and said : 'My God, give me the strength to convince him !'

In a little while I shall be taking this letter to the post in the same hand as my missal. You see what you drive me to. I would not have to write such things if I were yours.

This letter crossed the following one.

Pierre Costals   to Andrée Hacquebaut
Paris   *Saint-Léonard*

6 May 1927

Dear Mademoiselle,

My last letter was more cavalier than chivalrous. Almost as soon as it had gone, I was smitten with remorse. Forgive me for it.

Logically, that letter must have given you the impression that I was making fun of your predicament. In fact, not only do I not find it funny, but I feel it personally and respect it. However, I must tell you why, and you must take my word for it; for you will never understand how a man of my sort came to find himself in a similar situation to yours. I will not try and explain it to you. Apart from the fact that it touches all too closely on my private life, I cannot really explain it to myself. I have come to the conclusion that it was an ordeal of the kind that initiates have to undergo, or like the descent into Hades of the gods of antiquity who alternated between a sojourn on earth and a sojourn in the underworld.

Years ago, for several months – say six months – I was 'walled in' like you. I had a solid mass of tenderness all ready, God knows, to be given to more or less anybody as long as they aroused my desire (for I have never seriously loved anyone I did not desire). But I could not make contact. And I felt certain that the world was full of girls who would have been

only too happy to receive the tenderness and the pleasure that
I was only too happy to give them; and they longed for it in
vain, as I longed for it in vain. But still I could not make
contact.

Do you know, Mademoiselle, I brushed against people in the
street simply out of the need for human contact. I really did.
I was younger than I am today; my freedom was unlimited;
I had money to burn, and I've always been ready to pay for
my pleasures – and for the pleasures of those I love. But I
could not make contact. They were afraid of my desire, I
don't know why. I saw people steer clear of me to whom
I only wished to give and from whom I asked nothing in return,
except what they themselves desired. And yet it seemed to me
that my tenderness must be visible on my face, like perspiration, or like mist on a window-pane, blurring it. . . . I suppose
it cannot be seen in this way. People fled as I approached, like
sheep scuttling down the embankment on either side of a
road as a car approaches. The whole human race was trickling
through my fingers. There was something unforgettable about
the expression of fear in eyes one would have liked to close
with almost paternal kisses. Those girls one would have treated
like goddesses. . . . I don't know what was wrong with me.
Perhaps I had been guilty of some terrible infringement of the
law, and it showed on my face. Perhaps it was merely the
result of some misunderstanding, some calumny. . . . All around
me I saw people coming together and going off two by two.
But *I* could still make no contact. And it was spring, then
summer; these things always happen in summer (August is a
terrible month for the unsatisfied): the days are 'too beautiful', nature seems happier than one is oneself – Heaven knows
I went through it. And all the time this one obsession, and a
total inability to work, to tear myself away from this obsession. Loveless days going by one after the other. Another loveless day. Another day of defeat. And yet it *counted*, each day
counted and brought me nearer to the grave – a right that only
happy days should have. I have a horrifying memory of those
days, and a strong desire to help others who long to give but
can find no one to give to. It is a particularly tragic thing for
women, for all sorts of obvious reasons: their youth passes

more quickly, they are more dependent, more susceptible to other people's opinion of them, etc. I could almost take you to task for not complaining loudly enough about *your* case, as though you were not fully aware of your tragedy.

How did I get over it? I don't know. It just 'happened'. How? Just 'like that'. You will say this is a strange answer from a man who prides himself on being clear-sighted. But there it is. Nature, for a time, was against me; then she was on my side. Like a wind that changes during a game: now against you, now for you. Since then, I have put more trust in nature.

Let me conclude with a comparison similar to the one I made in my last letter. A bird flies into a room by mistake. It flutters around, seeking a way out. But there is none. Or rather there is, but the bird cannot see it, because birds cannot see everything, poor things. Suddenly it sees a thin streak of light – a half-open door. It swoops, and finds itself in a lumber-room lit by a paraffin lamp. But there again there is no way out, and again it beats against the walls. That bird is you, and the lumber-room with its paraffin lamp is me (you recognize my well-known modesty).

For, of course, nothing has changed as far as our relationship is concerned. Me, 'take' you (as you so nicely put it)? No, never.

Good heavens! For once, this is a long letter.

Believe me, yours sympathetically,

C.

P.S. I forgot to tell you that during the time I was unable to 'make contact' with women, I had four little sleeping companions, each one nicer than the next, whom I was very fond of. So I was only 'walled in' by a sort of mental blockage.

Costals' Notebook

At the Piérards'! O charming one! I want to lift her up in the palms of my hands, like a marine Venus in her shell. Exactly the right size for me: if she were smaller, I would overwhelm her; if bigger, there would be too much of her. She is much admired, which pleases me as though I were her papa. Dance with her. She dances so demurely that I wonder if she does it to tease me.

She came with the Saulniers. So, neither father nor mother. Divine absence! May it last for ever! If only girls knew how much they would gain by being foundlings.

No profound desire for her body. No sign of the tornado of desire – dry mouth, tottering legs, etc. An urge to say sweet, caressing things – an urge aroused by her, though these words could well have fallen on other ears than hers . . .

How like a little cat as she watches me write my name in a book I had brought her, as if she expected to see a little bird fly out of my pen. (Before setting out, I had solemnly kissed the cover of this book that I was about to give her.) Exactly like a cat perched on your desk watching you write. And again like a cat when we were sitting side by side and I felt her body leaning lightly against mine, like a river against its bank.

My hand on the arm of her chair in a caressing gesture, a gesture of possession almost. Once, but fleetingly, almost imperceptibly, she put her hand on my arm. Yet she is very reserved. Obviously she is pleased that she attracts me, but with an entrancing simplicity and naturalness. Not a grain of coquetry, in spite of her looks. Simply, almost negligently dressed. Is this an affectation? She claims not to like social life, not to like luxury, etc. Making allowances for a bit of affectation, which is conceivable, there must be some truth in this, for, being what she is, if she liked social life one would meet her everywhere.

Apart from what she says about her own character (she speaks from the heart when she speaks about herself – like most young girls), nothing, literally nothing memorable about her conversation. Her intellectual education is nil. But so much the better: schooling is for fools. A girl who has obtained some diploma or other, even if she later forgets all she has learnt, will still retain, it seems to me, like a pretty vase which once contained a nauseous liquid, the bad smell of the half-knowledge she once ingurgitated.

She is twenty-one, it appears. Let's say twenty-two. One wouldn't think it: she looks really young.

She spoke of her father: 'Papa used to be very interested in physical culture. He's a real enthusiast.'

'Is he ... does he have a profession?'

'No, he does nothing. ...' As she said this, she was visibly embarrassed. She's ashamed that her father lives on a private income! When she pronounced the word 'enthusiast' I gave a shudder, as though I had touched a snake.

She talked of one of her cousins. The fact that she had a cousin seemed to me strange, offensive, almost a provocation. O foundlings!

My behaviour was as bad as hers was good – taking her by the arm, propelling her to the buffet with my hands round her waist, trying to show off *urbi et orbi* that she was mine. How course and vulgar and naïvely pleased with myself! Like a cavalry sergeant. One often sees a man with a pleasant and intelligent face suddenly transformed into an idiot, his smile at once inane and conceited, his whole attitude at once awkward and affected. What has happened? He has just met a woman who attracts him. And inside him it is just the same. For the apparition of an attractive woman instantly lowers a man's self-respect, as sharply as a lump of ice lowers the temperature of a drink. Which is why anyone who loves humanity cannot love women. But *I* don't care a damn for humanity, and I love women.

I would have invited her to the cinema, but to have her see a film full of half-naked gigolos – no thanks! And anyhow, it wouldn't suit such an 1890-ish young person. The Opéra-Comique seemed rather to suggest itself. I told her I had a box for Tuesday. 'I'll ask my parents and telephone you.'

The box will be a *baignoire*,* and I shall have booked all the seats in it. Unfortunately we shall have those maddening musicians to reckon with, with their passion for noise. Ah well, if words are forbidden, gestures will have to do instead.

Of course, she may well refuse: because she hasn't the same degree of vitality as I have.

Next day – At one o'clock last night, my heart was still beating

---

*Big ground-floor box (behind the stalls) (*Translator's note*).

as fast as at eight o'clock in the evening when I left her. And then I was visited by a dream in which this chit of a girl betrayed me, as though I must realize that she was already capable of making me suffer. Oh, I didn't really suffer, but I felt a twinge.

Waiting for her telephone call: anxious all morning, convinced that the telephone would be out of order just at the moment she called, starting up at every bicycle bell in the street.

The telephone! She'll come! When I hear her voice on the telephone, Priapus himself could not outreach me – whereas, even when I was dancing with her, I could echo the words of the prophet: 'Tyre, though thou be sought for, yet shalt thou never be found again.'

I think of the day that voice will get on my nerves when I hear it on the telephone – and I shall leave France in order not to hear it any more.

How disgraceful of her parents to let her go out alone with Pierre Costals! A fine way to behave! Now, if anything happens, whose fault will it be? It's disheartening to see all moral standards crumbling like this in the France of 1927.

Wednesday – Opéra-Comique. *Madame Butterfly*.
After Madame Butterfly,
Ouch!

Yesterday a sergeant, today an undergraduate.

Not a sign of life from the object. Or rather, yes, one: in the second act she moved her chair a little away from mine. Can the object be virtuous? The thought sent a shiver down my spine. I was crestfallen: 'I'll have to start again from scratch....'

Paralysed. By her reserve. By the absurdity of a novelist kissing a girl in a box at the Opéra-Comique. I wanted to be 'ninetyish', but I had gone too far. A telltale remark by the usherette had revealed that I had reserved every seat in the box; how could the object not have guessed? The absurdity of this too carefully planned evening!

Not even the knowledge of my superiority over her from so many points of view could lift me out of my doldrums.

This knowledge became blurred, and I could only see what made me her inferior. She, a pretty twenty-year-old, and I an intellectual, an old thinking-pot of thirty-four.

Our conversation was a veritable swamp of platitude. I watched her hands, as though I hoped to see her twisting them in her anxiety at my failure to declare myself. When I said: 'It's frantically boring', she answered: 'Yes'. This 'yes' cut me to the quick; doubtless I expected her to throw herself into my arms, saying: 'How could anything be boring with you, my beloved?' The situation became so intolerable that I suggested we should leave. She said 'yes' once more without a moment's hesitation, which cut me to the quick once more. (How childish her 'yeses' are! The intonation of a doll when one squeezes its stomach.) We left, eyed by the usherettes with looks that powerfully suggested this thought: 'Well, well! There's a couple who must have been having a good time. But they can't hold out any longer, so off they go to the hotel.'

In short: a cold douche in the *baignoire*.*

The evening has made two things clear at least: that she is not in love with me, and that I am not in love with her.

Perhaps it was simply that, like racing cyclists, neither of us wanted to be the first to start. Perhaps her behaviour was calculated, to keep me in suspense. A rash calculation, then, for what's to prevent me from dropping her here and now? I'm not the man to persist if a woman refuses; there are a hundred more where she came from; they're all interchangeable. I'm glad to find that I don't love her any more than I did, and am therefore still free: I can take what I want from this game.

If today's set-back is not the sort of disaster from which one never recovers, it is the rock-bottom from which one may spring up even higher than before. What a leap it will be, with the impetus gained from the recoil. As a matter of fact I'm going to write to her: thus keeping the undergraduate touch. By means of this letter, I shall be reversing the situation, giving her back the initiative, driving her into a corner. My cards are on the table; now it's up to her.

---

*A pun here: *baignoire* = 'bath' as well as 'box' (*Translator's note*).

The ethics of honour, or simply the proprieties, were invented to provide an exact counterpart to natural ethics, thus allowing us to win both ways.

If Rosine is ugly and importunate, natural ethics to the fore: 'How could I be such a monster! Me, do such a thing to your venerable father! (or your husband, my best friend!).' But if she is attractive and aloof: 'How could I be such a boor as to remain insensible to your charms? I refuse to be so insulting.'

One finds the two alternatives in every field. If someone insults you: 'What! kill someone for such a trifle? Is that what honour demands?' or else, contrariwise: 'I killed him because I was insulted. My honour....' Etc.

Pierre Costals   to Mademoiselle Solange Dandillot
Paris   *Avenue de Villiers, Paris*

12 May 1927

You must admit, dear Mademoiselle, that last night was not quite the thing, and that indeed we provided a somewhat distressing spectacle. You made me very nervous – froze me in fact. Did you do it on purpose? Or am I simply a donkey?

It will come as no surprise to you, I think, to learn that I have a rather special feeling towards you. If you find it objectionable, let us leave it at that. I shall feel some regret, perhaps a twinge of pain, but I do not want to be importunate, and after all, the world is big enough. If, on the other hand, like an intelligent girl, you would like us to try our luck again, just tell me. Only in that case you must also tell me that you will allow me a certain degree of familiarity with you, and a modicum of those gestures which not only Nature, but Society itself, expected of us last night. Those august moral personages are at present overcome with amazement and wrath at our attitude; it is up to us to appease them. But you must make your intentions clear to me, for I do not feel inclined to offer you a purely platonic friendship, and even less do I feel inclined to be spurned by a woman, something that has never happened to me in my life.*

---

*This is a lie (*Author's note*).

Write to me or telephone me. But I'd prefer a nice letter; letters are more substantial. Not to mention all the advantages of the written word (I know what I mean, even if you don't).

Once more: failing a note or a telephone call from you telling me whether I behaved well or whether I behaved in an awkward and ill-bred manner last night, we shall not see each other again. It depends entirely on you.

Au revoir, my dear Mademoiselle, or adieu. It is possible that I am about to entertain for you a feeling with a touch of profundity about it (but I'm not yet absolutely sure). There is an impulse there that it would be a pity to waste. See if it displeases you or not, without considering my pleasure but thinking only of your own. And give me your answer with the same frankness and trust that I pride myself on having shown here.

Costals

Written by Costals in his diary

Have written her a letter that isn't up to much. How strange it is that when I write to an unknown or scarcely known woman who attracts me, I can avoid flannel only through passion or cynicism. The language of passion being out of the question, this missive is a compromise between twaddle and impertinence. She will enjoy the twaddle, will fail to notice the impertinence, and will telephone me within 24 hours.

(In fact I have no idea. I'm incapable of foreseeing her reactions in any given circumstance. In dealing with her I have the impression that I'm the Quai d'Orsay*: I do everything gropingly and by the grace of God.)

There's something poignant for me in imagining the happiness I might have given to other women with such a letter but have refused them. And this feeling has a great deal of charm.

The fact that I find it charming ought to make me feel that I'm a cad. Am I a cad? Brunet, at any rate, pays me compliments: 'Don't you think it's terrific to have a pater like you?' In fact, he's amazed: 'Why are you so nice?'

*The French Foreign Office (*Translator's note*).

The thing is that there are some people I love and some I don't. That sounds too simple. But it's the key to it all.

No, the heart is not affected, nor the flesh, but something is. Whence comes this obscure and passionate desire to please her? If only I could hear a tremor in her voice. . . .

Mademoiselle Dandillot did not write a 'nice letter'. She telephoned. The gist of her reply was: 'I must confess that I didn't really understand your letter. But I like you very much. So why don't we meet again?' They arranged to go to a concert. Costals chose the most expensive in Paris, because when one goes out with a woman it does not matter whether a thing is good or bad, but only that it should cost a great deal of money.

The entry of the female chorus conjured up a vision of lady prisoners at the gates of Saint-Lazare: ancient, deformed, sinister, incredibly frumpish. Then came the musicians, squat little fellows with handkerchiefs tucked into their necks like diners: *Froggy for ever!** The efforts of these poor wretches to look like artists (long hair down their necks, locks falling over their temples) were enough to bring tears to one's eyes. Sitting on metal garden chairs in an unbelievable church-hall décor – squalid 'foliage' and peeling 'pilasters' – they offered a spectacle which seemed so enchanting to some of the audience that they examined it through opera-glasses.†

---

*In English in the original (*Translator's note*).

†Need I point out that this chapter is a sort of leg-pull written by someone who allows himself an occasional flight of fancy, and that only those without a sense of humour could take offence at it? One can caricature what one loves all the more sharply the more one loves it. The things I have written or could have written about Algeria and Spain! Sympathy with music-lovers, gratitude towards musicians: such being my sincere feelings, I can allow myself to cut a few capers. And I seem to remember that in some of my other books I have spoken of music (church music, Russian, Spanish and Arab music, etc.) with a seriousness and enthusiasm which should, if necessary, excuse these pages (*Author's note*).

'If music softens manners', said Costals, 'it doesn't ennoble faces. There are about sixty musicians there, so I realize they can't all be expected to have genius written all over their faces. But why don't they give them masks, as in the theatre of antiquity, or hide them in a pit as at Bayreuth?'

Monsieur was *very* fastidious. However, Solange seemed to approve. But he felt that she was in a mood to approve of everything he said. He cast his eyes over the audience, and the extraordinary ugliness of these men and women, the squalid, grotesque and antiquated décor of the hall, made him look away. Literally repelled, his eyes swivelled up to the ceiling, in the hope of seeing the forms of a nobler humanity painted there. But on the ceiling too there was nothing but fussily decorated gilt plaster, blackened with dirt as though by factory smoke. It was obvious that generations had breathed in this hall. If Costals had not been with Solange, he would have left at once : it was almost more than he could bear.

Soon, the lights were switched on and platform and auditorium were brilliantly illuminated. It was a monstrous idea; both, in fact, should have been plunged in darkness.

As there was some delay in starting, people began to grow impatient and to drum their feet. But after a few seconds it died down. Then there was another little outburst, equally short-lived. Odd little gusts of bad temper in this crowd, odd because so brief. Even an outburst of patriotism would have lasted a few seconds longer.

At last the conductor lowered his baton and all the people on the platform began simultaneously to make a noise.

As the musicians frenziedly wielded their bows it seemed to Costals that he could smell the lady-violinists' armpits, and he was moved by this; it was the best part of the show, he thought.

Solange, sitting sideways, had moved closer to him. He stroked her smooth, clear neck. He noticed that she had brought her face close to his, as thought to enter his aura. Little islands of skin showed here and there through her blouse, like sand-banks in a white salt flat. The features of her face that he found unattractive he saw as emergency exits through which he could escape should the occasion arise, or as ambiguous clauses in a contract : that rather heavy chin would one day allow him to leave her with a light heart. He kissed the nape of her neck; she did not flinch (that little-girl odour of her hair!) And his blood stirred like foliage as his hand traced, through her dress, her suspenders and her long thighs. He was surprised that such a respectable girl allowed her thighs to be stroked in public. He had not realized that already she wanted anything he wanted.

'I think there's something ... how shall I put it? oppressive about that first movement (of the symphony),' said Mlle Dandillot, who was indeed oppressed, but for other reasons. 'Don't you?'

'I don't think anything.... Look here, tell me honestly, do you like music?' he asked after a moment with a suspicious look.

She raised her eyebrows as if to say: 'So so....' Then she said :

'What I don't like is church music.'

'Ah!' he thought, 'how unaffected she is! The delightful thing about her is that she has no interest in anything. So she doesn't try to dazzle you with specialized knowledge. And also that she hasn't an idea in her head, which for a woman, is the surest way of not having wrong ones.'

He put his arm around her. She was leaning right over now, almost lying on him. Pretending to pick something up from the floor, he kissed her body, scenting the rubbery odour of her suspender-belt through her skirt. From time to time he pressed his face against the nape of her neck and kept it there, as though to absorb, slowly, everything this woman had to give. 'No', he told himself delightedly, 'never has anyone behaved as badly as this with a woman in public!' He had always enjoyed being self-contradictory, and it pleased him to think that if he had seen another couple behaving in this way, he would have found it difficult to restrain himself from calling out to them : 'I say, what are hotels for?'

Leaning back a little, he saw behind Solange's back the young woman in the seat next to her; she was sitting well back in her seat, listening with her mouth half-open and her eyes closed. She was not pretty, but Costals desired her : (1) because he found it appropriate that, at the very moment he was caressing one young woman for the first time, he should desire another; (2) because she appeared to be asleep and this inevitably aroused in him the idea of taking advantage of her sleep; and (3) because it struck him that in order to experience such ecstasy from something as insipid as this music, she must be mentally deranged, and since he only liked simple, healthy girls like Solange there was something agreeable about wanting a deranged woman.

Suddenly the young woman flung her head back in a wild gesture, like the caracara bird when it has finished its call, the very picture of sensual delight. It was obvious that one of those sounds had penetrated to the most sensitive point of her being.

So Costals stretched his arm behind Solange's seat and placed his hand on the back of the other seat in such a way that the other woman's shoulder leaned against it. But the gentle pressure he imparted to it produced no reaction from the young woman, who was completely engrossed in her semi-quavers. He gave up. And in any case, since these contortions gave him cramp in his arm, the game was not worth the candle. Anyone foolish enough to imagine that all this was just a try-on, a sly and underhanded sacristan's trick, will be disconcerted to know that: (1) Costals really wanted to embark on a serious adventure with the unknown woman, to arrange a meeting with her, and (2) to do so without attracting Solange's attention (for example by passing a note to the unknown woman behind Solange's back) would have been excellent sport, like one of those feats at the circus during which the band stops, and therefore not at all the work of a sacristan but rather of an archangel.

The noise from the platform ceased and there was some applause, accompanied by demonstrations of hatred on the part of a few members of the audience against those who were applauding.

Thereafter the music took a new turn from which it was clear that this was the real classical thing.

'Well, do you like *this*?' Costals asked Solange.

'I don't mind it.'

'You don't.... Splendid! Absolutely splendid!'

'You don't understand,' she said, a bit nettled. 'The cubist music they were playing before this gave me the creeps. But this I don't mind.'

'I can see you don't care two hoots for it,' said Costals, 'and that's as it should be. You're a good child.'

'But I *do* care!' said Solange, with the woman's genius for squandering her advantage.

'No, no,' said Costals, chivalrous as ever, 'You don't care two hoots.' He was interrupted by a chorus of 'Ssh!'

Suddenly the most terrible cries rang out on the platform. It was as though a woman, at the very instant of giving birth, learned that she had not only lost all her money but that her lover had abandoned her. On hearing these yelps, Costals screwed up his face and instinctively tried to block his ears, but the hall exploded in a thunder of cheers. Such profound disagreements bring home to a man that a society is no longer for him. Costals remembered the truly 'immortal' pages in *La Nouvelle Héloïse* on the Frenchman's idea of music. 'They can appreciate no other effects but vocal outbursts; they are sensitive only to noise,' writes Rousseau.

'I don't think women are made for singing,' said Solange. 'Could that be profound?' the writer wondered. 'But what is profundity? A chamber pot is profound, too.'

Raucous voices (young people's?) were shouting 'Encore!' and people were still clapping: public manifestations of admiration in Europe are more or less what one would expect from the savages of Oceania. Three or four times the singers returned to take a bow. And Costals thought: 'Poor fellows!' The conductor, who was an obvious charlatan (for which reason he was admired, especially by the women), left the platform and returned several times, doubtless in order to receive several rations of applause. These re-entries were exactly like those of a clown. And yet the entire audience was in the seventh heaven.

Thereafter, as though to cure everyone's eardrums, the genii of music, or rather the bank clerks, played very softly: it might have been a clyster-pipe band. There were even moments when, literally, not a sound could be heard. These moments were magnificent.

Costals looked round the audience. A third of it was made up of people who spontaneously enjoyed the noise they heard; another third of people who enjoyed it only through an intellectual effort, remembering everything they had heard and read about each piece; the remaining third consisting of people who felt nothing, but absolutely nothing. All of them, however, adopted the most elegant poses in order to receive this manna. Pig-faced men with eye-glasses pretended that the slightest whisper in the hall spoiled their ecstasy. Pig-faced men in spectacles bent down towards their brats (for six-year-old children were to be seen in the audience, evidently brought there as a punishment for some grave misdemeanour) to draw their attention to some sacrosanct passage so that they should know once and for all that that was where they ought to feel moved. A number of women, like Solange's neighbour, considered it unseemly to do otherwise than keep their eyes closed. In unanimous mutual mimicry these people aped one another's earnest expressions, while from the platform the miasma of sound continued inexhaustibly to spread.

'They're depraved,' said Costals, casting a look of reprobation round the hall. 'Apart from the simpletons – for the donkey must have his bran.* At all events, an unhealthy place, and I wouldn't like to take the responsibility of chaperoning you here any longer. Shall we go?'

'Yes.'

Always that 'yes'! Had he said to her: 'Let's stay', or 'Come to my flat', or 'Let's go to Kamchatka', it seemed to him that her answer would have been the same: 'Yes.' And when he repeated it to himself with the same intonation she used, something stirred in his heart, like a bird in its nest.

So they left this temple of collective auto-suggestion. Costals remembered that when he was twelve years old his grandmother had taken him to another temple of the same sort. They were doing *Le Malade imaginaire*. When it came to the scene in which the actors pursue each other into the auditorium, the old lady, who from the beginning had shown signs of impatience, got up and said: 'Come on, let's go. It's *too*

---

*An untranslatable pun here. The French has *son*, which = 'sound' or 'bran' (*Translator's note*).

stupid.' An unforgettable impression it had made, on a child who was already only too inclined to judge for himself. *There* was a family in which received ideas cut no ice.

He could have taken a taxi, but preferred to see her home on foot: they both needed time to recover. He was so confident of obtaining whatever he wanted from her that he thought it advisable to keep something to look forward to: what, after all, would be left once he had taken her? Besides, for him it was a matter of principle that a self-respecting man should let a few opportunities slip. Accustomed to success in everything, he took pride in loading the dice against himself.

Not far from her house he stopped her underneath a street-lamp and stood in front of her, gripping her arms. Assuming no doubt that he was about to kiss her, she took a few steps backwards into the shadow – out of shyness or modesty. He drew her towards him; her arms hung limp, and she did not lift her face. As he bent down to kiss her on the mouth, she suddenly let her head fall so low that Costals' lips brushed the fringe of her hair. Putting a finger under her chin, he lifted her head and kissed her on the forehead; she remained quite still. Feeling a little dampened, he walked on, and she followed him. He had to force himself a bit in order to sound friendly as he asked: 'Do you want to go to the Bois after dinner on Friday?' Calmly, but with an eager expression on her face, she agreed. 'Your nose is shiny,' he told her. 'Powder it.'

As soon as Costals had turned away from her after saying good-bye, Mademoiselle Dandillot, instead of following him with her eyes until he had disappeared, which would have been the recognized thing to do, pressed the button on the outer door and climbed the stairway, the lift being out of order. As soon as she began the ascent, she had a painful intuition that she would be unable to reach the fourth floor, on which she lived, without something happening which she dreaded but could not define. She went up gripping the banister with one hand while the other kept contact with the wall, against which she scraped her hand-bag, tearing the leather on a nail. She reached the door of her flat, like an exhausted swimmer reaching a buoy, opened it, went into her bedroom, and sat down on her bed. 'What's the matter with me?' she said out loud, making a face. A late tram rattled past below; she winced and said, again out loud: 'Oh, those trams!' then winced again on hearing a motor-horn. Then she thought she had left the electric light on, not only in the hall but even in the rooms where she had not been; she went to see. By now her whole body was shot through with the sort of vibration that shakes a steamer when it pitches heavily and the propeller revolves outside the water. She lay down, her hands gripping the edges of the mattress, rolled over first to the right and then to the left, like the carcass of a dog being rolled over by the surf. She got up and removed her dress, so impatiently that she forgot to unfasten it and her head got stuck in it. She snatched a magazine from the table and tore it in two, her face still contorted, then tore the pieces in two. 'Am I going to have a fit of hysterics?' A sudden wave of nausea overcame her, and she felt herself turn pale. She went over to the mirror, overcome with an obscure desire to give herself a fright. Then her stomach heaved violently and sent her flying to the wash-stand, where, clutching the basin with one hand and holding her forehead with the other, she vomited.

When she felt better, she put on her night-dress and lay down on her bed without taking off her shoes. Her love for Costals became confused in her mind with the relief of having vomited. A sentence engraved itself in her head, mysterious and inevitable as an inscription in a phylactery: 'He has given me profound peace.' The whole of her life until these last few days seemed to her like a broad stretch of landscape, even and serene. Then a shell had fallen. And now the countryside was shattered and transformed, but the calm and the light remained the same. She turned over and stretched herself out on her stomach in a familiar, childish position, burying her fore-arms under the bolster to seek the coolness there, as one buries them in the desert sand, which becomes colder and colder the deeper one goes. She said again: 'He has given me profound peace,' and dropped her shoes off by scraping the heels against the side of the bed. Then she went to the book-shelf, took down the novel Costals had given her, got into bed, put out the light, and lay down still holding the book, which she slid under the sheet, a finger between the pages.

Thérèse Pantevin   to Pierre Costals
La Vallée Maurienne   *Paris*

15 May 1927

My Beloved,

I suffer, I am plagued with temptations, I suffer. Yesterday in church, while the priest was reciting the litany of the Blessed Virgin, I interspersed her name with yours. 'Heart most gentle. Heart most wild. Heart most wonderful. Heart without stain.' And I thought to myself that I ought to add: *Miserere mei*, 'Have pity on me.'

Have pity on me, Monsieur. I am a poor girl. Pity is the real miracle, not Our Lord's walking on the water. Pity is all-embracing and sufficient to itself. I think it can even dispense with an object.

Take me in your lap so that I do not die.

Marie

Write to me and tell me you have pity on me.

Andrée Hacquebaut   to Pierre Costals
Saint-Léonard   *Paris*

Tuesday, 19 May 1927

Your last letter crossed with mine. It has softened my rancour without reviving my ardour. You have a way of rubbing salt in wounds which you're ostensibly trying to heal. . . . You're a past master at distilling the sugar and the acid at one and the same time, at simultaneously licking and biting, like a wild animal. Are you by nature fundamentally good, but corrupted by a perverse intellect? Or fundamentally bad, but with enough decency to feel some remorse? Do you play at being good, or do you play at being bad, or do you just play? Perhaps it's a terrible law of nature that the superior man lends but never gives himself. In fact you've written as much : 'A creator who gives himself surrenders himself.' But *you* take the art of self-withdrawal to the ultimate pitch of refinement. Everything that comes from you is equivocal, double-edged. And the disturbing thing is that the first impression you give is one of simplicity and directness. You pour out poison and medicine in turn, almost simultaneously, but in such a subtle way that one is neither killed by the poison nor cured by the medicine. One remains in an ambiguous state which would be suffering enough in itself even if the elements of suffering were not dominant in it. Before your last letter I sustained myself on the horror I felt for you : for the one before was a masterpiece of pure malice. (Malice, that supreme banality, from a person one has placed above everyone else! And all that time wasted in fighting against one another, when it could be spent fighting side by side!) That horror had something solid about it, which I found almost restful. Your last letter – apart from the postscript, which must be a joke – shows so much understanding that one no longer knows where one is.... My heart goes out to you in spite of myself, as from a little sister to a big brother – that feeling which used to be so familiar to me. You stab me to the heart, yet it is with you that I am tempted to seek refuge. Then one says to oneself : 'If he understands so well, and yet does not lift a finger to save me, he is all the more criminal.' One feels more resentful towards you, and yet one cannot help having a sort of insane confidence in you. One can neither hate you wholeheartedly nor love you wholeheartedly : one adores you in a fog of anger and reproach, one hates you without being absolutely sure that it isn't love. Is that what you wanted, you who appear so passionate but are in fact so much in control of everything you do? Are you a sort of satanic alchemist concocting the feelings you want people to have for you with the same icy indifference as you measure out the feelings you entertain for others? Or is your attitude spontaneous, natural, guileless, unaware? Whatever it is, I don't know what you're like to those who do not love you, but I do know what you're like to those who do. *Flagellum amantibus*: a scourge to those who love him.

As for me, if you're playing some abominable game with me, which at this moment I'm inclined to believe you are (I mean at the very moment of writing these words, for at other moments I tell myself you're merely a child juxtaposed with a man rich in solemn meditation and weighty experience, Faust and Eliakim inextricably merged, in other words a monster – though if you are such a monster you cannot help yourself and are forgiven) – if you're playing a game with me quite consciously, I can only tell you I'm not strong enough for you, and cry 'Pax'. And in any case I'm not playing any more. You were once an element of vitality, of inner fecundity, of active torment in my life. Now there's nothing. You dry everything up, like the wind. You have mummified the tenderness, so fresh, so deep, so absolute, which I felt for you. Like a sort of white frost, you have blighted feelings which, had they flowered, could have brought forth wonderful fruit. So much so that you have relieved me (in this at least you operated a cure) of the misery and the fear of growing old. I wanted to stay young during the time I loved and was loved, because to my mind a woman of forty in bed. . . . But now, what does it matter? There are moments now when it seems to me that I can no longer give you anything at all, moments when it seems to me that you have pulled out by the roots everything that blossomed inside me, and that you could fall ill, even die, without my feeling anything. Quite honestly, even that time in Paris I wasn't all that sorry to leave you. I went home drunk, as it were, with a sort of deliverance, and for a week I was almost happy by comparison. As soon as I got home, I removed your photograph from the wall of my room. But it was really only a gesture. I put it back later. Why not? It was doing me neither good nor harm. I can see myself writing you a solemn farewell, and next time I come to Paris, asking you to kiss me like a sister, so that at least I shall have had one kiss from you. It would be the only thing I should ever have asked of you. Because I would have you know *once and for all* that I have never begged anything from you, your company, your friendship, your intimacy, or your love. I offered, and you turned me down; quite a different matter. My pride permitted me to offer. It would not permit me to beg.

Wednesday

As I have said: all I feel towards you now is emptiness, exhaustion – the very thing you wanted. And yet, this emptiness is itself a feeling, is still superfluous in my life. As long as you are still in my life, as long as I have still not cut all the threads that bind me to you, I shall not be available for anyone else. I shall *never* dissociate – my body to another, my heart to you. And if another should give me or allow me love, or its semblance, I shall not keep my friendship for you. (Not much loss. . . . For to have from a man what I have from you is to have lost him already. Nothing in the present, nothing in the future, nothing to remember. . . . And anyhow, a woman doesn't go on giving her friendship to a man who has refused it.) You are the only friend I could not keep in a normal life. Costals, the friend of the family, my children's favourite uncle, no, never! The reverse side of my feeling for you is nothingness, just as the reverse side of your sensual excesses is Jansenism. You will represent lost love for me, not friendship. You won't turn the torrent into an irrigation channel, nor the wild pony into a plough-horse. And so desperately, at the moment, do I need that normal life in which you can have no part, so desperately do I need to embrace reality rather than dreams, to hold in my arms a man or a child of my own, so grateful will I be to the nice ordinary chap who allows me to love him, that I shall give myself to him entirely, with my will at least. Even more than this, though I don't much care for children, in my desperation I have reached the point of wanting a child without a husband. Because, since the man refuses to be loved, and one cannot bear him if one does not love him, only the child can take one out of oneself. And so, whatever happened, I should no longer need you. Yes, I should infinitely prefer to have a beloved creature in my arms, *even if he didn't love me at all*, than to have his purest, most exclusive tenderness in his absence.

Friday

I can bear it no longer, I can bear it no longer. A human being has a certain capacity for suffering; beyond that, he

dies or finds release no matter how. Suffering cannot indefinitely remain suffering; it changes into something else. For four
months – ever since Paris – you have kept me living in a house
on fire. Either I had to die of asphyxiation, or jump out of the
window and break my back – which is what I have done.

I don't beg, I shall never beg anything at all from you. But
I tell you again, solemnly, irrevocably: if I have to give up
hope of being yours some day, life will no longer have any
meaning for me. After all, Costals, after all, I must live! Is
there not a single sentence in the hundreds of letters I've
written to you that might touch your heart even now? I want
to go on hoping, persuading myself that your attitude is the
result of scruples. When you come to realize, in six months'
or a year's time, that you're ruining my life, perhaps.... Perhaps between now and then you'll give me your love. Perhaps
you'll have ceased to believe that I'm a 'nice person' whom it
would be wrong to 'lead astray'. Perhaps curiosity – for my
body and what it can offer you – will have got the better of
you. If you had met me in a railway carriage, perhaps, for the
fun of it.... If I hadn't loved you, and had wounded you
or angered you, perhaps you would have done violence to me,
for the sheer pleasure of overcoming me and dominating
me.... (It's true that if I didn't love you I wouldn't want to be
yours.) I can still wait. A year or two more, perhaps.... My
youth is not yet over. I don't look my age, I've often been
told. If I hadn't admitted my age to you, you would think
me younger. All you can see in me is a black-clad provincial,
an earnest intellectual. Whereas, if I were at all happy, however illusorily, I would still be capable of so much playfulness,
such a blossoming out.

With you, as far as I'm concerned, it must be everything or
nothing. As I have told you, I no longer have any feeling for
you, nothing live, nothing that moves. But if you yourself
were to move, *it* would move. For what is latent beneath *it* is
not friendship but love. It could burst forth again, as a flame
springs up from what seemed to be nothing but dead wood
and ashes. If the worst came to the worst I could kill this
latent love, or at least stifle it, prevent it from coming to the
surface; what I cannot do is dilute it. In order to go on feeling

anything for you at all, I must have the certitude that one day you will be more than a friend. One evening we exchanged a lot of fine phrases, you and I – especially you – about friendship between men and women. Friendship between men and women is what music is to the instrument that produces it. Friendship between men and women is something totally disembodied and ethereal, something totally different from sensuality, but which can only exist through sensuality. Friendship is no longer possible between us without a pact, a solemn promise that one day it will be something else. One day? When? Whenever you like – in six months, in a year, if that is your whim. But what I must have is your firm promise, your promise on everything you hold most sacred. Then I can wait. Otherwise I can bear it no longer, not a moment longer. Unless I change the present, in which I am torn between hope and despair, into irrevocable past or potential future, unless I pull out the knife, I shall go mad.

A.

This letter remained unanswered.

The scene took place in a restaurant in the Bois de Boulogne. (Each of these restaurants in the Bois evoked contradictory memories for Costals: hours of intoxication when he was there with a woman he had not yet enjoyed; hours of deadly boredom when he was there with a woman who was already his.) Birds could be heard flitting from branch to branch, their shadows streaking the trunks of the trees as they passed. Above a lawless world, they flew to kill time.

He was saying to Solange:

'I'm not in love with you, nor you with me, and that's as it should be. For God's sake, don't let's alter it! So, you've never had any feelings for a man?'

'Never.'

'Never been kissed?'

'Sometimes, by surprise. And I fled at once. But never twice. If you only saw me snubbing people!'

'But look at those handsome young men. Why wouldn't you want them to love you?'

'I realize they have handsome faces. But what difference do you think that makes to me? What connection is there between my affection and a handsome face?'

'And yet I only fell for you because of your face!'

'Ah, but you're a man.'

'Never been deeply unhappy either?'

'No.'

'Never cried?'

'I don't know what it means.'

'Well, well!' he thought, 'here's the ideal cold fish.' At the same time he was surprised that she should allow him to stroke her hair and her legs and kiss her in public. 'It's all very inconsistent. . . . But what *is* consistent, except the behaviour of characters in novels and plays?'

As they were sitting down to table, a small child who was walking past with some other diners caught sight of Solange and stopped, entranced by her face. 'I don't know why children always like me,' she remarked. Costals, seeing the child's expression, understood why: because they were dazzled by her beauty. And this took him back, full of wonderment, to those days of old when beauty had a power of its own.

When the waiter said: 'As Madame wishes. . . .' Costals frowned: this 'Madame' raised the spectre of the nuptial Hippogriff. 'What's at the back of her mind? And her parents'? Mistress? Wife? Bah! Never mind all that. If the Hippogriff rears its head there'll be plenty of time to try conclusions once more with my old enemy.'

Costals had always been struck, not so much by the (perfectly legitimate) tendency of girls to see matrimony wherever they go, and to want men to marry them, as by their obstinate belief that he might consider marrying them, even if such a contingency was so improbable as to verge on the grotesque. It seemed to him that each one of them was accompanied by a Chimera – remember, a Chimera has claws – which they mounted at the slightest provocation, or no provocation at all, to gallop around in an element in which they were so much at home that they seemed to be capable of anything – that is to say in a cloud of unreality. He had christened this Chimera 'the Hippogriff', and the word had become a familiar one on his lips and on those of the young ladies who did him the honour of having designs on him. According to whether the idea of a possible marriage gained or lost ground in their imaginations (for in Costals' it was always in neutral) the Hippogriff was said to be thriving or losing weight. Sometimes Costals would 'feed the Hippogriff', sometimes the Hippogriff was 'insatiable', and one of the most chaste of these girls had even gone so far as to designate a certain part of her anatomy, with which she was obsessed, the 'hippogriffic part'. Costals spent his time fighting against the Hippogriff, endeavouring to kill the monster – in other words to convince his girl-friends that nothing in the world would persuade him to marry them. But, like all good mythical creatures, the Hippogriff, brought low, had no sooner breathed its last than it came to life again more fiery than ever. Nothing is more difficult than to persuade a young woman that one has no desire – none whatsoever – to dedicate one's life to her.

After dinner, when night had fallen, they strolled down the avenue des Acacias. Hardly a bench there had not been turned into a bed for a couple glued together; yet nobody threw a bucket of water over them, as over rutting mongrels. 'Perhaps they'll teach me some new tricks,' thought Costals. But no; at each gesture they made he scoffed: 'Why, I know that one, fat-head!' Dismal how limited the register of caresses is. These couples, as identical in their reactions as in their postures, exasperated him in the end, with their apparent conviction that they were the only people in the world, and the smiles they gave you to invite you to admire their happiness, which would end up with the vitriol bottle and the intravenous injection. Truly a gigantic miasma of vulgarity (literature, films, newspapers, sentimental songs ...) bore down on this unhappy man-woman combination. How bitter it was to be unable to escape it! After the tenth pair, Costals felt paralysed. 'In ten minutes' time, I shall be one of these puppets. Come on, I must take the plunge. Four or five more of these ecstatic couples and I'll no longer have the heart.'

He indicated a secluded path, making sure it was not one he already had memories of (no super-impressions – he was already too inclined to mix everything up).

'Shall we go down there?'

'If you like.'

They made their way through the trees, and came to a sort of clearing, where two iron chairs awaited them side by side, by special arrangement of the goddess Prema.

All at once he had her on his shoulder, her head thrown back, her eyes closed, offering her half-open mouth, not returning his kisses but letting him devour the inside of her mouth and her lips, never opening her eyes, never uttering a word. How was it possible that this slender form had become so solid and heavy in his arms? She was all corseted in rubber, armoured like a young Menelaus. At one moment she gave a little moan, as though she were about to burst into tears; from the way she clenched her lips against his, he guessed that she would one day have an aptitude for biting, and he felt her pointed nails scrape on his jacket, like the claws of a cat he had been holding in his arms thinking it was happy when in fact it was impatient to be off and would scratch him at any minute and escape. She took his wrist and gripped it more and more tightly, evidently trying to stop his embraces but failing to do so; and then a shudder ran through her. And all the time the paradise of her face lay open, motionless, and he was everywhere upon it with his mouth. She did not embrace him, did not even make the slightest show of doing so; she did not move her lips, never once returned a kiss. When he knelt down, she bowed her head completely, hiding her face. That she was his for the taking was patently obvious, but, as we have seen, he liked to proceed by degrees; besides, at that moment, sentiment was stronger in him than sensuality. And all the time he heard her rapid breathing.

From time to time he raised his head to recover his breath. A deep, protective silence seemed to have shaped itself to the very contours of their embrace. He caught sight of a stretch of water on their left that he had not noticed before; perhaps it had approached noiselessly so as not to take them by surprise. It glistened, motionless, beneath the thirsty trees. Fifty yards away from them there was a lighted car, with people who must have been picnicking on the grass, and children playing.

Never would he forget her face when she opened her eyes

for the first time and drew herself up – her eyes, normally rather screwed up, but now dilated, immense, staring at him without blinking. He scarcely recognized her; and she was seeing him for the first time; they were discovering each other. He said to her, as though she were really unrecognizable: 'Is it still you?' She said 'Yes', in a voice that was scarcely audible.

His watch pointed to half past midnight. 'We must go.' She got up without a word. Her hair had come undone, making her look like a little girl. She tidied it – in what a silence! It was he who handed her her hairpins, on the tips of his fingers. Then she stood in front of him, as she had stood the other day outside her house, smaller than he, her forehead bowed a little shyly, but her eyes still looking up at him without blinking, literally rooted in his. An unforgettable look, heart-rending in its directness. An unforgettable disharmony – or rather harmony – between her bowed, seemingly submissive head and this look of candour, almost provocative in its pride. She sought no higher than the face that was before her; her world stopped there.

He took her in his arms again, this time standing up, she with her head on his shoulder, he so intent on her mouth that he no longer knew who she was save by the taste of her mouth. He moved her from his left to his right shoulder with the same gesture – exactly the same – as that by which the matador transfers the bull from his left to his right side in the close *toreo*; with the same pose – exactly the same – as the matador adopts at that moment, feet firmly planted, slightly apart, back slightly arched; with the same grave expression – exactly the same – as the matador wears, and in his soul the same absolute mastery over himself and the other: intoxication and self-possession compounded in him as earth and water are compounded in clay. His domination over her was absolute, and he knew it. If he had said to her: 'Let's stay here all night', she would have stayed. If he had said 'Undress,' she would have stripped herself naked. She was subjugated. But if anything was equal to his domination over her it was his desire not to take advantage of it, or even to hurt her by pressing her too closely to him – for he could feel the play of his muscles, all that strength which, even if he were divested of intelligence, talent, money, would go on living within him for years to come, and tomorrow would make her happy. And his only precise sensations were the hardness of Solange's teeth, which he touched with his lips, and the scraping of her nails down his jacket, like one of those gestures people make in their death-throes.

They walked away unsteadily. He was holding her by the wrist. The lights had been turned off in the Bois; they had to go back as far as the Porte Maillot on foot, looking for a taxi. Now he was holding her left breast in the palm of his hand, and he felt it beat, as though it were the heart of creation beating in his palm. He made a few remarks, about the inconvenience of not being able to find a taxi. She made no reply. The impression she gave was of someone in a stupor, under some sort of spell. A little worried by her silence, he kissed her on the nape of the neck, as if to show her he still loved her. A young man called to them from a passing car: 'Not like that! On the mouth!' She did not laugh.

Still more worried, he asked her: 'What are you thinking about?' She replied: 'About this evening. . . . ' O little girl!

At last they hailed a taxi.

From the avenue des Acacias to the avenue de Villiers, the taxi brought back a dead girl. No sooner was she inside it than she threw back her head. During the quarter of an hour the journey took she said not a single word, her eyes closed, her mouth glued to his, as though it were from there that she drew her breath and if she left it for an instant she would expire. Once, the taxi slowed down and almost stopped under the multi-coloured lights at a crossroads, and a face only a few inches away looked in at them through the rear window. He disengaged himself and brought her little bunched fist to his lips and kissed her nails and fingers. But then she lifted her face a little for him to take once more, and this slight movement was the only sign she gave to prove that she was not unconscious. In the avenue de Villiers he woke her. He said good-bye to her and added: 'I'll telephone you the day after tomorrow.' She got out without saying a word, like a sleepwalker, or like a ghost.

The taxi drove off. At the first bar that was still open, he said to the driver: 'Would you like a drink?' At the counter, he drank two glasses of white wine. He stopped the taxi before they arrived at his house, to get some air. It seemed to him that the terrestrial globe was rotating far below him, and that he walked stepping from cloud to cloud.

Pierre Costals   to Mademoiselle Rachel Guigui
Paris   *Paris*

23 May 1927

Well, dear Guiguite, this is it: we're going to drop you. We've taken up with an angel of heaven, and we've decided to concentrate on her, being no longer of an age when each one has her share of us but all have us in full.* We would come to her half-heartedly, our palate would be jaded – and we want to experience the sensation in all its glory. We expected a long night, pierced at last by the dawn of her consent, but this angel was carried off her feet forthwith: we scarcely had time to desire her. It's very serious; physically not perhaps pure gold, but emotionally pure gold, and if we make light of it that is because it's our way. In short, my dear, we are in the heart of the sublime, and since that is a region where you have no place, we will keep you in suspended animation, with your consent, until the day, which cannot be far off, when our angel in her turn will have to clear out: the sublime, alas, cannot be sustained indefinitely. Upon which, we send you our love, together with some cash (provision has been made).

                                               C.

P.S. We use the pronoun *we* because we're accused of being conceited when we say *I*. It's true, *we* sounds much more natural – one should have thought of it before.

---

*Paraphrase of a line from Victor Hugo's *Feuilles d'automne* (Part I) on the subject of mother-love: '*Chacun en a sa part et tous l'ont tout entier.*' cf. p. 355 (*Translator's note*).

Extract from the Diary of
Mademoiselle Germaine Rival, Paris

Tuesday. – My last day here. Beautiful store-house dust that I shall inhale no more, behind these blocked-up, barricaded windows, amid the noise and disorder of crates being feverishly unpacked. And the little wooden staircase with its brass rail, that I shall descend once more but never climb again. It was like a companion-ladder in a ship. When I climbed it, I used to think the house was about to get under way and sail out to sea.

It was bound to come to this. When I took this job, C. did not reproach me in the least, although he must have been displeased: even when he's paying no attention to me, he wants to feel that I'm within reach. My new job was not likely to be more than a mild inconvenience to him, but the merest shadow of an inconvenience is for him a crushing burden. At the time he simply said to me: 'You won't stay a month. Imagine, a teacher! You're not one of them. They'll find an excuse to fire you.' He was getting at me through my pride. Three days later he became even more insidious: 'When they've thrown you out, I might perhaps take you to Italy.'

'Is that a promise?'

'A promise! Does *a man like me* ever promise anything?'

It isn't true, he promises all the time, but *a man like him* rarely keeps his promises. And never apologizes. 'I'm afraid I've changed my mind. You must take me as I am. Anyway, it comes under a statute of limitations.'

Even without promising, he put the idea of Italy into my head: that was all he wanted. Every time we saw each other he brought it up again: 'If you're sacked, and if we go to Italy, which, mind you, I don't promise. . . .' It was because of that 'if' that I eventually found a pretext and demonstrated with the others. I could have got myself fired for 'professional incompetence' (in other words, sabotage), but I couldn't face that: I, too, must be taken as I am. The motives of the demonstration were debatable. And anyhow I couldn't care less whether L—'s common law sentence was transformed into political expulsion or not. I didn't like L—'s face. Now I've been forced into giving the impression that I'm 'red'. Mummy is heart-broken. 'You who were brought up by the nuns!' and so on.

In this firm it isn't the manager who represents God for me, it's the cashier in his iron cage: deaf, dumb, blind – God personified. Another woman waiting on one of the benches in the hall, looking for a job, and there's nothing for her. That Renaud girl has just arrived with her narrow shoulders, her little face like a shrivelled lemon. It's hard at first, when you're only sixteen, and not used to it . . . She never stops thinking about her home, her pauper's lodgings, where at least she's not tied down and where she's sheltered from coarseness and abuse. That one over there has something wrong with her machine. She looks at me despairingly, appealing to me to come and help her.

'I don't know what's wrong, Mademoiselle.'

'Your driving-belt has slipped. I'll fix it.'

Now it's Lucienne, the one who says: 'I detest God.' (She'll get over that.)

'Mademoiselle, I've got a head-ache.'

'Go out into the yard, and come back in five minutes.'

'What if the manager sees me?'

'You can tell him I gave you permission.' She goes off. Then another says: 'Mademoiselle, Lucienne won't come back.' (Even the 'reds' are always sneaking on one another.) I reply: 'Of course, I hadn't expected anything else.' I can't get used to acting the part of a red. To show that I'm on their side, I should have to surrender my authority, but I just can't bring myself to do it.

(Yes, Andrée Barbot, you can stare at me, my girl. You won't get me to lower my eyes. You may drag a nervous smile out of me, but no more. You see, it's you who've lowered your eyes first. Nasty little beast!)

The five minutes are up, and Lucienne returns. I know quite well they're afraid of me. And I'm afraid of myself for having come to loathe these poor wretches. But apparently it's essential. 'Regard them as enemies. Be harsh.' They'll be talking for years about the hard-hearted overseer. As miserable as they. Perhaps even more so. Definitely more. But they don't rebel. What a flop, after all the drama! What a lot of 'no's' on the petition! Hardly a single 'yes', and a few signatures without either 'yes' or 'no'. And yet there were a large number of us who voted 'for'. What strikes one about nearly all of them is their lack of courage. Why should they rebel? Not only are they not shocked by tyranny and injustice, they actually like it: what they like is the fact of authority. And they don't like kindness either. If you're not unkind to them, they despise you.

I work with four men and sixteen women here. When I ask myself how many of them I shall say goodbye to, I can think of two men and three women. An interesting ratio.

Perhaps there's a password I don't know which would have made it possible for me to win them over. To be leaving without having discovered it.... To have received no help from anyone.... C., when I spoke to him about it, exploded: 'Me! Secrets of leadership from me! I neither give orders nor take them.' Of course, there's only one thing *he* wants: to escape.

Next day. – Worse than anything I had imagined:

'You know, we won't be seeing each other for a while.'

He could have told me anything he liked – that he was ill or something. But no, he always has to tell the truth.

'I've found a marvellous girl. Pure gold! I mustn't dissipate my energies right and left. I must come to her fresh. But when it's all over with her, we'll start again. It will be a matter of six weeks or so.'

He wanted to give me a thousand francs. His wretched money! I refused.

'You refuse? Just like an Arab!'

'What do you mean, like an Arab?'

'When an Arab is dissatisfied with the amount you give him, he flings it to the ground. And he doesn't pick it up again. But *you*'ll pick up the thousand francs. Because you're French. Because you're a woman. And because you have no reason to refuse it. I do something that annoys you. To make up for it, I do something that pleases you. What could be more reasonable?'

If he lied, I should feel strong enough to stand up to him.

But the way he puts things, there's nothing one can say. I didn't even mention Italy.

In the end I accepted. I shall buy a radio set with the money, and tell Mother I won it in the lottery. It's a 1,450-franc set, but I can get it for a thousand through Pierrette's boy friend. I asked C. to send me some records too, because he knows more about the latest music than I do.

No sooner had Costals and Solange sat down to dinner in the garden of this bogus 'hostelry' not far from the forest of Montmorency than Costals began to suffer. He hated all their fellow-diners, the men with their 'distinguished' airs ('Dear lady, doesn't this sky remind you of that Canaletto we saw in the gallery at Verona?'), the women with their faces set in a mould of boredom, stupidity and malevolence – all of them eaten up with self-esteem, and never more so, strange to say, than when they were apologizing to one another, all of them entrenched behind the barricades of their private language, their esoteric rites, their conviction of being a race apart, all of them irremediably exiled from everything natural and human, so much so that there were moments when they almost aroused pity, as though they were somehow cursed. There were a hundred and fifty people inside this enclosure, and the only sign of dignity was in the faces of the waiters, and the only sign of purity – a sublime purity – in a white greyhound.

It was not because they were rich that they disgusted Costals, but because they were so unworthy of their riches. Truly, it was a case of pearls before swine. There was not the slightest hint of envy in him, for the good reason that he himself either had what they had, or could have had it if he wanted it. But it was only by consorting with such people that he could obtain the things a writer of average talent can normally expect in France – honours, employment, 'position'. And he was incapable of consorting with them without feeling a disgust that was so painful to him that it was wiser to avoid occasions for it. As a result it was often said of him in those circles that he was aloof. And he was indeed aloof from 'those circles'.

There came a moment when his disgust grew so intense that the slightest pretext was enough to turn it into a physical revulsion. Seeing the expression of unbelievable stupidity on the face of one of these women, an expression intended to make it quite clear that she despised her husband (she was try-ing to look like Marlene Dietrich, and succeeding), Costals pushed his plate away and threw his head back. . . .

'What's wrong?' asked Solange. 'Do you feel ill?'

He had turned so pale that she was frightened. He apolo-gized without giving any explanation, and changed his place at the table so that he faced towards the forest and there were no longer any diners within his field of vision. It was not the first time that excessive disgust had caused this sort of revulsion. He had turned pale in the same way one day in the boulevard Saint Michel on seeing a parade of students, all wearing canary-yellow bow ties (a symbol?) and walking along with their arms round each other's shoulders bawling some-thing, behind a placard on which the figure 69 was scrawled. They were escorted by policemen, with one of whom Costals had exchanged a smile of gloomy commiseration; he could not bear to think that these men of the people might suspect him of indulgence towards the demonstrators. How, incident-ally, had the policeman managed to smile? In his shoes, Cos-tals thought to himself, forced by the exigencies of the service to accompany these brats of the rich and to watch the obscene mummeries inspired by their idleness and stupidity, he could not have restrained himself from hitting them over the head.

He had always been surprised by the patience of those who, in 'good families', were charitably referred to as *the lower orders*. He had always wondered why it was that the humble people of Europe and the natives of the colonies did not hate more. For it was obvious that many of them felt no hatred; and he was touched by this, without understanding why it was. Periods of social peace, he thought, are neither natural nor logical, however agreeable they may be for some people; revolt is the natural order of things. Whatever its excesses and incidental injustices (lamentable though they be) the day of revolt is the day when the situation becomes normal again and therefore satisfying to the mind: the age of miracles is over.

If Costals had been alone in these surroundings, or with old friends, or with his son, he would have gone to dine with the chauffeurs. Even supposing their language was not particularly fastidious, which was certain to be the case, they at least had an excuse, having had no education, no culture, no leisure. Whereas these people, who were spiritually so impoverished, had had every opportunity. And moreover the chauffeurs were concerned with something other than making a good impression and repeating what they thought it was the smart thing to say.

From time to time Costals gave Solange a sombre look. It was because of her that he was here. This was the price he had to pay for his liaisons with women, unless they were women of the people – the necessity to take them to vile places, fashionable drawing-rooms, grand hotels, night-clubs, theatres, smart beaches. They knew, of course, that they had to affect to despise these places when they were with him. They repeated what he said about them himself, and went even further. Such splendid indignations. But you had only to see them in these pleasure spots, livening up at once, preening themselves, strutting about, to realize that this was what they loved, this was where they felt most alive – even the nicest and the most decent of them, even the simplest. There was nothing to be done about the equation: woman=chichi. And Costals' past was full of relationships weighed down, not to say poisoned, by the shame he had felt at having to belie himself in order to amuse women by accompanying them in a way of life which he despised. Just as a man, thirty years after having left his adolescence behind, no matter how loving and devoted his parents may have been, associates them first and foremost with infinitesmal grievances – 'They made me spend a year studying law for nothing', or 'They made me wear flannel vests at the height of summer' – in the same way, no matter how much pleasure a woman had given him, Costals could not help thinking: 'The days she made me waste (not to mention the money) doing shameful things! For instance, it's because of her that – I still blush to think of it – I spent a

week at Deauville.' For the moment he did not hold it against
Solange that he had felt obliged, because he was with her, to
dine in a pretentious restaurant, but he carefully put aside this
motive for resentment – a generous resentment, so to speak –
to take it up again on the day he wanted to break with her.

Earlier that evening, as they drove through the forest of
Montmorency (passing motorists laughed as they saw him
kissing her like mad, and Costals laughed back at them in a
youthful, plebeian complicity he enjoyed), he had said to her :
'After dinner, at the *hostelry*, supposing I took a room ...
would you come up with me for a while?' She had answered
'yes'. Still the same *yes*! And now their dinner, begun in ill-
humour, was coming to an end with a sort of secret melancholy. There were times when he had taken girls in a sort of
Jove-like whirlwind which left no room for anything but the
glory of rape. At other times, such as now, he felt a twinge
of uneasiness at the thought that an act of such cardinal
significance in the life of a virtuous woman was bound to have
so much less importance for him. And then he thought : 'In
an hour's time I shall know how she does it.' Thereafter
curiosity would cease to sustain his feelings for her, and he
wondered what would become of those feelings once they
were left on their own.

'Did your mother ask you any awkward questions about
what happened between us in the Bois the other night?'

'Fortunately, no.'

'If she had asked you : "How did he behave to you?" what
would you have answered?'

She remained silent.

'I can see by your silence that you wouldn't have spared her
a single detail.'

'I've never kept anything from my mother.'

'Well, well, that's nice! You really have been well brought
up!'

'I've never kept anything from my mother because I never
had anything to hide.'

'Which means that if.... Ah! I see you have a grain of
intelligence after all.'

Now there occurred an enchanting scene similar to the one

the other night in the Bois. A little girl of about five broke away from a party of diners who were settling down to table and advanced towards Solange, gazing at her with an expression of wonder and delight. When her mother came to fetch her, she cried. Thereafter, they could not make her eat, because her eyes were steadily fixed on Solange. And Costals remembered what she had told him about the mysterious attraction she exercised over children.

She went upstairs to the room with great simplicity, without the slightest embarrassment. He was struck by this, and thought to himself (an ugly thought? no, the thought of a man who has lived): 'You'd think she had been doing nothing else all her life.' At first there were great photogenic embraces on the balcony, opposite the trees which glowed a sickly green in the lamp-light, while the sound of the orchestra rose from below. Costals applied himself. 'I must do it well. I must leave her a beautiful memory, worthy of this dear old moon and those rascally violins. Let's get it into our head that *éternité* is the anagram of *étreinte*.* Let's give her a whiff of eternity.'

Now she was lying on the bed, naked except for her shoes, which she had kept on, and her stockings which she had rolled down over them. She had undressed, at his request, without either coquetry or prudishness, with the same naturalness, the same simplicity which she had shown as she climbed the stairs under the noses of the hotel staff. Her legs were a little hairy – a charming trait in a young lady, provided she does not overdo it.

She embraced this gentleman awkwardly and without conviction, and the kisses she gave him – her first since they had known each other – were tight-lipped and decorous. She seemed to be saying to herself each time: 'I must kiss him. It's the thing to do.' But when, with his mouth on hers, he imparted to her the rudiments of the art, he sensed that, among all these caresses, she had at last found the one which suited her, which really gave her pleasure, and that now it was clear that her day had not been wasted. For minutes on end, in this unofficial intercourse of mouths, she gave herself quite as fully as in intercourse under its official form. When he

---

Etreinte=embrace (*Translator's note*).

asked: 'Would you like me to turn on the light?' (the first thing she had done on entering the room had been to switch off the light, but the room was flooded with moonlight), she said 'No, please don't', in a new voice, a voice transformed by emotion, the voice of a little girl, at once high and low, as though it came from far away, from a little Dandillot of another age who had remained in the depths of her being. Afterwards he was to call this voice her 'night voice', because she only put it on when they were making love – and the ship of love, when one is on it with little girls, always sails with its lights out.

Now he could no longer see anything of Solange's body, could see nothing of her but her face surrounded by her dishevelled hair, like the heart of a flower surrounded by its petals. It was as if the whole of this woman were concentrated in this great corolla: a woman-corolla.... At first she let him do what he wished, but soon she began to cry. 'No! No!' She cried for some time, with real sobs, while he fondled her without withdrawing from her, and he thought to himself: 'We know all about this.' Partly out of reluctance to hurt her, but mainly in order to keep some of the mystery and attraction for future occasions – while at the same time gratifying his fad of never taking advantage of an easy opportunity – when he let go of her he had not taken the decisive step. It is rare to be able thus to combine pleasure and virtue. Her sobs continued for a while after he had drawn away from her, then grew fainter, then stopped at last; in him, meanwhile, sensation was still as sharp as a fresh wound. They remained motionless and silent, lying there side by side, and he wondered if she was angry. Perhaps she was a false *ingénue* (it was a hypothesis which his mind could not entirely reject), piqued at not having been taken completely; perhaps, on the other hand, merely a little girl, vexed with him for having gone so far.... But suddenly, turning her head – cloc! – she kissed him on the cheek. The noise of a tree-frog jumping into the water.

He lay there for several minutes, silent by her side, and his thoughts began to take wing. There are elevations, religious or otherwise, which are provoked by fasting. Others – through the identity of opposites – can arise from the digestion of a rich meal, a process that transports us into a better world. With Costals, such elevations often took shape as soon as the carnal act had been accomplished, and they were all the more intense the more wholeheartedly he had thrown himself into that act. This was either because, having used up all his sensuality in the act, only the spiritual part of him remained, or because no sooner was he physically plugged in to a woman than he was filled with light – as when one plugs in an electric lamp – and this light was total: the absolute of sensation followed by the absolute of sentiment (there are certain souls that flow towards the absolute as water flows towards the sea). Almost all his most inspired work had been conceived during these post-coital periods. So now, as he lay by Solange's side, his thoughts turned to Thérèse, and he saw her soul threatened (from the Catholic point of view) without her suspecting it in the least. Yet he had had more than enough pity on her, and was weary of it.

The orchestra had stopped playing. The windows were wide open on to the warm night, and the dark foliage (the lamps had been put out) made a continuous rustling sound as it stirred, like the sound of rain. Now it seemed to Costals that Andrée was standing at the foot of the bed with her tormented face. 'I who feel, know, understand! I who have penetrated to the heart of your work more profoundly than if I were you yourself! And you refuse me what you offer unreservedly to this insignificant little creature, simply because she was born pretty!' Often the injustice of one of his actions would cause him a kind of enthusiasm: the pleasure that God feels when he contemplates his creation. This time, it weighed on him. Nevertheless, he began caressing Solange once more; since it was understood that he was biased in her favour, why make any bones about it? But he made up his mind to write Andrée a nice letter next day. (He did not in fact do so, being exclusively preoccupied with the religious thoughts evoked by a letter he was writing to Thérèse.)

In the taxi, she was less stupefied than she had been on the previous occasion. Several times she raised her head from her lover's breast and gazed into his eyes in silence, as though, after the event, she felt the need to get to know this person to whom she had given herself. And he, suffering her gaze, said to himself: 'My face is that of a man of thirty-four who thinks. How ugly people are who think, or profess to think!' He remained thus, under her scrutiny, like a soldier forcing himself to keep his head above the parapet: the terrible nakedness of a man's face, without powder, without paint, so brave compared with women's faces, which are always patched up. This lasted for what seemed to him a long time. Then she put her head back on his shoulder, as though she were surrendering for a second time.

As he felt he had the right to use the familiar form of address to her, whereas she still said *vous*, he asked, smilingly: '*Tu? Vous?*' And she replied, quite simply (without in the least meaning to be ungracious):

'I don't know how to say *tu*.'

He liked this remark, in which he saw a mixture of shyness and pride: the remark of an infanta.

Suddenly, after a silence, she asked him point-blank:

'Do you really love me?'

Rather foolishly, without thinking – and yet perhaps because he still had the feeling at the back of his mind that she might not be sincere – he said to her:

'It's I who should be asking you that question.'

She leapt up at this, and with a violence that he had neither seen nor suspected in her, she said:

'You have no right to say that to me! Haven't I given you enough proofs?'

She had drawn herself up like a little snake.

'You have no right!' Never would he have believed that she could use such a phrase. Might she be capable of passion? He also asked himself, with typical male cruelty, 'What proofs?'

'I,' she went on, 'I shall love you always, I know I shall And you, how long?'

'A long time.'

She made a face. Then he said to her:

'When I was sixteen – sixteen, do you hear – I had a little girl-friend of fourteen. I loved her as one loves for the first time, which is to say with a fervour one never recaptures.

And of course she said to me exactly what you've just said, which is a classic remark: "With me, it's for life. What about you?" And I replied: "For as long as possible." I loved her madly, and I was only sixteen; but I was as clear-sighted as that. I need scarcely add that six months later we had forgotten each other. You see, I like reality. I like to see things as they are,' he insisted passionately. 'People say one's unhappy when one sees things too clearly. I see everything clearly, and I'm very happy. But because I know what reality is, I know that one must never commit the future. What will your feelings be in a year's time? In six months? In three months? What will mine be? That's why I don't give you that "forever", which nevertheless I find quite natural on the lips of a young girl, and which touches me profoundly. I merely say "a long time", and I say it to you as a man who knows what "a long time" means. And it means a great deal. To know that one will love someone for a long time is a great deal, believe me.'

She did not answer.

When they parted, he wanted to give her some sign of encouragement, and said to her with a nice smile:

'I don't feel a bit tired of you, you know. . . .'

Later, he felt sorry for having doubted her. Not that he had doubted her in the strict sense of the word. He believed her to be pure of heart; he knew her to be intact of body. But he found it impossible, when faced with the 'no, no's' and the tears, and even the night voice, that unforgettable little schoolgirl's voice, not to think of all the counterfeits of these that abound among the fair sex. He was so convinced that Solange was 'genuine' that he found it almost vile of himself to have occasional doubts about her, even if these doubts were, so to speak, forced on him. For Costals' past injected into the present a whole accumulation of knowledge and experience that modified his vision of Solange, and there was nothing to be done about that. Nothing could alter the fact that for him she was only the latest, whereas for her he was the first. Nothing could alter the fact that he had known a great many copies before he knew the original, and that the original seemed less original after these copies. And whereas his attitude towards

168

Andrée caused him no compunction, he felt guilty towards
Solange, although he had done her no other wrong than being
what he was. For it is a fact that everything conspires to the
advantage of that which we love.

But there was another feeling that tended to make him
doubt Solange a little : he was astonished that she could love
him. Costals was devoid of literary vanity, and one of the
things he liked most about Solange was that she never spoke
to him about his books and never uttered the faintest word of
admiration. His vanity as a male, on the other hand, ran to
extremes. His first impulse was to assume that no woman he
desired would refuse to give herself to him. But whenever one
of them fell into his arms, at the same time surrendering something of her heart, he was taken aback, and repeated to himself the remark of Louis XV : 'I find it hard to understand why
they love me so much.' In this way he savoured alternately
the pleasure of believing himself invincible and the pleasure of
proving himself humble : there is a time for everything, says
the sage. That Solange could really love him he found hard to
believe. 'She's incapable of appreciating what is great and
superior in me. Poor darling, she has the brain of a water-flea.
So what can she find to love in me? What is there about me,
physically, that's worth loving? It's not at all clear.' This was
to ignore the fact that women, unlike men, go from affection
to desire. Thus two elements played a part in his distrust :
one which could be *stigmatized* in these terms : 'the disillu-
sionment of a cynic who corrupts simple innocence', and another which it is difficult not to describe as genuine modesty.
So his feelings were partly good and partly bad. Like three-
quarters of our feelings. Which is what society – which pre-
fers people to be either black or white, so that one 'knows
where one is' with them – will not have. But what nature –
which loves nothing so much as confusion – will.

'Nothing can alter the fact that I am by nature clear-
sighted – and clear-sighted *always*,' he said to himself as he
thought of the 'long time' he had opposed to her naïve assurance. 'And moreover nothing can possibly make me want not
to be. My clear-sightedness frightens people, but it never
frightens me. I'm amused by it ; it is a monster I've tamed.

But why "a monster"? Call it rather my tutelary spirit. It's thanks to this clear-sightedness that I lead a thoroughly intelligent life, doing only what I know I can do, and concentrating on that, never going off on the wrong tack, never wasting time, never being taken in either by others or by myself, never letting people cause me suffering and only very rarely being even put out by them. And as this lucidity of mine is combined with all the powers of imagination and poetry, through poetry I can enter the domain of dreams, and through the imagination I can enter the feelings of people who are not clear-sighted; and this allows me to take controlled holidays from my clear-sightedness when I think fit, and thus to win both ways. My life is not a superior life because, although my senses never fail me, my mind, my character and my heart are full of lacunae; but these elements are such that a superior life could be built upon them. As for my dear Dandillot, who is not me, I must see that she does not suffer on my account, and I shall do this sometimes by lying to her and sometimes by not lying to her, in short by letting myself be governed not by principles but by expediency, by flair and tact, with my affection as my guide. It is possible that in other circumstances I might muffle her up with illusions. But I had, at least once, to make her face up to things as they are, even though in future I may conceal from her a spectacle which it would be in the worst possible taste to impose uninterruptedly on a girl of twenty.'

Pierre Costals   to Thérèse Pantevin
Paris   *La Vallée Maurienne*

19 May 1927

Mademoiselle,

I have had great pity on you before God of late, as you requested me to, and a few hours ago, by virtue of some rather special circumstances, I saw your soul in a dream, and I saw that it was in grave peril. You are like those people who, on the eve of a revolution, believe they are safe because they are liberals. 'Afraid of the revolutionaries? Why should I be?

They know I'm with them at heart. And besides, if they condemn me, they'll have to condemn everybody.' The revolution
occurs; they are left in peace; they are exultant. Then they
are arrested and killed. You sleep in peace, seeing yourself
surrounded by such a crowd of petty sinners and false innocents that God must be obliged to spare them. But you ignore
the example of the Jews, who all perished in the wilderness
save two, and the whole of Scripture, which tends towards
the establishment of this doctrine. Jesus Christ tells us that
'few are chosen'; he warns that the way is narrow and rare
those who will find it. Christians read this with indifference:
they think it's all part of Christ's rhetoric.

A multitude of the damned can be seen in the churches at
eleven o'clock Mass, genuflecting and putting money in the
plate. Their extenuating circumstances are granted by the
Church itself, which has left them in their fools' paradise in
order to keep up the numbers on its lists. The contemporary
Church has no more right to invoke the example of a St
Augustine or the doctrine of a St Thomas without making
itself ridiculous than the dead humanism of our universities
has the right to claim descent from Greece or Rome: the
ancient world and the Middle Ages were tabernacles of a
spirituality which no religion or philosophy has been able to
continue or to transform.

The Church of Christ lasted a thousand years or so. I believe
(erroneously perhaps) that it survives only in monasteries and
convents. I dreamed of seeing you completely cut off from
the outside world, in a place where the affairs of the world
would revolve beneath your feet, as the affairs of heaven revolve above our heads. Even if nothing in Catholic doctrine
were true, you would have given me thereby a noble idea of
yourself, and that was not to be despised. If you were damned
in any case, it were better to be damned in a lofty and
singular quest than in the squalor that surrounds you now.
But you do not seem to have followed the advice I gave you,
to go and see a priest and let him probe your hidden depths.
I will not, therefore, pursue the matter. I cannot waste endless
time on you. The living, who merely pass by, can only interest
me in passing. And besides, if you yourself turn aside from

this path, so much the better : it is a sign that God did not intend you for it. There may be false stirrings of life in a dead soul : some people know this – from experience. I may have been mistaken about you.

You tell me you suffer. That could stand you in lieu of prayer, if you had no other way. Suffering is the prayer of those who neither think nor pray. I do not know the nature of your temptations, but I believe that to be tempted is a sign of God's grace; if you did not interest him, he would leave you in peace. Perhaps, in the state of peril in which I saw you, this temptation will save you. Even supposing that the temptation means not God's presence but his absence, there is probably not a single saint who doesn't feel God appear and disappear in his soul in rapid succession. The soul is like a sunny sky dotted with little clouds which veil it from one moment to the next.

I too have my temptations regarding you, and I am torn between them : the temptation to point you towards God, as one takes a dog by the collar and points it : 'Fool, that's where it got up', and the temptation to abandon you to your nothing-ness – which you will feel at last when I am no longer there.

Believe me, Mademoiselle, yours sincerely,

Costals

I must remind you that I am not a believer.... If I looked for God, I should find myself.

I reopen my letter to add this. I make no secret of the fact that last night, when I wrote the above, I intended to abandon you. You had let me down. But the other alternative remains. I shall have pity on you next Saturday at six o'clock in the evening; and I specify this hour because I shall be with someone from whom I can draw this power of pity. But beware – I shall have pity on you in a certain way, and in a particular direction. And you have no idea of the mysteries of pity. *I* know all about them.

Andrée Hacquebaut   to Pierre Costals
Saint-Léonard   *Paris*

1 June 1927

'Another endless letter! The girl must be mad! God, how mad the girl is! And how right Ecclesiastes (or Solomon) is when he speaks of the misfortune of falling into the dreams of an ardent woman!' That's what you're thinking, isn't it? Well, no, for once I'm not going to bore you this morning. I feel a little better.

Why do I feel better? I have the impression that in my last few letters I've rambled a good deal, and that now I see the situation more clearly for what it really is. First of all because I went to the hairdresser two days ago, which means that my hair now looks nice (it takes at least that long!), and looking at myself in the mirror with the thought that these horrible days must have added ten years to my age, I find my face more or less the same (indeed it's unbelievable how often I've been told since my trip to Paris how young and smart I look). And then because the weather has become overcast, there's no longer that intoxication of summer that seemed to mock my suffering – today's weather is like autumn, and next autumn, for me, will be *different*: I shall have other clothes than those in which I've suffered so much . . . a kind of superstition. . . . Hope has hoisted sail once more. Would you ever have thought that dull, grey weather could bring the promise of happiness?

Hope . . . promise. . . . That pact of hope constantly renewed with myself! That perpetual waiting! For four years now I've waited for a sign from you. I've given you everything, and had nothing in return. You haven't kissed me once in four years. If I were dead, would you give me a kiss at last? Why, oh! why, since it would cost you so little to leave me at least one souvenir which I passionately desire, when you have hundreds of such souvenirs and I shall never have another in the whole of my arid life? For one spontaneous kiss from you I would have given ten years of your friendship without a moment's hesitation.

There's an anomaly in your attitude: you love and yet you

give nothing. When one loves, one gives; it's a natural impulse. *Your* motto seems to be: 'Avoid giving at all costs.' It's so abnormal that I might be tempted to believe that you do not love me. But there's no question that you love me; I should have to be very blind not to have noticed it: women have an infallible instinct in these matters.

You tell me you do not love me. You try as hard as you can to persuade yourself of it. If I knew that you didn't love me, if I was certain that making love to me would be a penance for you, then I would give up of my own free will, for I'm too proud even to beg for anyone's love. But there it is. I'm certain that the opposite is the case. I know that, without having a devouring passion for me, you love me all the same. Was I dreaming when I read the tenderness in your eyes? Did I dream that the idea of our marrying crossed your mind when we visited the flat in the rue Quentin-Bauchart? Did I dream that you held my hand in yours on the 16th of May last year, that you held my arm and pressed close to me as we walked that day in the square des Etats-Unis, that you confided in me that same day, poured out your heart to me (about your regrets at not being a father)? Did I dream that once, when you were late for an appointment with me and I asked you why, you replied: 'Ask me rather why I came at all!' Do you know what made me aware of your affection? In May 1926, our legs touched in a taxi, and at once you drew yours away, sharply. I realized then that you loved me with your soul. 'The woman one does not enjoy is the woman one loves.' (Baudelaire)

If you are so sure that you do not love me, kissing me would be like kissing a stone. Why, then, do you resist so vehemently? Why don't you invite me to your house any more? Why don't you take me somewhere where we could dance and drink champagne? Then we would see what happened. It really is too stupid of you to pretend that you don't desire me, when you do everything in your power to exorcize this desire.

For four years, in your company, I have felt overwhelmed by your shyness. You want to make an advance, but you dare not. With women whom you don't love with your soul, you can dare all right. With me, you lose your head. Perhaps, too, you think me frigid! It was delightful for a time, but it has gone on too long. It's too absurd to be afraid of me.

If I were to take you at your word, if – however improbable it may seem – you did not want my love, there would be only one way of breaking it off, and that would be to convince me that you do not love me. But you couldn't because you *do* love me. You see what an inextricable jungle-growth you've got yourself entangled in! Inextricable for you – though a child of two could get out of it. You make me smile, you know. It just shows that a person of genius can be at the same time an idiot. Nothing could be more ludicrous than your attitude towards me – always on the defensive.... You poor, poor child!

Do, please, let yourself go at last. You hold yourself back, and you suffer from doing so. Is this wise? How can you allow the light I kindled in you to fade? How can you return to your barren, loveless solitude, when salvation is there, close by, with its naked arms outstretched, and its fresh face, and all the deep-down things inviolate? Never again will you find a woman like me. Never again will God hold out his hand to you.

Yours,
Andrée

P.S. My friend Raymonde has just left. I have always kept her informed – in a general way – about our *liaison*. She asked me how things stood. When I told her there was nothing new, she exclaimed: 'Don't you realize that he couldn't care two hoots about you?' When I explained to her that your reserve was a proof of your love, she laughed in my face. I'm ashamed of being a woman when I see women as coarse as that. However, I would like you to authorize me to write to her – after a suitable lapse of time – and tell her that at last you have made me yours. Thus I shall feel more at ease when I speak to her again. Yes, authorize me to say, not only to Raymonde but to one or two other *reliable* friends: 'Costals is my lover.' You would be giving me the shadow of that happiness of which you refuse me the substance. And after all, you owe me that much at least.

This letter remained unanswered.

Thérèse Pantevin   to Pierre Costals
La Vallée Maurienne   *Paris*

Sunday

Yesterday, Saturday, at the hour when you were having pity on me – six o'clock – I was seized with violent palpitations. The Angelus went, and I knew then, by an inspiration from you, that those who were ringing it were among the 'false innocents', that they were the Gentiles preparing to go through the pretence of celebrating Corpus Christi tomorrow with lying pomp, and I was horrified by the noise of the bell. I was seized with a violent shuddering – my body quivered like the withers of a horse – and fierce stirrings of the bowels. Then I gave a loud shepherd's cry – they must have heard it as far as Noison's. I began to groan, and lay down prostrate on the floor with my arms outstretched; I felt it was the only place where I would be at ease. I shook my head from side to side, as though dazed and befuddled by the state I was in. Meanwhile, as soon as I had prostrated myself, little Marcel (my sister's child, he's two) began to cry so loud that they couldn't pacify him, so I had to sit up and fondle him. Then I lay back on the floor, which made the child start crying again. I took him on top of me, and he stayed there quietly. But I went on groaning, I felt my bowels stirring, I said all sorts of things, about the spirit of Babylon, you, our marriage, 'Sigara, who is the symbol of thirst', Lucifer, 'created in rejoicing'. I pressed little Marcel against my breast, against my face, between my legs, I kissed him over and over again, he splashed about in me, he was our son, I was drunk with child. Mamma wondered if they ought to call the priest, but Barbiat said no. So then Mamma got the missal and read the prayers of the Mass, the *Te Deum* and the *Magnificat*. After a time

Barbiat took little Marcel away from me. Then I began punching myself repeatedly and violently on both breasts at once, and that relieved me a little. I was still talking, but I can't remember anything I said. I hid in a corner. I crawled about on my knees. I clapped my hands. I asked Barbiat to breathe on me, which he did, and then the same thing with Mamma. All the time I was crying to myself and moaning: 'Ah, I'm dying.' I must have looked frightful (it's a pity you can't see how ugly I am). Eventually, when I had suffered enough, I told Barbiat to beat my breasts with a bundle of firewood. He did so, very hard, and I was delivered.

My beloved, I can say no more. Let me know when you have another great pity on me. Oh, how I long for it! But not for a few days – it's too shattering for me.

Marie

PITY FOR WOMEN

'God created everything for man's happiness. There's no sin in any of it. An animal, for instance, will sleep in the Tartar reeds or in ours. It makes its home wherever it happens to be; it eats whatever God provides.'

TOLSTOY, *The Cossacks*

(Spoken by a Chechen peasant, the Chechens being at war with the Tartars.)

In the town of N—, in 1918, there was a little girl of twelve whose family described her as a 'quiet little thing'. She had no friends, and played silently at home by herself for hours on end; she sat through whole meals, too, without saying a word. She was known as a tomboy because she liked going for long, solitary walks or bicycle-rides, and showed little enthusiasm for girlish things. Also because she was brave : in boats, in the dark, or left by herself in some lonely shed, she never showed the slightest fear. And yet she was shy. If the maid forgot to serve her at dinner, she made no complaint and went hungry.

At school she was a fair pupil, though this must be qualified by the fact that she was a year behind. From twelve to fourteen, attempts were made to teach her the piano, without success. From fourteen to sixteen she was tried on the violin : a waste of time. After these four years and the expenditure of thousands of francs, it was at last conceded that this child of silence had not the slightest gift for making noise; later, a wireless set had to be got rid of, so greatly did this machine exasperate her. Then her father, who could wield a pencil rather nicely, thought he would teach her drawing : soon he had to lay down his arms. The fact was, she had neither inclination nor aptitude for anything. M. Dandillot became worried. In order to get her to 'acquire a personality' he would leave her for a whole hour, her cheeks on fire, sweating over a letter to an old uncle or to her godfather : her instructions were to write something 'original'. 'Original'. . . . M. Dandillot himself was considered something of an original. The son of a public prosecutor, after a year at the bar he had abandoned pettifoggery and with it any idea of ever making money, although his own fortune was no more than adequate. From the earliest days of French athleticism (he had been twenty-one in 1887) he had developed a passion for these things and had founded a sports club in N—. He was particularly keen on swimming, of which he had become the apostle. In his middle years, since he was by no means unintelligent or uncultivated, he had given up sport itself for the wider problems of physical culture, and resigned the presidency of his club – which from then on he condemned as heretical – to throw himself heart and soul into the natural health cults which were then taking root in France: a photograph taken at the Institute of Athletics in Rheims and published in *l'Illustration* around 1910, shows M. Dandillot heavily bewhiskered and clad as a Greek shepherd. He solemnly broke with his worldly life, went so far as to get rid of his dress-clothes – symbol of all the sins of Babylon – and thereafter concerned himself solely with the open air, the sun, diets, measurings and weighings, immersed in terrifying charts of all the things man must and must not do in order to remain 'natural', and in what might be called the hard labour of the 'natural' life – in short, forever harping on nature, although he could reach it only through the most preposterous artifices, which would have poisoned the life of any reasonable person, even supposing they could be reconciled with the obligations of a normal existence, which clearly they could not. At the age of fifty, still pursuing the path of 'purity', M. Dandillot began to 'tolstoyize': man, in order to be truly 'natural', must also remain chaste, and love his fellow men; thus the hatred M. Dandillot had always had for his father, from being a simple filial hatred, became as it were sanctified by the heads which the prosecutor had been responsible for lopping off. Shrewd, deceitful, stubborn, naïve, with a mind dappled like a panther's skin with patches of luminous intelligence and patches of dark stupidity; a bachelor by vocation though a father and a husband, with the qualities and eccentricities of the bachelor; and singularly uncreative, to the extent of not having managed by the age of sixty to deliver himself of the modest little treatise on the 'natural life' which he had conceived before the war and which would have been a mere compilation of his favourite masters.... But we shall not describe M. Dandillot further; he will do this for himself in what is to follow.

In 1923, Solange's elder brother died in Madagascar, where he had gone farming, and the Dandillots moved to

Paris. Solange was made to take a domestic science course.

Nubile at fifteen years and three months, she had gone through puberty without any of the turmoil – the sensation of being physically sullied, the depression, the indignation, the secretiveness, the anxious, furtive glances at the parents, the hurry to get away from them when they are together, the vows to renounce love 'forever' – which one often comes across in pure and sensitive girls at that age. When she had asked her mother how babies were born, she had done so out of boredom, not because she was really interested. Her hair, once golden, had gradually turned black. Her eyes had narrowed a little, and they had a bluish tinge which appeared behind her dark lashes like the Mediterranean behind a curtain of pines. She was so pretty that hardly a day passed without her hearing exclamations from the men who passed her in the street. Like the two workmen in Toulon, for instance: 'Take a look at that! Isn't she a beauty?' It sometimes happened that Southern labourers would stop working one after the other as she went by. For it was in the South particularly that she was a success: she was too natural for the Parisians, who only like grotesquely 'dolled up' women. Yet she remained quite unspoiled. She was always in the back row at church, always a little in the background at family gatherings. And it was incredible to see this ravishing girl going out in the morning wearing an old, dowdy, worn-out dress. Never in her life had she bought a fashion magazine, though if she chanced to find one she would read it with apparent interest. It was not that she did not enjoy being attractive, but her enjoyment was not sufficient for her to go to great lengths in order to achieve it; when she had passed a damp finger along her eyebrows and her tongue over her lips, she felt she had done a great deal. She never went to the hairdresser, wore no jewellery, and did not use scent or lipstick – only powder, which she put on badly. And this was neither affectation – which would have implied pride – nor a matter of principle – for she did sometimes wear jewellery or paint her lips for a few days, or spend a whole afternoon doing her nails, carefully getting together everything she needed and then, when she had finished, scraping off all the varnish and going up to the attic to ruin her hands rummaging in old packing-cases. She always wore royal blue, and nothing would make her give it up: she was greatly praised for this. But one day she set her heart on a wine-coloured dress.

The *Lycée* at N— was strictly run. In the top form, only one in every six girls had a lover. Solitary practices were unknown and Solange did not even discover what they were until she was twenty-one. Only a few of the girls had 'crushes' on others, and all of them, without exception, were from convent-schools. When Solange, one day, had been caught letting another girl smother her with kisses, her 'But, Madame, there's nothing wrong with it between girls' had been the cry of innocence itself. Once she knew, she repelled the girl's advances. But she remained the ideal confidante to all her friends, who were soothed by her placidity and her good advice. She listened to everything they told her and never said a word about herself. If the truth be told, there was not a great deal to be said.

As for men, nothing. Purveyors of flattery were sent packing, often with a flea in their ears. She liked dancing, but regarded the men who held her in their arms merely as a means of achieving that pleasure: she would as soon have danced alone. In a little book with a rose-pink cover she kept a list of the houses where she had been invited to dances, but she did not keep a list of her partners, even in the cotillions; she merely noted down indiscriminately the names of the young men and girls of her acquaintance whom she met at such parties. When first one, then another confessor in Paris (the provincial ones had been most correct) asked her questions which displeased her, she stopped going to confession altogether. Her religion became that of most Catholics: going to Mass on Sunday. She had no faith, and her life was in no way guided by religion; yet if she had missed Sunday Mass it would have worried her, and she would have gone into a church for a few moments. The habit of not going to confession increased yet further the power she had of keeping her intimate thoughts to herself and also of pondering over everything she did; instead of casting it all into a dark corner, she held on to it and turned it over in her mind. From that day (when she stopped going to confession), she became more intelligent and more conscientious. What may seem strange is the fact that she realized this.

Her mother and father loved her dearly, and with some intelligence. She loved them too in her way, which at first they had found some difficulty in getting used to. No sudden bursts of affection towards them, never a charming word, never a thoughtful 'attention'. She even disliked the 'attentions' they had for her: 'I hate being fussed over.' If her mother stroked her hair, she would frown and narrow her eyes even more. Her 'No's' were as famous as her silences: she would wake from her dreams at night shouting 'No! No! No!' As a baby, if someone merely glanced at her without saying a word she would scream 'No!', and she used to throw a tantrum immediately on entering the street where her grandmother lived, because the old lady was liable to paw her with maniacal affection. At the *Lycée*, she had not remained a boarder very long because she pined for her parents so. Yet when her mother came to visit her, the child would sit by her side in the parlour for half an hour without saying a word: it was her way of loving her mother. Her father nicknamed her 'Miss Silence', or sometimes just 'Silence'. 'But why didn't you ever say anything nice to me in the school parlour?' 'It didn't occur to me.' Once, when her brother had tortured a kitten in front of her, squeezing its neck until it no longer gave any sign of life, she had watched it all with her eyes starting out of her head and made no attempt to save the little creature. 'But you loved Misti, didn't you? Why didn't you call somebody?' 'It never occurred to me.' It was true: nothing ever 'occurred to her'. However, once one had resigned oneself to her cold ways, there was nothing to complain of in her behaviour. 'She's cold, but she's gentle,' her mother used to say, 'and she has never given me the slightest trouble.' Indeed, it was not that she did not love her parents, but rather that, while she felt at ease with strangers, she was shy with those she loved. And if, when punished by her father, she kept out of the way and sulked, she was burning inside with the desire to go and kiss him. Only it wouldn't 'come out'.

She really was a 'quiet little thing' until the day when, her brother having slapped her, she had a genuine fit of hysterics (she was fourteen). But even at the height of it, still no tears. 'If you had cried, you would have felt better,' the doctor said.

'But I can't cry!'

'You mean you can't cry in front of other people? Or you can't cry at all?'

'I can't cry at all.'

During the thorough medical check-up that followed this episode (the unexpected violence of her nervous reactions had caused some alarm) it was discovered that her heartbeats were abnormal in number and intensity. Three years later, when she was about to be X-rayed and the electric light was switched off in the laboratory, she had another attack. The family diagnosis was altered. She was no longer a 'quiet little thing'; she was now a 'suppressed hysteric'. The description was not such a bad one: everything that came out of her seemed somehow damped down, like a noise stifled by a wad of cork or cotton-wool.

Whatever their experience to the contrary, men persist in believing that a character must be all of a piece. Yet it is only in artificially-created characters that unity is to be found; whatever remains natural is inconsistent. Mlle Dandillot's principal characteristic was her naturalness. There was great surprise when, an elderly young man having proposed to her, she showed both pride and delight: with the character attributed to her, it was assumed that she would send him packing. And so she did, but only after having granted him two interviews. Later, she refused two other proposals. She only wanted to marry a man who attracted her (she had at least discovered that!). The trouble was that none of them attracted her. Her parents did not want to force her. In this they were right; but they should have taken her out more. As it was, since they did not care for society, she met very few people. So the three of them settled down to wait for the husband the heavens would send. The fact that Mlle Dandillot had firmly and vehemently refused three good matches did not however alter the family's verdict that she 'lacked will-power', any more than the handsome fortune her brother was piling up in Madagascar altered the family's verdict on *him* – that he was not 'practical'. He had never been able to mend a fuse: therefore he was 'not practical'. In certain circumstances, Mlle Dandillot showed will-power, and in certain circumstances she was fatalistic. It is this 'in certain circumstances' that people always forget. And yet, having so often heard it said that she had no will-power, she had come to believe it herself. But if she exerted her will so seldom, it was perhaps because there was little she desired.

And thus she reached the age of twenty-one, which she had only just arrived at when she slipped into this tale. A good housewife, adept at dealing with the upholsterer or the electrician, an expert on food and liking only the best, thrifty in the house and a spendthrift on herself, squandering her small allowance on silly things that gave her no pleasure, she was nonetheless still very much a child, fighting with her brother, climbing trees, rushing down the stairs four at a time. Disliking dogs – too frisky – and birds – too noisy – she liked cats, being very cat-like herself, and above all aquarium fish, perhaps because they were silent like herself, and cold, with neurotic reflexes (watch them as they twist and turn). She had a continuous succession of them, for after a week they would be found floating belly upwards: she had forgotten to feed them. She read little – a few snippets – and in the forty-odd books that made up her little library there were only three novels, which were there by pure chance; as for poetry, the less said the better: she hated it as she hated music. Even then she was far from having read all her books, though all the pages had been cut and the volumes carefully wrapped in transparent paper. She went to a dance about once a month, and had to force herself to do so, such was her hatred of 'dressing up'. At the last moment she would hesitate whether to make an excuse and not go, but once she was there she was happy as could be, never missing a single dance and always the last to leave: it was enough to wear her poor mother out. Whereas on the days when she did not go out she was in bed by half past nine. In society, she was sometimes thought to be stuck-up, because she carried her chin a little in the air (on account of her very heavy bun, which pulled her head back).

Whereas her brother, at fifteen, had impatiently shaken off everything that reminded him of his childhood, and lived only for the future, she did not think of her future, but awaited it passively, huddling over her past instead, hoarding her school-books, her prizes, her volumes of the *Bibliothèque Rose*, filing away, as it were, the whole of her childhood, every relic of which she would have preserved in her bedroom had not her father from time to time impounded some beloved* toy-rabbit or porcelain Infant Jesus and taken it up to the attic. All of which will no doubt gratify the reader, for a woman without childishness is a horrible monster. And yet, though she remained so close to childhood, she was incapable of talking to children as girls of her age usually can, and felt bored and ill at ease in their company. In her state of romantic solitude, she felt peaceful and happy. Of course she realized that the day would come when all this would change (for, let me repeat, she was not guided by any principle and there was no 'theory' behind her coldness) but she did not yearn for that day, and could not in the least imagine what sort of change it might bring. 'One shouldn't organize one's life, it's unlucky', she used to say. If she had had any precise feeling about her future, it would have been fear, fear of being less happy than she was now, fear of being, as she put it in her typical little-girl idiom, 'disappointed'.

Thus Mlle Dandillot lived, in a placid key which the author has endeavoured to emulate in writing about her.

(We have omitted to mention that from the age of sixteen, that is some twenty years before the age at which a man, and a man of mature understanding, begins to have a few notions as to how he should govern himself, Mlle Dandillot knew how the State should be governed. Not being clever enough to embrace all political convictions at one and the same time, she restricted herself to one: she was madly right-wing. She even belonged to an extreme right-wing group, and had intended to work on one of its charity committees; but she had only gone twice, being too right-wing to be able to settle down to it. We shall not mention the group to which Mlle Dandillot belonged, since she has given herself to a gentleman.)

---

*' But you never talked to your rabbit!' 'I talked to him inside.'

Andrée Hacquebaut
Saint-Léonard

to Pierre Costals
Paris

7 June 1927

Dear Costals,

Status quo. The weather's too hot, I haven't the energy to suffer, at least to suffer acutely. I'm certainly unhappy, and prefer to be unhappy because of you than apply myself to being angry with you; but unhappy not with an unhappiness that tears me apart, but with a torpid unhappiness, always the same. The state of mind of one still anaesthetized after an operation, of a detached convalescent, of Lazarus rising from the tomb – a kind of indifference and meekness towards the world. 'Let them do as they like. All that's over for me.' Do not however mistake this meekness for benevolence. I no longer wish to be frank, nor to give pleasure. Thanks to you, I have become like you.

How strange it is, but I must admit it : failure can be satisfying, or at least can give one a feeling of repose not so very different, I imagine, from the feeling achievement brings. I summoned up my courage and took the plunge. And I failed. You denied me the only thing in the world I wanted. And yet, in spite of it all, something has been gained. Now, all that is being reabsorbed. ... What difference is there, when all's said and done, between a body that has known pleasure and one that has not? Renunciation ! The peace of the woman who has renounced. If you knew how simple it is, when one has renounced all one's life. How quickly one gets used to it. My love for you was always, *a priori*, counterpoised by renunciation. My only error was to believe that that impossible love was in fact possible, to believe that tenderness and pity were enough to waken desire in a man, to believe that love could be created in another person as water can be got by turning on a tap. My sacrifices have always been made in advance. And self-imposed suffering is almost ecstasy compared to the suffering imposed on one by others. And then (even though I haven't had my fill of memories of you, not by a long way), I have taken so much from you that it makes it easier for me to renounce it all.

I must add that if you came to me today and offered me the two months of plenitude I wanted, I should be afraid. I felt passionately that it would be better to lose you after than to lose you before. But now I'm frightened. Some enthusiasm on your part would have been essential. To obtain that from you as an irksome duty . . .

You made it clear to me that the greatest gift my love could offer you was to give you nothing unless you desired and asked for it. And I sometimes think that my love was not so much love as a desire for self-glorification. I regarded you, in fact, as an instrument of my pleasure and happiness. True love would have meant searching, not for what pleased me, but for what pleased you; and thus giving up what I wanted of my own free will. No doubt I must have loved you very imperfectly, since I could not bring myself to make this sacrifice. Perhaps you loved me better than I loved you, since you did not love yourself in me. And perhaps it is now that I am giving you the best of my love. But a lot you care about that . . .

For the first time, I can tell you that there is no need for you to answer me. You would be bound to hurt me, with your genius for sadistic phrases, whereas in your silence I re-create and re-discover you, such as I once loved you.

Yours,

A.H.

I should also like to put to you a rather difficult and delicate question. I should like to know whether it has ever occurred to you that you might perpetuate my love by transposing some aspects of it into one of your books. This desire has nothing to do with vanity. It's simply that it would give me the feeling that so much suffering had not been entirely in vain.

This letter remained unanswered.

On the evenings when Mlle Dandillot came to the flat in the avenue Henri-Martin, the first thing she did was to switch off the light. And a sort of ritual had developed. He would undress her little by little, while she stood there small and upright in front of him, in her habitual pose, her head bowed a little, gazing at him without an atom of false modesty out of her dark blue eyes which seemed even larger and darker – almost black – in the dim light of the room, as if they had absorbed some of the night's darkness (which was why this night hung so clear above the world). And thus, half-naked, she would seem like a new person, and he would say to her: 'My little one, is it really you?' And sometimes she would answer 'Yes', as though it were a question which demanded a precise answer. And already this 'yes' was in her night voice, her voice of love, that extraordinarily changed voice of night and love, veiled and high-pitched like the voices of those who are about to die – her little girl's voice, her baby girl's voice, the voice of a woman newly-born and the voice of a dying woman.

And now behold him, vibrant, enveloping her in his coils, while she remains standing, motionless, wordless, only turning her head to follow him with wide-open, unblinking eyes. as the cobra, motionless on its coils, turns its head according to the movement of the snake-charmer's face. He moves as in more ductile air, in the infinite power he has over her; he kisses her now here, now there, according to his whim or with no whim at all; he rests his eyes now here, now there, and each time, as if bewitched, she removes some flimsy garment from the place his eyes have pointed to. Now she stands naked and utterly pure, and still he enfolds her in his coils. Her legs are warm and fragrant as freshly-baked dough. Her belt has left a red weal at her waist, as though she had been whipped. He pulls out two tiny hair-pins from her chignon, the only two he can find (for he is such a fool). She pulls out the rest and hands them to him, one by one, in silence, and their number never varies. Now she stands with her hair over her shoulders, over her breasts with their soft, dune-like curves, more than ever sunk into her childhood; and sometimes it happens that her hair is still damp, like a forest after rain, because she has come to him straight from the swimming-bath. He takes it in his hands, and first he kisses the ends of it, where it is her without yet being quite her, almost foreign to her, like a river which, at the end of its course, no longer knows its mountain or its source. Tracing it back along its

T—T.G.—G

whole length, he at last comes to her and the faint odour of her warm scalp.

He comes back to her face and meets again – like an old acquaintance – the scent of her face-powder which he had forgotten. He wraps her hair around her neck. He spreads it over her mouth and searches for her lips through it. With one lock for the moustache and the rest for the beard, he turns her into a young lady of Saint-Cyr in the role of Joad. And now she is naked in front of the window, practically on the balcony. He warns her, but she does not stir. On crossing his threshold, she has entered a magic circle. . . .

Lying down, she did not seem very different from what she had been the first time. She lay there, innocent and peaceful, as natural as a little goat in the midst of the flock. Nearly always she kept her eyes closed, and when she opened them, light with dark flecks, she created both light and darkness at the same time; and then she would look at him with astonishment, her face so close to his it made her squint a little. And she would give him short, sharp kisses, like a bird pecking, three, four, five at a time, like constellations; and then a single one, sudden, violent, like a ball shot at goal, or like a lightning flash. In between long silences broken only by a half-hour striking or a towel slipping from the towel-rail in the bathroom, he would say:

'What are you thinking about?'

'How nice it is. . . .'

O little girl!

'How silent you are!'

'When I'm happy I never talk.'

O little girl!

(When I'm happy . . . Andrée had written the same thing, but he had not thought it to her credit, because he did not love Andrée.)

Then he would tease her.

'I'm going to switch on the light.'

Whereupon her 'No! No's!' would break out with unexpected violence. And he: 'What do you mean, *no*? Have we, by any chance, a personality of our own?' (The possibility did not seem to please him; and besides, caressing a woman in the dark is like smoking in the dark: no taste). But when after a moment he asked her: 'What would you do if I suddenly switched on the light?' she answered: 'Nothing....'

O little girl!

And oh! that night voice as she said it, the incredibly child-like intonations, rising from the depths of her childhood as from a tomb – that other voice that came to her as soon as she was 'horizontal', like those chaste dolls which automatically lower their eyelids when one lays them on their backs.

It was on one of these evenings that he wrote this poem for her:

> Since you love me, I you (that's understood)
> Since I am wholly yours today – agreed?
> Since it appears that either finds it good,
> For I suffice you, you are all I need,
>
> Then lay against my breast, sweet age-old child
> (Don't fear those other heads; their trace is light)
> Your scentless hair and your long eyes, beast-wild,
> More deep, more dark, for having drunk of night.

And so it went on, but we shall quote no more, for we do not think it is worth a tinker's curse.

He never failed to express a little more tenderness towards her than he really felt, to add to that tenderness a sort of halo which spread it further. For instance he would sometimes say 'My little darling' at times when the words did not spring spontaneously to his lips, or else he would clasp her in his arms with greater vigour than his natural impulse called for. He knew that women tend to think one loves them less when one does not love them more and more, and that men, being poor at loving, must keep a constant watch over themselves if they do not wish to disappoint.

There were moments when he passionately wanted to be the man who would reveal her to herself. There were other moments when he had no such desire.

He still did not take her completely, for he wished to go on picturing this unknown territory before him, as when on board ship one looks toward that part of the sea where land will appear tomorrow. He would stop at the precise point beyond which he would have hurt her, as a dog that bites its friend in play will check itself delightfully and take care not to go too far. But their kisses were so voracious that the tip of his tongue was split and he had to give up smoking.

He was always afraid she might catch cold while naked, and would willingly have sacrificed part of his pleasure to have her put on some of her clothes again. She would complain a little: 'You treat me like a child.' To which he would reply: 'A person one loves is always a child.' Often he reminded her of the time, but she did not seem to hear. Sometimes they would stay together in this way until that supreme hour of night when the cats settle down in the middle of the road to attend to their toilet. Clocks chimed the hour, answering one another like cock-crows. He had the impression that if he had not said to her, 'Time to go, little one', she would have stayed there all night, as though her mother and father did not exist. In all their relations, it was never she who took the initiative. And he praised her for it. 'I hate women with a will of their own, and that is why you were always made for me.' (And yet, if we are to believe Schopenhauer, who sees a connection between will-power and sexual passion, he would not have been sorry had she willed a little more....)

Now she went off to the bathroom without being told, like a kitten that has been house-trained. Meanwhile he brushed the left shoulder of his jacket, where her cheek had left a cloud of face-powder like a milky way deep in the night sky. And now here she was by his side in the avenue, striking the echoing pavement with her short, mule-like steps. What had happened? Had anything happened? Here she was, exactly the same as she had been when she arrived that evening. Terribly womanly, when a moment before she had been such a schoolgirl. Terribly intact in appearance, and yet no longer intact. Terribly prim and proper.

He knew she never told them at home why she got back so late at night. The thought that she lied to her parents was infinitely pleasing to him. 'That way, we can talk.' He felt that this made her somehow more human.

Sometimes they walked hand in hand, like well-brought-up children who have been told to go and play in the park and be good – or like Tunisian gendarmes.

At about that time he had just published a new book, which brought him many flattering letters and reviews. He had taken as his motto Gobineau's phrase, which he twisted round to read thus: 'First love, then work, then nothing.' But his work was his writing, not the relationship between his writing and the public. To this he was more or less indifferent. He skimmed rapidly through both reviews and letters mechanically, without getting involved. Praise was to him like musical instruments being played in a silent film: he knew that they must be producing a pleasant noise, but he could not hear it.

He was saying to her:

'You really must try and see things as they are. Michelet says that it's most humiliating for the loved one to keep enough composure to be able to distinguish the truth behind the lover's fine words. *There's* a piece of nonsense worthy of the 'stupid' nineteenth century. To keep one's composure is never humiliating. And to see things as they are is always admirable. The fact, in our case, is that I am not in love with you. What I feel towards you is, on the one hand, affection tinged with tenderness, together with esteem, and on the other hand, desire. But all this does not constitute love, thank God. It makes up something which is my own particular formula, in which I am entirely myself, and which is wholly commendable: this last point alone would be sufficient to prove that it isn't love. For one likes a woman *because*, and one loves her *although*. Besides, experience leads me to believe that my formula pleases women, because according to my own observation they seem to need affection and tenderness more than love properly so called. You're not in love with me either, are you?'

She shook her head and shrugged her shoulders slightly, with an amused expression on her face – all this very young-lady-like and full of charm. And she said:

'Not exactly, no, I don't think so. . . . I mean I don't love you in a sentimental way.'

'There's one sure sign that you don't love me; you never ask me questions about my life. And you don't blush when your parents talk about me, do you? You've never looked me up in *Who's Who*? You never came round to the avenue Henri-Martin when we first met, to see the house I lived in? You've never scribbled my name on a sheet of note-paper for no reason at all?'

To each question she shook her head with the same gentle and amused expression on her face. True, the night after he had kissed her for the first time, she had gone to sleep with one of his books under her sheet. But that was right at the beginning; nature had blundered because it had been caught unawares. Never again had Solange done anything of the kind.

'It's true, isn't it? Before I brought you here myself, you never had enough curiosity to come and see where I lived? Then that settles it: you've never been in love with me. And that's how I want you to be. A loving girl, not a girl in love. I don't want you to get worked up about me. You would be bound to suffer, and it would be absurd for you to suffer on my account when all I want is your happiness. One must know how to handle the absurd, my dear, and I think I can say I'm a master of the art, but it should at least give you some pleasure. It's always stupid to suffer. To say that suffering is something great and remarkable is one of the worst lies spread around by the leaders of the masses (for political ends) and then taken up by the intellectuals (from sheer stupidity). At the end of your first fairly intimate letter you assured me of your 'tender affection'. I don't know whether it was a phrase you just happened to use by chance or whether you had weighed its meaning, but if it represented what you really felt, then it was magnificent, since it corresponds exactly both to what I feel towards you and what I expect from you.'

'I wrote that because it seemed to convey just what I felt.'

'Then, my dear, it's splendid, and I can see that we shall get on famously.'

And yet, that same evening. . . .

That same evening, when he asked her: 'Will you come to my flat for a while, later on?' she answered: 'Not tonight if you don't mind ... Perhaps we ought to space out our meetings a little. . . .'

And she added:

'When I come to visit you, afterwards I feel you're further away from me ...'

Although disappointed, he did not take her up on this. They were crossing the Place de la Concorde. He made a few remarks about the colour of the sky at that twilight hour. But inwardly he was turning to stone. Not only was he wounded in his male vanity, but it seemed to him as though she had locked the door on the future: how could he ever make love to her again after that?

There was a long silence, and then he asked her:

'Would you like me to take you home, or would you like to go somewhere?'

It was a terrible thing to suggest leaving her so early, contrary to all their habits, merely because of frustrated desire -- terrible for a girl of Mlle Dandillot's temperament; and terrible for him too. He had hoped she would answer: 'Take me home.' How could she not have realized that she had made the evening untenable? He was surprised at what he deemed her lack of tact when she said: 'Let's go somewhere.'

The cinema is the cesspool of the twentieth century. Whenever there is something vile between two people, it always leads to a session at the pictures. In the cinema near the Invalides where they finally landed up, she tried from time to time to make small talk. He, as though the muscles of his tongue had been severed, found it literally impossible to say a word. He was convinced that they were meeting for the last time. No, never had a woman said anything so humiliating to her lover; he had thought his caresses brought them infinitely closer to each other, but they made her feel he was further away! Now he wanted to wound her in his turn. 'She may as well know what I'm really like?' During the two and a half hours the show lasted, he never once opened his lips. As it was very hot, she sometimes put her handkerchief (her minute little girl's handkerchief) to her forehead, to her nose – to her eyes perhaps – and he wondered whether she wanted to cry. He noticed that one of her hands was resting in a rather unnatural way on the arm of her seat next to him, and thought she must have put it there so that he would take it and hold it in his. He did no such thing. Once or twice, too, she turned her face towards him without saying anything, as though asking to be kissed. The more he realized how base and vulgar, how petty and ridiculous – how bourgeois, in short – his attitude towards her was, the more he stuck to it. During the intervals he could read the thoughts on the faces of those around him : 'Such an exquisite little thing, and such a ghastly, sulking brute! Talk about pearls and swine!' What sickened him most about the 'scene' he was creating was that it seemed to him the very image of a conjugal row.

At last, the torture came to an end. They went out, still silent. Then she did something she had *never* done before : she put her arm through his. He was touched. This gesture seemed to say, with the utmost simplicity : 'Come back to me. Can't you see I'm not cross with you?' Yet, touched as he was by her gesture, at the same time he saw in it a way of hurting her even more : simply by not responding to it. However, when they reached the avenue de Villiers and passed her door without her showing any sign of stopping, he exploded. In a jerky, unrecognizable voice he blurted out : 'You have wounded me deeply. You have said the very worst thing a woman can say to a man. Now I can never touch you again. I shall always think that you let me make love to you out of complaisance, when in fact you feel nothing but disgust. . . .'

'Of course not, you know very well. . . .'

'To hell with girls – especially winsome, frigid little French girls who never know what pleasure is before they're twenty-six! After all, nobody has yet found any other way for a man to show his affection for a woman. No, there's no way out of it. I can't make love to you any more now. And as for playing at brother and sister, frankly it's impossible; I'm not that kind of man. You gave yourself, and now you've taken yourself back; but you did give yourself, and the taste of it will always remain. You opened the door on to a room filled with music, and now you have shut it again. . . .'

She said nothing. They went on walking, going round the block for the third time.

'And then, how can I dare talk to you again? What value

can you ever again attach to what I say? I told you a dozen
times: "Above all, you must be frank with me." And it's by
being frank that you've destroyed everything. You're being
punished for being what I asked you to be. And so from now
on I can neither talk nor act with you. It isn't your fault. It's
simply that our temperaments are incompatible. But I repeat,
there's no way out of it.'

Once again they reached her door. She would have gone on;
it was he who stopped. He held out his hand:

'Since we're seeing each other at the d'Hautecourts' tomorrow, we're bound to talk to each other again. But in fact
everything is over between us.'

He saw her raise her beautiful eyes towards him, full of
surprise, sadness and reproach, as a bitch gazes at the brute of
a master who has struck her for no reason. A taxi passed, and
he hailed it. His voice was so strangled that he had to repeat
his address several times before the driver understood it.

At home he found the bed prepared, and the armfuls of
flowers he had arranged for her. He threw himself on the bed
in an agony of suffering. Suffering from having made her suffer.
Suffering from having made her suffer although he loved her.
Suffering from having made her suffer for being honest with
him. Suffering from having deprived himself of her body.
Suffering because he suffered from having deprived himself of
her body, although her body gave him so little pleasure. Suffering because he suffered only in the basest part of his male self
(his sexual vanity) and because this male suffering was so very
puerile. Suffering, not least, because the room was so hot
(eighty degrees Fahrenheit). At intervals, a petal fell from a
vase like the chime of the half-hour. The intimate odour of the
girl's body came back to him obsessively, exacerbating his resentment, a wisp of fragrance that seemed to float about the
room like seeds borne on the summer air. Finally he thought of
going to the larder for a cold chicken which he knew was
there. He ate it, and his anguish died away. He even felt glad
that he had suffered a little. One must try everything once.

That night he had a dream. He dreamed of the old English
governess he had had as a boy. Never in his life had he

dreamed of her before. And try as he might, he could find no clue to what the dream meant.

He began to think about the woman, and a strange memory came back to him. He remembered his terror when, waking up in the early morning, he used to imagine that perhaps, during the night, she had gone away for ever. Then he would get up and go barefooted to the governess's room. Objects, clothes, everything would be in place: the Englishwoman had simply gone to Mass, as she did every day. But such irrefutable evidence was not enough to reassure him. He would tiptoe on to the landing and wait there with beating heart for the rattle of the returning governess's key in the front door (for, after all, he must have realized that she was at Mass). Then as soon as he heard the noise of the key, he would rush back to bed and pretend to be asleep. . . .

All this would have been easy to understand if he had had some sort of childish crush on his governess (he was then seven or eight years old). But nothing of the sort. On the contrary, he rather disliked her. She rapped his knuckles with a ruler when he made mistakes in his piano lessons, she left him – without a word – crying for half an hour at a time because he could not make head or tail of his arithmetic, she took the currants out of his fruit cake at tea-time, pretending they were bad for him when really she wanted them herself. . . He liked her so little that when she retired, although she settled in Paris, he had never once been to see her. No, however carefully he ransacked his memory, he could find nothing in his feelings for her except indifference tinged with resentment – nothing but indifference, with here and there those wild uprushes of passionate feeling, those torments of the tiny lover, at half past six in the morning, in the great, slumbering house. . . .

Costals began to wonder whether he did not love Solange.

The next day, a hop at the d'Hautecourts'. A few women's bodies would make it bearable. What would society be without bodies? One could see it wiped out without a murmur.

Arriving after her, he followed her with his eyes without letting her see him. He would have liked her discreetly to show her contempt for all these people; but no, she seemed at ease among them; was she, perhaps, one of them? She danced three times with a young buck. 'If they go and sit behind the buffet, or on the stairs, I feel – yes, I feel it as if it were happening at this very moment – that all the blood will drain from my face, will drain from my legs as if it were flowing away under the ballroom floor.'

He came towards her with an ugly expression on his face – an unwonted ugliness, a husband's ugliness. She greeted him, suddenly transformed, her face open, her eyes radiant with tenderness, as though nothing had happened the day before. He was touched by her unquestioning trust.

They danced. He was thinking: 'Am I going to be the ignoble male to the bitter end? Yesterday I was cruel and unjust because my petty sexual pride had been hurt. Tomorrow I shall debase myself by resuming my love-making, knowing that she merely tolerates it. This body in my arms in front of two hundred people – I have laid my head on its naked belly (an exquisite sensation); with my cheek against that belly, I have heard the rumbling of her intestines, like the faint sound of thawing snow. . . . In fact, by God, she's mine!'

And he let them see it all right. The dance over, an astonishing thing occurred. No sooner had they sat down beside each other than he put his hand on the girl's thigh (over her dress), and then let it rest on her midriff, as a lion spreads out its paw over the chunk of meat it has conquered.

Not in some secluded corner, but right in the middle of the room, surrounded by two hundred people. Not for a brief instant, but for a good half-minute, perhaps. Not in any dubious or 'advanced' company, but among well-bred, respectable people. That's what comes of inviting poets to your house!

He was deeply aware of the element of the grandiose in his gesture. Nothing licentious. The gesture of the couple. The primitive gesture of the lord and master, that of the ape with its mate: the essence of the couple. And he was also aware of the grandeur there was in the fact that she accepted it, that this reserved and modest girl did not flinch under his gesture, did not offer the least resistance, in the heart of that crowd, as though she did not care in the least, as though she were pleased even, that it should be demonstrated in this extraordinary manner, in front of everybody, what she was to the man she had chosen.

When he drew his hand away, yet another link had been forged between them. Invisibly, his hand was still upon her. That same evening she came to his house at the accustomed hour.

Andrée Hacquebaut   to Pierre Costals
Saint-Léonard   *Paris*

15 June 1927

Please read the whole of this letter.
Dear Costals,
I am far away, defenceless, sick with loneliness, crushed by such heat that it reminds me of that line of yours:
'The heat of the day sits, man-like, upon the earth.'
There was a big thunderstorm last night, and I was glad it woke me up since it gave me the chance to think about you. What was I saying in my last letter? I don't make a rough draft of my letters to you, and I'm afraid they must contradict one another terribly. I think I was telling you I had found a kind of peace ... Yes, I wanted, with genuine good-will, to safeguard our friendship through this ghastly business, although I know only too well how little a man cares for a woman's friendship when he cares nothing for her love. When you refused me, I thought: 'For him, of course, the woman who refuses herself is desirable, and the woman who offers herself is disdained. How childish!' But it has to be admitted: a disappointment, a refusal, makes what was desirable a thousand times more desirable. I can see it now with you.

Besides, how could I forget you? The fact that you are now a public figure (the same word for a 'public figure' and a 'public woman'! How appropriate....) makes it *physically* impossible. In order to be free of you completely, I ought never to open a newspaper or a magazine. And by the way, there's something I'd like to know.... Yesterday's *Nouvelles littéraires* (which I read – horror of horrors – in the deserted church,

204

because it's the only cool place here) brought me your poem:
'Since you love me, I you. . . .'
and I should like to know whether, when you wrote it, you
did not have me partly in mind. I very much doubt it, and
yet. . . . But no, of course not, it's addressed to someone else,
and I can just see you sneer: 'How naïve the girl is!' Naïve!
You have only yourself to blame: you could have made me a
woman, but you did not choose to. These amorous confidences
you spread around in the weeklies (isn't it nice to be able to
indulge one's exhibitionism in the sacred name of Art?) twist
the dagger in my wound, filling me with jealousy and desire.
It's too obvious: my love for you fills you with horror. But
what am I supposed to do about it? I think of you from morning till night. It oozes out of me. I was about to say like an
emanation, but the word is too pretentious; like sweat, rather.
You passed too close to me, you swept me, lonely little star
that I am, into your orbit, and you scorched me with your
fires. In all good faith, I still want to believe it is so. Man-
slaughter, not murder. You have annihilated me; I'm not
humiliated, I'm not torn apart, I'm stunned. You have made me
unfit for everyday life. I am like one of those antiques about
which dealers say to one: 'Yes, it's beautiful. It's worth a lot.
I can't buy it from you, though; they're not in demand just
now. But it's lovely, hang on to it.' I know I'm worth something, but no one has a use for me. And I shall end up by
hating myself, by destroying myself perhaps, as one ends by
hating and sometimes destroying those objects which antique
dealers find so beautiful but which nothing on earth would
make them buy. Yes, unusable. Because of you, I have nothing
to offer the man who might now come along expecting and
desiring someone intact; I would be giving him an empty husk.
It's *exactly* as if I had had a lover or a husband; my moral
virginity no longer exists. How can you not feel that all
this gives you a responsibility towards me, that you must
make amends? And by making amends I mean giving me the
satisfactions of the flesh to which I am entitled.

Your disinterestedness is a subtle form of perversion. You
told me once, parodying the motto of *l'Action Française*: 'We
stand for everything natural.' Oh, no! you are not close to

nature; that is perhaps your greatest illusion. It is saintliness you stand nearest to, but a sort of inverted saintliness, a diabolical saintliness. Ceaselessly preoccupied with you as I am, I learn a little more about you each day, in spite of your silence. I learn more about myself too. You once admitted to a certain 'curiosity' about me (and I have come to believe that it is the only feeling – a professional one at that! – you have ever had towards me). You might perhaps have desired me if I had not revealed so much of myself in my letters: it is the great misfortune of my life that, owing to my loneliness, nearly everything between us has happened by way of letters. But are you sure you really know me? Do you know whether, even *professionally*, a more intimate relationship between us might not reveal much more? Are you sure you don't actually *need* me?

You will never find me again unless, some day, you feel that need – but it must be total. I shall be your mistress or your wife, never again your friend. You will come back to me, if you do, knowing that I love you, that I adore you, that I have never wanted and do not want anything but your kisses and your arms around me. Are you satisfied? Is that clear enough? I feel a kind of wild relief in reaching these depths of self-abasement, in renewing the written proof of it, in giving you these weapons you will always be able to use against me.

Andrée

This letter remained unanswered.

'Just her legs alone, and I go mad!' he exclaimed, heedless of syntax. 'Look at that lovely little creature, old thing. Extraordinary how a pretty face can make you sit up. Suddenly, when you were sated to the point of not caring if you died, you want to go on living. Suddenly, if you had to write, you'd have forgotten how to spell. Eighteen, think of it! And arms even prettier than yours. And those vaccination marks! Enough to drive the archangel Gabriel to perdition. Quite frankly, my dear, I could gobble her up. She blows her little nose behind her newspaper (rather conservative in tone) so that

I shan't see her do anything so unbecoming. Then with her rosy fingers she stuffs the handkerchief back into her bag. Every time she catches me eyeing her, she moistens her lips with the tip of her tongue. And the way her shoulders shake when she laughs! And the parting in her hair, meandering all over the place! And her ears – I bet they've never known earache! And there's a hint of poverty in the cloth of her dress, in her little wrist-watch, that makes me swoon with desire. What power on earth could prevent me from desiring her? I'd like to know what her hair would taste like if I chewed it. I'd like. . . . She's worthy of desire, and so I desire her: it's only nature, after all, damn it! Oh, only *desire* her, you understand: I'm not breaking things up. But when I see those rather heavy veins on her pulpy feet in those sandals, then I tell you, old girl, I begin to feel like a man. Am I being wounding? Yes, I see I am. . . . I'm so sorry. . . . But what can I do, old girl? I belong to a sex which is the complete opposite of yours; I belong to the lecherous breed of men. What I enjoy is seeing what women are like when they surrender, and then comparing. . . . What is happiness, for those of my race? Happiness is the moment when someone surrenders. And incidentally, mystics often change their women, because attachment to one person is what is most contrary to the spiritual life. You too are a tiny star among thousands of others. And at dawn you'll fade away. . . . Ah! so I have wounded you? I recognize that way you have of smiling when something's gone wrong. . . . I haven't said anything unpleasant, though, have I?'

'Oh, no! Nothing at all!'

'And anyway, what I've been telling you was set to dance music, so to speak. You're not much of a sport, are you?'

'What's the good of explaining? You refuse to understand what you mean to me.'

'Yes, I do refuse. Because I ought not to mean too much to you.'

She turned her face towards him sharply, with a look of reproach. Then he said:

'I'm glad you love me, but I don't want you to love me too much. I'm glad my desire pleases you, but I don't want it to please you too much. For that would force me to exaggerate, to go beyond what comes to me naturally; in both spheres it would saddle me with a duty to reciprocate exactly; and this I dread, not only because it's duty (and duty doesn't suit me) but because it would drive me to artifice, which for the moment I'm entirely devoid of. What I want is for you to love me and to welcome my desire precisely to the extent that I love and desire you. And believe me, that's a great deal.'

Written the next day by Costals in the Bois, on the blank page of *l'Education des Filles*, which he was reading:

Two ravishing little things, fifteen and sixteen, straight out of Meleager, sitting on a bench with their mother who obviously.... Well, with their mother who knows a thing or two. (They were each swinging one leg, like two little donkeys swinging their tails in unison. Oh, to spend a night with one of those feet in my hands!) And it seems to me that merely by looking at them as I do, over there in the avenue de Villiers, suddenly, without knowing why, while she is sewing, her heart is pierced and it bleeds. O Nature, spare me from desiring others as long as I love her!

Mlle Dandillot's predominant feeling now she was in love was the fear that Costals might not love her enough and might abandon her. Faced with her first man, she was like a bas-relief changed into a statue – deprived of its support, suddenly alone and threatened on all sides. Before she loved, her nights had been uneventful. Now each night brought its dreams, always unpleasant dreams, though they never developed into nightmares. For instance, she dreamed that, cycling down a slope, she lost control of her bicycle; but that was all: there was no fall, no precipice. Or she dreamed that a cow broke away from the herd and approached until it was almost touching her, but did not attack her. Costals, the cause of all these dreams, never appeared in them: he was the hidden demon behind them. Sometimes, however, she dreamed, not about him, but that she was thinking about him.

There are women who are invigorated by love, particularly

a first love. Mlle Dandillot, on the contrary, ever since she had been in love, had physically declined. And it was fear of losing Costals that had weakened her. Often she felt below par, tired out, needing to sit down; when she had been standing for a while, her thighs ached.

At meals, the need to find an outlet for her nervous energy made her chew rapidly and vigorously. Having thus finished each course before her mother, she took second helpings to fill the gaps, and found herself eating appreciably more than usual. Then she noticed that she felt stronger after these large meals, and that as soon as she started over-eating, it was again in her thighs that she first felt better.

From then on, whenever she was due to meet Costals later in the day, she systematically took second helpings, which brought a smile to the face of the maid serving at table, a smile to which Solange responded sweetly, not knowing quite whether Suzanne had guessed her secret. She also had two cups of coffee, and could easily have managed two breakfasts. She was to be seen chewing away at peach-stones till they were worn down and cracked, as a dog worries a croquet-ball with its slobbery mouth. And although she was normally a non-smoker, she would now sometimes smoke two strong cigarettes one after the other. Yet Mme Dandillot noticed nothing (and as for her husband! . . .). Thus the servant saw what the mother didn't. It is said that mother-love is blind. Yes, indeed.

If Mlle Dandillot had not been such a good little girl, she would have known that a few drops of alcohol would have produced the same factitious vitality she obtained by ever so slightly stuffing herself. But she did not know this, or even guess it. And in any case the world in general does not know it either. Or rather it knows it *a little*, which is tantamount to not at all. A war-leader knows that, in battle, a good army is an army that is slightly the worse for drink. But he does not generalize from the fact as he should. A man who knew that there is no torment of love that a *really* good meal cannot dispel, at least for a few hours, a man who knew that physical and moral courage, poetic inspiration, devotion, sacrifice, may all depend on a good meal — that the most sublime flights of the soul may be due to the rotting flesh of dead animals — a man who knew all this could never be fooled by anyone. But the man who is on the brink of knowing all this shrinks from the knowledge. And if he does know it, he behaves as if he didn't. For man must live in the clouds.

On the other hand, Costals' meals before his meetings with Solange were very light. He was naturally so healthy and eupeptic that a little hotting-up would merely have decreased his lucidity, which he prized above everything. At these meals he even refrained from drinking, and thus weighing himself down, and only drank on the days when he did not love her so much. So that, when Solange was getting ready to leave, the first thing he did was to go to the wash-basin for a drink of water. And if Solange had failed to turn up at the rendezvous he had given her, which was always a few steps away from the house in the avenue de Villiers, his disappointment would have been offset by the fact that, after waiting twenty minutes, he could dive into the nearest wine-shop. He had elevated into a philosophy of life what had at first been no more than a delightful characteristic: to love (and to be capable of doing) in everything its opposite. Thus fate, whether it gave him a yes or a no, satisfied him equally. And he was always on velvet, which was very pleasant for him, and even satisfied his mind, for he held that only dullards and mock philosophers conceive of life as a struggle.

She had said: 'Come and have tea with me on Sunday. Mummy and Daddy are spending the day with some cousins of ours in Fontainebleau, and it's the servants' day off. We shall be alone in the flat.' The idea of making love to her in her own house, in her own little-girl's bedroom, had set him on fire.

It was an exquisite sensation to find her alone in the empty house and to see her switch off the front door-bell. But soon he noticed a slight sore on her lip, and dark rings under her eyes which intensified the depth of her gaze. She confirmed what he had guessed; and his feelings took on a new note of solemnity, as when the piano pedal is pressed down. These were the times he always loved best in women, when he knew them to be unwell: this weakness in them fanned his heart as much as his senses. However much they protested that they hardly felt it, he fussed and worried, convinced that they were simply being brave and really needed nursing. He had always had a tendency to pamper women, even sports-women, in spite of the impression they sometimes give of having more stamina than men.

And now they were in the drawing-room, sitting side by side on a sofa. The cloudy summer day seemed more like autumn. At first they had talked about trivialities (but how touching she was when, gazing straight in front of her, she would swiftly turn her head towards him whenever he said something particularly nice or striking). He had asked her to take him into her bedroom, but she, who usually agreed to anything he asked, had this time firmly refused. He had asked her to show him some photographs of herself, but she had not been photographed since she was fourteen – so lacking in vanity all these people were! Eventually he came to a subject which was very much on his mind. The last time she had been to his house, he had embraced her with an ardour so intense and so frequently renewed that at the end of the evening, while he was getting dressed, he had been overcome with a sort of nervous prostration: he had suddenly gone silent and numb, and heavy with weariness. He had to make a real effort to drag out a few commonplace remarks as he escorted her home. So now he explained that men, after having given too generously of themselves, are subject at times to such temporary diminutions of vitality, that this is a normal and recognized phenomenon, and that, assuming she had noticed it, she should excuse it in him. But had she in fact noticed it?

He had put the question almost casually, and was surprised and a little worried when she said 'Yes'. Did she notice everything, then?

'What about the other occasions?'

'Then, too.'

His surprise increased. On other occasions, either this collapse did not occur, or if it did, it was so slight and fleeting that he thought he had managed to conceal it under a renewed outburst of caresses. 'Goodness! The girl sees everything!'

'But how astonishing! You really did find me distant, those other times, when I was taking you home?'

'Yes. I wondered why. Whether I'd disappointed you. . . . '

He started explaining afresh, citing the *Omne animal post* . . ., offering to show her medical textbooks. Meanwhile he kept gently tugging at the little hairs above her elbow (a detail worth mentioning, after all). Suddenly he fell silent. It seemed to him as though his eyes were being opened at last.

'But then, when you said to me: "Afterwards you seem further away from me", is that what you meant?'

'Yes.'

He repeated the words to himself: 'Afterwards, you seem further away from me.' For the first time he realized it could be interpreted in two different ways: either that, after their love-making was over, Solange felt colder towards him, or else that she felt that he was colder towards her. An abyss separated the two meanings. How had he managed to see only the first and not the second?

'Look here, Solange, this is extremely important: did you feel you were further away from me after we'd made love, or did you, on the other hand, find that I was further away from you, colder towards you?'

'I found you colder towards me. I could sense in you the reactions which you've just described, as a blind man feels a Braille text with his fingertips. But I didn't know there was a purely physical reason for it.'

'What an incredible misunderstanding! I understood just the opposite. But why on earth didn't you explain? You let me sulk for hours and make a frightful scene, and all the time you say nothing, you just stand there gaping at me like a sick calf. . . . When all you had to say was: "It's *you* I find so cold, afterwards. . . . " '

She made a slightly impatient, rueful gesture.

'You know how hopeless I am at explaining. I've told you often enough. The more I saw you going off on the wrong tack, the more paralysed I became. Often when I'm with you, I feel stupefied. . . . The first time, in the Bois . . . if you had told me to jump into the water, I would have done it.'

'Yes, I know. And may I point out to you that I did not do

so. But still, I've never known such an incredible misunder-standing. You could never put anything like it into a novel. Nobody would believe that a twenty-one-year-old Parisienne, in the year 1927, could allow herself to be upbraided for hours by her lover for having said something which merely expressed her fear of seeing him grow cooler towards her, in other words for expressing nothing but affection, and all because she's hopeless at explaining? But you're crazy, my dear girl, absolutely crazy! A real little artichoke, on a railway embankment!'

'Why a railway embankment?'

'Because that's much nicer, of course!'

With a feeling of deep tenderness he took her in his arms. Never, no, never had she seemed to him so like a child, so defenceless, so vulnerable, so susceptible to the suffering which everything in life, and especially he, would ultimately inflict on her. He remembered the gesture she had made when, not knowing how to break down his moody silence, she had – for the first time – slipped her arm through his, as a scolded dog puts out a paw to obtain forgiveness. In that instant, a com-plete upheaval occurred inside him: he saw that she was infinitely weaker than he had imagined, and he realized too that he loved her far more than he had imagined – while at the same time the only complaint he had ever been able to make against her had lost its justification. In that short moment she came really close to him, to what was essential in him. What joy he would have felt in killing anyone who harmed her now! Then he bent down and kissed, not the top of her shoulder, which was bare (for this might have seemed like sensuality), but that part of her shoulder which was covered by her clothes.

Then the conversation drifted. With the same kind of feeling that had caused him to kiss her blouse and not her skin, he was now holding the edge of her dress. Eventually, prompted by their surroundings, the talk settled on Solange's family.

'My brother wasn't very clever: the only thing he was capable of was making money.... I don't love Mummy and Daddy in the same way. I love Mummy in an indulgent way: she's so superficial! Daddy has much more finesse. Besides, he's so ill. . . . ' (M. Dandillot was suffering from cancer of the prostate and his days were numbered.) 'The point about men like my uncle Louis is to get the maximum of approbation for the minimum of risk.' ('What a splendid definition of the bourgeoisie!' thought Costals.) 'My religion? I'm not a believer, but when I see a paper like' (there followed the name of a weekly with a particularly 'Parisian' tone) 'it makes me almost want to be a Christian again. I tell myself there must be more to things than *that*.'

And finally, this scrap of dialogue:

'None of the young men of my generation seem to have a sense of duty. Whereas a man like you. . . .'

'Seriously, do I look like a man with a sense of duty?'

'No. But you are.'

'You're a sly one! Yes, of course, as soon as one's in love, one can't help having a sense of duty.'

At first, Costals had seen Solange as a doll. He had taken her as one takes a woman for a waltz and then brings her back to her chair. Later, when he knew her better, she seemed the product of the kind of upbringing which teaches that it is impolite to express one's own opinion, and that one should always agree with the other person. He had snubbed her when she said, as girls so often do: 'I'm a bit of a freak.' 'You're not in the least a freak. You're exactly like any other girl.' He had snubbed her again when she said she was 'misunderstood': 'That's what all women say when there's nothing in them to understand.' He had regretted not being able to tease her to his heart's content, because she wasn't witty enough to answer back: 'She would only feel offended and hurt.' He had once paid her this compliment – a considerable one, though its limits are obvious: 'I have never heard her say anything either stupid or vulgar.' He had seen her as soft and self-effacing, in fact an ideal heroine for a French novel. And yet, confirming from his own observations in society that she was telling the truth when she said she had no friends, he was inclined to infer that she must be worth something, since solitude and worth are synonymous. This worth did not, however, go further than 'magnificent negative qualities', and he still thought of her what St Teresa says of herself: 'Thou art she who is not.' His predominant feeling towards her was admiration for her beauty.

But now it was as though he were watching a photographic plate in a bath of developer: gradually, as on the plate, new details of Solange's personality emerged; gradually her complete image was taking shape, and this image reflected great credit on her. Her qualities of perception and judgement, so shrewd and so sensible, were not in themselves so very unusual. But he did not expect to find them in her. He discovered how little he knew about her, and in particular how much better she was than he. Even her voice was a new discovery. Until then, he had known three voices of hers. Her society voice, rather affected, which she adopted not as a pose but on the contrary because she was shy. The voice she used when she talked to him, about which there was little to be said. Her 'night voice', full of pathos, a voice from another world, with its childish words springing from the depths of her past like birds from the bottom of a well. And now there was this new voice, calm, utterly simple and serious, with its soothing quality, its indefinable intonations which made him think: 'Exactly the way girls of the aristocracy speak.' He said to her:

'I'm talking to you as if I'd known you for years, and I'm glad. I'm ashamed of the coarse way I treated you at first. As though you were a tart. Forgive me. . . .'

'It doesn't matter. I would have overlooked everything, since I love you. As a matter of fact I did overlook everything. . . .'

'Overlook what, for God's sake?' he wondered. 'Bah! the fact of having given herself, no doubt.' It was clear that she had judged him – perhaps with the same 'indulgence' with which she judged her mother. At other times he would have found this rather irritating. Now it only raised her in his estimation.

'You're in a lower key today. What's happened?'

'Only that I feel more at ease with you now our misunderstanding has been cleared up. Before I knew you, I was afraid of the future. Then, when I was with you, I wasn't afraid any more. And then that misunderstanding occurred and, ever since, I've felt like a bunch of flowers tied too tight. Now you've loosened the string and the flowers can breathe again.'

'Oh! we're in full poetic flight, I see. . . . I'm sorry! Even when I'm very serious, moved in fact, I can't help joking. Besides, I love teasing you.'

'I know. I'm beginning to know you.'

'You said something a moment ago.... What was it that you "overlooked" out of affection for me?'

'Don't you know?'

'I can guess. It's true: you, such a good girl, to give yourself to me like that, like a falling leaf.... When I think of the moving speech I had prepared to make you give in! And lo and behold! Like a falling leaf.... It must have been written in the stars. You have every virtue, including the principal one of having given yourself without any nonsense. For a woman who isn't easy isn't a real woman as far as I'm concerned. And I ask you, what would all those virtues have been to me if you hadn't given yourself with such dazzling promptitude?'

'When I gave myself to you, I had already given you everything.'

'*Cosí fan tutte.*'

'To tell you the truth, it wasn't the act itself I "overlooked". But ... all the secrecy ... that hotel, the first time.... '

'Like a falling leaf,' he said again. 'Like a little artichoke one picks.... And yet there are women who put up a show of resistance even when they've made up their minds to surrender. The last stand.... '

'I loved you too much to resist you. That at least is not a *così fan tutte.*'

'It's very extraordinary indeed,' he said gravely.

Languidly, with the sickness of the lunar cycle upon her, she was half reclining in the crook of her lover's arm, like a small strip of moss in the damp hollow of a rock. When Costals had entered, two cats had fled: not all cats are heroes. Now they kept coming back, walking across the room, going out again, coming and going as silently as ghosts. At moments their presence could be guessed by the sound of a creaking floorboard, now here, now there.

'You really ought to be taken in hand; you'd be well worth moulding,' he said, after a silence. 'That's quite clear to me now.'

'That's always the way. The man shapes the woman as he wants her to be, and she acquiesces.'

'Except that the man doesn't know what he wants. Is there anything more foolish than the male? And besides, he may not be interested. I love you, I want your happiness, and yet I don't feel like moulding you. Do you know why?'

'Yes.'

'What do you mean, "yes"? I bet you haven't the slightest idea.'

'You're not interested in moulding me because you have enough to do moulding your books.'

'Really, you are fantastic! You've hit the nail on the head. I have better things to do than to create individuals. The reason why Rousseau put his kids in an orphanage was that he wanted to write _Emile_. All the same, it's rather horrible. You've backed the wrong horse, old girl.'

'Oh! no, I haven't.' (She put her hand on his.)

'Yes, you say that now! We'll talk about it again in two years' time. . . .'

'But shouldn't love go on increasing all the time? That's the only way I can imagine it.'

'That sort of love isn't my line at all. Mine is more like a waterchute.'

He smiled as he said this, so she smiled, too. And they ended up in one another's arms.

'She lacks inspiration,' he thought to himself. 'Yes, I've put my finger on it. But she's a fine girl all the same.' How openly she had always behaved towards him! Trying to please him (changing her way of dressing, for instance, in accordance with chance remarks he made) but without a trace of coquetry; giving herself without affectation or artifice or pretended flight; so discreet (never asking him anything about his life or telephoning him first, or, on the telephone, saying more than was strictly necessary); not obtrusive or 'interfering' in the least, when there are so many women one eventually has to push away with practically the same gesture one made to pull them towards one; completely devoid of 'pose'; so far removed from the easy tricks used by others to captivate him, in an age when it is the men who are pursued by the girls; and even going to the unbelievable lengths of never – not once – making the slightest allusion to his literary work, whereas all the women who tried to worm their way into his life first tried to unlock the door with the key of admiration. He was grateful to her, too, for knowing nothing about the mediocre literature of the day and, knowing nothing, keeping quiet about it rather than trotting out the usual clichés, grateful to her for being so innocent of all snobbery, of all unhealthy – or even healthy – curiosity, of any wish to play a part or push herself forward, of any admiration for false values or false riches, for being so different, in a word – and apparently to her detriment, although she was infinitely superior to them – from all those bogus, snobbish, loud-mouthed, empty-headed bitches who were the flashy partners of so many prominent men in Parisian society. He was grateful to her for all this, and his spirit soared in an uprush of simplicity and trust.

'You see,' he said, 'the fact that you're a decent person is far more important than you probably imagine. For a long time now, a very long time, people have been working both inside and outside the country – and God knows with what calculated hatred – to make France a place where anyone with any decency must feel an exile. It's been a long and arduous business, because France was a good nation, basically sound. But at last it has been done. Dare I admit it? I who identified myself so passionately with my country in my youth and during the war, find that there are moments now when I not only feel no loyalty to it, but I even feel a violent need – which arises, and this is the serious part of it, from all that is best in me – to reject it entirely. Well, meeting someone like you, who are French, checks this impulse, and one thinks : "No, I can't desert". . . . '

'But there's nothing extraordinary about me. I can assure you that I know lots of girls like me, and there must be many more who are better.'

'It's possible – although, believe me, I tried a good many before I found you : "maiden trials", in racing parlance. But the whole effort of society – perhaps the whole effort of mankind – seems directed at showing off worthless women and making them appear interesting. Women complain of being misjudged. Why then do they allow the worst of their sex to take the limelight? And why do they swallow so easily every male suggestion that tends to make them appear grotesque and degraded? Why such a failure to recognize their own interests? Nearly always when women debase themselves – by some hideous fashion, some obscene dance, some idiotic way of thinking or talking, it's men who have put them up to it. But why don't they resist? Everyone knows that a woman's body, when it's no longer young, tends to become a ridiculous and often repulsive object, a joy for cartoonists, whereas a man's body, as old age draws near, keeps in much better shape. Morally it's the same thing. When a woman is morally not much good, she becomes abominable: it's either one thing or the other. When a woman is ill-bred, lacks decorum, she is a harpy.'

'I thought you only liked easy women.'

'I like women with a sense of decorum who are easy at the same time.'

'Oh, I see.'

'Do you know what a harpy is? Well, I should say bitch, if I were the sort of man who used such expressions. All the women who put on airs, the vamps, the flirts, the "Hallo, darling!" women, all the women who get their pictures into the glossy magazines, all the women I include under the heading of women-who-want-their-faces-slapped are harpies. It is the harpies that all the theologians, the philosophers, the moralists have been aiming at for thousands of years in heaping scorn and anathema on women; but they were wrong in not indicating clearly that it was those women, and them alone, whom they condemned. Which brings me back to my question: why don't decent, sensible women defend themselves against these harpies? Don't they realize the harm the harpies do to them? Women's worst enemies are women. I was telling you just now that, when I meet the sort of woman I take you to be, I feel more kindly towards my country. But it goes further: I feel more kindly towards the whole of your sex and ready to treat it more honourably. For if men behave badly towards women it's because they're afraid of them, because they're obsessed by the harpies. Most of the caddishness, the desertions, broken engagements, etc., that women suffer from are due to the fact that, however sweet and loving a woman may be, the man thinks he can detect the harpy in her, either hidden or potential. So he turns on her, or else he bolts: either way he treats his natural companion as an enemy. And that is why, among your sex, the good pay for the bad.'

'All the same, hasn't there ever been a harpy in your life?'

'Never. And I take no credit for keeping them at bay, as I can't stand them anyway. Me, have anything to do with people like that? Never! As far as they're concerned at least, I shall die intact. I have never loved and I cannot love – more, I cannot bear – any woman who is not simple and straightforward. When I was out in Indo-China, I saw most of the officers – men with the power of life and death over hundreds of their fellows – manoeuvred like pathetic puppets by the worst kind of women, sewers of shame, hideous, vile, ravaged, but full of airs and graces and the same grotesque poses one sees in film stars (ah! the female spy must have a fine time in the French army!). And now and then I would say to one of these men: "How could you?" And he would answer: "There's no one else; I have to take what I can find." And I would say: "Marooned on a desert island, with no other woman in sight, I'd rather make love to a Great Ant-Eater than to one of those pretentious bitches, however ravishing." If I'd had my way in one of those colonial outposts, I'd have had them all deported or clapped into jail. I'd let my men go with native women, with men, with kids, with donkeys, with the leaf of the prickly pear*, anything but those women. The harm they do in our colonies is unbelievable.'

She saw that he was full of a sacred fire, and remembered reading in her history books how the revolutionaries, during the Terror, killed for the sake of virtue. Nevertheless she approved. Then, when Costals started joking again, she said she would go and make tea: such eloquence deserved it.

'Have you any idea how to make tea?'

'You don't know me.'

'Come on, then, I'll teach you. And you'll see the cats playing the cello.'

---

*The *raquette* of the prickly pear, much appreciated in the wilds of Africa (*Author's note*).

'Do your cats really play the cello?' he asked, for everything always seemed possible to him.

'No, but they stick a paw straight up in the air when they're washing, and then they look as though they're playing the cello.'

'That image doesn't seem quite accurate to me,' he said, like the honest craftsman he was in the art of writing.

He followed her into the kitchen. The cats had preceded them, but they were not playing the cello. The black one must have had cold paws, for she had covered them with her tail. While the grey one doubtless had a cold tail, for she had placed her paws upon it. The black one opened her eyes as they came in. The grey wondered whether to do the same, then kept them closed, to show her contempt. A deep silence reigned in the kitchen, punctuated by the disproportionately loud tick-tock of a huge alarm-clock, which emphasized the silence instead of breaking it. The silence was even deeper here than in the drawing-room, for the kitchen overlooked the inner courtyard and the whole building on that side was wearing its Sunday look, meaning that it looked uninhabited. The kitchen windows, open on other days to disgorge the wail of gramophones and the chatter of maids, were closed. The drawn curtains were marked at the level of the hasp of the window-bolt with a dark patch which showed they had been pulled back over it all week and gave them the special crumpled look of housemaids' Sunday dresses.

Solange put a kettle on the stove, and Costals picked up a volume of the *Bibliothèque Rose* entitled *The Holidays*, which was lying on the table. Solange said that she had lent it to the cook's daughter, who had come up from the country to spend a few days with her mother.

'The Comtesse de Ségur! You can't imagine how well this book fits in with what I was thinking about you a moment ago. Of course, the "model little girl" is you! "Marguerite de Rosebourg" is you! All my childhood comes back to me with this little red book, and this time you're in it. How delightful!'

Standing, they turned over the pages of the book which lay before them on the kitchen table.

'The holidays were drawing to a close; the children loved

each other more and more,' Costals read. 'Isn't it charming! I feel that you and I, too, love each other more and more.'

'Oh, yes,' she said childishly, turning her face towards him. Then she leaned her head against his, as people are supposed to do when they are reading the same book. He pushed the window to, lest anyone should see them. The room became a little darker. Solange read:

'Marguerite threw herself into her father's arms, and he kissed her so hard that her cheeks became quite crimson.'

They laughed, for one day he had remarked that her face was all flushed with his kisses. And they kissed madly.

'The divine Comtesse!' he exclaimed. 'Her books breathe the very soul of the nobility. They make one drink to the dregs the bitter draught of low birth. All the good characters have titles, all the bad ones haven't. At least one knows where one is. Ah, ha! Here's a sentence which seems to concern someone I know: "I shall now ask Sophie to explain to us how the accident happened".'

'Is it me that sentence is supposed to concern?'

'Dear Rosebourg, wasn't there ever, in your girlish life, a little accident?'

'Which one?' she asked, and he laughed, charmed by her innocence.

The water began to sing in the kettle. Solange was about to take it off the stove, but he stopped her.

'Let the water sing its little song; you can see it's enjoying it. It seems to me that I can hear a thousand different noises in this room which at first seemed so quiet, in the same way as one gradually begins to make things out in the dark as one's eyes get used to it. Can't you hear lots of tiny noises round you?'

'Why, yes!'

'What do you mean, "yes"? The cheek of it! Only writers are allowed to have any imagination. You deserve to be put to the test: tell me, please, what are the voices you profess to hear so clearly?'

He put his face in his hands. She said:

'There's the noise of the tap dripping into the sink – a dull, muffled sound. There's the noise of the water dripping from the

bain-marie into the metal pan below – a quick, sharp sound.'
('The *bain-marie*!' he thought. 'Oh, ho! isn't she knowledge-
able!') 'There's the noise of the water spitting from the kettle-
spout on to the stove – like a locomotive getting up steam.
There's the noise of the steam lifting the lid with something
like a big sigh of contentment . . .'

Smiling into the palms of his hands which still covered
his face, he repeated:

'. . . with a big sigh of contentment. . . .'

'All these noises occur at regular intervals. But then there
are the free-lance noises. Can you hear the little tap-tapping
of the chair on the tiles? That's the black cat scratching herself. The table's creaking: it's as though it were stretching its
legs, lazily, because it's Sunday. In fact it's as though these
noises only exist on Sundays, as if all the household things
were having a day off. And the alarm-clock beats time for the
whole little orchestra, as potbellied and self-important as a
ballet-master from the *commedia dell'arte*.'

'Well, well, old girl!' said Costals, lifting his face. 'This is
certainly a day of revelations. Where do you get it all from?
The gift of observation and the gift of imagery: the two fundamental gifts of the craft of writing, you have them both. And
to think that I had quite made up my mind that you were
totally lacking in imagination. . . . Oh! here's something else. . . .'

Catching a few drops from the tap in her palm, the girl
sprayed them over the hot-plate of the stove, where they
evaporated with the rustle of a silk dress. She said:

'They're running, running, as if to escape their impending
evaporation. . . .'

Costals watched them with the look people have when they
stare into the fire.

'Yes, like soldiers running, running before being blown to
smithereens by exploding shells. How they hate to disappear!
And it's you who thought that up!'

She made as if to stop. He implored her:

'Please kill a few more for me. . . .'

Again she scattered the tiny drops. And again she stopped.

'More! I could go on forever watching them vanish into
oblivion.'

'One would think you enjoyed it.'

'It reminds me of the remark made by a general in Darius's army in the middle of a battle. Every time one of his men fell, he said: "One more fool the less." It's true he was a philosopher-general – a breed that shouldn't be encouraged.'

Leaning over the table, she flicked through the book in the red and gold binding.

'I'm looking for a sentence in *The Holidays* which always used to move me when I was a little girl. . . .'

In the silence, the genie of dripping water, the genie of boiling water, the genie of fire in the stove – a fire that never went out, as in the most ancient myths – the genie of the motionless cats and even the genie of this melancholy day, this strange winter day in the heart of summer, re-created the familiar world of Costals' early childhood, with its cats, its nursery rhymes, its kettle, its Hans Andersen's *Fairy Tales*, its musical boxes, its New Year almanacs, Humpty Dumpty and *La Tour prends garde*, Cadichon and Kitty Darling, all the magic fairyland of Old France and Old England adapted for the edification of rather strait-laced little boys. And it was she, the most silent genie of them all, even when she spoke, it was this unobtrusive Cinderella ('If I were to disappear for a week, I don't believe my parents would notice, I take up so little room in the flat'), it was she who, with a wave of her wand, had reawakened this universe for him. It was this stranger who had reopened his nursery door and given him back the savour of his past.

'There!' she exclaimed, 'I've found it! You know, the sentence I found so moving when I was a little girl. Paul says to Sophie: "So you had forgotten me?" And she answers: *"Forgotten you, no, but you were asleep in my heart and I dared not wake you."* '

Costals glanced at the book and read the sentence himself. Why did he feel it was somehow familiar? He blinked in an effort to remember. Suddenly it came back to him, and a shiver ran through him. Long ago, his mother had said to him about those very lines exactly the same thing that Solange was saying now: 'When I was little this sentence touched me deeply. I used to whisper it to myself over and over again. . . .'

He had always been happy to talk of his mother to Solange. But this time. . . . To think that, at a distance of so many years, his mother and this young girl had been moved by the same words! He said so to Solange, without comment: his heart was gripped by something too strong for words. It seemed to him as if some mysterious sign had descended upon her.

'What about the nightmare of the Maréchal de Ségur in the haunted house! Could it have frightened a boy? It used to terrify me. . . .'

Silently they read the story together. Costals reached the place where the Marshal, as the spectre puts the point of its dagger to his breast, kisses the Star of the Holy Ghost on the ribbon of the Order and the spectre, seeing this gesture, spares his life. He reached that passage, and then a strange thing happened: his eyes filled with tears, and he began to tremble.

Trembling, and his eyes full of tears, he said:

'When I was a child and came to this passage in the book, the tears would come to my eyes as they have today. I cried because the Marshal had been saved for being brave. And because the ghost was not too wicked to be moved by his courage. And I too, like the ghost, am not so wicked that I can't still cry, even now. And I owe this to you! You have transformed me into what is best in me. You have brought me back into the atmosphere of my family, to the days when I was a good person, living among good people. Whereas now I live among literary men, and have become a humbug and a rake. What would my life be worth, but for the time I spent in the war? I should never have been a decent person, except when I was a child.'

He bent down and placed his forehead on the open book.

'I'm doing as you do when you switch off the light, so that you may no longer see this face of mine, this man's face with all its unpunished crimes.'

Standing against the sink, she was stroking his hair. He took her other hand and clasped it in his – so warm, like a

handful of sand. Then he raised his head. He felt a terrible urge
to tell her the truth about himself. It was an urge that he felt
fairly frequently. It was nearly always into base souls that he
cast this truth, for there it was more likely to disappear. But
it could be cast into a pure soul; there was no rule against it.
So he said to her:

'If a certain lode in me were to be followed up, an unbroken
succession of good actions would be found. If another, a
succession of horrors. Not petty horrors, judged by this code
or that – according to local customs – but really hideous things
which the universal conscience can never forgive. Yet if I had
not done these dreadful things, what an abyss of despair I
should be in today, and above all tomorrow, when I am old.
It is not from a desire for self-abasement that I accuse myself
before you. It is because I want to see things as they are, and
for you, too, to see them as they are, without flinching, because
that is what is good.... No, no,' he said, his eyes blurred,
sensing that she wanted to speak, 'let me surrender to this
spirit that sways within me. Let me be what I am!' he
exclaimed passionately. 'What was I saying? Ah, yes, the
lodes.... Well, sometimes, these lodes run parallel, but sometimes they cross, and when they do they interweave in
arabesques, twining playfully about each other. And sometimes, too, it happens that they dissolve into each other, the
best and the worst blended together, indistinguishable from one
another. And in the evil I do there is a part I like and a part I
dislike, just as in the good I do there is a part that I enjoy and
a part that leaves me cold.' (One of the cats sneezed.) 'Certainly
I enjoy evil, but I think I enjoy good even more intensely. However, I'm not so sure about that.... Do you remember greet-
ing me one day with the question: "How's your morale today?"
And I replied: "My morale is fine, but so's my immorale."*
That's what you must understand. Beware of preferring your
own image of me to the reality. You must take me with all my
"outbuildings", the stables and the latrines. However that may
be, it is this pleasure in goodness which you have reawakened
in me. And what you must know is this: that I've enjoyed

*The pun works better in French, where the words are *le moral*
and *l'immoral* (*Translator's note*).

and will go on enjoying the harm I have done and will do to others, but that never – and I say it in all solemnity – never will I enjoy the harm I may do to you.'

He slid on to his knees on the tiled floor, trembling all over with the effort of resisting the pleasure he would have liked to give her by asking her to marry him. As she was half-sitting on the edge of the sink with one foot dangling, he kissed the hem of her skirt, then removed her grey suede shoe, and taking her foot in his hands, pressed it to his lips at the spot where the stocking had a small darn. Often, he had kissed her face on the places where her features were a little defective, thinking that, while in her perfection she belonged to all men, in her imperfections she belonged to him alone. Now he kissed the darn in her stocking because it introduced an unexpected hint of poverty into his idea of her, a faint possibility that the apparent affluence in which she lived might not be altogether genuine; and the thought that he would one day wrong her seemed to him more odious than ever. And the knowledge, underlying all his other feelings, that she was a little unwell today, added new warmth to these feelings and brought them to the boil, as the flame nearby had brought the water to the boil.

'You,' he said at last, 'you, so quiet and good, as though to appease the Fates. It's strange, I wish you well. What a mysterious thing it is to really wish someone well! What is essential is that you should always be happy. Once you are out of my hands, of course, because as long as we're together.... I so much want to keep the damage I shall do you to a minimum.... Don't love me! Don't love me!' he exclaimed vehemently. 'It's the only chance you have of not being unhappy because of me. Ah, yes, there's another: you must realize that I'm mad. I'm not *only* mad, but I'm mad *as well*.' (He felt her toes moving beneath his lips; at the same time, in spite of the intoxication of the moment, it struck him that her foot was rather thin, and he would have preferred it to be a bit sturdier.) 'Marguerite de Rosebourg,' he said, raising his head, 'I ask your pardon for the future. It is the divine part of my soul (though I don't believe in God, I have no reason not to believe in him), it is the divine part of my soul that asks your pardon in advance for whatever harm I may do you; and I ask you this while mentally kissing the glittering Star of the Holy Ghost which I, too, wear invisibly on my heart. Remember this well, Rosebourg: I shall do you harm, but the harm I do you will give me no pleasure.... Am I boring you?' he asked, seeing the grey cat giving a jaw-splitting yawn. And, because of this ludicrous association of ideas, his laughing self was reawakened and took over once again. Throughout this entire speech, it was as though he had been swept now right, now left by opposing gusts of wind.

He straightened up, and then, standing in front of him, she rested her forearms against his chest, either from some immemorial girlish instinct, or because she had seen it done in films. She had not raised him up when he was kneeling. She had not wept when he wept; the time had not yet come when he would know how to make her cry. With a confidence that nothing, then, could have shaken, she had listened to him as one listens to a child babbling in a dream. She said: 'I know you will never do anything to hurt me.' He was disturbed to think that she knew him so little, and said to himself: 'What can I do against such trustfulness?' Meanwhile the sky had cleared, she had opened the window (canaries were chirping in a cage which had just been put out), and their long embrace was visible to the outside world. He thought of this, but did not close the window, as if something new had occurred which gave them a right to embrace publicly. Thus they remained, merged with each other like the sky and the sea on certain days when the horizon is no longer visible in a great, smooth, even splendour. Then they parted, well pleased with each other.

That night, after the five hours they had spent talking with passionate truthfulness and sincerity, and with no caresses (he despised the very thought of them) – all of which was new in their relationship – Costals was unable to sleep. The esteem he felt for her kept him awake. This esteem had created in his body a tension of a wholly virile kind which he had not experienced during their chaste hours in the kitchen and which was not, even now, accompanied by the faintest lustful image.

'The *Précieuses*,' he thought, 'used to distinguish "tenderness based on esteem".* This is a case of tension based on esteem.' Till then he had never suspected that a feeling of a purely moral order could have such an effect, and he was greatly astonished.

He was perfectly aware that he had treated Solange that day as though he were engaged to her, and that it was impossible for her not to have noticed it. For the first time he envisaged the possibility of being weak enough some day to bestride the nuptial Hippogriff with her if she should ever decide to confess to such a desire. He knew for certain that it would be the purest folly. He knew that marriage – of which he had always said, in the words of Don Quixote : 'It is impossible that I should ever conceive of being married, not even to the Phoenix' – would wreck his future : as a writer, because of the obligations, the nervous wear and tear, the need for money, the time-wasting it would involve; and as a man, because his independence was for Costals a necessity as absolute as the air which kept him alive. The Hippogriff, once straddled, could only lead him to Hades. But the idea of marrying Solange was an abyss that had suddenly opened before him and might suck him down.

Supposing the marriage did take place, it was inevitable that a day would come when he would have to get divorced, both to *save his work* and to *save his soul*. But if Solange had done him no wrong (and he was sure she would not have), and if she refused to divorce him, how could he regain his freedom? All night long this prospect weighed him down like an incubus. At last he realized that the only solution would be to murder her. Not to murder her openly, and be condemned, for that would place him in a situation where he would be unable to continue his work and pursue his love-life. But to murder her in such a way that he would not be detected. For instance, by toppling her over the rails of a ship. Or by taking her out to sea in a dinghy. He had already thought it all out in other circumstances.

Le Tendre sur estime – from *la carte du Tendre* in Mlle de Scudéry's novel *Clélie* (*Translator's note*).

Of course, killing her would be a hideous crime. But what if there were no other way of recovering his manhood? 'Am I then a monster? No, I'm just like everyone else. Sometimes better than others, sometimes worse. I'm like seven people out of ten. And if seven people out of ten are "monsters", there can be no such thing as a monster. It may seem strange that, on one and the same day, I should not only love this girl enough to consider marrying her, but that I should also contemplate murdering her – not for any jealous motive, but simply because she would be in my way. But many other things in men's souls are equally strange. Of course, since it's the idea of marriage, and it alone, that is responsible for fathering this homicide plan, the simplest thing would be not to marry her. Alas, it isn't as simple as that. It's like an abyss sucking me down.'

He had thought that the night would dissipate these musings like evil phantoms. And, indeed, when he awoke, the possibility of marriage had lost a great deal of its substance. Not enough, however, to prevent him from taking an immediate precautionary measure, painful though it was.

He was due that day or the next to send to a monthly review a long story about a man who poisons someone for fear that he will 'talk'. All the emotions through which the man passes before committing the deed, and the technique employed, were minutely described over some sixty pages. It was a piece of documentary evidence which, should Costals ever fall under suspicion, would tell fearfully against him. 'A man capable of thinking up a murder with such hallucinatory precision cannot be far from committing it; he has already almost committed it in spirit.' He could just hear counsel for the prosecution! Regretfully Costals wrote to the editor of the review to say that he was unable to deliver the promised story.

At the same time he wrote to Andrée, for he felt sorry for her because he was happy.

Pierre Costals
Paris

to Andrée Hacquebaut
Saint-Léonard

21 June 1927

Dear Mademoiselle,

A small cousin of mine,* sweet and open-hearted if something of a rascal (thanks to his father who's quite impossible), was out on an excursion one day when he suddenly decided to telephone his father. 'Hullo, is that you, papa?' 'Yes, what's the matter?' 'Nothing, except that I'm happy and enjoying myself, and I just wanted to let you know.'

Yesterday I was happy. Happy in a kitchen. And, my good-will having been awakened as a result of this happiness, I wanted to 'let you know', and also to ask how you were. Tell me *briefly* (not more than two pages). I have an idea you've been writing to me lately, but I confess I don't remember what you said in your letters; I must only have read the opening sentences. I won't ask whether you're happy, as I know it isn't your fate to be happy. But still, how's it going?

So long. You can't imagine how benign I feel at the moment. 'Opportunity not to be missed.'

C.

I had never seen the inside of a kitchen before. It's an astonishing place; all sorts of possibilities. And to think that it was there all the time!

If this novel conformed to the rules of the genre as laid down in France, the scene in the kitchen between Costals and Solange would have been placed at the end. Everybody would have been delighted: the pundits because, in a novel constructed in the French manner, that is to say a *logically* constructed novel, the culminating scene must come at the end, and the moralists because this scene seems to foreshadow a union between the principal characters. And thus the novel, by ending on a *vista of blue sky*, would have been edifying from beginning to end, for French novels, like Christian souls,

---

*Costals' bastard son.

always preserve the possibility of redeeming themselves *in extremis*.

But life, which knows nothing of living, foolishly presumes to ignore the conventions of the French novel. In the story we are here relating, as it really happened, that scene in the kitchen, in which Costals and his sweetheart discovered together some estimable areas of their souls, was indeed a summit, but with all the drawbacks of summits. For, the summit having been reached, one must perforce descend. That scene had no aftermath.

When they next met, Solange was taciturn, almost morose. Perhaps she had her reasons. Perhaps she had none. Perhaps, even, she was no different from her usual self, but they had climbed too high. A multitude of small signs made him doubt whether she loved him deeply. Her face did not light up at the sight of him. . . . A fortnight had elapsed, and she still hadn't had the snap-shots she had taken of him developed. . . . Whereas so many women overwhelmed him with solicitude, there was never anything of the kind from her. . . . Once she said to him : 'Neither you nor I are infatuated with each other. That's a sign of the solidity of our attachment.' The 'neither you' was an echo of what he himself had said to her about his not being in love with her. But the 'nor I' seemed a bit chilly.

He thought : 'She's like a shaded lamp. The light is there all right, but it lacks radiance.' And indeed, as soon as they were apart from each other, it was as if Solange's personality, after all rather frail, was, as it were, swallowed up by that of Costals. When he was with her, he believed in her integrity. When she was absent, all that was tortuous in his nature began to ferment again. Distrustful as a prince and always prone to believe that others wished him as much harm as he felt capable of doing them, he had unwittingly substituted his own turbulent spirit for that of the girl, and soon found himself confronted by a detached, blurred image of Solange, which was no more than a projection of himself. He had re-created her in his own image.

He had once asked her : 'What did you think of the way I made love to you that first evening in the Bois?' She had answered that she had been extremely surprised, though not shocked, and that the sensation had been disagreeable. He was inclined to exaggerate her physical coldness, and comparing the poor quality of her responsiveness to that of, say, Guiguite or certain others, he sighed; for sexual enjoyment, he could only give her five out of twenty. And he consoled himself with theories, all deriving from that tedious habit he had of drawing a sharp dividing line between the sexes: 'Men only love with the heart when they have first desired with the senses. With women it's the opposite: first they love with the heart, and from thence flows desire. Ugly men are loved, ugly women are not. A woman in love doesn't mind if her lover hasn't shaved for two days, whereas no man would kiss a bearded woman.'

At other times, this coldness in Solange did not displease him. It provided him with an excuse, opening the door through which he too would one day escape to undertake the divine conquest of some new little partner. Had she remained the Solange of 'Kitchen Sunday', he might eventually have married her. But if she were the first to show signs of wanting to break it off, then he would break it off himself with total indifference. The only person he ever missed was his son, and in any case nobody is irreplaceable. Hence one of the most significant traits in his character was that he was almost devoid of jealousy, which he characterized as a 'shopgirl's sentiment'. Whether the girl fell madly in love with him, or whether she threw him over, made no difference to him at all. He would adapt himself to either contingency with the same promptness and the same contentment: more passionate as she became more passionate, more forgetful if she chose to forget him. Such was the amplitude of his inner keyboard, and his mastery over it, that he could draw from it at will whatever he wanted.

Nevertheless, prepared as he was to believe that their liaison was on the wane, he decided that it would be unfair to her to postpone the regularization of their position any longer. The state of *demi-vierge* could not forever satisfy a soul with a thirst for the absolute. The time had come to bring Mlle Dandillot into a more clearly defined category.

With this end in view, they were at his flat one evening, in the room which he called 'the tomb of the unknown woman', when suddenly. . . .

> Who's that ringing at my door
> Said the fair young la-a-ady

Yes, who, well after half past nine? . . . The servant was out. He saw her start up suddenly from the bed, her eyes wide open, and tried to calm her down. An electric sign outside threw splashes of red on to her arms and shoulders, while the glow from the lights of the city, shining in bands through the slats of the shutters, streaked her face with light and darkness as if she were behind the bars of a prison (this figurative prison was her love for him, little though he realized it). The doorbell rang again, and then a third time, with insistence. She slipped out of bed and hurried to the bathroom.

He followed her, and found her getting dressed. He begged her not to. But she was shaken. A minute went by, while she sat, half-dressed, on a chair. And suddenly the bell rang again, and fists began to pound on the door of the flat.

This time Costals was worried. Solange was now fully dressed. There was no one there but a respectably attired young damsel, whose parents must be aware that she often visited him. But he did not think of this: he was simply a frightened man who has heard fists pounding on a door behind which he is in bed with a girl.

Meanwhile the banging had stopped. He tiptoed into the hall, to make sure no one was waiting behind the door. There, on the floor, lay a visiting card. Andrée!

'Your letter touched me so much that I felt we must talk things over and get our bearings at the earliest opportunity; so I caught the first train. I know you're at home, because the windows of one of your rooms are lit up. But never mind. . . . Please write to me express at the address below, tomorrow if possible.'

So this woman wasn't content with pestering him from a distance. She had to ring his bell at half past nine at night, and bang on his door like a drayman, and watch his windows like a spy. She, whom he did not love, had to disturb him in what he did love.

He told Solange that it was only 'some imbecile of a friend', but when he asked her if she wanted to call it a day, and she pleaded her shattered nerves, he said to her:

'Don't apologize. You'd hear bells ringing and fists banging the whole time. . . . Even I, after nine years of peace, I can't hear a knock on the door without being reminded of machine-guns. Let's finish the evening in the Bois. Tomorrow I'll pick you up at a quarter to four in front of your house, and we'll go to my country place.'

This was what he called a garden studio which he owned, off the boulevard du Port-Royal, where they sometimes went.

Then he wrote an express letter to Andrée, the Angel of Treachery reading over his shoulder.

Dear Andrée (*it was the first time in five years he had called her by her Christian name*):

I am so looking forward to seeing you again! If I could have guessed that it was you just now, I would of course have opened up, even though I was in night attire; but so lonely! Come tomorrow, 25th June, at four-thirty, to 96, boulevard du Port-Royal, and ring three times. It's a little 'folly' I've had there for some years. We shall be undisturbed.

Yours,

C.

P.S. In writing to you I am behaving treacherously to another woman. Sweet treachery.

They went out. The stars were dancing about like motes in a sunbeam. He stopped the taxi at a post-office, and handed the express letter to Solange.

'You post it, just to please me. You may read the address. You see it's to a woman. . . .'

She gave him an anxious, questioning look.

'It's a woman I'm punishing.'

'What are you punishing her for?'

'For not loving her.'

Back in his flat, he wrote in his notebook: 'Here on my balcony, at a quarter to twelve, I savour to the full the exquisite tang of treachery. It is such a pleasurable state that I wonder how one can ever relinquish it without some grave reason. Above the town, the sky glows like heated iron. An emerald breeze gently fans my face.'

Next day, at four, Costals and Solange arrived at his Port-Royal studio. Situated at the end of a small garden, this studio was like every other studio, and so not worth describing (the bachelor apartment in all its horror). There was, however, one thing peculiar to it: a number of show-cards, which Costals had had made following an American fashion then becoming fairly widespread in France, were lying about on the furniture. One of them bore this inscription:

LADIES!
NEVER OFFER GENTLEMEN
MORE THAN THEY ASK FOR

Another:

THIS GENTLEMAN
DOES NOT MARRY

And another:

THIS GENTLEMAN
NEVER RETURNS LETTERS

It was not in awfully good taste, but youth will have its fling. And the highest moral altitudes are all the more pleasurable if one comes down to earth occasionally.*

'None of this is meant for you,' Costals said to Solange. 'Don't worry, I shall give you back your letters. And now, follow me.'

At one end of the studio was a staircase leading to a tiny loggia, which Costals called the dovecot because, perched high as it was, it did bear some resemblance to a dovecot, and because human doves did nestle there at times. He also sometimes called it his *columbarium*, by virtue of an old saw according to which funereal thoughts stimulate pleasure, though he himself had little need of such stimulants.

'Well, my pet, no more nonsense; now's the time for you to take the plunge. On this bed, shortly, you will become a

---

*Untranslatable pun here. The French is *pied-à-terre*, = 'feet on the ground' and also 'bachelor flat' (*Translator's note*).

woman. So you'd better get a good eyeful of the décor, if what they say is true, that the act still has some importance for a girl in spite of everything. And it has! A moment like that is like an oil-stain that will spread over a woman's whole life. So try and do it properly. For the time being, though, the only thing I ask is that you should stay here and keep mum. In a few minutes, I shall have a visitor downstairs. You see this curtain? Behind it you'll hear everything, and see everything too, if you draw it aside a little. without being seen. Goodbye for now. If you get restless, you'll find plenty of books on morals lying around. Here, for instance: Louis Ménard's *La Morale avant les Philosophes*. You'll see the progress morality has made since then. Splendid chaps, the *Philosophes*!'

He went downstairs and settled in an armchair. For a moment, his eyes vacant, he wondered how he would tackle the scene with Andrée. Then, with the touch of arrogance that woke in him at times, he decided that such a question was not worth his bothering about, that Andrée did not deserve to have a set speech prepared for her, and he made it a point of honour not to think about her any more. He flicked through a magazine and thought of Solange, hidden and yet present, like God perhaps.... Whereupon he plunged into a sort of lucid confusion, was seized with a gust of spirituality, and composed some lines, which he jotted down:

> O God! Hide then yourself but in appearance,
> Not in reality.
> And when you withdraw deep into your silence,
> Listen to me.

At four thirty-five, Andrée had still not arrived. At twenty to five still nobody. He was glad she was late, as it was further justification for the cruelty he was about to inflict on her. The fact was that he would cheerfully have suffered insults, dishonour, desertion, the loss of all his money; but he could not bear to be kept waiting. He always told his women, from their very first meeting: 'The chief qualification of a woman in love is punctuality. Everything else is secondary.' He had told Solange, too. He had a notebook in which he kept a record of the number of minutes his girl-friends kept him waiting, and when the total reached five hours, he broke with them – at least in principle. Not without warning them three times, at the end of two, three and four hours, in accordance with an old Arab precept: 'Warn the snake three times before you kill it.' To date, after six weeks, Solange's total only came to one hour seven minutes. A very decent average.

At a quarter to five, the bell rang and Andrée appeared. 'Ah! there you are, my dear Mademoiselle. The burnt child still risks the fire, eh?' On shaking hands with Costals, she held his for a long time, which the writer found far from agreeable. Mlle Hacquebaut, who was usually content with a dab of powder and a touch of lipstick, had today really made herself beautiful, but in a Saint-Léonardesque style: glaring red lips and irregular blotches of dark powder. Her legs were bare, which could have been explained by the heat, though the real explanation lay elsewhere. Her face looked parched and emaciated, like that of a literary gentleman who has had to wait too long for a good review (a plant without water). And there were dark rings under her eyes such as Costals had never seen there before: blue, purple, glossy, huge, spreading out like a fan, or the wake of a boat, nearly up to the temples – terrifying in the broad light of day. He thought she must have developed a taste for solitary practices.

She glanced round the room and read the show-cards.

'No, dear Mademoiselle, you are not really in a house of sin. The worst that ever happens is that I occasionally shut my cat up in here with some tom when she's on heat. But one or other of them always seems to lack interest. The tom, usually. Isn't nature odd? Some day I must shut the tom up here with a mouse. It might sharpen his desire.'

'Yes, his desire to eat her up, after torturing her for hours. And you would be watching them through the window, gloating. I can see it all!'

'What a lurid image you have of me,' he said with disgust.

Still, he had her there in front of him, completely at his mercy, and he wondered what would be the best way of making her suffer. For a sort of chemical reaction had taken place in him since the day before. For nearly five years he had restrained himself from wounding her, for five years he had been waiting for the present moment. All that pity, that kindness, that forbearance had been transmuted by last night's irruption into an element which was chemically their opposite: cruelty. Like milk changed into blood. 'Milk or blood, it's all the same. I love both milk and blood, like the *manes* of antiquity.' And all the effort that had gone into his benevolence now went to reinforce his cruelty. 'I felt heroic, and that's a feeling I dislike.' Now he could give rein to that other self that had been stifled so long, now he could drop the weight he had been holding up for five years. The strength to make her suffer began to wake and stretch itself within him, and he watched the girl as a wrestler measures up his opponent, wondering what sort of hold to try on her. 'She once wrote to me, paraphrasing Cleopatra's words about Antony, in Shakespeare: "For thy bounty, there is no winter in't." Why, in the first place, should I show myself bountiful to her? Don't know. And then, why should there be no winter in my bounty? Winter's a very fine season, when you look at it in relation to the others. Blessed are those who blow hot and cold together. If the souls of the just are like good trees and good pastures, as the Gospel says, they must love winter as well as summer, drought as well as plenty, darkness as well as light: it needs a little of everything to make a man. All the seasons exist in me, one after another. I am a revolving cosmos that presents every point of its surface to the sun, one after another. One after another! Always one after another! Now she'll see what it costs, five years of pity from a man like me.'

'I see you have bare feet,' he said nonchalantly. 'In Algiers, when young Frenchmen of the upper classes want to seduce a girl who also belongs to the upper classes, they take her by car to the forest of Bainem. There, if she refuses, they wait until nightfall, then take her shoes and jump into the car. She gets back as best she can, barefoot. The forest of Bainem is twelve kilometres from Algiers.'

'Poor things!'

'Well, it teaches them to stand on their own feet, no pun intended. We must defend ourselves, mustn't we?'

'Defend yourselves! Poor helpless males! Either defending

themselves against women who refuse, or defending themselves against women who throw themselves at their heads. But I,' she said (with sudden volubility, rushing the words to the point of stammering, as though all of a sudden she had started rushing down a slope), 'whatever you may have thought, I never threw myself at your head: I never begged; on the contrary I offered. You refused. Of course, to be loved takes away part of one's freedom. But so does everything that has to do with life. By simply going on living, you accept the tyranny of time and space, the weather, the need to eat and sleep. . . .'

'My entire life is based on one thing: getting rid of everything that isn't essential to me.'

'If you really had to be afraid of something, you could have chosen something else to be afraid of besides love – mine, at any rate. But however that may be, you can't say I've forced myself on you. I went out of your life in silence, and so I have remained. Shall I tell you? I was utterly fed up with you. With you, and with this wretched love that has never fed upon anything but itself. And then, just as I imagined you must be thinking: "Now she's dead all right, and she'll never stir again," you wrote to me, you shouted "encore" to bring me back on stage, as if you had enjoyed my little tragi-comic act. Oh! you know how to keep women in suspense all right. Why did I come? First of all, to show you I wasn't sulking. And then because, in spite of everything I wrote, I hadn't given up. The only way you could have made me give you up would have been to tell me you didn't love me. But that you've never done. Not once, in four years and nine months. Not once. You've always run away, but you've never really broken off. And then, after running away, you return to the attack with redoubled vigour.' ('My head! My head!' thought Costals, putting a hand to his head in the gesture of Achilles tearing his hair.) 'I came here in order to hear these words from you, if that is what I am to hear. To hear them from your own lips. Whatever happens, this abscess must be lanced.'

'Well, we'll see about that,' he said cheerfully, not yet clear as to what he was going to say or do.

From her spotless legs, her made-up face, he guessed she

must have prepared herself with minute care. He could also guess why. Yet the seam of her dress had come unstitched in places, the lace edge of her petticoat, showing at her throat, might have been cleaner, and her nails – pointed and varnished – retained a thin streak of black under the artificial pink, which made him wonder whether she thought black finger-nails an additional attraction, as negro women do their lip-plates, or a measure of hygiene like the dirt on Arab babies which their mothers preserve religiously because it is a guarantee of good health. Slatternly people, in their occasional attempts at cleanliness, always overlook some detail that betrays them. And it is the misfortune of women that men can bear negligence in a man but loathe it in a woman.

Nevertheless, all this time, Costals had been smiling at her, and smiling so naturally that he was not even aware of it. He smiled at her (a) because he had a natural gaiety which expressed itself in that way, a kind of artless vitality, like one of those electric currents, innocently blue, but deadly; (b) because he was grateful to her for the pleasure he was about to derive from making her suffer; and (c) because, in spite of everything, he still rather liked her. (Through all their debates and discussions he had never stopped liking her, and that was no doubt one of the reasons why he tormented her.)

When he had taken a good look at her, Costals shifted a vase of flowers on the table in such a way that his face was hidden from the woman who loved him. She moved her chair sideways so that she could see him again. Once more he shifted the vase.

'Why don't you want me to see you?'

'Just to annoy you,' he said gaily. 'But there, I'll be nice.' He pushed the vase aside.

'I've really been an awful fool, haven't I?' said Andrée. 'If men only knew how stupid women can be, they'd pity them instead of torturing them.'

'Women keep on begging until one gives them something. But one can give them pretty well anything. Pity, for instance. In any case, men do give it to you, though without realizing it. They call their pity love. On the whole, what brings man and woman together is pity far more than love. How could one fail to pity women when one sees what they are? One doesn't pity an old man : he has reached the end of his cycle, he has had his day. One doesn't pity a child: its helplessness is but momentary, the future belongs to it. But a woman in her prime, at the peak of her development, look at her! Woman would never have conceived herself to be man's equal, if man hadn't told her she was out of "niceness".'

'Sometimes, it seems, this pity turns into desire.'

'Of course. Everything changes into everything else. What people call "love", "hate", "indifference", "pity", are only momentary phases in one and the same feeling. And we must thank God that pity is only a momentary phase. Otherwise it would annihilate us. We should escape from the enslavement of love only to enslave ourselves to pity. One can make people do anything by exciting them to pity. Do you know one can die of one's pity? Consequently, everything that is done out of pity turns out badly, except perhaps what is done out of pity for greatness, and you won't find that sort of pity every day. Half the doomed marriages in the world are marriages in which one or the other has married out of pity. When I was wounded during the war, the more the civilians at railway stations pitied me, the more I despised them. I felt their pity put them so utterly in my power! I could have got them to sign cheques or hand over their daughters, anything I wanted, and all this without deserving it, or putting on an act. It was revolting! Still, one might as well take advantage of it, and it seems to me that now, if I coveted other worldly goods than those I already possess, I should be less inclined to acquire them by exploiting the stupidity or the vanity or the greed of my fellow-men than by exploiting their pity.'

A butterfly flew into the room through the open window and (ignoring Andrée) fluttered around Costals as though asking to be stroked. But it is not easy to stroke a butterfly.

'I'm beginning to understand,' Andrée said slowly. 'The only feeling you have ever had for me is pity. The only feelings you ever have for women are desire, irritation and pity – never love. So you arrogate to yourself the right to pity women! Do you realize how ridiculously nineteenth-century you are? "Poor unfortunate" women! Michelet! Oh, no! please, not your pity! I've had enough of those life-belts of yours that hit one on the head and send one under. Please don't throw any more. Women don't need your pity. You're the one who should be pitied.'

'Why? Because I don't love you?'

'Because you love nobody. You have no wife, no home, no children, no object in life, no faith. And perhaps it's because you're ashamed of all that that you come and huddle close to those who do love – that you call them back to you, as if you were one of them. And you're not, oh no, you're not! A leper, that's what you are!'

'Yes, it's exactly as I said: because I don't love you. But really, Andrée Hacquebaut, take a look at me: do I look like an unhappy man?'

'It's a mask, a grimace.'

'The grimace of the literary man is intended to make him appear *un*happy. They all want to look like Pascal. "M. Thingummy's Pascalian anguish." There are two certain recipes for admission to the Academy: a book on Racine, and a book on Pascal."

'You admitted it all to me, don't you remember: "I lie all the time"?'

'I remember very well. I said that in order to give you a false idea of myself. And besides, what I say to you is of no importance. It's in their work that you must look for men like me, not in what they tell you.'

'One has only to look at your photograph in this week's *Vie des Lettres* to see that you're not happy.'

'One has only to look at my photograph in this week's *Vie des Lettres* to know that the photographer had disturbed and irritated me. Come, come, my dear girl, this is a perfect example of reaction 227a.'

'I don't want to know what reaction 227a is. It's sure to be something unpleasant as usual. . . . What *did* you mean?'

'I'll tell you – it's quite nice, really. As you probably know, all women react in the same way to a given stimulus. There's nothing mysterious about women. Men have led them to believe they were mysterious, partly out of chivalry and partly as a bait, because they desire them. And of course the women fall for it, and even improve on it. It's always the same: at first sight, in a gathering of women, when you see them all saying the same things, laughing at the same things, etc., you feel that they form a kind of interchangeable substance. Then if you get to know one of them and develop a warmer feeling for her, she begins to appear very different from the others, the others can tell you nothing about her, she is an enigma to you, and so she will remain until you have conquered her; for it was desire that made you believe all this. Once conquered, she soon appears exactly like the others again. So one sees that in reality all women's reactions are automatic and can be foretold in advance. These reactions can be classified, and that is what I have done, identifying them by numbers. Reaction 227a is the classic reaction whereby a woman, because she is unhappy, tries to convince the man she loves that he too is unhappy. Not only because she wants to comfort him and "mother" him, but because it exasperates her to see the man happy, and happy without deriving his happiness from her. Men too, of course, often exhibit reaction 227a, but in them it arises exclusively from desire. And then nearly all Catholics, both men and women, also have a similar reaction: they want to convince unbelievers that their situation is desperate. In that category, the reaction is numbered 79PC. PC stands for "practising Catholic" as opposed to the non-practising variety.'

'I don't know what women can have done to you to make you speak of them in such terms. They must have made you suffer dreadfully. Oh, of course, I forgot – I mustn't say that! It's reaction 227a. You just wait, though: one day you'll be rid of women for good. I've often wondered what you'll be like when you're old. Well, you won't be much to look at. I could tell you exactly what wrinkles you'll have: I can already see the first traces of them, like the light pencil strokes with which a painter begins a sketch. It's true, there are lines on your forehead which weren't there three months ago. . . .'

He began to laugh, delighted by her naïve rudeness, and feeling slightly attracted towards her. He wondered which of his different selves to bring into play. After all, had Solange not been there, he would not have minded 'taking' Andrée. 'The nape of her neck isn't too bad. But is it enough? Six of one, half a dozen of the other, as they say. But even so!' For the first time, he felt a sort of desire for her, more especially, perhaps, because of the rings under her eyes. Perhaps also because he found her repulsive: 'The strong alone relish horror.' He watched a fly in the ash-tray on the table in front of him, which had been quietly feeding on the ash and cigarette ends for three minutes with as much apparent enjoyment as if it had been jam – so drunk with ash that one could have picked it up with one's fingers. So it was with him: everything was much of a muchness. This sudden upheaval of all his feelings, of his whole policy towards this girl over the past five years, would have had its comic side. He felt no hatred towards her, merely indifference with if anything a certain liking, and from this indifference anything might emerge. He did not mind making her deliriously happy: why not? She deserved it. He did not mind making her deliriously unhappy: she deserved that too. It was just as rational to make her suffer in order to compensate for all the unwarranted good he had done her, as to make her happy in order to compensate for all the un-warranted harm he had done her. And in any case, was there any need to behave rationally at all? Everything came easily and spontaneously to him, just as it did when he sat down at his desk in front of a blank sheet of paper. Costals' inhumanity did not arise from an inability to experience human emotions, but rather from his ability to experience them all equally, and at will, as if all he needed to do was to press the appro-priate button. There are those who rebel against the arbitrary nature of the laws that govern human lives; others are not even aware of it. Costals was aware of it, but rather than suffer from it, he chose instead to worship it. For his whole existence was governed by this one thought: since the world offers so many reasons for joy, only a fool would choose to suffer (since suffering has to be paid for in this world and is unrewarded in the next). After having suffered for some years from seeing the decline of France, he had decided to enjoy this decline (for patriotism, not being inborn, can be lost as easily as it is acquired). He had reacted in the same way towards social in-justice, and in general to the whole problem of evil. 'If I were to suffer because of all the evil in the world, my life would be a torment, and therefore an absurdity. So let's enjoy that too.'

He debated for a moment whether to arrange a meeting with the young woman next day in order to pleasure her? But would he be able to recapture the feeling he now had for her? Suddenly, Andrée's ridiculous remark came back to him: 'You've no idea what a woman's will-power can do,' and at once the problem was settled; for there still remained all the reasons he had had for the past five years against going to bed with her, with the added irritation of remarks such as this. Nevertheless he no longer felt the same desire to torture her. The idea of staging a melodramatic cat-and-mouse act ultimately repelled him as being too facile and vulgar. He decided, therefore, to bring matters to an end without more ado. 'Forgive this interruption, but it's now five thirty. I must warn you that my landlady is calling at six o'clock. If there's anything you particularly want to say to me. . . . '

'But isn't it you, Costals, who have something to say to me?'

'Me? What would I want to say to you?'

He saw Andrée's face harden in an instant, like the faces of those women who, after swaggering into the police-station with their tawdry jewellery, are told by the superintendent that he will have to detain them. His good genius tapped him on the shoulder: 'Don't be unkind.' 'Why not? I'll be nice to the other one in a moment.' 'What about this one?' 'Another time.'

'Your attitude towards me is a perpetual insult, and there are times when I wonder how I ever managed to put up with it. . . . '

'I've often wondered about that myself. But it's surprising what women will put up with from a man. . . . '

'Of course, when they're in love. But *you're* only interested in abusing your power. The life of a man like you is dreadful, monstrous!'

'A writer worthy of the name is always a monster.'

'Taking advantage of certain people and thwarting the others. Never in tune with other people. Destroying everything in the germ. Your life is one long series of abortions – your own, and those you inflict on others. Have you forgotten what you once wrote to me? "It's too easy to make women unhappy. I leave that to the gigolos"?'

'That "once" was a long time ago. It was at the time when

you yourself wrote to me: "A girl is never the first to tire of platonic love." Besides, you're intelligent enough for it to be worth while making you unhappy. You can make use of your suffering.'

'No, no, don't you believe it! I'm not intelligent enough.'

'But to suffer because one loves: isn't that a kind of happiness? What if your suffering ceased? Wouldn't you miss it?'

'It's easy for you to talk.'

'I don't know, it's the sort of thing women say.'

Now she was afraid of him, with a sort of animal fear, the fear one has of a madman when one is locked in the same room with him and has seen a murderous glint in his eyes. Frantically she sought to placate him.

'Please don't try to be cruel, Costals. It doesn't come naturally to you – you have to force yourself.' (She was trying to persuade him that he was kind, just as other women tried to persuade him that he was 'a Christian at heart'.) 'Is having loved you my crime?'

'Why yes!'

'Why no!' she said vehemently. 'Why must you take revenge on me? I've never done you any harm, and I've suffered a great deal from you. My anger was only a form of inverted misery. I paid for it as I paid for my sulks – which you didn't even notice. I beg you not to destroy this pitiful peace of mind so painfully acquired after three months of struggles and tears. I said to you once: "Rather than this silence and this uncertainty, bludgeon me until I have the strength to escape from you." Now, I say: "No, for pity's sake, spare me these blows." What would I have left of you, if you were no longer even kind to me?'

That she was afraid of him gave Costals no pleasure. All he wanted was to be able to make her suffer with a clear conscience.

'You admitted the other day that your love was not up to much, since you preferred your happiness to mine. For once, I ask you to prefer my happiness. Let me make you suffer. Then I shall love in you the pain I have caused. In this way I shall become part of you, and so love you. For five years you have given me the pleasure of resisting you; now give me the pleasure of being cruel to you. Women always refuse to recognize the degree of falsehood, calculation, weariness and charity in the love men bear them. With me you will see it all. And it will do you good! It will teach you something about life. You see, the important thing is not to let life stagnate. Life is always kind to the virile.'

'But who said I was virile? Is it my business to be virile? I'm a woman, damn it, a woman, a woman!'

'Still, women have a sure way of preventing themselves from suffering.'

'What?'

'Looking at themselves in a mirror when they're unhappy. They'd change their expression at once. And there's another recipe for automatically putting an end to your suffering. That is to try and imagine what you will be like in five years' time. You know perfectly well that, in five years' time, you will have ceased to love me, and that the whole of this episode will seem to you as ludicrous as the items they print in the newspapers under the heading "A Hundred Years Ago". A new sand-hill piles up and buries the old one. Just put yourself in the place of Andrée Hacquebaut at thirty-five. It only needs a little imagination.'

She was about to answer – to explode – when a sort of centipede appeared on the table and began to saunter nonchalantly around. She had a horror of such creatures.

'Kill that ghastly thing!'

'Why? It hasn't done me any harm.'

'What about me? Have I done you any harm?'

She crushed the insect with a newspaper. He gave her a nasty look.

'Mademoiselle Hacquebaut, you exhaust me. The other day I was in a kitchen with a little girl who made me very happy. Being happy, I wanted you to be happy too, and that is why I wrote to you. Last night, at half past nine, you came and banged on my door like a drayman. I was with that same little girl: everything had been arranged so that I should make a woman of her that night. And you dislocated the whole thing. However, since you had come because of me, I did not want your journey to have been in vain, and I made this appointment with you. We might have had a good hour and a half in which to talk pleasantly, if you had not contrived to turn up a quarter of an hour late. Now I really don't know where all this is getting us.'

'What are you after? Are you trying to make me so sick of you that I shall leave you in peace? So that's why you brought me back! To tell me of all your filthy goings-on with a scullery-maid! It's just as I always said: you're incapable of loving your equals. . . .'

'I'm not interested in equality in love because it's the child that I look for in a woman. I can't feel either desire or tenderness for a woman who does not remind me of a child.'

'That way you'll end up in gaol as a satyr.'

'Satyriasis is only an over-developed form of masculinity.'

'And so this is your "goodwill" – the goodwill you spoke about in your letter! This moral trap you set for me, carefully prepared as you prepare everything. . . . Well, did you or did you not emerge from your peaceful existence to write to me: "Opportunity not to be missed"?'

'That was a joke.'

'When Nero hurled himself at one of his courtiers with a dagger, and missed, he used to laugh and say it was a joke.'

'Oh God! Have we got to Nero now?' He heaved an exasperated sigh, pressing his fingers against one of his eyelids. 'I can't help it if I like joking, can I? Life has infinite charm as soon as you stop taking it seriously. But you women are all the same; you always think I'm joking when I'm not, and that I'm not joking when I am.'

'Why won't you admit that what you wanted to do was to watch the effect of your refined tortures on me minute by minute, to watch my thoughts and feelings struggling inside me, just as you might watch ants or Martians devouring each other while you, with your horror of getting involved, keep well away from it all. You like to have me within reach, as a cannibal chief keeps his favourite white man, cutting himself a slice from time to time. . . . Oh, yes, it's a splendid thing, your pity for women! What would it be like if you hadn't any? The pity one feels for a chicken just before wringing its neck.'

'I admit that, on occasion, I've behaved like a bit of a charlatan towards you. But not now. A while ago, yes, I wanted to make you suffer, and I even asked you to allow me to do so. But not now. At this moment, I feel very sympathetic towards you.'

Then she saw something which seemed to her extraordinary. She saw an expression both deep and solemn appear in Costals' eyes, and the word 'fraternal', that once she had loved to repeat to herself in thinking of him, rose to her lips as the one word which could describe what she felt towards him at that moment. But the expression quickly faded.

'Do you believe I could ever be generous towards you?' he asked, wishing to give her a false hope.

'I can no longer believe in you or in anything that comes from you. You have deceived me too often, wilfully misled me. Oh, men, men! Pits of horror and mystery and utter inconsistency as opposed to women, even the least stupid and the least affectionate of whom can do nothing but love, can do nothing but spend their lives returning good for evil!'

'Perhaps rather less is demanded of them. As for men's inconsistency.... Men are more inconsistent than women because they're more intelligent.'

'Oh, you and your intelligence! All I say is this: if, as you pretend, you have the smallest spark of feeling for me, then save me. Save me, Costals. To you it means nothing, to me it means life itself. And surely I have a right to live!'

She was only a few inches away from him, and her eyelids were now closed. She stood thus, with lowered lids, like someone expecting a blow – a little wraith-like, with her great hollow eyes, and burning with the desire to abandon herself. The only sound was the faint patter of sparrows' feet on the sky-light. Then, as Costals said nothing (and although she had not seen him raise his eyebrows when she said 'Surely I have a right to live', as if to say: 'Is it so important?') she moved away a few steps, her head bowed, saying in an odd voice: 'I'm sorry, I've got a speck of dust in my eye.' She turned to the wall and dabbed at her eyes with her handkerchief, silently (no snuffling). Costals waited for her to stop crying, endless though it seemed. 'There's still time,' he thought. 'One word, and I could make her madly happy.' But he said nothing, and she came back to the table. Then he took a step towards her. Suddenly his eyes fell on Andrée's right hand, and he saw what he had not seen before: while all her other nails were long and pointed, the nail of the middle finger of her right hand was cut short. He looked up at the dark rings under the girl's eyes, and his eyelids flickered with the gust of desire that swept over him. But it was too late.

'Did you break your nail?'

'Oh no,' she said, 'it's nothing.' And quickly she closed her fist. Her head was bowed.

'Off you go now, my dear. I think we've come to the end of what we have to say to each other.'

He thought she might be armed, and was going to kill him, or at least slap his face, and in order to be able to ward off the blow, he moved still closer to her, as modern bull-fighters stick close to the bull's flank in order to be 'inside' a blow from its horns. She raised her head, looked surprised, and stared at him motionless, with her bruised eyes. He realized meanwhile that she did not intend to kill him, that the idea had not even crossed her mind, and he thought: 'Really, these Frenchwomen!'

'Costals, I shall probably never see you again. I just want you to answer one question: are you aware of what you're doing?'

'What, me? That's a good one. If I weren't aware, I wouldn't be guilty.'

'What do you mean by that? Am I to understand that you *want* to be guilty?'

Without answering, he took her gently by the arm, and opening the door, escorted her along the short garden path to the door that led into the avenue. (There was a wing-shaped cloud floating in front of them.) 'Shall I kiss her on the forehead before throwing her out?' The reasons for and against such a gesture were equally balanced. The door-bell had been out of order for some time: it was not supposed to ring when the door was opened from the inside, but in fact, about every other time, it did. 'If it rings, I shall kiss her.' He opened the door. Silence. A twittering of birds, weaving a trellis of song above their heads. She went away.

He closed the door. He had an intuition that she would come back, that she would knock, that something would happen. But no, nothing: he had never had any luck with his intuitions. Back in the studio, he listened a moment longer, then went upstairs to the columbarium.

'Well, my little one, what did you think of all that?'

Solange was still standing behind the curtain in the attitude she had adopted for eavesdropping. And she looked at Costals with perplexed and feverish eyes. Her cheeks were flushed, too, as when he switched on the light after covering her with kisses for hours (that face of hers, a little swollen by his kisses), although today he had only kissed her three or four times, and that an hour and a half ago. And her hair was somewhat wild, because she had not wetted it that morning.

'Well,' he asked again, 'what did you think of that little scene? A real performance, eh?'

'I wish I hadn't seen it. When you made me read some of that woman's letters, I felt sorry for her. But after seeing that, I have no pity left.'

When he had got her to read some of Andrée's letters, she had been shocked by what she considered a lack of delicacy on his part, although he had not revealed the name of his correspondent. She had told him so, and his reply was: 'I'm taking the hat away.'*

---

*'To return to the conduct of the Comte de Guiche, the secretary also told me that, being present one evening at the Queen's card-table where the princesses and duchesses are seated around the Queen while the others remain standing, the Count became aware that the hand of a lady, his mistress, was busy in a place which modesty forbids me to name and which he was covering with his hat. Observing that the lady's head was averted, he maliciously raised his hat. Everyone present began to laugh and whisper, and I leave you to imagine the confusion into which the poor creature was thrown....

'He played similar tricks upon ladies daily, and yet they continued to seek his company.' – Primi Visconti: *Memoirs of the Court of Louis XIV.*

'What do you mean?'

'You'll be told when you're a big girl.'

Now again she was shocked, out of some obscure sexual solidarity, that he had made her a witness to the humiliation of one of her kind. But such was her faith in him that it never occurred to her to wonder: 'Will this happen to me one day?'

'It does one good to see you again. To see a woman who still lives in the world of reality. It's true, you're one of the few women I know who isn't crazy. Literary men attract crazy women as a lump of rotting meat attracts flies. We're landed with every kind of loneliness and repression: they want food for their dreams! You're the exception that proves the rule, and as an exception I love you.'

'But then why bother to reply to them?'

'Ah, well! When I see flies on a piece of meat, I say to myself: "Everyone has to eat".'

He had taken her in his arms, inhaling the warmth and freshness of her face and sliding a hand under her shoulder-strap (he was a real terror with shoulder-straps: he had only to look at them for them to snap), hungry to get back at last to something he really desired, and with the same ardour as if he were returning to her after a long absence; and he was indeed returning from a distant country, from the nether regions where dwelt the people who did not attract him. And it was as though he were about to give voice to the sort of little strangled yaps with which a dog will greet the return of its master, be he good or bad. He said to her:

'I bring you my cruelty while it is still warm. This cruelty is my tenderness for you; they are one and the same thing. Kind? Cruel? It's all the same. As one quenches one's thirst with a cigarette. Water would refresh you, and the cigarette burns, yet they're the same thing. Don't try to understand. You saw that girl? There are masses and masses of them around! All the women I've refused because I didn't find them attractive. Drown the lot of them, that's all they deserve – like Carrier's executions in Nantes. And in fact that's how it usually finishes: rrrop...I open the trapdoor. Quite seriously, what she ought to do now is commit suicide, so that I'm really rid of her. I showed you that little episode so that you should see what happens to women I don't care for. There's a girl who started from nothing, who brought herself up entirely on her own in the worst possible conditions, who is cultivated, sensitive, intelligent, extremely gifted, and who has been in love with me for five years. If I weighed her merits against yours, yours would be non-existent. But I don't love her. I've never given her anything, never kissed her, never held her hand. Because I don't love her. You, on the other hand, come along, you attract me, and I give you everything; my attention, my affection, my sexual vigour, my intellect. Remember that, if one day you have reason to complain of me, which you surely will. You have had everything, for no good reason. There's no reason why I should have given everything to you rather than to others, no reason for such a preference or such a partiality. Where did I read that line that always runs through my head when I think of you?

I know not why 'twas you I chose.

What are you? A little thing like so many others, a dewdrop in the meadow. You might have had all the "negative qualities" in the world: do you think that would have stopped me? All you had to do was please me, and you couldn't help that. Picked out almost at random. That's how life goes – everything a matter of chance. Why this rather than that? *In reality*, there is no reason, or what reason there is is absolutely unimportant. For you, everything; for the others, nil. There's a terrible injustice there, and that is what I like about it. Not that I don't love justice too; I enjoy them both in turn. I had to tell you all this. In any case, you know that I enjoy telling you unpleasant things. It's part of my love for you.'

She listened without really understanding, with a certain bewilderment that was natural enough. But she belonged to a world where writers were thought of as 'literary chaps, not to be taken too seriously'. As for him, he was glad that she did not answer, for whatever she had said would doubtless have been very different from what he himself thought. He went on :

'There are so many worlds that are foreign to you. The world of knowledge. The world of justice. The world of suffering. The world of responsibility. You do not even suspect their

254

existence. And I am only aware of them in flashes. A rocket soars, lights them up for a moment, then they are plunged in darkness once more. My darkness.

'Yet I devote time and attention to you, I give you part of my substance, there are times when I speak to you as if I were speaking to some unknown world. How many of my words have reached their target? What a lot of wasted shots! Am I right, or am I wrong? A little girl. A little twenty-year-old bourgeois Parisian girl. There are those who will say: "So that's what you spend your time on! When the social structure.... When whole nations.... When empires.... Aren't you ashamed of yourself?" And there are others who will say: "This little soul is every bit as important as the soul of an entire nation. All the suffering caused throughout the world by the war weighs no more than the tears of this chit of a girl. If there was nothing else in your life but the fact that you treated her lovingly, you would have fulfilled your human role here below, you would have worked the tiny human plot that is allotted to each of us." Which of these two viewpoints is the right one? A vulgar and meaningless question. Both of them are right. You must immerse yourself in one of them until you have exhausted it, and then do the same with the other. They're two aspects of a single truth. Fancy writers tell us that truth is a diamond, but what they never stop to consider is how many facets this diamond may show. And now, quiet! Don't try to answer. There's no need for you to understand, as there's no need for me to know that you haven't understood.'

He went and closed the shutters,* drew the curtains, and modestly turned over a little card from a press-cutting agency which bore the legend 'WE SEE ALL' in large letters. His soul was still smouldering, as if under the influence of some life-giving spirit: this delectable brew was his cruelty to Andrée. He flung Solange, fully dressed, on to the bed, and straightened her legs out. From then on, he was like an apache trying to pin a man to the ground. Usually he dared not squeeze her too

---

*The columbarium overlooked the gardens of a convent (of which there were many in the district). The convent bells could be heard, and the nuns could be seen from the windows. The author has refrained from exploiting the too obvious contrasts.

hard for fear of hurting her: she was so young! Now for the first time he was brutal with her, and although this was partly from necessity, because she struggled, it was also calculated, for he was determined to leave her with an unforgettable memory. She screamed, 'No! No!' with her mouth wide open and her head lolling from side to side, and he drank in her breath which no longer had the odour he knew but an odour which came from deeper down, as though her cries drew it up from the depths of her being. He could keep her head still only by seizing her tongue between his teeth and clenching them when she tried to move. And with every limb he systematically manhandled this thing which was Mlle Dandillot. Suddenly everything became easy and he let himself sink into a new sensation. She closed her eyes, and her plaints ceased. Meanwhile he was absorbed in his sensation, mediocre though it seemed. It gave him no more than an intellectual satisfaction: 'Well, that's done!' And he sniffed vaguely at this woman's face, as a lion, tearing chunks off the meat it holds between its paws, stops now and then to lick it.

With one of the handkerchiefs embroidered for him by Andrée Hacquebaut, he wiped Solange's forehead and the curve of her nostrils, so divinely moist. Her head, having slipped between the pillows, was now tilted even further back, so that the long, pale curve of her neck and throat assumed more prominence than the face itself, on which there appeared a look of such complete surrender that he pressed her eyelids closed in alarm. Her lips were parted a little, disclosing the small teeth like those of a sheep's head on a butcher's stall. There are three smiles that have something in common: the smile of a corpse, the smile of a gratified woman, and the smile of a decapitated beast.

He scrutinized her thus for a while, attentively. He was trying to differentiate her, to see in what way she was more than a mere body, more than an instrument for his caresses, more than a mirror in which to observe his own pleasure.

He stretched himself out at her side. His soul, already clouded with intimations of sadness, took flight and hovered in realms remote from her. It was the primordial moment when man asks, as in the Gospel: 'Woman, what have I to do

with thee?' The primordial moment of pity for women. Outside, the sky must have clouded over, for the room was now
almost dark. He had visions of flabby, white-skinned women,
women of infinite depravity, who lie in one's arms at nightfall
as the lights spring up one by one around the city, and who
say: 'Look ... there's a light ...' and whom one goes on holding, out of pity, making them believe that one loves them, out
of pity. This memory brought back others: the whole of his
life opened out like a peacock's tail, and all of it, past and
future, was dotted with faces like the golden circles on a peacock's tail. He felt pity for this young creature alive at his
side, her face nestling in the hollow of his left shoulder, where
so many faces had lain. (If that shoulder had been a photographic plate, how many superimposed faces would have been
visible there, and what a hideous monster the composite face
that eventually appeared. . . .) He felt pity for her for having
placed herself in hands such as his (and yet, had he detected
the slightest little ruse or merely precaution on her part, to
protect herself, he would have held it against her). He felt pity
for her because he did not love her more, could not find more
reasons for loving her – and because for him she was but one
among many, whereas for her he was the only one – and
because of what she believed he was giving her, when in fact
it was impossible for him to give it. He thought: 'One spends
one's youth loving people one cannot possess fully (through
shyness), and one's maturity loving people one cannot possess
fully (through satiety).'

One of his arms lay under Solange's head, but his face and
body were turned away from her. There was a moment when
he betrayed her so cruelly in his thoughts that he put out his
hand to seek hers and comfort her, as if she must have guessed
what was going on inside him (and also because, now that he
no longer expected anything from Solange, he felt he must be
doubly kind to her as though to counteract the suspension of
his love). She turned and, without a word, kissed him on the
cheek – still the same childish kisses, in spite of all that had
happened. She had emerged from her stillness to do this, as a
solitary wave rises above a calm sea. A cry burst from his
heart: 'She can suffer because of me, but I cannot suffer

because of her. I love her, yet it is not in her power to make me suffer. This game must end, this abominable one-sided game, so harmful to the weaker of us.' Then a voice rose: 'You say you love her, yet she cannot make you suffer: therefore you do not love her.' And he answered: 'Why must I always be lumped together with other people! I love her but she cannot make me suffer, because I am not like everybody else. I am not so easily hurt.' He was suddenly seized with a passion for truth that was either dazzling light or cloudy obfuscation, either a glory or a vice (one of his women had called it his 'catastrophic honesty'); he wanted to say to her: 'Little one, my darling little one, I had better warn you now: I do not love you enough. You too will have to stand aside for someone else. The day will come when I shall have even forgotten your face. I am of the wandering race of men. The day will come when I shall love other women, different women. Perhaps it has happened already!' (this was not true). 'Perhaps already I have stopped loving you. . . . Perhaps I have never loved you at all, my darling child. . . .' But he knew that she was like all the rest, that she too, like the great ones of the earth, lived and fed almost exclusively on lies, and would soon die if the lies were to cease, and that Truth, anyway, is *ipso facto* reprehensible and punishable by law since, as everyone knows, she goes about naked. He said nothing, but squeezed her hand more tightly. 'The main thing is that she should be happy.' Then, with her face buried in his neck, she made a cooing noise which it would be feeble to describe as being like the cooing of a dove, for it literally was the cooing of a dove. He asked her what it meant. She answered, 'It means I'm happy,' in the same far-away voice, as of another self, the ghost of the little girl she had once been, speaking from the depths of her subconscious where it had sunk long ago.

Then he remembered that there had been other women beside whom, lying thus after the act, he had not felt the same impulse to escape – others beside whom at such moments he had thought: 'I could die quite happily, like this. Now I really wouldn't mind dying, like this.' But lying there beside Solange, he did not say this to himself; no, he did not say to himself that he was ready to die.

'The main thing is that she should be happy.' Once again, his lucid mind laid bare the underlying meaning of the words. And he saw that it hardly differed at all from what he had felt for many, many others, of the most diverse kinds (and what does it matter how a person behaves towards those he loves; his behaviour towards the rest is what really counts). He remembered the emotion he had felt on reading the words of that splendid old fossil Captain Hurluret in *Les Gaîtés de l'Escadron*, when he is eventually retired: 'I've been forty years in the service, and the only thing in all that time that really counts for me is the fellows I've stopped making fools of themselves and getting into trouble, the fellows for whom barrack-room life has been a little more tolerable thanks to me. And if, later on, there are some of them who remember their Captain and say: "He wasn't a bad sort, after all," I shall have had my reward.' On reading this, Costals had raised his head from the book. It had struck a deep chord in him, and he thought: 'I am the same sort of chap as Hurluret. Of course, there are other things in me, but I'm Hurluret as well.' And now he realized that underlying his words about Solange, his wish for her 'to be happy', was something not so very different from what he had felt towards his men during the war: 'Are the men happy? Is there anything wrong?' – or at home towards the servants, always going out of his way to see that they got their fair share of pleasure in this world – or towards the hired native in the colonies, getting up in the middle of the night to give him an extra blanket because he had heard him cough in his sleep – or towards the almost unknown vagrant he had sheltered under his roof as a guest, and with whom he identified himself through the mere fact of this hospitality. And so it was for all that race of men and women encountered by chance, to whom he had given more than any other man would have given in his place – given not for the sake of 'principle', not because he believed that good was preferable to evil – given without even any preconceived ideas about the world, for he had come to the conclusion long since that no definition holds water, that 'the people' are not this or that, that 'natives' or 'women' or 'Frenchmen' are not this or that, that all is in everything, that the good are also bad and the bad also good – given, finally, without the least thought that it might be counted to his credit somewhere, in the hearts of these men and women, who had promptly forgotten him, or in the eyes of public opinion, which knew nothing of his actions, either before those human tribunals where the riff-raff dispense injustice, or before that supreme tribunal in which he did not believe and of which all he could say was that if it existed, and if one day he were to appear before it (as he no doubt would, having always lived without giving much heed to the Law), hundreds of people would come and bear witness in his favour. And he saw that there, too, Solange Dandillot was one of a crowd, and he pitied her for not being more clearly set apart.

He lay there, no longer thinking about her. 'What are you thinking about?' she asked, a little alarmed by his silent day-dreaming. 'About you.' A slight, very slight and tenuous thread of boredom pierced his consciousness. Then he thought: 'One day I shall put that image of her teeth, like those of a decapitated sheep, in one of my books. I *use* her!' At the thought that he *made use* of Solange, his throat tightened as if he were about to cry. But suddenly another thought leapt up like a dolphin out of a calm sea: 'I've been told often enough that I was wrong, "criminal" even, in not taking a girl who offered herself to me. Nature, society, public opinion, are you satisfied now? Well? I bet I still haven't got it right.' Amused by this thought, he was encouraged to say some things which he found a bit difficult. He sat up, and leaning over her, said with a smile: 'Well, my little Dandillot, now you're my mistress! You see the way things happen.... Now see if you can get away from me.'

She frowned a little, and he smoothed out the furrows with his thumb.

'You said "no" when it happened, so your honour is safe. ... There's another thing, rather less agreeable. Do you know what a woman does when she....'

He gave her some pharmaceutical advice in a whisper. He would have liked the room to be darker still, as dark as night. Several times he repeated: 'I'm ashamed to have to tell you these things....' But it was not 'these things', or having to say them, which made him feel ashamed: he knew that there was nothing shameful about them, that on the contrary they were beneficent and therefore moral. But he was ashamed of having said them so many times before. Eventually she got up without saying a word, and disappeared into the next room.

He sat down in an armchair. From the bathroom came the familiar sounds of the different water-pipes. 'Now she's doing this, now she's doing that. . . .' The almost identical similarity between this moment and hundreds of others he had been through plunged his soul in melancholy. 'For her, it's something so new, so surprising. . . . For me it's all so stale.' His melancholy would have been less had his pleasure been really spectacular. But far from it; and he was well aware that Solange had derived no more pleasure from the act than he had.

She came back, and with her hands on the arms of his chair, leaned over him, compassionately, in a very 'womanly' gesture; they were like two castaways flung up together on the shore. But so completely did she seem to share his sadness that this sadness vanished. He went and sat on the divan, and made her sit beside him. Then he said:

'Yes, all this is very painful. And yet, when I showed you that woman just now, although it was indeed for the reasons I explained, it was also in order to show you what becomes of a girl who doesn't do the necessary when she should. You see, there's only one way of loving women, and that's by making love to them. There's only one way of doing them good, and that's by taking them in one's arms. Incense needs warmth in order to give out its perfume; women too need that particular warmth to give out theirs. All the rest – friendship, esteem, intellectual sympathy – is an illusion, without love, and a cruel illusion, too. For illusions are the cruel things: with realities one can always get by. You remember the words of St Paul: "The prudence of the flesh is the death of the soul." I know many unsatisfactory marriages where the trouble is entirely due to the husband's "respect" for the wife: a wife should be treated like a mistress, and not just in fits and starts but all the time; whether it's easy or not is irrelevant. That silly little get-together we had just now disappointed you, no doubt, as it did me; but it takes six months for a young Frenchwoman to learn how to be properly excited. You've only got to touch an Italian or a Spanish girl and she practically swoons; but French girls are slow starters and it's the devil of a job to give them any pleasure: I usually reckon six months to get things right. Perhaps some harm may come from my having taken you; but since you love me, it would have been just as hurtful – to you – if I had refrained. And in any case you're twenty-one. Of course I don't mean it's the autumn of a woman's life, but all the same, the way things are going now. . . . Why, in this year's Miss World beauty competition, the age-limit was twenty-two. . . . Come, my beauty, let time work for you. The day will come when you will sense my desire from afar, and will welcome it. We shall be attuned to each other like a pair of runners in a three-mile race – both working hand in glove. We shall speak to one another in our silences. You will want what I want, I shall want what you want. So you'll no longer want darkness when you are in my arms; you will want broad daylight, the better to see me with, and you will see me. . . . What will keep me going when I am old? The books I have written and the pleasure I have given women.'

She stroked his hair, then clasped her hands archwise over his head and rested her forehead against his chest, bowing so low that all he could see was her hair, in a gesture of utter submission.

They went out. An old man was sitting on a bench feeding the birds, and she made a detour so as not to frighten them away. In the streets, a few radiant faces were almost engulfed by the repulsive, virulent magma of the unloved and the unloving (not to mention the notorious ugliness of the Parisians). And he was filled, for the hundredth time and yet as freshly as ever, with that regal sensation of walking side by side, as though her legitimate owner, with a woman who attracts stares and almost shouts of admiration. She still addressed him as *vous*, though oblivious of the delicate pleasure he derived from being thus authorized to say *vous* in return. With this *vous*, Costals was able to deny the intimacy of their relationship, to create, alongside the reality, another order of things that belied it.

From time to time he put his hand on her waist, for a second only, as if to make sure that she was still beside him. But soon she put her arm through his. It was only the second time she had done so, the first having been on the night of their great misunderstanding. On both occasions, it was after having seen him troubled: he was touched by this. Soon, however, he began to feel uncomfortable. For the fact was that ever since he had first gone out with a woman he loved at the age of nineteen, he had always obstinately refused to keep in step with his female companions; he found it ridiculous and humiliating for a man. So they jolted along for another fifty yards, and it seemed to him painfully symbolic that a man could not walk straight because the woman who loved him, and whom he loved, was holding his arm. Finally it was she who, breaking step as soldiers do on the march, fell into rhythm with her lover. He noticed this and was pleased. Soon, however, it wasn't enough for him. That weight on his arm seemed like a chain. The very gesture with which, poor child, she had thought to bring them closer together, had only made him feel impatience and scorn at being coupled. He took advantage of a traffic jam, as they were crossing a street, to detach himself gently. And then, having regained his freedom, he felt a wave of tenderness towards her.

She was dining with friends in the centre of town. They passed travel posters showing Algerian belly-dancers (for the benefit of French tourists) shoeshine boys (for the benefit of British tourists), all the symbols of that devilish human invention, travel, which for inconvenience, exhaustion, danger, time-wasting and nervous wear and tear has no rival except war (the only difference being that travel costs you the earth whereas at least one is paid for going to war). What they inspired in Costals was not so much a desire to be sea-sick in Solange's company as an urge to make a great splash on her behalf, which, now that she had given herself, would no longer look as though he were trying to buy her (this feeling comprised a mixture of delicacy and vulgarity, as is so often the case with questions of money): he could feel the banknotes quivering in his wallet like thoroughbreds at the starting-gate. He said to her:

'You know, old thing, I like squandering money on women;

it's one of the things I pride myself on. When I am old and
poverty-stricken, with only a pension of eight hundred francs
granted me by the Society of Literature and the proceeds of
the subscription launched for me in the *Figaro* to live on, I
like to imagine that all the money I ever spent on the women
I loved will be reconstituted somewhere in tangible form and
that I shall depart this world satisfied with what I have done,
my eyes fixed on that mountain of gold – which, if you'll forgive the expression, I shall call "the gold of my loins". This is
why I regret having spent so little on you when we were out
together. I get the impression that I'm out with a decent
woman, and that's a sensation I don't like at all.' (Since when
this note of insolence with her? Wasn't it since.... Ah,
wretched males, even the best of them!) 'Listen: those are
bank-notes, made to be changed into happiness; and that's
something I know all about, for I won't deny I've had my
whack at God's creation. Do you want to come away with me
somewhere for a couple of months? I say two months, because
that's just about the time it takes to get through a good love
affair, but it might be longer – until one of us has had enough.'
('One of us' was a charming euphemism. He knew perfectly
well that he was always the first to break off.) 'Anywhere you
like. Persia. Or Egypt. Or Transylvania. Or Pennsylvania. Or
Mount Ararat. And I really mean it: you name the place and
off we go. In my life as in my art, I'm ready for anything:
what's difficult is to really want something, but this time I
somehow believe I do. And so it's all right, because I love my
desires. I have the impression that God has given you parents
who want your happiness above everything else. You will
come back armed with two months' happiness: a splendid
weapon to face the future with. You will then be admirably
placed for marrying. You are no longer a virgin – though,
taking one of those linguistic liberties which are the privilege
of great writers, I shall continue to call you a girl, for I am
too fond of youth to resign myself to using the word "woman"
unless I really have to: it sounds so old and pompous – you
are no longer a virgin, but from what I know of men, and if
you have any wit at all, your husband won't even notice it.
Besides, even if he does, he won't say a word: we're not

savages in France! Then, either he'll make you happy and you won't regret me, which is what I very much hope; or else you'll be unhappy, and then I shan't be far away. We'll get you a divorce if need be, and go back to good old Ararat. This trip can either remain a secret as far as you're concerned, or be made public. In the latter case, it will redound to your eternal credit. You never bother about your own glory, so one has to look after it for you. But it can also be kept very secret. I've been on a dozen honeymoons in my life, and nothing has ever leaked out. And I would go to gaol sooner than give away a woman I loved. All in all it's a plan against which no objection, social, moral or otherwise, can hold water. Of course there are always those who will say: "Sir, you're a revolting cad" – to which I would reply: "Far from being a revolting cad, I'm a spirit of the air. Of course it's not your element, etc. . . ." You see, when one wants to give pleasure to somebody, one mustn't look too far ahead, or bother too much about the consequences. When one wants to give pleasure to somebody, it's the same as when one wants to produce a great work of literature – it must be done with a kind of studied insouciance: because if you thought about it too long you'd never do it at all. . . .'

For a moment he dreamed of seeing the beauty of the world with her, unveiling it to her, becoming merged with her as part of that beauty. Then his day-dream disintegrated, wandered, took another path. And he realized that though he did want to go on such a journey, he wanted to go alone. And it was true that, when he remembered all the wonderful places he had seen – every one of which he had visited at least twice, once alone and once with someone he loved – or when he wanted to use them in his books, it was always the time when he had travelled alone that came to his mind most vividly, most magically and most potently. For it is a major law of nature that we are no longer entirely one when we are two. If God said 'It is not good that man should live alone', it was because he was afraid of the solitary man. And so he weakened him by providing him with a mate, in order to have him at his mercy.

But he quickly repelled the sirens of solitude: 'After all,

whatever I made of it would be for her. To give pleasure to someone who deserves it is not to be despised. . . . '

Under an archway he pulled her towards him. His lips hovered above her face and eventually came to rest on one of her eyelids, where they remained for what seemed an eternity.

As they were about to part, he said to her :

'You know, one day I'm going to put in one of my books an image that occurred to me about your teeth – "like those of a decapitated sheep".'

'How horrible !'

'But it's true. And so it has to be said. You don't mind my making use of you in my books, do you?'

'Not at all. On the contrary, I'm glad to be useful to you in your work.'

'Well said. . . . You're not the first, mind you. . . . But still, well said. . . . Now I shall be able to love you even more than I do already.'

He gazed at her fondly. But just then an expression crossed her face which spoiled her prettiness. And it struck him that if ever he allowed himself to be finally caught, and married her, it would again be out of pity. And he was afraid of his pity.

Back in his studio, he was tidying up the bed when he saw traces of blood on the top sheet. He reflected that the sheet would go to the laundry, whereas fifteen years earlier he would have kept it as it was, as a souvenir. He felt a pang as he realized once again that he was not sufficiently open-hearted towards her. As though to make up for this, when he went to bed he searched for Mlle Dandillot's blood-stains on the sheet and placed them against his heart. And he fell asleep feeling somehow protected by the affection he felt towards her.

During the days that followed, Costals awaited some sign of life from Andrée : a letter, a telegram or a visit. . . . The concierge, the servant, everyone was warned – a little ridiculously – to bar her passage. Ah, if only he could have had her deported to the Island of Dogs near Constantinople, or to some other equally God-forsaken spot! But nothing happened.

'Perhaps she's killed herself.' The thought filled him with profound satisfaction.

It is a peculiarity of most young girls to wish to show their
parents to the man they love, even when these parents are
total idiots who will alienate him at once. Costals was invited
to lunch at the Dandillots'.

The advent of 'the family' invariably provoked three reflexes in Costals. Terror at the threat of the Hippogriff: 'I
know what they're after!' A feeling of ridicule, this being
for him a basic element in the concept of the family. And
animosity, for he could not but detest all parents, who represented the potential enemy. On this occasion, these reflexes
combined to put him in a state of excitement to which the
thought of the risk he was running and the ordeal to be overcome contributed greatly.

Solange had sought to make the prospect more alluring by
saying: 'You'll see, my parents are very likeable.' 'Likeable
to whom?' he thought to himself. 'To her? What do I care!
To me? How does she know?' It reminded him of the people
who tell you on their invitation-cards, by way of encouragement, what you will be given to eat or drink: 'Tea, Sherry,
etc.' (The vulgarity of European manners compared to those of
'savages' – the Chinese, the Arabs etc.)

Mme Dandillot had the dimensions of a horse and the aspect
of a policeman. To reconcile the two, let us say that she
resembled a police horse. She was a head taller than her husband and Costals. To his horror, Costals recognized in her a
caricature of her daughter. The same nose, though misshapen,
the same lips, though colourless, the same expression, though
deadened. The resemblance could not be said to be frightful,
since it was natural; it was nonetheless startling: 'At fifty, my
mistress will look a similar fright. In fifteen years' time she
will be as plump as a partridge already. It's a warning from
heaven; there's not a moment to lose.' He was appalled to
think that Mme Dandillot knew all about their liaison and that
perhaps, in certain circumstances, she had dictated Solange's

behaviour. The thought that Solange was incapable of lying oppressed him now like sultry weather.

M. Dandillot, on the other hand, had an appearance of such nobility that no one would ever have taken him for a French-man. Close-shaven, and with hair as thick as a young man's, though nearly white, he reminded one a little of the 'family Doctor' as seen in advertisements for patent medicines. His smile, which was delightful, revealed a row of perfect, gleaming teeth. But all his features seemed to be drawn with pain. Clearly he was a doomed man. At table, M. Dandillot said nothing except for a few polite words.

It has often been said that nothing reveals a man's character more than his home. The Dandillots' interior bespoke an absence of taste rare even for their social background and for Paris. A few quite handsome objects stood cheek by jowl with a mass of vulgar and pretentious junk – inexcusable for people in their circumstances: it was all fairly opulent-looking. Costals could have understood a bachelor engaged upon some great work putting up with such surroundings out of in-difference to externals and contempt for them. But a 'worldly' family, and this ravishing girl! That Solange had not compelled her family to have a decent-looking home, that she could tolerate this obscene décor, told heavily against her: there must be something of the same inferior quality in her that enabled her to feel at home in it all. And it seemed to him even more serious that she should have no hesitation in show-ing it to him, no suspicion of the uneasiness it might cause him, or what it might make him feel about her.

Mme Dandillot said that her daughter had never had a day's illness ('She's beginning to boost her wares'), and that she did not care for scent or jewellery. When Costals said he did not much care for them either, she simpered: 'Another thing you have in common.' ('She's already treating us as if we were engaged, blast her!') She also sang her husband's praises, pre-sumably so that Costals should not think she had married a corpse. If one were to believe her, M. Dandillot had more or less created French sport. He had run various sports clubs, encouraged the young, been 'a man of action'. Costals choked back the retorts that rose to his lips: that action is like an

itch: you scratch, and that's all; that the only action worthy
of the name is inside oneself; that all men of action, when
you press them about it, can ultimately think of nothing to
say, so little justification can they find for it, etc.

Solange, her nose in her plate, said not a word. She was
embarrassed beyond belief to see Costals in the midst of her
family. Embarrassment hardened her features, gave her a sly,
ill-natured expression. What family life can do to people! An
angel of sweetness transformed into a *femme fatale*. Anyone
who saw Solange now for the first time could not have helped
thinking: 'She's a perfect bitch. Beware!'

Costals and Mme Dandillot talked about nothing for an
hour. In order to be sure of pleasing the writer, and also to
avoid saying anything stupid, Mme Dandillot would repeat,
after a suitable interval, precisely what Costals himself said.
Costals having expressed the view, over the hors d'oeuvres,
that 'journalism does not prevent a real writer from getting on
with his work', Mme Dandillot declared with an air of wisdom
over the coffee, as if it were a truth which Costals needed to
be convinced of: 'You know it's quite possible to produce a
good book and also write for newspapers.' Costals felt more
and more ridiculous, and humiliated at the idea that he was
here as a possible fiancé. A fiancé! A 'son-in-law'! Braggart
though he was, he could not shake off this feeling of humiliation.

He looked at these people and despised them for not looking
after their daughter better. 'Whether out of vanity, or
immorality, or calculation, or irresponsibility, they have let
her go out with a man like me, and I find it hard to believe
that they don't know I sleep with her. Perhaps they think I'll
marry her, but how do they know? A girl who was obviously
cut out to be a virgin, who was the personification of the
chaste young girl, and they don't do anything to protect her
against herself, the swine. No religion, no tradition, no education, no self-respect, no backbone. My role is to attack, I know,
but it's up to society to defend itself! Yet whenever I try to
conquer people's bodies, or trouble people's minds and spirits,
it's always the same: no defences! Soft as putty everywhere.
I play my game, but they don't play theirs!' From then on,
the thought of having parents-in-law so lacking in decorum

made the possibility that he might one day allow himself to be drawn into marrying Solange even more remote than ever. Nevertheless it must be noted that had the Dandillots been high-minded people who would never have let their daughter go out alone with him, he would have railed against both them and her, and would promptly have discarded her with a jibe against prudery. Despising them for being high-minded, despising them for not being so, he held them as though in a vice, and Solange with them. He would screw it tight the day he stopped loving her. The machinery was ready.

After lunch, a visitor was announced. Mme Dandillot and Solange went to entertain her in the drawing-room. M. Dandillot asked Costals to join him in his study. Costals thought: 'If he says: "I entrust my daughter to your care" (he felt a lump in his throat), I shall reply: "She will be like a little sister to me." It's not a phrase that commits me in any way. For as my mistress she's like a little sister to me.'

In his study, M. Dandillot let himself sink into a low arm-chair. He suddenly seemed tiny, like a fly shrivelling up just before it dies. The outline of his emaciated thighs was visible inside the trouser legs. We shall refrain from describing the study, for we know that novel-readers always skip the descriptions.

'Monsieur Costals,' he said, 'I am not the sort of person you think me. If I hardly spoke at lunch it was because I have been eating my meals with Mme Dandillot for thirty-one years, and we have said all we had to say to each other. I have lost the habit of talking, or rather I've acquired the habit of talking to myself in my room. As for you, I prefer to talk to you alone, as I want to talk to you seriously. However, there's something about you that bothers me a little, and I should like to get it off my chest before I start talking about myself. May I speak with absolute frankness?'

'You can always try, and we shall see,' said Costals, who this time could feel the baleful Hippogriff literally breathing down his neck.

'Now, now!' said M. Dandillot with a smile, pretending to see it as a joke. 'I owe it to the man who wrote that great book' (he pointed to one of Costals' books which was lying on a table nearby) 'to be absolutely frank. Well, here goes: why do you wear that?'

He pointed to the red rosette of the Legion of Honour in Costals' buttonhole.

'I don't like making myself conspicuous. If I had refused ...'

He was about to add: '... I should have appeared to be making a great deal of fuss about it,' but stopped short, sensing that he was about to put his foot in it.

'Well, if you had refused? I'd like to show you something.'

Solange's father rose, took a sheaf of papers out of a drawer, and handed Costals a cutting from the *Indépendant de N—*, dated July 1923. The headline read: *Our fellow-citizen, Charles Dandillot, refuses the Legion of Honour.* A lyrical, or rather cautiously lyrical, editorial introduction was followed by the letter written by M. Dandillot to the unfortunate custodian of the scarlet flood.

Sir,
I understand that you wish to propose me for the Legion of Honour.
I have dedicated my life unostentatiously to the youth of France. I did not do so in the hope of a reward which must be shared with all and sundry.
Furthermore, I am now fifty-seven. Allow me, dear sir, to express one wish: that in future the Government will employ men better qualified to select the people who have done something for their country.
Believe me, etc....

Costals saw in this letter the resentment of a man who had missed being decorated at thirty, and nothing more. 'As a way of thanking a man who has had a kind thought, it's not too badly put together.' The fact that M. Dandillot had communicated his masterpiece to the *Indépendant de N—* also seemed rather significant. M. Dandillot then embarked on a lecture about 'purity'. Costals knew this one well, having delivered it himself on occasion. His real opinion on the subject of honours was that they belonged to the category of things designated by Epictetus as 'indifferent'. But it was obvious from this letter that M. Dandillot attached great importance to honours.

While the latter was searching through the folder, Costals had cast an author's eye on the cover of his book (writers throw surreptitious glances at their names in print much as pretty women – or women who think themselves pretty – glance at their faces in mirrors) and noticed that hardly more than a dozen pages of the 'great book' had been cut. It is true, of course, that one can perfectly well 'place' an author after having read only a dozen pages by him.

When he had finished his lecture on 'purity', M. Dandillot said: 'Has Solange told you that I haven't long to live? It's not absolutely definite, but I'm fairly certain of it.'

'Mlle Dandillot has never said anything of the kind.'

'I shall be dead within a month. The end of all illusions!'

'For me, death will be the end of all reality.'

'For me, the end of all illusions. I'm going to die at the age of sixty-one. And for a man who has been living for the past thirty years in accordance with certain natural principles which could reasonably have been expected to promote both youthfulness and longevity, it's a bit of a fiasco. Sixty-one! The age at which everyone dies. And yet, think of it: for over thirty years I've lived with all my windows open, never touched alcohol, never smoked. For over thirty years, do you hear, not a drop of hot or even lukewarm water has ever touched my face or body, even when I was out of sorts. For over thirty years, I've been up at six every morning doing my exercises naked. And only a year ago I was camping in the mountains, walking twenty-five miles a day with a rucksack on my back like a young man, my head bare to the sun and the rain. Even if my face is lined, my body, up to a month ago, was still that of a young man. . . . Even now,' he added, pointing to his stomach, 'you mustn't think I have a paunch. I have to wear a flannel belt, and that accounts for the thickness. Actually I have a very slim waist. In short, I've lived a *natural* life: you realize what that means, *natural*? And in spite of all this to end up dying at sixty-one, at the mere threshold of old age. When heaps of people who have lived the softest, most artificial lives, go on living into their seventies and eighties. So now I say to myself: it wasn't worth it, I've been had.'

Costals, too, felt that it hadn't been worth it. He remembered the words of the Scripture: 'I shall suffer the same fate as the foolish. Why then was I more wise?' He said:

'The main thing is to know whether it was a sacrifice for you to give up wine, tobacco, etc. . . .'

'Often, yes. Particularly getting up at six. But I was determined to conquer myself. If I had had to struggle for my livelihood and that of my children, I should have told myself that the effort was not wasted. But no, I've always lived on my private means. If I have struggled, it has only been against myself, a kind of luxury. And now I tell myself: I've taken all that trouble for nothing. You see, Monsieur Costals, there's no point in being brave about life. And yet I feel obliged to go on, to see it through to the end.'

He threw back his hair with a sudden jerk of the head – the gesture of a young boy, or a horse tossing its mane.

'Why see it through to the end?'

'Am I to betray the ideals of thirty years? Am I to deny everything I have stood for? I know too many people who would have a good laugh, or should I say a nasty laugh? To every one who came near me I presented the image of a certain type of man. It is my duty to maintain that image to the end, even if I was mistaken. Look, my eyes are dead, my heart is dead, my spirit is dead. I know what would buck me up: champagne. But how could I possibly ask for it? It would look as though I were ratting on the whole of my past life. No, I refuse to be a deserter.'

'What an aberration of conscience!' thought Costals. 'That's how one turns into a living lie, when one imagines one is "pure".'

'I'm going to die,' M. Dandillot went on, 'but if I make the slightest allusion to the fact, I'm told I'm an alarmist. But hush. . . .'

There was a noise in the next room. M. Dandillot said: 'Walls have ears, you know. . . .' His expression was that of a child caught red-handed. When the noise had stopped, he went on:

'Yes, I'm going to die, and they expect me to be cheerful. I have to pretend that I don't know I'm dying, so that my family can go on enjoying themselves with a clear conscience.

When I'm at my last gasp, I shall have to say something memorable that my family can pass on to future generations. What about you? Will you make a historic remark on your death-bed?'

'I trust I shall preserve some decorum on my death-bed, and that means no historic remarks. If I were positively compelled to say something, I think I should ask the public's forgiveness for not having expressed more satisfactorily what was in my heart. . . .'

'You're a public figure, that makes it different. *I* thought I had the right to stop acting now, after thirty years of it – the right to three weeks' sincerity before I vanish from this world. But on the contrary, the farce has only just begun, and it will soon be in full swing! Yesterday the doctor came, and he had to give me a very painful injection. I was longing to complain, just to hear them say "Be brave", so that I could shout back at them: "Be brave? Why should I? When I've hardly an ounce of energy left, because I've spent it too lavishly in the service of others, I'm expected to use it up putting on an act for your benefit. This corpse of mine must buckle to and step out smartly so that you should all feel better and not have to despise me. Well, go on, despise me then! What difference will it make to me where I'm going?" That's what I should have liked to shout at them. Instead of which, I acted the Roman, the man of iron – not a sign of fear, not a moan. And while they were admiring me (at least I suppose they were) I was despising myself for my absurd heroism.'

'And so,' said Costals, 'you lie to yourself, and worse still, you do it to impress others.'

'What do I care about the opinion of others! Perhaps if they'd shown some gratitude for the example I gave. But all they did was treat me as a lunatic. "Dandillot never eats tinned food because it's not natural . . . Take off your scarf when you see Dandillot, otherwise he'll pitch into you: don't you know he breaks the ice to go for a swim in winter?" My wife laughs at me openly. Solange pretends to take my ideas seriously, but I know she only does it out of kindness. My son used to do the opposite of what he knew to be my principles, on purpose, simply to annoy me. So the results have been negative all along the line. Not only have I set an example which nobody followed, but it's also possible that the example was not worth setting. And yet, it might all have been very different if, like you, I had written something.... Ah, yes, you've nothing to worry about!'

It occurred to Costals that the world would believe that M. Dandillot had died of cancer, but perhaps in reality he was dying from not having received the recognition he felt to be his due. As lamps need oil, so men need a certain amount of admiration. When they are not sufficiently admired, they die. The only way of softening the last days of M. Dandillot would have been to flatter his vanity. Costals was touched, too, to see the old man so naïvely, or so nobly, envying the achievement of a writer of thirty-four. The tragedy of not being able to express oneself suddenly struck him as being quite horrible.

M. Dandillot spoke warmly of Costals' future : 'You'll get everything you want, etc....' But there was a sting in the tail : 'Nevertheless, in spite of all this, your standing with the public is not what it ought to be. I don't know whether you're aware of the fact....'

'He's embittered,' thought Costals, 'so he's determined that I should have reason to feel embittered too. It would console him a bit. And yet he's obviously well disposed towards me. Ah, well! One mustn't expect too much of people.'

The whole thing seemed to him all the more exquisite for the fact, of which he was still firmly convinced, that M. Dandillot had never read more than ten pages of his work.

The writer went on :

'My dear sir, you must not think that your lessons have been in vain. You are giving me one this very minute which confirms my own way of thinking: that it's madness to restrain oneself except for the most powerful reasons.'

Moribund though he was, M. Dandillot was still sufficiently alive to contradict himself madly, which is the essence of life itself. The conclusion Costals had drawn was not at all to his liking. He protested :

'Everything that's good in the world was born of restraint.'

'I don't believe a word of it!' said Costals sharply, thinking to himself: 'That's the sort of tawdry platitude with which poor old humanity tries to justify all its sweat and tears.'

'Let me go on believing so, at least,' said M. Dandillot. 'If everything I've done has been in vain, let me feel at least that I rose above myself in doing it.'

It was then that Costals realized the extent of the old man's defeat. And he felt a great surge of pity towards him.

It occurred to him that Seneca had written more or less what M. Dandillot had just said. He told him so. But at the mention of Seneca, M. Dandillot burst out angrily:

'Don't talk to me about those humbugs! I used to fill up whole exercise-books with quotations from the moralists: I'll make a bonfire of them all before I die. Where did I read that splendid expression the other day: "a dunghill of philosophies"?'* Really Monsieur Costals, you as a literary man must admit that you need a typist who can copy a manuscript intelligently more than you need a new conception of the universe. Those charlatans! I love life, I get nothing but enjoyment from it, and yet I'm supposed to be pleased at the prospect of leaving it for ever! Doctors probe my inside, and I'm supposed to find the pain enjoyable! I've known old men who talked with serenity of their approaching end, who, knowing that death was imminent, continued to go about their business as if nothing was the matter. Well, they were all blockheads, idiots. Intelligent people are afraid, paralysed by fear. Those scoundrels of philosophers should be locked up in padded cells if they believe what they say. And if they're just laughing at us, they should be made to laugh on the other side of their faces. Yes, I'm surprised no emperor ever thought of exterminating the whole brood of philosophers at one fell swoop, on the same grounds as the early Christians.'

'For a dying man,' thought Costals, 'he seems a bit worked up. But perhaps it does happen that way.'

M. Dandillot closed his eyes for a moment with an expression of intense fatigue. 'That's what comes of walking twenty-five miles a day at the age of sixty,' Costals said to himself. 'Alas! one can't use up one's energy with impunity. But one mustn't

---

*Panaït Istrati (*Author's note*).

say so. We must go on playing boy-scouts!' His eyes still closed, M. Dandillot raised his forearms and let them fall on the arms of his chair in a gesture of resignation and sadness.

'What I want is sleep. But Mme Dandillot and Solange keep waking me up to give me medicaments. The medicaments don't help, and sleep does; but no matter, I must be robbed of sleep because of the medicaments. Right up to the very end, one must behave according to what's "done", and not according to reality.'

Costals, who had imagined that this lunch was a trap set by the nuptial Hippogriff, and that M. Dandillot had got him behind closed doors in order to enumerate his daughter's assets, was more and more surprised to see that there was never any mention of her, or rather that M. Dandillot included her in the group – his 'family' – of which he spoke with such lack of warmth. And he began to think that Mme Dandillot alone knew what was happening between himself and Solange. Either she accepted it, because it gratified her pride, and looked no further, in which case the Dandillots were rather odd people. Or else she wanted to give their liaison the flavour of an engagement, for the sake of appearances, but just the flavour, not the reality. Or she had made up her mind to see the thing through to the end. But in any case it looked as though M. Dandillot had been left out. And this was quite natural, since he would soon be dead.

M. Dandillot opened his eyes again, and with a vague motion of the hand (at about the level of the books) which seemed to take in everything in the room, said:

'What do I care about all this! Mere trifles to help the living to kill time. Now my eyes are open, and it's all lies. The clock shows the wrong time, because it's stopped. The barometer is out of order. That Corot there is a fake. I won't talk about the books. Everything is false, and yet it's so much a part of the atmosphere we breathe that, as soon as we discover what a fraud it is, we die, as drug-addicts do when deprived of their drugs.'

Suddenly he sat up straight, as though pulling himself together.

'I am grateful to you for two things. For not having tried to delude me about my condition. And for not having tried to console me. You see, if anything could console me, it's the thought that I'm dying a natural death, that I'm not dying for a "cause"....'

Costals did not answer. M. Dandillot added :

'It's quite possible, though, that my death may be other than a natural death. I've something there' (he pointed to a cupboard) 'that will hasten the end, if the pain proves too much for me to bear. Two tubes of veronal. Dissolve, drink, and it's all over.'

'Yes, but supposing the dose isn't strong enough and you recover – think what hell your family would give you!'

'Do you think so?' M. Dandillot said with a small, child-like smile. 'Nonsense, with veronal there isn't a chance of recovering.'

'Why not use a revolver?' said Costals, adding, with a grin : 'Afraid you'll harm the family's reputation?'

'Yes, because of Solange. Besides, revolvers kick, and there's a chance of missing.'

'Not if you aim at the bone just below the temple. No, the real risk is that the gun might jam. I know all about that. Filthy guns. Worse than anything – false security. If one really wants to kill someone, give me a good knife any time. No one has ever found anything better.'

'Since I can't kill myself with a knife, I'll stick to veronal. Do you think it's cowardly to kill oneself?' ⟨

'The people who call it cowardly are those who are too cowardly to do it themselves.'

'That's exactly what I think.'

There was a silence, as if they were both aware of having exhausted a subject. Then M. Dandillot went on :

'I've spent forty years doing things I didn't enjoy, and doing them of my own free will. As a young man I sweated over law-books in spite of my wretched memory, although both my family and I knew quite well that I would only be a lawyer for appearance' sake, and only for a year or two. I married without love, or self-interest, or any particular taste for marriage. I had children because my wife wanted them : I don't mind telling you that Solange was not at all welcome.

I took a flat in Paris, although I loved nature and solitude, because it was "the thing to do". I went on taking the waters year after year, long after I'd satisfied myself that they did me not the slightest good. I did all this without any good reason, simply because everyone round me was doing the same, or because I was told I ought to do it. And now I'm going to die without knowing why I've led a life which I disliked, when there was a time when I could have made for myself a life I would have enjoyed. Isn't that odd?'

'Not at all. Men let themselves be dragged into things: it's the rule. Men live according to chance: it's the rule.'

Suddenly the door opened. Mme Dandillot appeared, and addressing her husband, said:

'I came in to see whether you needed anything.'

'No, thank you.'

'Don't you want the window open wider? You of all people!'

'No, the noise tires me.'

'I see your bottle of Eau de Cologne is empty. I'll send out for another.'

'No, Eau de Cologne's too cold....'

'We can't heat up Eau de Cologne, I'm afraid. Well, I'll leave you to it.'

For a few moments, Costals and M. Dandillot remained silent. There could be no doubt that Mme Dandillot, behind the door, had heard all or part of their last few remarks.

M. Dandillot resumed in a lower voice:

'If only I could go to a nursing-home! If only I could see new surroundings, new faces, before I die, instead of those I've been seeing for thirty years. But it's a dream: even that is forbidden me. Do you know the only occupation I find tolerable in my present condition? Burning my correspondence. Forty-five years of correspondence. If one added up all the hours one has spent writing letters or doing other equally futile jobs, one would find one had wasted years of one's life. You are still young, so I'll give you a word of advice: never answer letters, or only very rarely. Not only will it not do you any harm, but people won't even hold it against you: they'll soon get used to it. As for me, by destroying my correspondence I'm saying *no* to the whole of my past life. And I find pleasure in doing so, and also in depriving Mme Dandillot of the pleasure she would have in rummaging through my affairs. . . . It's odd that I should talk like this to someone I don't know.'

This way of casting one's innermost secrets into the void was familiar to Costals: more than once he had done the same with Solange. Unwittingly M. Dandillot was returning the mysterious trust he had had in the girl; and the thought made him ponder.

'My wife,' M. Dandillot continued, 'my wife's religion is that of the average Frenchwoman: she doesn't practise, she doesn't take the sacraments, but she goes to Mass on Sundays. Solange claims to be an unbeliever, but goes to Mass with her mother, and would be upset if she missed it. But Solange doesn't really know. . . . You know her: she's still in bud. As for me I've always been a pagan. You can't love nature as I do and Jesus Christ at the same time. Besides, we have an infallible proof that Christianity was inferior to the great pagan philosophies: the fact that it triumphed. Everyone knows the kind of things and people who triumph' (with an embittered smile). 'It isn't that I don't admire Christ's teachings. Any religion will always redeem itself from ridicule by charity. But St Paul ruined everything. And so, one of the firmest tenets of my moral code was: not to have a priest at my death-bed. This is still my intention, needless to say. But after the inner upheaval I have recently undergone, I must confess that this "gesture" seems to me less significant than it did. And you, Monsieur Costals, may one ask where you stand in regard to religion?'

'I'm an "old Christian", an old Christian *de sangre azul*. But of course I have no faith and I don't practise.'

'Ah! I'm very glad. I couldn't shake hands altogether honestly with a man I knew to be a believer, whatever his religion. Here, give me your hand, will you?' (He clasped it firmly.) 'Well, now, in spite of that, do you intend to have a Christian burial?'

'I should like my body to be carried straight from my death-bed to the paupers' grave, and buried there not too deep, so that the dogs can dig it up and eat it.'

'Splendid. But what about the priest? Would you see a priest if you were about to die?'

'It depends. If I were dying in the bosom of my family I think I would. For two reasons. To please those around me at little cost to myself, since they would ardently wish it. And to be left in peace. It must be horrible to be pestered and persecuted at such a time, when all one wants is to be left in peace. Shall I tell you exactly what I think of this particular manifestation of religion? It has no importance whatsoever, and to struggle against it is to give it an importance it doesn't deserve. But if I were to die far from home – which is my dearest wish – if no one mentioned priests, I should certainly not call for one.'

'You're probably right. "It's of no importance": that's about the long and the short of it. Take this room, for instance: everything is in order, everything classified, labelled, easy to find. Well, if I had been untidy, what difference would it make now? Another example: I've always bought things of the very best quality, on principle. Yet a fifteen-hundred-franc suit or a seven-hundred-franc suit both fray at the cuffs after the same number of months. So that one needs a new suit just as frequently, whichever one buys. Which means that it's really of no importance whether a suit is good or bad, just as it's of no importance whether a man is good or bad.'

M. Dandillot pressed his right wrist against the bridge of his nose, between the eyes, as though to filter the light which he found so tiring in spite of the fact that the shutters were three-quarters closed, and his magnificent hand hung limp alongside his cheek.

'I used to worship the sun,' he said. 'I believed it cured everything. I believed that whatever was wrong with one – pneumonia, an ulcer, a broken leg – one had only to lie in the sun to be cured. Yes, I believed this, from the bottom of my heart: it was pure fetishism. And I taught the same thing to hundreds of youngsters. And now, whenever the sky is the least bit bright it hurts me. I can't bear it any more. If I went out I would stay in the shade. (To think that I may never again see a cloudy sky!) Is there, then, one truth for the living and another for the dying? I was intoxicated by the beauty of the world and its creatures, quite disinterestedly, I may say, for I was never a womanizer. Now every living thing seems to me offensive, and I feel ready to hate them all. I've given up reading the newspapers. What do I care about all that, since I'm leaving it? My wife wants to take me out for a drive in the Bois. Well, I refuse. I don't want to see the beauty of the world any more, since I shall soon be unable to enjoy it. It would hurt me, and I don't want to be hurt.'

'It's strange that your reaction to light should be exactly the opposite to that of the dying Goethe.'

'There you go again with your great men,' said M. Dandillot impatiently. 'What do I care about Goethe! Let him die as he wishes: no one can set me an example any more. Goethe also began to study natural history at the age of seventy-five, and one's supposed to think how admirable. Well, I'm with Montaigne: "What a foolish thing is an abecedarian old man!"'

Costals was a little shocked. Out of conformity he had hypnotized himself into believing that Goethe was one of the great beacons of the human spirit, though in his heart of hearts he considered him grossly overrated.

At that moment Solange came into the room, the lady visitor having departed. And Costals experienced the odd sensation of finding the presence of someone he loved importunate.

As M. Dandillot made no move to send his daughter away, Costals took his leave after a few moments. In the hall, he ran into Mme Dandillot:

'I can't understand what's the matter with my husband. He groans when he gets out of bed. He groans when he puts on his trousers. You'd think he was doing it on purpose. And yet he's a man who has had a great deal of character all his life.'

'You can't understand what's the matter with him? The matter, dear lady, is that he's dying.'

'In the first place, thank heaven, it's not at all certain. And even if he does believe his life is in danger, isn't that just the moment for him to show his mettle? When can he show it, if not in times of stress? But do you know what he said to the doctor yesterday? "Don't hurt me, doctor." "But you won't feel a thing ...'' "Yes, yes, I know how you doctors talk. Well, *I don't want to be hurt*, do you hear me! Let others put up with suffering if they like, I won't!'' It's rather painful for those who love him to hear him talk like that in front of strangers.'

Costals mumbled something and left. 'So,' he thought, 'he brings me here so that he can unburden himself, and he lies! He'll be dead within a month, and he lies! God, what a bunch!'

<table>
<tr><td>Andrée Hacquebaut
Cabourg</td><td>to Pierre Costals
Paris</td></tr>
</table>

30 June 1927

Read this or not, as you please. This letter, which will be my last, is simply to tell you that I KNOW.

Crushed by you, with a temperature of 101 degrees – the fever of grief, nothing else* – on the point of becoming seriously ill or going mad, I had to have an immediate change of air and came to stay with a friend in Cabourg. At the Casino here I met a whole group of women writers and poets, and among them Baroness Fléchier.

'Costals?' she said. 'Not only has he never held a woman in his arms, but never in his life has he even desired one! He admitted it to me himself.'†

Then she talked about Proust. I plunged into Proust, whom I had never read before. What a revelation! The scales dropped from my eyes. It's all blindingly clear. *M. de Charlus is you!* ...

It's all there, everything! You love strength – like him. You go for long walks – like him. You don't wear rings – like him. All the details tally, everything speaks against you. The other day in your studio, you wore a shirt with an open collar. And

* Pure invention. She had no fever but, because of her 'emotional upset', a boil on the thigh.

†See p. 123.

then there was the time you drew my attention to your big, square-toed English shoes such as nobody wears in Paris. You mentioned your delicate feet! In fact it was an affectation of virility, an alibi.

And the contradictions in your attitude towards me! The same 'inconsistency' we find in M. de Charlus. And your ups and downs. 'The very ups and downs of his relations with me,' as Proust writes of Charlus.

You said to me in the avenue Marceau: 'See how much I trust you. I talk to you as I would to a man.' You bet!

And that 'delicacy of feeling that men so rarely show'. One can deny you all sorts of things, but never delicacy of feeling.

Again, you once said to me that young men were fools. Charlus says it too. 'What impresses us about this man's (Charlus') face is a certain touching delicacy, a certain grace, an unaffected friendliness. . . .' Just as I used to say to everyone about you: 'He's so natural and friendly.' Fool that I was! It's absolutely frightful to be plunged into this underworld. It has changed my whole vision of the world.

And what was it you said about your character Christine in *Fragility*? 'I transformed myself into Christine.' Those half-admissions, which Proust also draws attention to! You reminded me of Flaubert's remark: 'Madame Bovary is me.' But Flaubert was obviously a pansy: he never married, there was only one woman in his life, and above all there's that phrase in *Salammbô* about certain Carthaginian troops whose 'friendships' made them more courageous, so it seems. (At that rate, I'd rather have an army of cowards.)

And your complete lack of jealousy, which you have often spoken to me about and which you describe as 'an almost sublime common sense'. That cannot be called manly. Jealousy is one of the basic characteristics of the male.

Now I understand why you did not find me more desirable. And to think of the tortures I went through, the time I spent staring at myself in the mirror! Now I understand why you did not need me. Of course, you were half woman yourself!

You, Costals, possessed but not possessing! Dominated but not dominating! Seeking in love the same self-abasement that we women seek. The very thought of it sickens me. You have befouled the face of the earth for me, after having filled it with radiance.

Since I knew nothing about this form of debauchery, and the ladies in the Casino knew nothing about it either, judging by the questions they asked one another, I overcame my nausea and consulted a medical dictionary (Labarthe's) which I found in my friend's library. I discovered that members of this infamous sect 'paint their faces'. And I've been racking my brain trying to remember whether that fresh complexion of yours. . . . And the thought that you might be strolling along the boulevards with 'a handkerchief, a flower or some needlework' in your hand, as Labarthe puts it. . . . And to think that I had my copy of *Fragility* bound in green morocco, now that I know that green is the favourite colour, the symbol by which these creatures recognize each other! Oh no! it's too frightful! It's stifling me, it's killing me. . . .

I have shut the dictionary, and I won't bother with any more documentary evidence. Even if these descriptions are a bit fanciful, they are quite enough for me and I shall stop there. You may well say that women refuse to face reality, that they are always burying their heads in the sand, etc. Well, have it your own way, but for me it's all very simple: there are a certain number of horrible things in the world which I prefer not to know about. My dignity as a woman, and eventually as a wife and mother, forbids it: I should be sullied for ever. Let the world do as it likes – I personally have the right to ignore as much of it as I please.

For five years now you have prevented me from marrying. Because of you my youth has been wasted – in fact my whole life has been wasted, for youth is all that counts in a woman's life. And wasted for whom? For the *wretched creature* you are! Can you imagine the tragedy of a woman who has made one of these people the very incarnation of manhood, and who suddenly, one day, has this revelation? And you haven't even the merit of being original, for there are heaps and heaps of them, and you're nothing but a pathetic snob, a slave of decadentism and putrefaction, a mere hanger-on of the Gides and the Prousts, those imbeciles, rotten to the core with intellectualism, sterility, aestheticism, instead of honestly fulfilling their duty as men, men who are useful to others and to their country.... And not only did I love *that*, but I also loved its work! And since your whole attitude both towards me and towards society is totally insincere, your work must be the same. I can no longer believe a single word you have written. Your work is mere empty rhetoric, a monument of bad literature. If there were a spark of honesty left in you, you would break your pen in pieces. The only thing left for you to do is to creep into your hole in silence, pursued by the jeers of normal men and healthy women.

The love I had for you, I have given to another. You have no right to it, for one does not accept a love of which one knows oneself to be unworthy, one has no right to cultivate the friendship of a pure and chaste young woman when elsewhere.... My letters were addressed to a semblance of a person. I demand that you return them to me: they have fallen into your hands by mistake. And I am ashamed of them. What I loved was the man behind your work, the man of your false creation. It is as if I had given myself in the dark to someone I thought I knew, and at dawn discovered that I had been caressing some nameless creature, some half-man, some hideous hermaphrodite.... Are you aware that this kind of horror could lead one to suicide? Are you aware of that?

But in this tragedy of mine, I have one consolation. The thought of what I have escaped. When I think, when I think that I might have been touched by you! Whereas now I could not bear you to touch my hand, even with gloves on. Yes, to think what I have escaped!

I despise you.

Wednesday

I don't want you to take me for a dupe, but nor do I want you to think me cruel. I want you to read what I wrote to you yesterday, but I don't want it to be your last impression of me.

I am writing to you with infinite sadness. But it is not for myself that I feel sad, today, it is for you. Ah! times have changed indeed! You have pitied me enough, now it is my turn to pity you. You loved me, let us say, like a sister; I feel today that I might come to love you with the compassion

286

and forgiveness of a mother, and that makes me more serene.

Yes, how sad it must be to be a monster! It makes one's heart bleed. I beg you to try and extricate yourself if there is still time. You are unhappy, and no doubt it was because you were unhappy that you took refuge in these refinements of vice. And now you are doubly unhappy; though perhaps you are not entirely guilty. I implore you, in the name of all that is sacred in the world, in the name of our memories (for you did love me, after all; only you could not, for obvious reasons, go all the way, could you?), abandon the path you are on. If ever my letters meant anything to you, if ever they helped you, made you ponder, please consider this one seriously: it is a solemn adjuration. Drag yourself up from this Abyss. Get back to the world of real humanity. Become a *man* again!

If only for the sake of your talent as a writer. To think that *you have never held a woman in your arms*! How can you not feel that you are incomplete, that your whole outlook on the world is falsified thereby, and your art so much the poorer?

When one is ill, one looks after oneself. But one must have the will to be cured. You must acquire that will.

This very morning, I had a talk with one of the doctors here. He told me there were various kinds of treatment, both physical and moral, for gentlemen of the Charlus type. I enclose herewith the names of some Parisian psychiatrists who have apparently effected such cures. Put yourself in the hands of one of them. But first and foremost say to yourself, and repeat it, sometimes even *aloud*, after taking *a slow, deep breath*: 'I want to become a man.'

These recent events, though they have shattered me, have brought me back to religion. God at least does not let one down. You know that I had more or less given up practising. But for the past five days, I have started going to church again daily. I no longer say, as in the past: 'O God, make me happy.' Now I pray for you. And I shall continue to pray for you until you are *saved*.

Farewell. I forgive you. Believe in my immense pity.

A.H.

Pierre Costals   to Armand Pailhès
Paris   *Toulouse*

My dear Pailhès,

Epigraph to this letter; the words of the Scripture: 'A woman's love is more to be feared than a man's hatred.'

Object of this letter: A man's rage finds vent in violence. A woman's rage finds vent in stupidity. It is this second point we shall now demonstrate.

I am sending you, duly 'registered',* a document which seems to me quite remarkable. You can return it to me when I have the pleasure of seeing you in Toulouse ten days from now.

A woman rejected because she is not attractive enough welcomes with transports of delight an absurd allegation by an old literary crone about the man who has 'insulted' her. The allegation justifies her in her own eyes by convincing her that it was not because of her looks that she was rebuffed, and at the same time avenges her by showing her 'insulter' in an 'infamous' light. In other words, she is shown the portrait of a person unknown, who in no wise resembles the insulter, except, shall we say, that they both have two eyes, one nose, etc., perhaps even the same colour of hair. Blinded by her passion, she recognizes the portrait as that of her insulter; if she were before a judge, she would take an oath on it. But it is not enough for her to execrate him; she has been pitied, so she must pity in her turn: her scorn is transmuted into pity. And finally, since in spite of all this she still loves, and since reality, by deceiving her hopes, has thrown her back into darkness, she begins to pray for her insulter, and is thus enabled to crown her triumph by congratulating herself on her magnanimity, and perhaps to pursue her relations with the insulter, without damaging her self-respect, by means of bi-weekly letters twelve pages long in which she will continue to talk to him about himself under cover of the supreme Being.

*A pun in the original: *recommander* = 'to register' (a letter) and to recommend' (*Translator's note*).

For, on the labels of cages in zoos, the males are indicated by an arrow, which means that they pierce the hearts of women, and the females are indicated by a cross, which means that they take refuge in the Crucifix.

The case of Andrée is all the more extraordinary for the fact that Andrée is a very intelligent woman – really somebody.

You know my ideas about the automatism of female reactions. All the reactions you will find here have long been classified and described. The reaction which causes a rejected woman to accuse her 'insulter' of being a M. de Charlus is No 174. The reaction whereby an unhappy woman tries to convince the man she loves that he is unhappy too is No 227a. The reaction whereby a desperate woman turns to Christianity is No 89. The reaction whereby a desperate woman pretends she is ill in a final attempt to arouse in her lover that 'pity for women' which they long for and disapprove of at the same time is No 214. This last, it must be admitted, is no more than adumbrated in the case of Andrée. And it must also be admitted that one of the most typical reactions, No 175, whereby a rejected woman accuses her 'insulter' of sexual impotence, has not yet manifested itself here. In spite of this lacuna, there is in Andrée's graph something so classical and so pure, in a word, so perfect – in its vulgarity – that the mind derives from it an equally perfect satisfaction, a satisfaction as delicious as it is possible for any sensation to be: the sort of satisfaction astronomers must feel when they contemplate the acrobatics of the stars. I can also see myself as the chemist who, having put two solutions in a test-tube, watches the vicissitudes of the combination; knows what the final result will be, though the layman does not, and knows that it will be very unexpected for the layman; and at last sees these elements assume precisely the form, the colour and the density which nature intended. But the most splendid thing of all is that the curve of Andrée's progress, classical though it is, is at the same time absurd. There is in it, at one and the same time, something both baffling and foreseeable. *And in this it is the quintessence of nature itself.* Andrée is not afraid to write that the fact of having recognized me in M. de Charlus has 'transformed her vision of the universe.' I daresay my own vision of the universe, if I had one, would be transformed for less. . . . To remain in the same key, and since nothing less than the universe is in question, I may say that the Cabourg letter inclines me to believe that a celestial economy *really* exists, – which up to now, *pace* the priests and *pace* Voltaire, I had been rather inclined to doubt.

All this might also provoke a few reflections on the lack of psychological understanding in women, which I have always found rather striking. Most of them are quite out of touch with reality. If one cared to go back over the whole of Andrée's behaviour one would see that time after time she makes the grossest blunders, with a regularity that is as startling as it is baffling. She believes she's pretty, she believes I love her, she believes I have no children, she believes I'm M. de Charlus, she believes I'm unhappy, etc. You'd think it was something to do with a bet. And I repeat, Andrée is a woman of almost exceptional intelligence. You will say, perhaps : 'It isn't women who lack perception, it's women in love.' But since they're always in love !

Mistaken about what men are and what they think, women are also mistaken about the way to go about winning them. A woman maddens you by coming into your room while you are working, or by giving you little presents, or by badgering you too often, or by bringing along her friends, who are not yours. You are on good enough terms with her to speak out frankly. Well, she stops for a while, and then starts again. A woman delights you by her lack of affectation. You tell her so again and again and you castigate all affected women. Well, sooner or later she herself begins to get coquettish and indulge in little wiles. All women without exception spoil their chances with you by their inexhaustible demands for money, and the time comes when the pleasure you derived from them has been poisoned at the source; and so you break with them. Demanding nothing, they would have had everything, one would have been so touched. But no, they can't help it : you might almost think there was something that forced them to be so clumsy.

And just as women deceive themselves about their men, they deceive themselves about their children (girls or boys, though much more so with boys, of course). That 'maternal instinct' we hear so much about is nothing but a fraud. No mother ever knows what goes on in the mind of her child, nor what ought to be done for it. I could write a book on the subject, composed entirely of 'true stories', a few of which were provided by my own mother, for there are exceptions to everything. Any man who dares to look life in the face, whether he be a moralist, a doctor, a teacher (religious or lay), or a psychiatrist, will tell you so. But they will only tell you privately. They will never say so in front of a woman, or in public. They would never print it either, being far too frightened of public opinion which is created by women. Even the great Tolstoy himself said to Gorki: 'When my body is halfway into the grave, I shall say what I really think about women, and quickly slam down the tombstone over my head!' To my knowledge, Herbert Spencer alone had the courage to write: 'A mother's intervention is often more harmful than her complete abstention would have been.'

And grown-up sons, too, are well aware of their mothers' delusions about them, their profound lack of understanding. But they too will never say so; they will hardly admit it to themselves. They are sorry for their mothers: always this pity for women.

As for me, I have a son, and he is what I love most in the whole world. That is why I was determined to *protect him from motherhood*. I arranged that his mother should have absolutely no rights over him. And I put him in charge of a woman *who is not his mother*; he stands a better chance that way. As you know, the 'maternal instinct' of cats does not always prevent them from devouring their young. There's a terrifying symbol there for you: I may well have preserved my son from being eaten up.

Such, dear friend, are my reactions to Andrée's little effort, on the purely general plane. On the personal plane, I find it almost unbearably funny. I almost feel inspired to do a burlesque commentary on the whole thing. For instance: Andrée says that in loving me she took me for someone else. But that's quite commonplace: when you kiss a cat, you think you've kissed a cat; well, if you look closer, you find you've kissed a flea. And so on.... This kind of thing doesn't get one very far, but I feel madly inclined to go on: the absurdity of it all is intoxicating.

I never had much faith in Andrée's friendship for me, because I knew she was in love with me. I pretended to believe in her friendship, in the same way that, as a writer, I pretend to believe in the demonstrations of friendship of some of my confrères, even though I know they hate me like poison. And now, how am I to behave towards her? I might have been able to put up with her insults: there is something in me that rather enjoys being insulted,* like that famous shark Alain Gerbault writes about, which, while being eaten up by all sorts of other fishes, 'seemed not in the least to resent being torn to pieces'. What I cannot stand is her stupidity. I love and venerate, in a truly religious spirit, stupidity in pretty women, so long as it is sweet and passive. But the braying stupidity of an ugly woman, no thanks. (Incidentally, have you noticed how her stupidity, born of her anger, has affected her style – 'decadentism', a capital A for 'abyss', etc. – she who nearly always wrote so naturally and powerfully? And the intoxication with which she writes the word 'pansy'! It's obvious that she learnt it only yesterday, and wants to show how up-to-date she is. Just as Brunet, at the age of four, when one taught him a new word that caught his fancy, would go round bawling it out for a whole afternoon.) Now it's my turn to write Andrée a similar letter, fifteen pages long, in which I shall tell her exactly what I've thought of her from the beginning.

But it isn't only stupidity. If I were eighteen and Andrée the first woman I'd come across, I might have said to myself: 'This is what love must be like. It's bound automatically to turn into something squalid. It's the nature of things.' But I can't think that any longer: I've seen so many women and girls who, disappointed, abandoned, even betrayed, have managed to retain their dignity (not to mention their critical faculties) and have gone on wishing their tormentors well.

---

*'My self-esteem has always increased in direct proportion to the damage I was doing to my reputation.' – Saint-Simon

So, no forgiveness. And besides, I've had enough of forgiving all the time. A fifteen-page letter.

This episode prompts three further observations.

The first is that I have never been insulted by a pretty woman; always by ugly ones. When some unknown woman writes me an insulting letter, I know she is ugly.

The second is that the sublime Andrée seems cut out to be a literary critic, by which I mean a Parisian literary critic, vintage 1927. The way in which, in identifying me with Charlus, she 'proves' that an object which is black, as black as ink, is white, as white as chalk, shows how well she is qualified for such a role. She would put her pen to delightful articles in which she would demonstrate how some purely lyrical novel was in fact a work of realism, or how some obviously euphoric writer was really a manic-depressive; she would show how Morand is a Baudelairean, Giraudoux a proletarian writer, etc. And she would soon be widely esteemed, since the important thing for a critic (I mean a critic in Paris in 1927) is not to write the truth but to write something that has not been written before; not to possess a sound judgement, but simply to concoct pieces which will be 'taken up' in other journals.

And thirdly. You know how fond I am of secrecy, and of covering up my tracks. The Arabs, who are experts in this form of sport, maintain that the lion obliterates his with his tail; and it is said that one of their sultans had his horse shod back to front. 'Hide your life as the cat hides its excrement,' says the Egyptian proverb. Let us be clear about this: the secrecy I like is not the kind of secrecy practised by the majority of people, but the kind that deepens the more one confesses and shows off. Next to the 'aristocratic' pleasure of displeasing, of which, God knows, I have amply availed myself, there is the pleasure of being taken for something one is not, provided that it is a little to one's discredit. I do not know whether this pleasure can be called aristocratic, but it titillates me. Well, the maenad of Saint-Léonard has given me an idea: I would not swear that some day or other I might not include a Charlus in my collection of masks. Nothing could be simpler: I would merely have to start abusing women from the *intellectual* point of view, and the public is so obtuse – and moreover so ignorant of my carefully concealed liaisons – that it will inevitably deduce that I despise them from the *carnal* point of view. And then ... then my horizons broaden. Can you understand how? Can't you see how much less distrust I shall arouse in parents, how much easier my parthenomachy will become, if I am classified as 'a gentleman who does not care for women'? Indeed, Andrée may well have injected a new dose of happiness into my life. This woman I rejected may well be worth twenty to me. God grant that she may hear of it some day!

I conclude, my dear Pailhès, by sending you my warmest greetings, and a quotation from Juvenal: 'A woman's resentment is implacable when humiliation spurs on her hatred.'

C.

All the same!

For fifteen years, to have been transfused with the power of women as an organ is with air, and to have reverberated with it; one's travels, one's comings and goings, one's disappearances, one's long 'literary silences', everything that appeared inexplicable in one's life, all that to have had no other cause but the erratic race of women; to have spewed forth the world (how often!) in everything that was not love; to have sacrificed everything but one's art to one's private life, and that private life to have been exclusively devoted to love; to have suffered, more often than not, only from the suffering one was forced to inflict on women, or rather on young girls, for every adventure with a young girl that does not end in marriage is doomed to end in suffering and unhappiness; to have had one's whole life constricted, weakened, slowed down by a constant preoccupation with not hurting them; to be unable to read the words 'little girl' without feeling in one's throat the first spasms of tears; to be unable to hear a girl admit to having failed her *bachot* without longing to worship her; to be unable to see a spelling mistake in a letter from an unknown girl without kissing it – and then to be taken for a M. de Charlus by an intelligent, cultured, perceptive woman who has the whole of one's work at her finger-tips. Mind you, it is not the Charlus thing that frightens me. 'What we call unnatural is merely unusual' (Montaigne). The 'unnatural' is nature itself, as a torpedo-boat destroyer is no more and no less than a torpedo-boat. The silly woman talks of my 'Abyss'; but our abysses are elsewhere. No, what frightens me is the darkness that divides one soul from another. In spite of all appearances, she has never understood me in the least, since she could be so utterly mistaken about me. And I haven't understood her in the least, since never, never, would I have believed her capable of being so mistaken. Baudelaire was right: there's nothing that is not based on misunderstanding. I knew it, but how one forgets, or rather how the mind forgets! Forgetting is so essential to it that the mind might well say: I forget, therefore I am.

Pierre Costals   to Andrée Hacquebaut
Paris   *Saint-Léonard*
               (Please forward)
               3 July, 1927

Well, dear Mademoiselle, that was quite a letter you sent me! But what of it! My gratitude to you still has the upper hand: a man who professes to study the human heart cannot but rejoice at not having missed that. For five years you have given me your friendship. You are giving to me still by withdrawing it.

I think we have nothing more to say to each other for the time being. But I know you: doubtless you will come back to me one day. And I know myself too: doubtless I shall welcome you as if nothing had happened. However, let us not rush things. You must need a breather.

Please rest assured of my warmest regard. I follow your various moods with interest.

                               C.

P.S. I am sending you by the same post the book on Cosima Wagner which you told me you wanted to read in one of your letters last winter and which I've just discovered by chance on a second-hand bookstall.

Madame Blancmesnil   to M. Pierre Costals
Avranches (Manche)   *Paris*

2 July 1927

My name will mean nothing to you, but the name Thérèse Pantevin possibly may.

Do you remember these words : 'Should I ignore those cries? I haven't the heart to. . . . Perhaps there are forces in you that might be consecrated. . . .' And then : 'On Saturday next at 6 p.m. I shall have pity on you.' Then a month's silence, which you probably did not even notice : what did Thérèse Pantevin matter to you? For you this correspondence was merely a game. But what you must know is the result of your little game, and the reason for this silence : three weeks ago my unfortunate cousin was taken into the lunatic asylum at Avranches. Will she ever come out again?

Thérèse Pantevin, the daughter of well-to-do farmers, full of bestial pride ever since her childhood, thought herself a genius because of her teaching certificate. I too have my teaching certificate. Do not therefore imagine I am envious. Envious of a poor madwoman! Lazy, scornful of manual work, bigoted, full of absurd intellectual pretensions – how she despised us! Shutting herself up with her repressions in her farm at La Paluelle; and then discovering the works of Costals. Costals, the one and only man capable of understanding her! She breaks with her friends, with her dearest pupils, everything, in order to read you and meditate on your work for days on end in her room, poring over all the photographs of you which she had cut out of the newspapers, and which were found on her. . . . Finally she writes to you. . . .

And you who, even though you are young and know nothing about life, in spite of all your pretensions (I have only read one of your books, but that was enough to make me detest you), you, who cannot after all have been so blind as not to guess my cousin's mental state from her letters, instead of throwing these letters into the waste-paper basket, you answer them, you add fuel to the fire. Vanity or sadism – what other motive could have prompted you? You were safe, you knew perfectly well that the little peasant-girl with her hair pulled back from her temples (she had sent you a photograph) would never come up from the depths of the country to pester you in your marble halls and that in any case, even if she had the impertinence to do so, you would have had her thrown out by your flunkeys.

In April, she leaves home to catch a train to Paris to see you. Her mother stops her in time and locks her up. In May she escapes again : we have to have her arrested at Vire by the gendarmerie. She flung herself on her knees in front of them and said : 'Let me see him for just five minutes and then you can arrest me !' They were obliged to keep her in prison for the night until we came to fetch her. Then, in June, she has a fit of hysteria. . . . That, Monsieur Costals, is what you have done.

And then there is the poor, wretched mother who has had to sell her farm to pay for her daughter's keep and who, at the age of sixty and more, has undertaken to read all the books of Pierre Costals in order to find out what sort of man is responsible for the ruin of her daughter and herself.

And now, Mr Great Writer (!), now that I have forced you into an awareness of your responsibility in all this, what do you propose to do about it? In case there is a shred of humanity left in you, which I doubt, I should like to point out that your victim's boarding fees at the asylum are 15,000 francs a year. If you should feel it your duty to contribute towards them, you could deal directly with me. I would hand over whatever you sent me to Mme Pantevin, who is hardly capable of dealing with such matters herself. If, on the other hand, you choose not to reply, we have your letters to Thérèse Pantevin and we shall know what steps to take.

Antoinette Blancmesnil

Written by Costals on a blank page of this letter:

'For you this correspondence was merely a game.' Played with Andrée, yes, sometimes. With Th. Pantevin, never. The opposite of a game. Put her on her guard against confusing the sacred and the profane. Snubbed her so that she would take against me. Urged her, not to enter a convent, which would have been presumptuous of me, but to go and see a priest who might help her to discover herself. Tried to give her the impression that she was a real person (which indeed she was). Simply and solely pity. Pity all along the line, without an atom of malevolence. Pity, sympathy, understanding and respect.

Imprudence? Agreed. But *every contact with another human being is imprudence.*

The imprudence of generosity – that's more like it. Any action undertaken out of pure generosity always turns back upon its author as automatically as a boomerang returns to the man who threw it. *Without exception.* Anyone subject to generous impulses can, as a matter of course, and in advance, be classified as a victim.

This being so, the tragedy is not that the Pantevin affair should have earned me such a letter: that was but the logical consequence of the premises. The drama, the tragedy, is that Thérèse Pantevin is very probably not mad at all. She has been put away at twenty-five because she was in touch with the higher regions of the spirit: being different, she was envied, that is to say hated. Thérèse Pantevin has been put away by the people she lived among for having been superior to them.

And what do I care even if she was mad, seeing she was suffering!

If I believed in God, I would pray for her.

Andrée Hacquebaut   to Pierre Costals
Saint-Léonard   *Paris*

8 July 1927

Dear Costals,

I no longer know where I am with you, and I no longer know *what you are*, and I am writing to tell you so, although I am well aware how much I must lower myself in your eyes with these eternal 'last letters'. As if it wasn't enough to be crushed by you in Paris, I had to go through it again with

that revelation in Cabourg. And now, this : in my indignation
I wrote to several acquaintances in Paris, people in the know.
I asked them why they had never warned me about you, and
they wrote back calling Baroness Fléchier a lunatic and telling
me that 'nothing could be more grotesque than to believe such
nonsense'. So now I no longer know what to think. There are
still moments when I believe that the woman was telling the
truth, but they may simply be the moments when my suffering
is too great. At other times I doubt. I suppose this uncertainty
must be pleasing to one who once wrote to me that he liked
nothing better than 'the fringe of uncertainty where one thing
merges into another.'

However, something new has happened to sustain me. I am
no longer the thirty-year-old spinster whom no man had ever
taken in his arms, to whom no man had ever said : 'My little
one.' Now I too have my joys*, which are just as good as
yours, whatever they may be (oh! this frenzy to know what
sort of pleasures you enjoy . . .). Now I have other friends
besides you, and *they* don't invite me to second-rate restaurants.
So you needn't despise me unduly any more. Nevertheless you
must know that even if I get married, that night of love I
asked from you will always remain a hope for me. My life will
never stir again until you yourself make a move. If you are not
what I thought you were in Cabourg, if you should realize
one day that I mean something to you, that you want me in
your life, body and soul, that I am as irreplaceable to you as
you are to me, if I should ever seem worth the perturbations
and anxieties that love inevitably entails for the man who
loves a woman and considers her worth it all, then send for
me and I shall be yours, whatever man I may belong to at the
time and whatever the ties that bind me to him.

Good-bye. I have loved you very very much, and I love you
still. As for you, nothing can alter the fact that you allowed
yourself to be loved. I feel that if I heard you being attacked
as I did the other night in the Casino at Cabourg, I could not
and would not endure it at any cost. However cruelly you

---

*Pure invention. This 'man' who was supposed to be part of
Andrée's life did not exist (*Author's note*).

have wounded me, there is something between us which can never be lost or destroyed. And then, perhaps my name will live on in the character you will draw from me in that novel you promised me.*

A. H.

But to think that some day, perhaps, you will marry! If you were to marry a rich woman, I could at least console myself with the thought that she was giving you something I could never have given you. But if you should marry a woman no richer than I am! It's enough to drive one mad!

This letter remained unanswered.

'There is something divine in serious illnesses.' *Saint-Cyran.*

Costals received a note from M. Dandillot saying that he would like to see him two days later, at four: 'We shall be alone.' In the same way the daughter had said: 'Do come, we shall be alone.' What it is to belong to a family! Whereas many dying people write in a firmer, better-formed hand than usual, because they make it a point of honour to do so (as a drunk man will try to indulge in the refinements of calligraphy), M. Dandillot's handwriting was falling apart, and meandered all over the place: a corpse of a hand, preceding the other corpse. His letter was written in pencil.

M. Dandillot was now confined to his room. As Costals entered, a male nurse came out – a man with the sort of face one would not care to meet in a dark wood at night. The first thing M. Dandillot said was: 'Isn't there a bit of a sick-room smell in here? I get them to burn aromatic paper, but I don't know whether.... The only real dignity, you see, is health. And God knows I used to be a healthy man. But now!'

His voice had become a little shrill, and weak, like the voice

---

*Pure invention. Costals never promised her anything of the kind (*Author's note*).

of a man who hardly speaks any more, who no longer has the strength, and who has anyway lost interest in the sounds he emits. His eyes seemed to be veiled by leukoma. He was unshaven, and proceeded to explain why:

'I've done enough for people. Why should I shave for them? Why should I be nice to them? I see now that one should never try to do good to people one doesn't love. Nothing requires more naturalness and spontaneity than doing good. There too I went wrong by forcing myself. And besides, the good we do is poisoned by the fact that we do it the wrong way.'

'One should never try to do good to people one doesn't love,' Costals repeated to himself, thinking of Andrée.

Costals had realized from their first meeting that M. Dandillot was only interested in himself, and he liked him for it. But now that death was drawing near, he saw him shrink even further into himself. He had always thought it natural for old men to be selfish. How the devil could they love the world after having endured it for a life-time?

'My oldest friend has just left,' M. Dandillot said, unconsciously picking up Costals' train of thought. 'We've been cronies for fifty years. Do you know what we talked about? For a quarter of an hour he described his plans for a trip to Egypt, India and Ceylon, going into ecstasies about all the wonderful things he'd see. He spent the next quarter of an hour asking me for letters of introduction for his son. And for the last five minutes – the last five minutes of our friendship, since I shall be dead by the time he returns from his trip – he scolded me very severely for living in a room with the shutters closed. That's what a man says to the friend of half a century who is on the point of death.'

'It's simply lack of imagination.'

In a dense cone of sound, the piercing cries of the swallows came surging in from the trees in the avenue.

'And the veronal?'

'Always ready.'

'You'll never take it. We once had an old cat at home, who developed an incurable sore by scratching himself. So we had him put to sleep. Then my mother felt remorseful. "Even with his sore he might still have enjoyed a few happy hours." When you're on the point of swallowing your veronal, you'll say to yourself: "Perhaps I might still enjoy a few happy hours".'

'I haven't taken the poison yet because the pain isn't bad enough. What I feel most of all is tired. Tired! And do you know what makes me so tired? It's having done too much good all my life, having obliged too many people. I was destroying my correspondence the other day. And do you know, I sometimes went through ten or fifteen letters in succession and every one of them was a request for some favour or other or to thank me for a favour I had done. And if you allow that only one person in two ever thanks you for something you've done, it will give you some idea of the number of people I've obliged – and for what, ye gods? Remember this, Monsieur Costals: the people we help *never* deserve it.'

'I'm lucky enough not to be obliging, so I'm not a good judge. But how a man of your calibre...? Only fools are hurt by ingratitude. Isn't generosity just another way of saying "Return to sender"?'

'What makes me tired is not the ingratitude with which my generosity has been repaid, it's the generosity itself. So futile! Such a waste of time! Ah! Be selfish, Monsieur Costals.'

'But I *am*.'

'Well then, the world is yours.'

Then M. Dandillot went on to say that he was so tired that he would be glad to die. He expounded, as if it were his own, Mechnikov's theory that a man dies only because he wants to. He proclaimed: 'I hate people who are afraid of death, like the Pascals, etc. . . . ' Costals was glad to find him in this frame of mind, since it relieved him of the necessity to put on a solemn face.

'That said, I wonder why I've lived at all,' M. Dandillot concluded with a gloomy stare.

'You've lived because you could not do otherwise,' said Costals impatiently. 'Nearly all men's lives are corrupted by the need to justify their existence. Women are less subject to this infirmity.'

'If I had been happy, I shouldn't feel the need to justify my existence: it would justify itself. But I have not been happy, and I've discovered that that is why I'm dying at sixty-one, instead of seventy or seventy-five as I should logically have done with the principles on which my life has been based. Can you realize what it means to have lived for forty years without ever meeting an intelligent person? And I'm so tired of people who aren't intelligent. . . . '

'It takes a lot of searching to find an intelligent person. . . . '

'And now I meet you, just as I'm about to die!'

'It's better that way. We should never have got on together.'

'Why not?' M. Dandillot asked, shyly.

'Because I should have grown tired of you.'

'How can you say such a thing to me?' M. Dandillot said, flabbergasted.

'Because I know you won't understand.'

'Yes, I'm stupid, aren't I? And boring too.' (A terrifying expression of bitterness spread over his face.) 'Boring . . . people have made it plain to me often enough. I should have loved to know whether my wife really thought me an imbecile, or whether she merely pretended to, just to be disagreeable. It's true that I actually do become an imbecile when I'm with her.'

'Haven't you become more intelligent since you've been ill?'

'Yes, I think more.'

'If you'll forgive me, I don't believe you really think. Not real thinking. I myself don't really think. I've often tried to see things clearly, but the time goes by and I still don't understand a thing.'

'You consider that I think like an amateur, isn't that it? My family have always looked on me as an amateur. If I'd had a job of some kind, it would have been different. For ten or twelve years now, they've made a habit of ignoring what I say. It would be impossible to climb back up that kind of slippery slope even if there were still time. Even if the Minister came in person to decorate me in this armchair, they *wouldn't understand*. Did I show you the letter I wrote to the Minister refusing the Legion of Honour?' (With a scornful emphasis on 'Legion of Honour'.)

'Yes, you did.'

'Forgive me, my memory goes at times,' he said with an absent stare. 'Did I tell you the story about the man who was prepared to sacrifice ten years of his life for the sake of the Grand Cross of the Legion of Honour?'

Costals shook his head.

'A friend of mine has a brother aged seventy-two. This brother is unhappy because he considers that, according to the promotion schedule, he should have had the Grand Cross a couple of years ago. My friend said to him jokingly one day: "I believe you'd rather die in a year but be promoted at once than live another ten years without it." "Of course I would," the brother answered, without a smile. Isn't life wonderful?'

'It is. I couldn't have done better if I'd created the world myself.'

M. Dandillot smiled, under the impression that Costals was being blasphemous. He did not realize that Costals was in fact very fond of Catholicism. Then he frowned in an effort to re-focus his eyes, which had grown vacant again, and which now wandered from one object to another until they finally came to rest on a drawer of his filing-cabinet.

'Would you be kind enough to get that drawer out? It contains all the correspondence I had with my mother when I was a young man. I should like to give it to you. We'll make a parcel of it. If *someone* comes in and asks you what it is, you can say that it's press-cuttings about physical culture.'

'Someone!' Costals was still rather surprised at the way M. Dandillot 'annulled' his daughter, as it were, passed her over in silence, or let it be understood that she was one of the people he despised. And just as he had been irritated by Solange's irruption into the room the other day while he was talking to her father, he was now forced to the conclusion that any reference to her would have lowered the tone of their conversation. She seemed so unimportant compared to the kind of preoccupation with which he and M. Dandillot were absorbed; even more, she seemed unimportant compared to M. Dandillot himself.

'This is the second time we've met, and yet you want to give me your mother's letters!'

'Who else can one trust if one doesn't trust strangers?'

'Give them to me some other day.'

'There may not be another day.'

'Of course there will!'

'So you really think I may live a bit longer?' said M. Dandillot, his face brightening, although not so long before he had professed himself happy to die.

M. Dandillot then asked for paper and string and began to parcel up the letters. They kept slipping from his fingers; he could scarcely move without dropping something or other.

'Everything falls ... everything falls.... Things run away from me. They can sense the corpse.'

And as Costals drew nearer to him to help him with the parcel, he said:

'I should be glad if you would tell me frankly whether my breath smells. I've changed so much since I've been ill. I looked quite a different man six months ago, you know. People thought I was only fifty-three or fifty-four.'

Among the letters, Costals noticed some press-cuttings. They were reports of social functions dating back to 1890, and M. Dandillot's name had been underlined in red pencil. He had repudiated his worldly phase to the extent of ostentatiously selling his evening clothes, and yet his vanity was such that he had kept these pathetic accounts of provincial parties for forty years, simply because his name was printed there. Ah, nature had indeed erred in refusing M. Dandillot the gift of expression. He was born to be a man of letters.

'What is your motive for giving me these letters? Am I to destroy them? Am I to keep them without reading them – in which case, what's the point? Am I to read them, and if so, on what grounds?'

'I'm giving them to the novelist. Read them, and you may find things that are of use to you in your novels.'

'Well, well! what a bunch!' thought Costals once again, rather flabbergasted in spite of himself. 'I knew of course that there were female readers one had never met in one's life who sent one whole notebooks in which they described their conjugal life in the most intimate detail "in case it could be of some use". But a man! And what would the late Mme Dandillot have had to say about it all? Would she have been pleased to know that her letters to her son would eventually be handed over to a stranger – for after all, I am a stranger to him – to be

305

"made use of"? Humanity? A swarm of thoughtless idiots.'

M. Dandillot's hand went up to his forehead.

'Those swallows,' he said, 'what a din they make! Swallows, sunlight, everything that's good exhausts me. Just now there was a workman singing on the landing: you may have noticed that the staircase is being painted. You can't imagine how true his voice was, and I thought to myself. "He's in overalls, he doesn't wash, he's coarse and vulgar, and yet his voice is so pure, so tuneful.... A voice from another world",'

'And that voice tired you too?'

'No.'

'I had the impression from the way you began that you were about to tell me that the workman's singing tired you like everything else....'

'I'm sorry: I can't remember how I began. These gaps in my memory....'

He began to fiddle with the medicine bottles on the table beside his armchair.

'In fact you don't know whether the workman's song pained you or pleased you, any more than you know whether you really welcome death, as you said earlier on, or whether it horrifies you, as you have also given me to understand. You find it both horrifying and acceptable, simultaneously. Just as the workman's song simultaneously exhausted you and did you good.'

'I don't know,' said M. Dandillot, like a schoolboy who has been asked which way the Gulf Stream flows. Before saying this he had clenched his fists (the nails must have dug into his palms) as though he were making an effort to pull himself together.

'I was wondering why I liked you,' said Costals with a sidelong glance at a pattern on the carpet. 'Now I know. It's because you are like me. And you gave me your mother's letters, because you know that I'm like you: I've only this moment realized it.... O God! give him eternal life!' he added in a passionate murmur, his eyes on the carpet. M. Dandillot gave a start:

'What did you say? So you believe, then!...'

'Me, *believe*?' hissed Costals with withering scorn. 'The words just came to my lips. It doesn't mean a thing.'

'The last time, you fortified me in my unbelief. And now you throw everything into doubt again. And at this late stage – when I am so weak! Men, like nations, never stop declining from the moment they start hearing about God. I can't help it if the moral dregs of mankind cannot do without religion. But you, if you have a religion, at least you should be ashamed of it and keep it dark.'

'You are about to die. Could you not concern yourself with something more important than God? You told me just now that you used to be a healthy man. A healthy man doesn't bother about God.'

'But it was you who.... You pretend to be an atheist and you think about God all the time.'

'What you say is simply ludicrous. I might have expected some such cheap psychological commonplace from you.'

'How you enjoy insulting me!' said M. Dandillot in a milder voice and with even a friendly gleam in his eyes.

'Yes, I like being rude to you. It's because you often say things which exasperate me. Here you are, on the verge of death, trying to brush up your conception of life, like a school-boy mugging up his syllabus three days before the exams. But don't worry: even if I enjoy insulting you, it doesn't in the least affect my feeling for you.'

'I'm not worried. You don't worry me at all. Does that surprise you? But why do you despise me?'

'I have a right to, if I despise myself, as I in fact do. Just as I have a right to kill if I don't mind being killed myself.'

'You mustn't despise human nature so. You know it has some admirable virtues.'

'I despise it in its virtues too.'

'Why are you smiling?'

'Because I can see myself in the mirror,' replied Costals, who had just caught his own reflection in the mirror and found it amusing.

'My exams! That's exactly it,' said M. Dandillot, smiling a little in his turn. 'Will I pass or fail my entrance to paradise? Whichever way it goes, eternity is now opening out in front of me. You, I imagine, even if you believed, would distrust an eternity that hadn't been tailor-made for you....'

He was still fingering the bottles and tubes of pills on his table. One of the bottles fell.

'What I distrust above all is eternity as such. If God existed, he would by definition be intelligent, and in that case he would never have created anything permanent.'

'There's a brand-new proof of his non-existence.'

'I always thought "proofs" of God's existence were the last word in human stupidity, but I see that those of his non-existence can go even further.'

'No matter, I like your proof.'

'And I prefer dry port,' said Costals, hoping that M. Dandillot would offer him a glass. Perspiration was soaking through his shirt and moistening his face as though he had just emerged from a river. Life was oozing from his body, shamelessly, in this liquid form.

'Is it true, Monsieur Costals, is it really true that it was only a figure of speech?'

'I swear it. It would take too long to explain. . . .'

It was on the tip of his tongue to say: 'In three weeks' time you'll be a dead man. Why should I bother to explain anything to you? My passions alone interest me.' He did not say it, but mentally turned away from him as the Greek gods turned away from corpses. And at the same time he had a horrible sensation of loving what was doomed in this man.

'Tell me you believe in nothing,' said M. Dandillot, convulsively seizing him by the hand.

'I believe in nothing. And it's because I believe in nothing that I'm happy.'

'The happiness of the man without God! Thank you,' said M. Dandillot, looking him in the eyes with an unbearable expression of gratitude. 'Oh! those swallows! Why swallows in July? It's in September that they congregate before migrating. But everything's at sixes and sevens, isn't it? You do agree with me, don't you?' he insisted. 'There are no laws governing the world. I find the thought so comforting.'

He was silent. But soon his face, which had relaxed, began to express discomfort. In a few seconds, he was deathly pale, and sweat broke out all over his forehead.

'Are you going to die?' Costals asked softly.

'No, but please ring the bell, quickly! I must go to the lavatory, at once. Yes, I'm subject to these ... Everything's going slack inside me ... Please go away. I'm so sorry. And don't forget the letters. ... '

Costals rang the bell, then went to the door and called the nurse, and as soon as he arrived, slipped away quietly. 'How much longer will he last?' he thought, feeling as exhausted as the dying man. 'When will I be able to stop suffering on his account, and to tell myself that it *really* is too late?' In the avenue, he sank on to a bench, and fanned himself with his hat. Then he lit a cigarette. 'He never even offered me a cigarette, on the pretext that he was dying.' Above him, the swallows still clamoured shrilly.

He opened one of the bundles of letters. He read the first ten, skimmed through the next twenty (there were well over a hundred). They were a cross-section of what is supposed to be the most sacred thing in the world: the trusting, tender relationship between a mother and her son. A cross-section of human love, in its purest and least questionable form. And yet the whole thing was triteness itself, not to say inanity; it was nothing, nothing, nothing. There was a drain-hole nearby. Costals tied up the letters and threw down the drain the love between Mme Dandillot and her son.

A week later, on the 15th of July, by means of a telegram from Solange delivered *poste restante*, Toulouse, Costals learnt of the death of M. Dandillot.

A natural death? Or had he taken the veronal? Presumably a natural death. In any case the question was totally irrelevant. He was dead: that was all there was to it.

For a long time he wandered aimlessly through the streets, holding the telegram in his hand. He felt limp all over; anyone could have jostled him without fear of reprisal. Soon his eyes were wet with tears. 'I bet there isn't a passer-by who doesn't think it's because a woman has let me down.'

He continued his conversation with M. Dandillot: 'Here I am weeping over you who, egotist that you were, probably never shed a tear over anyone. And yet you tried to give me a taste for the future, a future that you knew you would never see.'

In the restaurant, he was unable to eat. He sat there gloomily, unable to hide his grief: 'People must think I've got money troubles.' But he was thankful to be in Toulouse on the day of the funeral. Nothing on earth would have induced him to get mixed up with that sort of mummery.

Back at his hotel, he wanted to write to Solange and her mother. But he found himself writing 'Mons ...' on the envelope. So he took another envelope and wrote on it: 'Monsieur Charles Dandillot' and the address, and he kept this envelope in front of him. The thought that he would never have to write this name again brought the tears back to his eyes. 'Why weep for a man after he is dead? It's during his life, and *for* his life, that one should weep. It's better to be dead than to be only half-alive.' He remembered the tears he had shed, some years earlier, over the death of a great writer, tears that would subside for an hour and then burst out afresh as if their source had meanwhile been replenished, so much so that eventually his mother had observed testily: 'You didn't cry like that when your father died.' And he savoured to the full the words that now sprang to his lips: 'Never again will I make friends, because one suffers too much when one loses them.' They were the self-same words old ladies use when their little doggies pass away (but then, was M. Dandillot his friend?). He decided to send merely a telegram to Solange and her mother. They did not interest him.

In bed, incapable of sleeping, he jerked his leg up and down over the sheet in an incessant movement, like a dying horse pawing the ground. An immense community of suffering linked him with those dying horses, an immense chain stretching between him and them.

After a while he remembered something that had struck him in a letter from his son. One of Brunet's school-mates had just died of meningitis, and the child wrote: 'I feel awfully sad, but let us hope I shall get over it.' Costals, too, hoped that he would soon get over it. 'It's nature that has wounded me, and it's nature, too, that will heal me through oblivion. The day will come when I shall feel as indifferent to M. Dandillot's death as to the memory of his daughter. Since for the very same reason that I am weeping today I shall have ceased to weep tomorrow, then my weeping today is merely a game.'

At four in the morning Costals woke up and thought: 'A girl living alone with her mother is almost bound to fall. A boy likewise. So powerless is the mother, unless her power is evil. But Solange has already fallen. How stupid; M. Dandillot died for nothing.' He went back to sleep.

Solange Dandillot   to Pierre Costals
Paris   *Poste restante, Toulouse*

18 July 1927

Why this silence, nothing but that telegram to my mother, did you not promise when you left to write to me within three days? and can you not feel that I am all the time on tenterhooks waiting for the next post?

This intolerable existence has now lasted five days, I beg of you, put an end to it. I implore you to come to my help. I'm at the end of my tether.

Or else it means that you have gone away for good and are going to abandon me. Then you must say so, it's better than not knowing.

All my love,
Your
Rosebourg

I am enclosing a stamped addressed envelope with some paper inside, if you don't feel like writing, you only need to write your name on the paper, nothing more, and I shall know that you are not abandoning me.

My poor papa was buried this morning. What a void it has left for us! I shall write again to tell you how he died. We were so glad that he agreed to see a priest.

Costals' Note-Book

Well! So much for cold little Rosebourg!

With her letter in my hand, I wandered through the crowds, my eyes on the ground and biting my lips with emotion.

So she, too, in her turn has begun to howl like a beast, to screech like a cat locked in a cellar. She too has gone mad in her turn. It took Andrée four years to go mad. G. R. one. Undstein six. Claire one. But she has gone mad in two months. That's what comes of being a quiet little thing.

As Andrée's desperation subsides, hers begins to rise. Always these female lamentations, this music of flutes and tears that accompanies me all through my life.

(Her punctuation is inexcusable.)

Like the sorcerer's apprentice, I have unleashed this virgin love, this wild element of which I am no longer the master. At the Opéra-Comique, she was well behind me. Then she gained and gained, moving much faster than I, and caught up with me, and has now overtaken me. I have the feeling, almost, that she is starting again when I've only just arrived.

Is there, perhaps, some slight exaggeration in her letter? As I, at the age of sixteen, used to date my love letters two in the morning when they were written at two in the afternoon. This sudden outburst is so surprising! Had Solange been a little more 'demonstrative' with me, such a suspicion would never occur to me. Perhaps the poor child is paying now for having been so discreet and reserved. How unfair that would be. But what can I do about it?

I accept her love.

I agree to enter into the world of duty.

Sweet duty, since I love her. But duty all the same, and duty has never suited me.

However, I accept this love. With respect. With gravity – that intermittent gravity of mine which, in spite of everything, always comes into play when it is needed, if only at the eleventh hour. With ... the word escapes me; I meant to convey that her love does not displease me, that I do more than accept it: I welcome it.

And now, another matter.

Her indifference to her father's death! That postscript. She thinks of nothing but me, and I feel ashamed for both of us.

And yet she's a nice girl. Of course, fathers are not made to be loved by their children. Such is nature, and Brunet, tomorrow, with all his niceness.... But getting used to nature is always a painful process. We always expect it to be the extraordinary that takes us aback, when in fact it is the ordinary that is so terrifying.

Whenever I have visited the recently bereaved widow or orphan of someone I was more or less indifferent to, I have felt that I was more deeply moved – more sincerely moved – than was necessary: I seemed to be teaching them a lesson. It was *always* they who were the first to change the subject.

Pierre Costals
Toulouse

to Solange Dandillot
Paris

20 July 1927

Peace, my child. Peace, peace, peace everlasting to little girls. Why all this frenzy? An artichoke is always cool and collected.

You ask for reassurance: I give it to you. Peace, my darling little girl. Peace in the present. Peace in the future, as far ahead as it will please you to want me in that future. Total and absolute peace. Gaiety and serenity of mind in trust and in peace.

I have held you against my heart at the peak of my solitude, and you were alone there also, yet protected. You may remain there as long as you wish; I shall not go away from you. I love you, and what is rarer, I love the attachment you have for me. I shall never leave you until you have left me.

I have heard it said that a woman in a situation such as this should be put to the test. I do not put what I love to the test.

I have heard it said that one loses a woman by loving her too much, that an affectation of coldness, from time to time, brings better results. And so on. I shall play no such tricks with you. No tricks at all. I am not one of those people who see love as a battle; it is a notion I abhor. Let love be truly love – that is, let it be peace – or let it not exist at all.

Why this terror of my absence? What more could my

presence bring you? You are here, silly one, did you not know? In the daytime, like a little shadow, you glide quietly by my side. At night I go to sleep with you in my arms.

And my body thinks of you too. It wakes in the night and reaches towards you, as a dog stretches out its neck asking for a drink.

I have followed up your preoccupations in the order in which they appear in your letter. I have spoken first of you and me. Now a word about your father.

I do not know whether you loved your father, but I met him twice and loved him. I do not know whether you respected your father, but I met him twice and respected him. I had the impression that he was someone superior to you.

You think of no one but me, and yet you hardly know me. The casual way in which you refer to your father's death in your letter shocked me, although I understand it; exactly that: I understand it and am shocked by it. Granted, you are 'in love'. But I would have you know that love is not an excuse, but an aggravation. Precisely like drunkenness, which the insane justice of men treats as an extenuating circumstance, when it is an aggravating circumstance.

Must I be the one to make you realize what sort of man your father was?

I want you to be the person you ought to be. And you ought not to be *altogether* the person who wrote that letter.

There now, my little one, I send you my fondest love. Other men, perhaps, will love you more than I do. I love you as much as I can love you. I cannot do more.

C.

The punctuation of your letter is inexcusable.

Pierre Costals   to Mademoiselle Rachel Guigui
Toulouse   *Paris*

20 July 1927

Dear Guiguite,

Two whole months since we last met, and since I last wrote to you.

3I4

When I discovered the angel you know of, my first reaction was to drop you: one fancy drives out another. I gathered in my scattered affections from right and left in order to concentrate them all upon my angel and to make them into something powerful, like heat concentrated in a burning-glass. This adventure gripped me; I was full of it. In reality I was disregarding not only my own nature, but nature itself. Nature accumulates, and a well-endowed man does so too; in him, as in nature, there is room for everything. My angel is what she is; *you* are something else, and that is enough to make me want you as well. And so I trust that in your kindness you will see fit to resume your place among my delights.

Of course, as you remember, I had intended that we should eventually get together again. But I thought that would be when I had grown tired of the angel. Quite the contrary, my feeling towards her has never been so serious, so deep, and so strong: affection, supported by the twin pillars of esteem and desire. And it is on the tide of a great uprush of feeling that I have for her at the moment (as a result of a note received from her yesterday) that I am reverting to my natural instinct and the guiding principle in accordance with which I cannot have only one woman in my life.

Besides this, I love intelligence. And that is why, whatever my team of the moment, I must always have a Jewish mistress in the batch. She helps me to put up with the others.

I shall be in Paris on the 25th. Come on Tuesday, the 26th, the feast of St Barnabas, at 8 p.m., to Port-Royal. We'll have dinner, and afterwards you shall see what you shall see.

Goodbye, my dear; I stroke you with my hands, and even send you a kiss, for, as you know, my sensuality is of the tender kind. You, too, are a very sweet girl, and that is why my affection for you is so real. But get ready to make me happy, for I badly want to be. Thinking of you, I feel a spasm of fuliginous joy, comparable to the transports of the mystics or the final spurt of a flame. And lastly, after such a dose of the sublime, I yearn for a love that is not disinterested.

C.

Pierre Costals   to Mademoiselle du Peyron de Larchant
Toulouse   *Cannes*

('*to be given to Brunet*')

20 June 1927

My pet,

I do not like doing things behind your back; what's more, I cannot. I must tell you therefore that I wrote to Mlle du P. five days ago asking her whether by any chance you mightn't have done something really naughty, and begging her to tell me the whole truth. She answered that there had been nothing out of the ordinary run of your day-to-day tomfooleries.

Now this is why I wrote to her. Not a day passes without my thinking of you at length, and the time I spend thinking of you is always the best part of the day, however good the rest of it may be. But this time it was a dream. I dreamt that, taking advantage of a moment when the chest of drawers in Mlle du P.'s room was unlocked, you poked inside it and took out some money. And this dream was so striking, so plausible, so coherent from beginning to end, that I could not help wondering whether it might not be a mysterious warning, and so wrote the letter.

This dream made a profound, almost overwhelming impression on me. I felt more forcibly than ever before what a terrible blow it would be for me if I were no longer able to think well of you.

There are several people for whom I feel a certain affection. But this affection, sincere though it is, goes only so far and no further. Like a motor-car which one knows has only so much horse-power in its belly. The affection which I feel for you, on the other hand, knows no obstacles, never reaches a limit. It belongs to another, infinitely higher category.

The affection I feel towards those other people does not preclude my being able to do without them, my being able to tease them, or wound them even, or see them in distress without suffering from it or doing anything to relieve them. The affection I feel for you would preclude all that. Not once in my life has it occurred to me to try to upset you, or to let you be upset when it was in my power to prevent it, or even to keep you waiting for a pleasure which it was possible for me to grant you at once. For this belongs to another, infinitely higher category.

When I emerge from the atmosphere generated by those persons and return to yours, everything, with you, seems so simple. That is because I really love you and nothing is simpler than loving, just as nothing simplifies things more.

Nevertheless, my affection for you is not altogether un-assailable. The affection I feel for the various other people is at the mercy of those people themselves, who may cease to deserve it, but also at the mercy of my moods, my lassitude, the exigencies of my work and my need for independence. The affection I feel for you is at the mercy of you alone – by which I mean that in one eventuality only could it weaken: if you became unworthy of it.

It's a sort of miracle: for fourteen years (or let's say eight – since the age 'of reason'), I have never had anything to re-proach you with, you have never done anything to offend me. I observe it all, as one observes the perilous feats of an acrobat, thinking: 'If only he can hold on to the end!' And I say to you, with all the force at my command: change, since in nature everything must change, and at your age especially one may change utterly within a fortnight; change, but in your essence remain what you are. Let there be a solid, steadfast nucleus in your nebula (ask Mlle du P. to explain what a nebula is; I would do so myself, only it bores me stiff, and I'd be at a bit of a loss to do so anyway). As you know, I allow you considerable scope for your idiocies, more so than any other father would allow his son; that is because, in my opinion, they do not affect what is really important. But in matters of importance do, I beg you, be on your guard. What I want passionately is to reach the point where *it would be in-conceivable that I should have any anxiety on your account*, as regards your intrinsic quality; a point where you would represent complete calm and complete security to me; and that another living creature besides myself should represent complete calm and complete security to me is the most extra-ordinary thing I can imagine, since in effect it hardly belongs to this world. But it must be given to me, and by you and you alone: no one else means anything to me. You are the only person who has permanently engaged my affections, which are not easily engaged by other people. In fact, you are the only person I love, since the word can only be applied to that feeling which strictly extends to infinity, from which infinite demands can be made, with no more trouble than there would be in asking for water from the sea. Were the feeling I have for you to collapse or merely to fissure, it would mean the collapse or fissuring of the whole of myself. It would shatter me.

When one truly loves someone, there is no need to tell him so : that can be left to inferior people. And as you know, I never do tell you. But that dream frightened me, and I felt the need to set something of it down for you on paper. Keep it (this may be asking a lot), and let us now move on to the absurd business of your bike. . . .*

Mlle Marcelle Prié   to M. Jacques Picard†
Rue Croix-des-Petits-Champs   chez M. Pierre Costals
Paris   avenue Henri-Martin
                                                                           Paris
                                                              20 July 1927

Jacquot,

I am here in the café like last Sunday, alone of course, since you have deserted me. I've been waiting for you for six days. What does your silence mean, love? If you didn't want to see me again, then why did you call me back? So you were just making fun of me, were you? I'm not having you throw me over like this, my boy. We've got to meet again, do you hear. Come on Tuesday at 10 p.m.

Do you know when I first realized you had had enough of me? In the Underground, coming back from the boxing match. I wanted to kiss you and you kept turning your face away. So I said to you : 'Don't you love me any more, then?' 'Yes,

---

*The rest of this letter has no bearing on our story (Author's note).

†Costals' manservant.

PITY FOR WOMEN

but don't kiss me like that in the Underground. It's not right.'
'Are you ashamed?' 'Yes, I'm ashamed.' It was plain enough.
Please be straight with me. I'm the victim of my passion for
you. I wanted to love you, to guide you a bit in life. You're
twenty and I'm twenty-five, but really the different in our ages
is much bigger than that. Oh! I would have been prepared to
do without marriage, since you didn't want it, but we could
have been together, or just met on Sundays; it would have
been better than nothing. Now you don't want it any more.
You're free! But you'll regret it later. Your youth would have
been all my happiness. But you never understood me, and now
it hurts more than ever, my heart bleeds with loneliness and
with all this waiting and not being able to make you see.
Honestly, Jacques, do come one last time, and then I'll leave
you to do exactly as you please.

If you can't come tomorrow, I'll wait for you all week till
Sunday.

I kiss those eyes I used to love.

Marcelle

This letter remained unanswered